Quantum Leap

Quantum Leap

Rainie York

To order additional copies of this book, contact:
Xlibris
1-888-795-4274
www.Xlibris.com
Orders@Xlibris.com
799753

For Courtney

AUTHOR'S NOTES

REGARDLESS OF HOW real my characters seem to me, Quantum Leap is a work of fiction. Certain aspects of the book, however, are very real. These include Reiki, a Japanese energy healing system; Transcendental Meditation (TM); and quantum science principles relating to energy that underly Rebecca's discoveries in the story. Perhaps Albert Einstein said it best:

> "Everything is energy. That's all there is to it. Match the frequency of the reality you want, and you cannot help but get it. It can be no other way. This is not *philosophy*. This is *physics*."

CHAPTER 1

Justice Is Served

May 29

REBECCA JEAN PULLED her bedroom door closed behind her. The latch snicked softly into place. Walking lightly on the balls of her feet, she moved across the room to her desk. To her computer. Now that she had decided to do this, she was feeling a sort of guilty glee. What she was about to do could get her into trouble. Probably *big* trouble. But no one would ever believe it, not in a million years, so how could she get caught? And besides, it might not even work.

No. Deep down, she knew it would work.

She set her water bottle and popcorn carefully on the desk beside her laptop. More trouble if her parents knew she was eating in her bedroom. Stupid, pointless rules! She made a face as she settled herself in her chair and rolled close to the desk. She felt a sense of power and anticipation as she opened her Events folder and scanned the titles. There were three.

But not like this one.

Her finger tapped lightly on the mouse. She leaned back in her chair, raking a hand through her hair. She gazed at her laptop, her mouth pulled into a little pout. She sat forward again. She righted her paper clip holder; Tinker must have knocked it over. She gathered the loose paper clips and fed them one at a time into the container. Each one jumped to the magnet with a satisfying little click and lined up around the top of the holder. She set the tape dispenser and stapler side by side, aligning their edges just so. She nibbled on her popcorn, swallowed a sip of water. She reached for the mouse again. Her other hand found its way into her hair, and she unconsciously twirled a lock around her index finger. Around and around.

Stalling, whispered a voice in her head.

She nodded to herself, and her right hand settled again over the mouse, her fingers curled around the small device. She took a deep breath and clicked a new file open. She was surprised to realize she was singing softly under her breath — words to a Dire Straits song her mother and grandmother both loved. Without thinking, she titled the piece Louisville Slugger.

Closing her eyes, she took a deep breath and exhaled slowly. She took another deep breath. Exhaled. When she opened her eyes, she began to type. The pads of her fingers tingled as they moved deliberately across the keys. She stared fixedly at the screen, but her attention was on something else. Something . . . distant, and a little dark. A new story began to form. A new Event was being set in motion. The Fat Man was going down. He was mean and a tyrant. It was only fair. It was justice.

CHAPTER 2

How It All Started

May 3

REBECCA WAS DREAMING—A strange, disconnected dream. In it, she was carrying a box. It was full to bulging, but she didn't know all the things it held. She knew she needed to sort through the box to find something important, and she had to put it down to do that. But she couldn't find a good place to set it. She thought about just dumping everything out, but for some reason, this frightened her. She needed to look at the mess inside one thing at a time. The box was getting heavy, and she was tired of carrying it around. On top of all that, it seemed to be making some sort of noise. Was it going to explode?

She suddenly found herself at the edge of a cliff. Interestingly, she now knew she was dreaming. And if she was dreaming, she could just wake up! Couldn't she? Apparently not. She hurled the contents of the box over the cliff but, oddly, the bits and pieces merely floated about, some brushing against her face or clinging to her clothes. She threw the box with all her might. She knew it was going to explode; it was still making that tapping sound.

Rebecca pulled herself from the dream, panicky and breathing hard. The box was a heavy weight behind her knees. She jerked her legs away, and it responded with a surprised "Mrrrt . . ."

"Tinker . . ." Rebecca sat up in relief and pulled a big saffron-colored cat into her arms.

Tinker responded by settling against Rebecca's chest—a solid, *real* weight, her purr rumbling in Rebecca's ears and her whiskers tickling Rebecca's cheek.

"Tinks." Rebecca nestled her face into the warm fur. "Icky dream," she murmured.

Tap. Tap. Tap.

How could that be? Surely she was awake now.

Tap. Tap. Tap. "Becka . . ."

Still holding Tinker in her arms, Rebecca looked around her room. She shook her head to clear it. Movement pulled her attention to her corner windows. The high windows of her basement suite looked onto a limited and leafy view of one of her mother's shrub hedges and one corner of the patio, respectively. Most mornings, Rebecca checked the weather through the restricted opening beneath the neatly pruned shrubs. Did she have a little patch of blue? Gray drizzle? Were the bushes shrouded in white or shuddering in wind? At the present moment, beyond all belief, the shrub view was filled with her little brother, Andy, and the grinning, slobbering face of his Labrador-mix mutt of a dog, Scoundrel. Rebecca stared, uncomprehending.

And then, "Andrew Lawrence Coleson! What on *earth* are you doing in my shrubs!" Unequivocally the voice of her mother. "Scoundrel! *Bed*!"

Scoundrel dropped immediately to his belly and wriggled backward out of the bushes. The blond head of her little brother froze momentarily, and then Andy too began a rearward withdrawal. A disembodied hand grasped the back of Andy's pants to hasten his retreat, lifting his lower half clear of the ground. As Andy's body was tugged unceremoniously backward, his arms flew out in front of him, as if in supplication. Surprised blue eyes met her own.

He was mouthing something to her, but she couldn't make it out. This was more puzzling than the dream! She glared at him in mute fury. Andy's surprised look morphed rapidly to one of sheepishness, and then to alarm as his evacuation from the shrubbery was hastened by another sharp pull on his belt.

"OMG, look at you! Now you'll have to change your clothes before school."

"Aw, Mom . . ."

"No argument!" Andy's protest was cut off. "You get your butt upstairs this instant, and I don't want to hear a peep . . ." Andy's feet made a little hop. "Not a *peep*! Now *march*!"

Rebecca guessed Andy had been about to protest. He should have thought better of it, given that their mother had used all three of his names, not to mention swear words. Seven-year-olds, however, weren't renowned for their deep thinking.

Rebecca watched as two pairs of feet disappeared across the patio. This was way too much to process so early. Especially after the weird dream. She could still feel the urgency of that dream. She leaned back against her pillows with another deep sigh. Tinker settled comfortably in the crumpled covers.

Tap. Tap. Tap.

Rebecca jerked upright and whipped her covers aside. Dislodged again, Tinker jumped off the bed. She turned offended green eyes on Rebecca. "Tinks! So sorry."

Rebecca slid out of bed and stood in the middle of the room for a moment before padding over to the window seat. She pulled the shutters closed. Too late now, but the action was still satisfying. She shook her head again as she sank onto the cushioned seat.

Okay, she thought. *Okay, it's Friday.* Aloud she muttered to herself, "Get a grip." Friday. Homework would be light. Maybe she could even get it all done in Home Room last period. Sam was coming this morning . . .

Sam! She and her best friend were to walk to school together this morning.

"OMG, Sam! What time is it?" And then the tapping again.

"Becks?" Softly, from the other side of her bedroom door. "Are you up?"

Rebecca crossed her room in long strides and flung open her door to find Sarah Ann Morgan standing on the other side. Tinker flashed past Sam's ankles without so much as a backward glance. Rebecca pulled her friend inside, shut the door, and leaned against it.

"Sleep late?" Sam's smile was impish.

Rebecca shook her head. She ran her hands through her tousled hair and latched on to a generous handful. The state of her honey-blonde locks was not improved. Neither was her grasp of the morning's events. "It's been totally bizarre this morning," she said.

Sam perched on the end of Rebecca's bed, her look questioning.

Rebecca stared at her. "Andy . . ." She shook her head again. "I dreamed . . ." No. Not that. "I just . . ."

It was no use. In that moment, she didn't have the words or the will to explain. Instead, she picked up a pillow, smacked Sam with it, and disappeared into her closet, one hand still clutched tightly in her hair. Sam settled more comfortably on the bed as Rebecca rummaged for something to wear.

Thumps and muttering came from the closet. "Geez, no way." There was the sound of drawers being yanked open and slammed shut, hangers clattering, a soft thud followed by a muffled exclamation. "Geekers," drifted out. And then, "Stupid rules!"

Eventually, Rebecca emerged in faded jeans and a bra, a midnight-blue sweater top clutched to her chest and a white, denim jacket in one hand.

"Good look." Sam cupped her hands beneath her ample breasts, joggled them up and down, and smirked at Rebecca.

"They're new." Rebecca ignored Sam's innuendo. She smoothed her hand over the soft fabric of the sweater. "Mom got them for me." She tossed the jacket onto the bed beside Sam.

"She said the blue would bring out my eyes." Rebecca batted long lashes and vamped before slipping the sweater over her head and disappearing back into her closet. A shoe came flying out. More muffled thumps. A heartfelt curse.

Sam picked up the short denim jacket. "I like it. It'd be great with those white sandals AJ had on yesterday. Jeez, they sure made her tall!"

Rebecca's head popped out of the closet, a fierce scowl describing her face. "Wouldn't it just! Too bad my father is such an obsessive nerd." Her father's beliefs on a host of issues, including dress code, were a source of ongoing annoyance to Rebecca.

"You know how my dad is about his stupid rules," she continued, still frowning. "I don't see how wearing shoes with heels could ruin my character. But Dad seems to think it would. I think fewer rules would be an asset to my character development. Give me a chance to, you know . . . develop."

"I'll trade you for my dad," said Sam.

"Mmm. Maybe not." Rebecca's voice floated from the closet. She didn't like Sam's dad. He was kind of creepy, and she felt uncomfortable being around him.

Sam was still holding the little white jacket, her face thoughtful. "White," she said. "It wouldn't be very practical in the barn." She let the jacket fall to her lap.

Sam was happiest when she was on the back of a horse. Or anywhere near a horse, for that matter. She spent every possible moment at her uncle's ranch north of Colorado Springs. Sam didn't talk about it often, but Rebecca knew Sam's eagerness to be at the ranch was, in part, to be away from her father.

Rebecca reappeared from the closet. Sam nodded in approval.

"Nice." She fingered the material of the little blue sweater. "Enhances your assets."

"Nice T-shirt." Rebecca changed the subject.

"Thanks." Sam drew her shoulders back, and the faces of England's '60s Fab Four leered from her T-shirt. She flashed long fingernails painted in the same vibrant yellow as the shirt.

"What do you call that color? Banana slug?"

Sam laughed, running her brightly lacquered nails through tousled curls. "More like Yellow Submarine," she said.

"Oh, yeah. I hadn't thought of that."

"Get your shoes and let's go eat. I'm starving."

Rebecca shoved her feet into plain, flat sandals, and the girls headed up the stairs to the main floor. They found Andy at the kitchen table. He was in clean clothes and had freshly combed hair. In front of him was a plate of scrambled eggs and bacon. He was fiddling with a banana—you couldn't say he was eating it, exactly. Scoundrel sat on the patio just outside the French doors. One ear was cocked up. The other drooped down. His weight shifted from one front leg to the other as he gazed hopefully at them through the glass.

"Where's Mom?" Rebecca asked.

Andy shrugged. "She's here."

"Where here?" Rebecca gestured around the sunny kitchen.

"In the office . . . ?" Another shrug. Clearly, Andy was in a funk.

"And just what was that display of genius in the bushes this morning?"

Andy had the grace to look a tiny bit discomfited. "Mom said to tell you Sarah Ann was coming up the street."

"And you couldn't just knock on my door to tell me?"

"You really hate it when I wake you up knocking on the door."

"Oh, and pounding on my window under the bushes I love?"

Andy had no response for this. He hunkered down in front of his plate and nibbled on a piece of bacon. His expression suggested he felt the day wasn't shaping up all that well.

"What do you want for breakfast?" Rebecca's attention turned to Sam.

"A bagel would be good," said Sam.

"I don't think we have any. Except the frozen kind. And they're yucky," said Rebecca.

"What about those?" Sam pointed at a white bag on the counter. Large, block lettering on the side of the bag proclaimed The Diner. "They wouldn't be yucky."

"OMG! Dad must have gone out for those!" She snatched up the bag and held it under her nose. "Mmm. These're the best."

Sam nodded. Rebecca pulled two bagels from the bag.

"Just a half for me," said Sam. "They're huge."

"I could eat a whole one," said Rebecca pointedly.

"Then do," said Sam. "But I only want a half. My jeans are getting sort of . . ."

"Tight?" Andy smirked at Sam, his mouth full of bacon.

Sam sighed in resignation. "Yeah."

Rebecca sliced a huge bagel and pushed the two halves into the toaster. She gave Sam an appraising look. Sam was solid and fit. Her round figure filled out her jeans, and her T-shirt fit snugly across her full bosom. Rebecca was a little awed by Sam's breasts, but it was a secret she kept to herself. Periodically, Sam made a half-hearted attempt to lose a jean size. It rarely lasted long, and it was seldom effective.

"Strawberry cream cheese?"

"Sure!"

Andy got up from the table and set his breakfast plate, barely touched, in the sink.

"You'll never make it to lunch, sport," said Rebecca. She rummaged around in the pantry until she found some cookies and snack bars. Forbidden for school snacks. Of course.

"Here." She shoved the booty into Andy's backpack and ruffled his hair. He slipped his small shoulders into the straps.

"Thanks." It was a mumble. Andy shuffled for the door and his bus.

Later, when the two girls left the house, they were in high spirits. The day was off to a good start, in spite of its weird beginning. It was a perfect early May morning on Colorado's Front Range, sunny and bright, but cool. Just right for the new sweater and jacket. The promise of the weekend was only seven class periods away. Sam linked her arm through Rebecca's as they headed down the tree-lined street. A little breeze lifted Rebecca's hair from her shoulders and tangled Sam's curls around her face.

"Sweet," said Sam. She lifted her face to the breeze.

"Yeah." Rebecca took a deep breath.

"If only I were riding Skydancer out instead of . . ." She didn't finish the thought. Instead, she said, "Are you working on a new story?"

"Mmm. Why do you ask?"

"Because you usually are." Sam was matter-of-fact.

"Yeah. That's me. Just lame." Rebecca pursed her lips, her eyebrows drawn together.

"It's not lame!" Sam protested. "Do you think it's lame that your grandmother is an author with about a zillion books published?"

"Well, no. I guess not." Her expression clearing, Rebecca said, "Nanna's books are pretty rad. And it's twenty-one."

"Seriously? Your grandmother has written twenty-one books?"

"That are published. So far." Rebecca nodded.

"Wow. Twenty-one. Good number."

Rebecca grinned. "Yeah. Totally." Her expression turned pensive. "Remember those Ariel stories I used to write? Where Laney turned into a mermaid? Now, those were lame."

"Not for a third-grader!" Sam laughed. After a moment, she asked, "Have your stories always been about Laney?"

"Pretty much."

"She's sort of you, isn't she?"

Rebecca looked startled. She didn't answer right away. "You know, she kind of is," she said at length. "But braver than me."

"How so?"

Rebecca considered. "Laney's pretty . . ." She searched for the right description. "To the limit," she said finally. "She'll do about anything, and she never worries about stupid stuff. Like rules. Getting caught. Fitting in. You know my dad. My life is totally about stupid rules."

"Well, yeah." Sam frowned. "Like I said, I'd trade."

Rebecca just shook her head. "When I'm writing a story, I feel free." She smiled. "And in control. That's totally the bomb."

"Totally." Sam nodded. "I feel that way when I'm riding," she said wistfully. "Free, I mean." She was quiet for a minute, and then she said, "You did sort of have a fixation on mermaids for a while."

"You mean sort of like you're fixated on horses?"

For this there was no defense, and Sam made none. She just laughed. The sound was filled with light and music and acceptance.

"You should write a story about meeting some hot guy. Not from Front Range. Mysterious. Bad news, somehow."

Rebecca's insides tightened for an instant. She ignored Sam.

"You could have Laney meet him." Green eyes teased. "Especially since she's 'sort of you.' Put her in a tight sweater and let her flaunt her assets. I assume Laney has admirable assets and isn't afraid to flaunt them?" Sam pulled her shoulders back and thrust round breasts forward. She wriggled her shoulders. Paul and Ringo's faces danced on the yellow T-shirt.

Rebecca shoved Sam playfully and pulled her jacket closer. "Laney would do it."

Sam dropped her pose and nodded but said nothing.

As they approached Front Range High School, the sidewalk began to fill with other students. Sam and Rebecca glanced around.

"Where is everyone?" There was no sign of Tyler, Alexa, or Zoe.

They passed through the big doors, still looking for their other friends. The smell of school greeted them. Books, chalk, bodies, strong cleaning solutions. It was hard to describe and unmistakable at the same time.

"See you at lunch," said Sam.

"For sure." Rebecca waved at Sam's retreating figure.

CHAPTER 3

It's a Normal Day, Mostly

May 3

R EBECCA'S FIRST CLASS was algebra. She liked the orderliness of math. Its predictability. And she was good at it. She didn't much care for the teacher, though. Mr. Hammond was fat and sloppy, which felt jarringly at odds with the precision of math. She could have forgiven him for that. Maybe. But he displayed blatant partiality toward the jocks. It wasn't fair. Plus, he smelled funny, and he was mean.

Jackson Middleton was in this class, and he was a perfect case in point. Tall, blond, the star freshman quarterback, Jackson was one of Mr. Hammond's favorites. Jackson could do no wrong. Rebecca had known Jackson since fifth grade. She didn't consider him a friend exactly. He was too . . . extreme. But he was a constant in her life. She was drawn by his enthusiastic assault on each day and his cheek with respect to adult rules. Where Jackson was, there could certainly be a good time. But he was erratic. Dangerously unpredictable. Most days, she didn't know what to think of Jackson. Mr. Hammond's seating assignment (what a nerd) placed her across the aisle from him. He was always trying to con her into sharing her notes, or answers, or whatever it took to get around doing actual work himself.

And there he was. As Rebecca slid into her seat, she raised her mental guard. Jackson was sprawled in his desk, long legs extending into the aisle toward her. Just at the bell, Josh Kenyon barreled into the classroom. Jackson's face split in a grin.

"Telluride! Extreme champion!" Jackson and Josh high-fived, bumped fists, and went through a series of gestures, smirks, and grins.

"Jacks! What's happenin', man?"

Rebecca was a little in awe of Josh Kenyon. She loved that he walked his own line. How hard would that be, she wondered. Like Jackson, Josh was a freshman football star, but he played no other school sports. His first love was mountain biking, and especially fat-tire racing. When he wasn't actually on a bike, he was usually doing some sort of training. Josh had beaten the favored racer in the final run in a big race at Telluride the previous summer. The victory had earned him both a trophy and his nickname. Tyler had filled Rebecca in on these facts; she seemed to have a lot of them. Rebecca thought Ty might have a secret crush on Josh. No big deal. Ty had a lot of crushes.

Josh dropped his wiry frame into the desk in front of Jackson. Jackson fake-slapped Josh on the back of the head and then leaned across the aisle and twined his fingers in Rebecca's hair.

"Hey, darlin'," he said.

She jerked her head away and glared at him.

Jackson just laughed. He pushed the hair from his eyes in a habitual gesture and slouched back into his seat, long legs again extended. He crossed one ankle over the other.

"S'up, Becka?" he asked.

Rebecca could think of no response, so she just shrugged.

"Becka plays hard-to-get." Josh punched Jackson in the shoulder for emphasis.

Rebecca turned a level stare on Josh. "Grow a brain," she said. She was secretly pleased at her comeback.

Jackson fake-slapped Josh on the back of his head again. "Yeah, grow a brain, man."

Josh grinned. Jackson laughed. Rebecca tried to think of something clever, but her mind had gone blank.

The classroom door opened, and Mr. Hammond lumbered in. He moved toward his desk with a heavy tread. Josh faced the front of the room. "Hard-to-get," he said under his breath.

"Nah, Becka's just Becka." Jackson winked at her.

So what did *that* mean? Rebecca had no idea. She straightened in her desk, schooling her face into a neutral expression. At least she hoped it was. Mr. Hammond growled at the class. The rest of algebra was taken up with a pop quiz and practice problems. Rebecca settled into the work and tried not to think about Jackson.

***

Second-period science. Wrinkling her nose at the smell, Rebecca scanned the room for Tyler. Ty's dark-auburn hair made her easy to spot. Rebecca dropped her books on the table and pulled out the chair next to Ty.

"What're we doing today?"

"Don't know," said Ty. Her thick red hair, pulled into a tight ponytail, lurched from side to side as she shook her head.

"Look at this." Tyler pulled a CD from her book bag and slid it toward Rebecca.

"The Beatles at the Hollywood Bowl," Rebecca read the title. "Is that a big deal?"

"Oh yeah! They did concerts there twice during their early tours in America. The original album came out in 1977. Dad says it's pretty rare." Tyler ran a hand over the CD with reverence. "Sam will be green."

"Yeah. Totally." Rebecca nodded, but she wasn't so sure. "So do you really like the Beatles all that much?" she asked. "I mean, beyond the cool T-shirts and stuff?"

"I like them enough." There was a note of caution in Tyler's voice.

"It's just that . . . I never notice you actually listening to Beatles songs."

"How would you even know what I listen to when you're not around?" Ty was cool.

"Okay. I don't," said Rebecca. "Except for what you talk about listening to."

Tyler held Rebecca's gaze but said nothing.

"What I mean is . . ." Rebecca fidgeted under Tyler's steady look. Jeez, why had she even said that about liking the Beatles?

"Just say it, Becks." Tyler folded slender arms across her chest.

"I just wondered if maybe you do all this retro stuff . . . I mean, there's some really good old music . . ." Rebecca shifted in her seat and adjusted her chair. Tyler still said nothing. Rebecca took a deep breath and said in a rush, "I just wondered if maybe you do all this retro stuff to get in good with your dad."

"What if I do?" said Tyler.

Rebecca blinked in surprise. She opened her mouth and then closed it.

"What wouldn't you do to get your dad to notice you? If he lived three hours away and on the other side of some mountain."

Rebecca's breath caught. "Oh, Ty!" Her heart constricted, and she unconsciously pressed the heel of her hand to her chest. "I never thought of that. I don't know what I'd do if my dad was . . ." Rebecca couldn't finish. "Even with all his stupid rules . . . I'd do anything." Rebecca shook her head. It didn't bear thinking about.

Tyler slipped the disc back into a pocket in her book bag and carefully closed the zipper. She pulled out her science notebook and placed it on the table.

"Jeez, Ty. You're not mad, are you?"

Tyler's posture softened, and she gave Rebecca a little smile. "No. It's okay."

Rebecca didn't think it was really okay, but she didn't know what to say. She was still searching for words when two cheerleaders walked by. Brittany Something and Clarity Austin. Brittany's smart designer bag slapped the side of Ty's head as she went by. Brittany glanced back at Tyler but moved on without so much as a word. Ty rubbed her head. Rebecca glared after Brittany.

"Bitch." Rebecca's voice was soft but venomous.

"For sure," muttered Ty.

The cheerleaders settled noisily at another table that was all jocks. They were suddenly all smiles and brazen flirtations.

"Okay, people!" Mr. Gonzales called for quiet, looking pointedly at the table where Brittany and Clarity were causing a stir. He opened his fat teacher's text and began to drone on about review topics. Rebecca and Tyler flipped open their binders. Tyler paid careful attention, taking notes in a precise hand. Rebecca's mind wandered. Only half listening, fingers twined into her hair, she twirled a lock around one finger. She glanced a time or two at the cheerleaders' table. She doodled in her Laney folder and idly wrote "Bitch" in bold letters.

With the period bell, the girls gathered up their books and headed together for English.

"Thank God that's over. I hate science." Tyler shook her head, and the ponytail swayed.

"Can I review your notes?" Rebecca asked hopefully.

"Sure." Tyler nodded. "If you'll take my next test for me."

"You know I would," said Rebecca. "Maybe you'll do great on the next one."

Tyler looked dejected. "If only."

"You might," Rebecca insisted. "You do great on all the other work."

Tyler's slender shoulders sagged, but her eyes were fierce. "I tell myself every test this will be the one that doesn't totally freak me out." She grimaced. "But then it does."

Rebecca didn't know what to say. Tyler in a funk felt off. Heavy. Rebecca switched her book bag from one shoulder to the other. "You'll get it, Ty." She wasn't sure she believed that, so why would Ty?

"That's what Dad says." Ty sighed.

They walked in silence to their English class.

Seating in English was grouped into what Mrs. Lindzer called study pods. A study pod was a table accommodating six students. The same as in science, where they were just plain tables. Rebecca and Tyler's pod included Jackson, Brittany-the-Bitch, and Clarity, and a boy Rebecca didn't know well—at all, really—Travis Scott. He was dark haired and quiet and felt kind of intense. Clarity and Brittany spent most of the period making eyes at the boys, leaning forward so their low-cut tops flashed generous views. Jackson and Travis didn't seem to notice, but it would be hard not to. Rebecca unconsciously pulled her white jacket closer around her.

The assignment was boring. Once she completed it, she doodled notes in her Laney folder.

***

Drama. Her last class before lunch. Rebecca slid into a chair and looked around. She nodded at a senior, Charles, across the aisle from her. Drama was a mixture of students from all grade levels, which was too cool, although she sometimes felt nervous around the juniors and seniors. Also cool in that there were no books and rarely any tests. You could sit anywhere you wanted. And spontaneity was the rule. You never knew what was going to happen. None of Rebecca's best friends were in this class. It was better that way. Sometimes she sort of pretended to be Laney, and there was no one who knew her well enough to tell the difference. On this morning, Mr. Tilson breezed into the room, a brilliant smile lighting up his deeply tanned face. Rebecca thought he was funny and kind of cute, in an older sort of way. He must be at least thirty. She settled into her chair, expecting a fun class. It usually was. The day did not disappoint.

***

After drama, Rebecca hurried to the cafeteria. She burst through the double doors and scanned the room for her friends. Everyone was there. Alexa Jensen's tall frame was draped in a chair, long legs stretched out in front of her. She wore red high-heeled sandals. They were propped on her book bag, which had been tossed carelessly on the floor. Straight, medium-brown hair in no particular style fell to her shoulders. She pushed red-framed glasses up her nose and waved casually as Rebecca approached. As always, when Rebecca saw AJ, she was struck by her friend's arresting appearance. The heavy-framed glasses, careless posture, and unremarkable hairstyle did not conceal the fact that AJ was beautiful.

Zoe sat next to AJ, appearing tiny and neat by contrast. Her mass of dark hair was held back by a vividly colored scarf. Her face was quiet and composed. Big dark eyes turned in Rebecca's direction.

Rebecca felt a rush of affection for her first BFF. She raised one hand in a gesture the girls had shared since first grade. Zoe's eyes widened with pleasure, and she signed back. It was a little thing. But it felt huge. Rebecca couldn't remember how it had started or what it might have meant to six-year-olds. It was just something she and Zoe, and sometimes Sam, had always done. It felt like a reverent *I see you.*

Tyler was perched on the edge of a chair—you couldn't really say she was sitting on it. The heels of her feet were tapping on the floor. She waved her hands as she talked, and the ponytail jittered a frantic dance. Sam was across from Ty. Booted feet, crossed at the ankles, rested on an empty chair. Only half listening, she absently tapped full lips with one yellow fingernail.

"Becks!"

"Hey, AJ." Rebecca's eyes lingered wistfully on AJ's sandals. She tossed her book bag on an empty chair and scanned the lunch marquee.

"Mac 'n' cheese. My fave." And she hurried off.

Rebecca came back with a steaming tray of cheesy pasta. Tyler was mimicking the cheerleaders' attempts to get Jackson and Travis to notice them in English. Her minimalist chest was not up to the challenge, and the others were breaking up. Rebecca laughed with them, feeling a warm sense of belonging. She always felt somehow . . . more . . . when she was with her friends. More confident. More relaxed. More whole. More than her regular self. She took a generous bite of macaroni and cheese and leaned her elbows on the table, looking around at her girlfriends. At times like this, she loved being in high school.

***

Lunch was followed by government studies, which was usually lethally boring. Today was no exception. Rebecca barely listened, thinking instead about Sam's suggestion for a Laney story with a mysterious dark-haired boy. She couldn't get the idea out of her head. She scribbled ideas in her notebook, and feeling confident and bold, she wrote "Author's Notes" in a side margin with a green Sharpie. She lost herself in her ideas, and when the period bell sounded, she looked up in surprise.

Gathering her things, Rebecca hurried for French class. Zoe was waiting at the stairs.

"Bonjour," said Zoe.

"Bonjour." Rebecca smiled back.

Zoe rattled off a sentence in rapid French, and Rebecca looked at her in amazement. "Your grandmother arrived?" she asked.

"Oui, c'est vrai," replied Zoe.

"What did you just say?"

"Yes, it's true," said Zoe.

"No, I got that. Before."

Zoe shrugged. "It's Acadian French. Corrupted by years of living in Louisiana with Cajuns. So Grand-mère says. It doesn't really compute to anything we do in class."

"Could've fooled me," Rebecca said. "Nice you get to practice when you're at home."

"Not really," Zoe said. "Textbook French doesn't have much in common with Cajun street French."

"Or Cajun swamp French?" Rebecca kidded.

Zoe gasped. Her brown eyes went wide, but she giggled. "Grand-mère would cut out your insides, roast them over a fire, and feed them back to you with a nice bourbon if she heard you say that."

Rebecca laughed. Zoe's grandmother was quirky and funny, often so upbeat she was sort of over the top. Rebecca could imagine Zoe's grand-mère doing a lot of crazy things, but going anywhere near a swamp wasn't one of them.

"French would be more fun if I thought there was some chance of, say, going to France and speaking it," Rebecca whispered.

"Or meeting a sexy, exciting Frenchman," said Zoe.

"Oui!"

"That's the only word you'd need for a sexy Frenchman," whispered Zoe.

Rebecca elbowed Zoe and stifled a giggle. She tugged the denim jacket a little closer.

No sexy, exciting Frenchman materialized before the end of class, and Rebecca and Zoe trudged out of the room and down the stairs speaking English.

"I have to go," said Zoe.

"Go where? You won't be in Home Room?"

"Dentist appointment." Zoe bared her lips, showing white, even teeth.

Rebecca's mood dipped a little. "I'll still have Sam," she said.

"Sam's doing a make-up exam. For a Monday, she was 'sick' and stayed at the ranch."

"Jeez! So just me in Hammond's haven for jocks?"

They had reached the bottom of the stairs, and Zoe headed toward the big, double entrance doors. Rebecca stood in the hallway, students jostling her as they hurried past.

Zoe turned back. "There's always Jackson." Her face lit up in a mischievous grin.

Before Rebecca could answer, Zoe was gone.

CHAPTER 4

The Fight

May 3

REBECCA WALKED INTO Home Room alone and slipped into a seat. She usually enjoyed the unstructured class with her friends, in spite of Mr. Hammond's excesses. Not today. At least she could knock out all her homework. There wasn't that much, except for the algebra problems Mr. Hammond had piled on. After that, she could think about the ideas she had scribbled down in government studies. She thought Sam was only partly right about Laney. Laney was fearless and with it; she made her own rules and didn't care what anyone else thought. She was in control of her own life. No. It wasn't so much that Rebecca and Laney were the same. It was more like Laney was the person Rebecca wished she could be.

Rebecca sighed. She pulled out her algebra book and tackled the first problem. Absently, she twined the fingers of one hand through her hair.

She was working on her last problem when she felt, rather than saw, Jackson hanging over the desk behind her. She hadn't even noticed him come in.

Algebra, English, Home Room—Jackson was a constant throughout her day. Sometimes she almost liked him. Not in a girl-boy way! No freaking way! Jackson was way too . . . well, just too much, for that. Most of the girls Rebecca knew thought Jackson was hot. Okay, he wasn't hard to look at. He could flash his FIGJAM grin, and every girl in the room would go all gooey eyed. Girls could be so gullible. Brain dead, that's what it was. Where Jackson was concerned, Rebecca's feelings usually ran between cautious amusement, annoyance, and outright fury, coupled with a gut-level certainty that he was the devil in blue jeans. He had three personae—the flirt, the pain, and pure trouble. She wondered which one he'd be today.

"What'd you get for that one, Becka?" Jackson purred.

The flirt. Rebecca knew without seeing his face that Jackson had put on his most seductive smile. The lopsided "I'm so freaking good—just ask me" grin.

"Work it out for yourself, Jackson," Rebecca said.

"I really like your hair." Jackson leaned in close and made sniffing noises in her hair.   She shook her head, leaning away from him.

"Mmm. Is that . . . strawberries?" Jackson's nose was practically buried in her hair. It could have been a little bit flattering, but Rebecca refused to be drawn in.

"Really, Jackson," she said. "We've had the same practice problems all week." She turned to look at him, her expression bland. "You did do the practice problems . . ."

"Come on, Rebecca. Don't be a nerd," Jackson wheedled.

So now the pain. "I am not a nerd just because you're too lazy to do your own algebra problems." Annoyance had not yet grown into aggravation, but it was on the way. She turned back to her work. She closed her algebra book and put it in her book bag, pulling out her story folder at the same time. "I'm working on something. Do it yourself."

Jackson shrugged still closer. She resisted the temptation to turn around again, but she thought he must be practically lying on top of his desk. He changed his tactic.

"I'll bet you help people all the time, a sharp girl like you."

Rebecca ignored him, or pretended to, as she opened her folder and pulled out the page with her story ideas. "Author's Notes" in bold green ink jumped off the page at her. It had seemed fun when she did it. Now she felt a little weird about it, kind of exposed.

"Author's notes . . ." Jackson was still leaning over her shoulder. "What class is that for?" Reaching a long arm around her, he slid the page off Rebecca's desk.

Rebecca whirled to face him. Mild annoyance skipped over aggravation and blossomed into immediate fury. "It's not for a class. And give me that!" she hissed.

Jackson's smile now held an edge of satisfaction. "So what have we here? What's so special about some notes?"

"It's none of your business, you retard!" Rebecca made a grab for the page, but Jackson slid backward out of reach, landing in his seat with a solid thud. The desk creaked in protest. He held the page above his head, blue eyes daring. Rebecca sprang to her feet, but Jackson was quicker, sliding out of his desk and dancing away from her.

"You want this?" he asked, smiling innocently. White teeth flashed as a grin spread across his face. He held the page out to Rebecca. She made another grab for it, only to have Jackson whip it once more out of reach.

This was futile. Rebecca bit her lips and forced herself to stand still. Her scowl caused Jackson's grin to widen. For a long moment, she glared at him, fury smoldering inside her. She felt herself grow cold and calm even as the anger built. She felt detached from herself, like she was out of her body and watching from somewhere else. Was this Laney? Still she didn't move. Jackson's grin slipped a little. He relaxed a tiny bit.

Rebecca lunged.

She hurled herself into him and drove one elbow with savage force into his solar plexus. Jackson grunted and doubled over, his breath rushing out in a loud wheeze. Rebecca stomped a foot on his instep. She grabbed a handful of his hair and wrenched his head down. Jackson let out a wheezy yowl. Still doubled over and gasping for breath, he fended her off. She almost had it. Her fingers touched the paper; her hand closed over it! Jackson twisted away at the last second. Rebecca heard a sickening ripping sound, and the paper separated into two ragged pieces. A new level of fury boiled through her, and she gave Jackson's hair another vicious yank. He howled again and tried to duck and pivot away. It was something he did playing sports all the time, but he had never tried to execute the tactic with someone swinging from his hair.

Rebecca clung with manic fury, pummeling his chest with the hand that now clutched the bottom half of her notes. Every time her fist thudded into him, there was a *whoof* from Jackson and a little *skritch* from the paper. Jackson still managed to keep the other half just out of reach. Oblivious to anything around them, they danced a savage ballet in the middle of the aisle. It was only seconds, really, but time seemed to have slowed to a crawl.

"*What is the meaning of this disruption!*"

Mr. Hammond's voice thundered at them from the front of the classroom. Jackson and Rebecca froze in mid-struggle. It might have been comical had it been someone else. Someone else pounding on Jackson, gripping a handful of his hair in one hand, a piece of crumpled paper clutched in the other. Someone else nearly sick with outrage. Someone else who had created an awesome spectacle in Home Room. A part of her seemed to watch from a distance. That part observed that Jackson was bent in a half crouch, his head hauled awkwardly toward her as, even now in frozen pantomime, she tightened her grip on his hair. Responding to instinct or stubbornness, he still managed to keep her notes out of reach, gripped in his fist like a trophy. A tangle of arms and legs, faces red and twisted into grimaces, they remained locked together in their now-motionless pas de deux.

Mr. Hammond's voice came again. "Jackson! *Miss* Coleson!"

They disentangled from each other. Jackson straightened, rubbing his head and then his solar plexus. Rebecca smoothed her hair and adjusted the blue sweater in an effort to gather herself. Feeling naked and exposed, she tugged her jacket closer and turned to face the front of the room where Mr. Hammond glowered from behind his desk.

"You will approach *immediately!*"

Rebecca's fury was seeping away, leaving embarrassment and humiliation. The "other" self vanished, taking with her any sense of detachment. It felt all too real now. With a sinking feeling of defeat, Rebecca made her way up the aisle. She was only dimly aware of Jackson following behind her. They came to a stop in front of Mr. Hammond's desk.

"To what do we owe this unconscionable display?" demanded Mr. Hammond. He scowled first at Rebecca and then at Jackson.

They stared at him. Neither of them spoke.

"Well? *Explain yourselves!*"

Jackson shuffled his feet. Rebecca wished she could sink into the floor. They were both mute. And then they both spoke at once. Mr. Hammond raised one hand. He looked at Jackson.

"Sorry, Mr. Hammond," said Jackson in his best "I'm a jock I can't help myself" voice. "I was just playing around. I guess it got a little out of control."

Mr. Hammond grunted. He turned his angry gaze on Rebecca. "Miss Coleson?"

"He took my notes . . ."

He didn't let her finish. "I'll take that."

Mr. Hammond glanced down at the severely abused paper and back up at Rebecca. "Not much here to get so upset about," he said and dropped the tattered sheet on his desk.

"He has the other half. He took them and wouldn't give them back." Her heart was pounding, her voice was shaking. Her throat was thick with the threat of tears.

Jackson held out the mangled paper. "Here," he said. "Sorry, Becka."

Rebecca grabbed the torn page, smoothing it against the front of her jacket and folding it to hide the vivid green "Author's Notes."

"Well, then," said Mr. Hammond. "No particular harm done, it seems. But you will both refrain from disrupting my class in such a manner in the future." His voice was stern. He frowned at Rebecca.

"Yes, sir," said Jackson meekly.

Rebecca looked at Mr. Hammond in disbelief.

"Miss Coleson?"

"Yes, sir," muttered Rebecca. She gritted her teeth. "May I please have the rest of my notes?" She gestured at the crumpled page lying on Mr. Hammond's desk. Mr. Hammond waved his hand indifferently. Rebecca took it as a yes and grabbed the paper. He dismissed them with a careless gesture.

"All right, class," said Mr. Hammond. "Tyson and Ali have finished their round. Let's everybody get back to business."

There was laughter from the class. Her face flaming, tears of humiliation and frustration barely held in check, Rebecca turned and followed Jackson between the rows of desks to their seats. Time seemed to have slowed again, and it felt like an endless march. Her chest was so tight her breath came in shallow gasps. A sick sensation boiled in the pit of her stomach. Along with it, however, smoldered a burning resentment. It simply was *not fair!* Jackson seemed unperturbed by the horrid scene, grinning at two idiot-jock buddies as he sauntered toward his desk. *Jackson the Jerk*, she thought. She wished he was dead. In fact, she wished she was too.

Rebecca reached her seat and collapsed into it, hunching down in an attempt to become as small as possible. Invisible would be even better. She heard the jests thrown at Jackson by his buddies.

"Pretty sorry, Middleton!"

"Taken down by a girl!"

Josh made a loud sucking noise on the back of his hand. "Teacher's pet, Jacks," he snickered.

Jackson just grinned. "No way, Telluride," was all he said.

The boys bumped fists. Desks scraped the floor as they briefly arm-wrestled. No reprimand came from Mr. Hammond. *Figures,* Rebecca thought. Her emotions were a gut-curdling mixture that threatened to evict her lunch.

As the clock crawled toward the hour, Rebecca buried her face in a textbook. She was not reading. She was simply marking time until the end of the period and escape. When the final bell tolled at last, Rebecca shoved her book into her knapsack and darted for the door. She melted gratefully into the melee of students, wanting to put as much distance between herself and Home Room as possible. Eyes on the floor, she plowed headlong into another student.

"Oh, sorry . . ." Rebecca muttered an apology, her head still down.

"Hey, Becks!"

The familiar voice made Rebecca look up. AJ! The red-framed glasses were knocked askew. Their arms were entwined almost as though getting ready for a slow dance. AJ gazed down at Rebecca from a height enhanced by her high-heeled sandals. She straightened her glasses with one hand, still holding Rebecca's shoulder.

"What's up?"

Rebecca couldn't speak. Her face was twisted with emotion and the effort to hold back tears. She tried to shrug out of AJ's grasp, but AJ held on.

"Becks, what's the matter?"

Rebecca shook her head wordlessly. She let AJ pull her out of the flow of students and into an alcove housing a glassed-in trophy display for various sports achievements. She was still afraid to speak, afraid she'd lose it completely if she so much as opened her mouth.

"Come on, Becks, spill," urged AJ quietly.

Rebecca shook her head. She trusted Alexa. They all did. Unruffled by drama, mostly disinterested in gossip, it was not easy to unsettle AJ. When things got crazy, AJ got cooler. Even so, Rebecca didn't think she could tell her about the scene in Home Room.

AJ waited, her calm gaze holding Rebecca's. At last, Rebecca gave in, the fight draining out of her. She slumped against the trophy case, the glass cool on her hot face. Still shaking her head, she said, "It's that stupid Jackson. And Mr. Hammond. And my notes . . ." Rebecca's voice was ragged. For a moment, she couldn't continue.

AJ prompted her. "What has Jackson done this time? And what does Mr. Hammond have to do with it?"

Rebecca brushed at her eyes with the back of her hand and then poured out the entire story in a rush. Anger boiled in the pit of her stomach; frustration was a tight fist around her chest. The unfairness of it—there simply were no words. AJ listened without interrupting. Finished at last, Rebecca forced out a deep breath and said, "I wish that stupid jerk was . . ."

"Was what?" asked AJ.

As Rebecca searched her mind for something sufficiently hateful to give Jackson his just desserts, her gaze fell on a freshman football trophy next to a team photo. Surrounded by the rest of the players, Jackson knelt in the front row, holding a football and grinning. The idiot grin. The "See me, I'm a star" grin. The cocky FIGJAM grin.

Rebecca landed a vicious kick on the display case. AJ draped a long arm around her shoulders and steered her toward the front entrance where students were still streaming out toward sunshine and freedom.

The casual but intimate gesture was comforting. Rebecca felt a tiny easing of her anger and frustration.

"Just you and Jackson today?" asked Alexa. "Where were Zoe and Sam?"

"Dentist appointment. English makeup exam." Rebecca grimaced.

There was a pause before AJ asked, "Why do you let him get under your skin so much?"

"You would too." Rebecca was sure of it.

"Well, if I did, I sure as hell would never let him know it," said AJ.

"You know it's not that easy, AJ!"

"Maybe. But it seems like it could be important." The two girls navigated a group of students on the steps. "You don't . . . um . . . *like* him, or something, do you?"

"AJ!" Rebecca wrenched herself from AJ's encircling arm and turned to stare at her.

AJ continued. "I only ask because it seems like maybe you overreact to Jackson sometimes. He's just a stupid boy. What's the big deal?"

"You know it's not just today!" Rebecca exhaled in a huff. "He's always bugging me and pestering me and copying my notes and trying to get me to do his homework. He always gets away with crap, and he *never* gets caught—or if he does, he never gets what he deserves! Just because he's a stupid football star. He just grins that stupid grin. It would so serve him right if he . . . if he . . ." Rebecca trailed off. She was too wound up to think clearly.

"If what?"

"I don't even know if what! I get him in every single one of my classes, and he's always in my face!"

AJ murmured a noncommittal "Mmm . . ."

"It's *so* not fair!"

"You couldn't possibly believe high school has anything to do with being fair," said AJ. Her voice was soft, but there was an underlying edge.

"Well, it's *not* fair!" Rebecca insisted stubbornly.

"I know, Becks," said AJ. She sighed. "There's my ride." She nodded in the direction of the passenger drop zone. "Speaking of one of God's gifts." Her nose wrinkled. "Do you want a lift?"

Rebecca followed Alexa's gaze to a battered pickup truck idling at the curb. AJ's brother, Tom, a senior football star, sat behind the wheel, his arm resting casually on the frame of the open driver's window. His body language radiated self-assurance; the confident tilt of his head suggested he was used to winning. He was bantering with another jock, and Rebecca would have bet just about anything their conversation was about football. *Or some other stupid activity involving stupid boys and a stupid ball*, she thought.

"No. Thanks, AJ." Rebecca sighed. "I think I'll walk."

Alexa nodded in understanding. "You're sure? You're okay?"

Rebecca nodded.

AJ hesitated. Then she said, "See you Monday, then." She gave Rebecca a quick hug and headed toward the waiting truck.

Rebecca stood motionless, watching AJ go. A loud creak accompanied the opening of the passenger door. AJ threw her backpack to the floor and slid with athletic grace onto the seat, drawing long legs in after her. The door creaked again before it slammed shut. Rebecca stared after the truck until it disappeared around the corner and out of sight, the expression on her face now closed and unreadable. Abruptly, her blank expression was replaced by one of anger, and with an irritated jerk of her shoulders, she headed toward the street and home in a determined walk.

Rebecca's eyes were fixed on the sidewalk, but she wasn't really seeing it. Now that she was alone, her semi-calm state was slipping away. She was angry—really angry—with that dumb head Jackson. She was embarrassed and humiliated. She felt a helpless sense of unfairness. Things had spun totally out of her control, not that she'd had much to begin with.

It was just too much. Her thoughts were a jumble. The fight. Fat Mr. Hammond who let the jocks get away with everything. Jackson stealing her notes. That's where it had started. With those stupid stories she couldn't seem to stop writing!

Even as her thoughts whirled, she knew the stories weren't stupid. She *liked* writing stories and didn't think she could stop writing them even if she wanted to. The stories seemed to sort of write themselves when she had a good idea. She could see that maybe it wasn't a totally bad thing, but it did make her feel . . . apart. Different. She didn't want to be different. Okay, maybe just a tiny bit different, but not so different that she stood out from everyone else like a vulture droid at a picnic. High school was hard enough.

That dumb Jackson had really gotten under her skin this time, and she had totally lost it. And Mr. Hammond was *such* a waste of life! She thought furiously to herself, *Why are guys so universally lazy, stupid, and annoying? Is it a congenital thing? Some deficiency in their DNA mapping? Are they all damaged at birth?* And what would Laney do?

She paused in her fuming to consider the question. What *would* Laney do?

Rebecca trudged up her street, curiosity now moderating her anger. Laney could get even. But *would* she? She thought maybe Laney would want to even the score somehow. Mulling this over, Rebecca let herself into the house.

"Becka, is that you?" Rebecca heard her mom call out. "Help yourself to a snack. I have a conference call in two minutes." Rebecca's mother worked in the field of complementary and alternative medicine. Rebecca wasn't entirely sure what that entailed, truth be told—fewer knives and pills and more other stuff, she guessed— and most days, her mom worked from her home office.

"Sure." Rebecca mumbled an answer. She dumped her backpack on the bench in the mudroom and headed to the kitchen. She opened the refrigerator and scanned inside for something to eat. Nothing looked interesting. She repeated her search at the pantry, disappearing into the cool, spice-scented space. Nothing there, either. How could they have all this stuff in the house and still not have anything she wanted to eat? She found a little bag of cheese puffs. Forbidden for after-school snacks, of course. She snagged the puffs.

CHAPTER 5

Jackson the Jerk

Still May 3

NIBBLING ON HER cheese puffs, Rebecca trudged down the stairs to her bedroom. She wasn't supposed to eat downstairs, but in her present mood, she didn't care. There were so many rules! Rebecca usually found her room peaceful and cozy. Right now, her little suite failed to cheer her.

Sighing deeply, she plopped down on the corner window seat and pulled a large stuffed bear into her arms. She hugged it to her chest and buried her face in the soft fur. Restless, she put the bear aside. One window was still shuttered following the scene this morning in her mother's shrubs. She stared with unseeing eyes out the other window with its view of the back patio.

She yanked those shutters closed too, shrouding the space in half-light. She wandered around her room. She picked up another stuffed animal, punched a throw pillow, straightened some books on her shelf. A binder containing some of her stories caught her eye, and she picked it up. She flipped absently through the pages, her thoughts scattered. An odd sense of detachment settled over her again. She looked over at her desk, her eyes lingering on her laptop. Her earlier thought resurfaced. *What would Laney do?* Still holding the binder, she crossed the room and perched on the edge of her chair. She opened the laptop and stared at the blinking cursor. She typed in the password and clicked on the word processing icon. Her fingers noodled at the keyboard. She wasn't thinking about a story exactly, or anything at all, really.

Jackson the Jerk. Her fingers tapped out the letters, but her mind was far away.

Suddenly furious all over again, Rebecca flung the story binder across the room. It bounced once on the bed, pages fluttering wildly, and came to rest teepeed on the floor between the bed and the wall. Rebecca straightened at the computer, her face set in a grim mask. She settled her fingers on the keyboard. Slowly and deliberately, she began to type.

> Laney stood on the curb in the light rain. She saw Jackson racing his bike through the parking lot. Skidding to a halt, he waved to Josh, who was flirting with two cheerleaders. Jackson walked his bike in their direction. A large black sedan turned down the parking aisle. Jackson didn't see the car until it was too late. With a yell, he threw himself out of the way. Almost. There was a scream from a bystander, the sound of metal contacting metal, and then a sickening crunch as Jackson's bicycle was crumpled beneath a tire.
>
> A fat man struggled to free himself from the car and waddled to where Jackson sat howling on the curb, rocking back and forth and cradling one ankle in his hands. Mr. Hammond! Jackson had been run over by the champion of jocks! Laney watched impassively. Onlookers gathered at the scene, kids talking excitedly, teachers urging them to move along. One teacher pulled out a cell phone, punched at the device with one finger, and then spoke urgently into it.
>
> Laney turned and walked deliberately into the building, muttering under her breath, "Jackson the Jerk. Serves him right."

Rebecca paused. She stared at her computer for a long moment. Then she took a deep breath, hit Save, and typed The Jerk in the title box. She clicked out of the program and closed her laptop. She nibbled on some cheese puffs. She retrieved her story binder from the floor behind the bed, smoothed the pages, and placed it on her bookshelf. She sat two stuffed bears side by side on the window seat. She opened her shutters and then walked out of her room, closed the door, and ran up the stairs. Reaching the main floor, she called out, "Hey, Mom, what's for dinner?"

CHAPTER 6

Saturday and Denial

May 4

SATURDAY MORNING. REBECCA stretched and then curled onto her side, pulling Tinker into the curve of her body. Her little clock said 9:30.

"Hey, Tinks," she murmured. She kissed the top of Tinker's head and nuzzled her face into the soft fur. Tinker purred her contentment.

A little piece of brilliant blue sky was visible beneath the shrubs outside her window. Her mood matched the sunny day. She dropped another kiss on Tinker's head and slipped out of bed. She stretched again, yawned, and headed for the closet. One hand on the doorknob, her eyes fell on her computer, and a little thrill of unease fluttered in the pit of her stomach.

No! She would not think about the story. She turned toward that little piece of blue sky. It was a perfect day, and she would tolerate nothing less.

She dressed quickly in old jeans and a sweatshirt and tucked earbuds into her ears. Moving in time to music only she could hear, she stripped the sheets off her bed, bundled them into her arms, and headed up the stairs.

Maggie Coleson looked up in surprise as Rebecca ducked into the laundry room and started a load of wash.

"Where's my youngest daughter?" Maggie teased. She held a spatula in one hand and her coffee mug in the other. "You know, the one who's never around when it's time for chores on Saturday morning."

Rebecca ignored the teasing and gave her mother a sunny smile and a big hug. Her mother set her coffee down and hugged her back, ducking her head to lay her cheek against her daughter's tawny hair. Rebecca nestled into her mother, breathing in the familiar scent of lemon verbena.

"Andy hasn't eaten?" Rebecca looked at the pan of bacon sizzling on the stove.

"He had cereal," said Maggie. She turned back to the stove. "This is his second breakfast. And your dad hasn't eaten yet. Do you want eggs and bacon?"

"Mmm. No. Maybe just an egg." Rebecca looked at her mother. "Mom, if I get my chores done right away, do you think Sam and Zoe and I could go to a movie tonight?"

"Perhaps," said her mother with a smile. "Some movie in particular?"

"There's a new Taylor Hunt movie out. *The Girls*. He's got three girlfriends and tries to juggle them all and not get caught," said Rebecca. "I've seen previews. It's pretty hilarious."

"It's so gorgeous today," said Maggie. "You should do something outside."

"I'll do something outside today, and then do the movie tonight." She slipped on a face that was innocent and imploring and adorable all at the same time. At least it was supposed to be.

Maggie laughed. When she was like this, Rebecca was hard to resist. "I don't suppose I have a problem with that. Where is it playing, and how were you thinking of getting there?"

"It's at the new mall. I thought maybe Lissa . . . " Rebecca broke off as her older sister came into the kitchen.

"You thought I what?" said her sister.

Rebecca turned toward Lissa, dropping the "adorable" expression. She favored her sister with a million-watt smile.

"That may make all the boys swoon," said Lissa, "but it doesn't make *my* brain go all mushy. You want something, Becka."

Rebecca nodded. "I was hoping for a ride to the movies tonight. At East Oaks." The million-watt smile morphed into a hopeful expression.

Lissa looked at their mother. "I was planning to meet James at Best Booksellers this evening," she said. "I guess I could drop Becka off. Who else is going?"

Rebecca threw herself at Lissa, arms wrapped around her sister in a suffocating hug. "Oh, thank you, Lissa. Just Zoe and Sam. The show starts at six forty-five. Can you drop us off at six thirty and we'll meet you at the bookstore after?"

Lissa unwound herself from Rebecca's clench and nodded. "Sure."

"Sam and Zoe can come here. For dinner, Mom?" Blue eyes appealed once again to her mother, who nodded, giving in without a fight. "And we can drop them off at home after the bookstore?" Rebecca smiled again at her sister.

"Sure," said Lissa. "Anything else while you're on a roll?"

"No." Rebecca tried to look demure. She quickly gave it up. Singing softly under her breath to a tune coming from the earbuds, she danced out of the kitchen and down the stairs to call her friends.

Lissa and her mother shared a look. "She's the limit," said Lissa.

Maggie Coleson just smiled.

Rebecca threw herself into the rest of Saturday. She helped her father organize his workbench in the garage, which left Jack Coleson wondering if doing it by himself might be much easier. She walked Andy to the park, where he met Jimmy Norton and Jimmy's mom. She helped her mother plant spring flowers in the big pots on the front porch and back patio. This consisted mostly of occasionally handing her mother a bag of soil amendment or a six-pack of colorful plants and scraping weird designs into the dirt with a trowel. Busy. That was the main thing. To stay busy enough that the tiny niggle of unease in the pit of her stomach could be forgotten or disregarded.

Sam and Zoe arrived spot on time. After a quick supper and a hasty washup of dishes, the three girls piled into Lissa's Prius to head for the movie theater. Zoe and Rebecca climbed into the back seat. The middle was piled with Lissa's stuff, so Sam slid into the front passenger seat. Rebecca sighed with inward relief. This day was nearly over, and the Taylor Hunt movie would be far too delicious to allow for errant thoughts of . . . well, any kind whatsoever. As she and Zoe compared notes on what they had heard about the movie, Rebecca noticed that Sam and Lissa were talking earnestly. This seemed a little unusual; it gave her a little tingle in her solar plexus. But she dismissed it.

When Lissa pulled to the curb in front of the theater and the three girls clambered out, Rebecca heard Lissa say, "Talk to my mom," and Sam nodded her head. And then they were rushing to queue up at the ticket window.

CHAPTER 7

Sunday Rituals

May 5

SUNDAY WAS FAMILY day. The Colesons started with a habitual Sunday breakfast. This was Jack Coleson's wish—that on Sunday morning, the entire family sit down together for a meal. Her dad prepared favorite dishes, and they had what he called "meaningful conversation." He usually kicked things off by asking Andy what the best part and the worst part of his week had been. Rebecca had loved it when she was little; now it was more trying than fun. As she slid into her place at the table, a niggle of disquiet stirred in the pit of her stomach. She wasn't sure of the high point of her week, but she knew unequivocally what the low was.

Jack was just settling into his chair when Lissa said, "I need another job."

All eyes turned to Lissa. Maggie paused with her napkin halfway to her mouth.

"But you love the doll shop!" Rebecca could hardly believe what she was hearing. "And you pretty much get paid to play with dolls."

"I do," said Lissa. "To both of those things. And I have plenty of time to study, which is great. But the pay sucks, and I'll have expenses at college, even if I have a full scholarship."

"It's good to think ahead," said Jack. He dug into his breakfast.

"Do you have some leads? Or at least ideas?" Maggie's voice was carefully neutral.

"What about Mrs. Mason?" asked Jack. "Isn't she sort of . . ."

"Is she really crazy?" Andy interrupted.

"Andy," Maggie gently reproved her son.

Rebecca took a big bite of egg. "Mmm. Great omelet, Dad."

"Thanks, Princess."

"I do," Lissa said again, nodding at her mother. "I've been thinking about it a lot." She took a sip of coffee. "I do love the dolls."

"Yeah, tough job," said Rebecca. "Maybe I could do that part."

Lissa looked thoughtful. "You know," she said, "that's not a half-bad idea."

Rebecca looked up. This was getting interesting.

Lissa continued, "I'd like to have something a little more substantial to, you know, look good on my admissions forms." She took a bite of egg. "In addition to making more money."

Maggie nodded. Jack looked skeptical but kept silent.

"So what are you thinking, Liss?"

"Well, the rock shop," said Lissa carefully. Her father opened his mouth, and Lissa went on before he could speak. "It's way more than crystals and incense." She looked pointedly at her mother. "There's been a major re-do. It's pretty awesome. They've added regular massage, but also energy massage. Reiki, hypnosis, life coaching, yoga—and they're adding even more classes. There's even a holistic chiropractor who's going to start work there."

Now Maggie was fully interested. "I did not know that," she said.

"They've done some expansion and refurbishing and changed the name. It's called High Health Center now."

"I like it," said Maggie.

"There's a medicinal herb garden in the back. Part of Mrs. Mason's estate. And a couple aroma therapists work out of the shop." Lissa was reeling her mother in.

"Interesting," Maggie said.

"Do the rumor therapists *live* out there?" asked Andy. "Like, in the herbs?"

Rebecca nearly choked on her eggs. She sneaked a look at her mother, who was biting her lips behind her napkin, her eyes sparkling with suppressed laughter.

Lissa was barely keeping it together. Smiling widely at Andy, she managed to speak in a calm voice. "*Aroma* therapists, Andy. You know, an aroma is a smell. Aroma therapists make things from different plants, and then we can breathe in the smells, and they can be good for us."

"Oh." Andy considered this. "Like how? How can they be good for us?"

"Like helping us sleep," said Lissa. "Or making you feel relaxed if you're stressed out."

Maggie nodded in approval. She said softly to Lissa, "Well done."

Jack didn't notice any of this. He was frowning. "Is there some sort of opportunity?"

"Well, you know what they say," Lissa said. "The best way to get a job is to make up the one you want and then pitch the hell out of it. Convince them they need it."

Andy grinned at his sister's profanity. Maggie threw Lissa a cautionary look. Jack was still on point.

"And what do you think they need?" her father persisted.

"Well, maybe they could use an advocate with a connection to the energy/alternative community. Like CAM. Sort of like a . . . facilitator, maybe." Lissa looked at her mother.

"Who'd have thought," mused Maggie. "And Mrs. Mason knows about alternative healing modalities?"

"Absolutely. She owns the rock shop. And she's the driving force behind it."

"Hmm." Maggie seemed to be at a loss for words.

Jack was not. "This sounds like a job for your mother," he said. "And it's a bit of a stretch from that to sustainability."

"Maybe not so much," said Lissa.

"They have a college for stainability?" asked Andy, his mouth full of toast.

"*Sus*tainability, Andy," corrected Lissa.

"Right," said Andy. "Like Dad and I did to the deck last summer."

Rebecca and Lissa burst into laughter. Their parents tried to keep straight faces, but this time, it was just too much.

Andy looked, first, perplexed and then offended. When Lissa could talk, she explained sustainability to Andy.

"Do you have to go away to college? Why don't you just stay with us and dress dolls at the shop?" Andy sounded wistful.

"It's not for another year, Andy," said Lissa. She ruffled her little brother's hair, and he briefly leaned his head against her hand.

Rebecca was touched watching them. The thought of Lissa leaving for college made her a little sad too. But maybe she'd get Lissa's larger room downstairs. Surely that would ease the sting of having her sister leave home.

For a few minutes, it was quiet around the table except for the clinking of flatware against dishes. Lissa broke the quiet. "Mom, how much does veterinary medicine embrace alternative practices?"

"Not much, I don't think," said Maggie. "But it's a little outside my frame of reference. Why do you ask?"

"Just something Sarah Ann said last night," said Lissa. "Made me wonder."

"What did Sam say?" Rebecca remembered Sam and Lissa in earnest conversation on the way to the movie. A little twinge of anxiety prickled in the pit of her stomach.

"Something about a lame horse being put down . . ."

"No!" Rebecca's fork fell with a clatter onto her plate.

Lissa put a hand on Rebecca's arm. "They haven't done anything like that yet."

"But they might? Which horse is lame? Not Skydancer!"

"I don't know. Sam didn't say."

"Why would she ask you?" Rebecca demanded.

"She asked me about my chakra pendant." Lissa fingered the long, narrow pendant hanging from a chain around her neck. "And one thing led to another. Energy healing came up somehow. And she asked if it could work for horses." Lissa looked at her mother. "I'm sure it would, but I thought maybe you'd know, Mom . . ."

"Jimmy Norton got another lizard," said Andy in a seven-year-old's perfect non sequitur. He looked around the room hopefully.

"Is it another bearded dragon?" Lissa smiled at her little brother.

"Maybe. Wait, no, it's a . . ." Andy paused, his brow furrowed in concentration. "I forget," he said. "But it's pretty cool." He looked hopefully at his mother.

"Probably not," was all she said.

"What about you?" Jack looked at Rebecca.

"Me what?"

"Your week," her father said calmly, as if there had been no mention of a weird lizard or murdering an innocent horse.

"I just had my low point," said Rebecca. "Hearing that a lame horse might have to be put down and wondering what that might do to Sam." Her voice was grim.

"You'd pull her through it," said Lissa.

Rebecca glared at her.

"You're an unusually close group of friends," said Lissa. "Especially you and Sam and Zoe. You'd have her back. Help her get through it." Lissa looked at her mother, and Maggie nodded.

"You are an odd little group," said Jack.

"Jack!" Maggie was aghast.

"Dad! What do you mean? We aren't odd at all . . ." Rebecca's chest felt tight. This was more than distressing. Her father thought her *odd*?

"I just mean . . . diverse," Jack said lamely.

Rebecca pushed her chair back and carried her dishes to the sink.

"Come on, Becka," her father pleaded. "I didn't mean anything. Don't be mad."

"I'm not mad, Dad." Rebecca's was voice carefully neutral, and she refused to look at her father. "Mom, can I go up to Zoe's after we get the dishes cleared up? Until it's time to leave for Nanna's?"

"She's coming with us today, isn't she?"

"No. Her grandmother's here from New Orleans."

"Yvonne Cotard? Oh, I love her!" Maggie beamed. "Such a character."

"Yeah, well . . . so long as no one thinks she's odd or something."

"Sure, Becka. You can go for a while." Maggie threw a warning look at her husband as she brought her own dishes to the sink. "And no one thinks Yvonne Cotard is odd. She's much too powerful for that. She is clearly and unapologetically her own person."

"We're not all done here," complained Jack.

But it looked like they were.

Maggie brushed a kiss on Rebecca's cheek. "We'll leave at four. You know the drill."

Rebecca did. Another Sunday ritual was visiting her grandparents a few miles outside of town. This wasn't mandatory. Rebecca rarely missed, but it was because she wanted to go. She had always loved being at Nanna's house. She had countless memories of happy times there. She remembered making sugar cookies and decorating them for holidays. Any holiday, not just Christmas. Nanna said sugar cookies were nonpartisan when it came to holidays. There had been cozy nights snuggled in front of a fire when Nanna had read to her, movies with popcorn and peanut butter crisps. Games out on the deck. Pappa teasing her. Pappa was like a big bear. Cuddly and sort of scary at the same time. Were bears cuddly? Well, to another bear, probably. Rebecca smiled to herself at the image.

Later, settled in the back seat of her dad's big pickup, Rebecca leaned her head against the window. Zoe's house had been wild. Mrs. Cotard—Mme. Cotard, she corrected herself—had been, as usual, wildly upbeat. Rebecca wondered absently if the old lady was a little crazy but instantly felt bad about it. *Powerful and unapologetically herself.* That's how her mother had described Mme. Cotard. That would be a really good thing, wouldn't it?

Don't you need to know who you are before you can be unapologetic about it? Was that Laney's voice in her head? This was new. Sometimes Rebecca felt she was thinking Laney's thoughts, especially when she was writing, but Laney didn't usually just drop into the conversation. Also, Rebecca thought Laney was being a bit snide.

Rebecca thought about Mme. Cotard. Nanna was like her in that she was powerful and unapologetically herself. Beyond that, Nanna was kind of hard to define. She had a way of making Rebecca feel special. But she could be as tough as an iron spike. She expected the best of people and accepted nothing less. She was diminutive in size, but no one mistook that for fragility. Nanna's hair was silver, and expression lines described her face, but she was full of life and energy. There was a little framed motto on Nanna's desk that said, "Be curious, and expect miracles." Maybe that was the best way to sum up Nanna. Curious and expecting miracles.

The truck pulled to a stop beneath a grove of big cottonwood trees and stands of lodgepole pine. Andy clambered down and dashed for the house. Rebecca slid down more slowly. She followed her parents up the flagstone path and into the house.

"I have cookies," she heard Nanna say.

"What kind?" Andy asked.

"Peanut butter," said Nanna. "Of course!"

"They're the best!" Andy threw his arms around her. "Are the trains set up?" he asked.

"Aren't they always? You remember how to turn on the power?"

Andy nodded. "Thanks for the cookies, Nanna!" And he ran for the basement stairs. He'd be down there for hours. Or at least until he ran out of cookies.

"Are you coming, Dad?" Andy's voice carried up the stairs.

"In a bit," Jack called back.

There were hugs around. Rebecca noticed that her mother lingered in Nanna's arms, too. Maggie Coleson was several inches taller than her mother, and she bent her golden head to rest it on Nanna's silver one.

"Is Dad home?" Maggie asked Nanna.

"No. He's . . ." Nanna paused and made a vague gesture with one hand. "Somewhere in the Southeast. He had several sites to visit starting early tomorrow."

Then to no one in particular, Nanna asked, "Cookies for anyone else?"

Jack tapped one finger against his chest. Nanna nodded at a crystal canister filled with chocolate cookies. He helped himself to a handful. Maggie took one. Rebecca shook her head.

"How can you be a daughter of mine?" said her mother, laughing. "What happened to your chocolate gene?"

"Try these," said Nanna. She handed a plate to Rebecca. "Pumpkin-pecan."

"Nanna!" Rebecca exclaimed. "My most favorite! Oh, thank you!" Rebecca took the plate in both hands.

"Those look good," said her father.

"There are more, Jack," Nanna said, and she pointed to a covered tin on the counter.

Rebecca helped herself to several cookies and then passed the plate to her father. He took a cookie and pulled her into the curve of one arm, giving her a gentle squeeze. She nearly purred with contentment, the exchange over breakfast at least temporarily forgotten.

"These are yummy, Nanna," Rebecca said around a mouthful of cookie.

"I take credit for the peanut butter and chocolate cookies," Nanna said. "The pumpkin-pecan are April's. I asked her to make them especially for you." Nanna gave Rebecca an affectionate hug.

Rebecca hugged her fiercely back. She was so happy her throat felt tight. She didn't try to speak.

April was Nanna's helper and a very close friend. Rebecca's earliest memories included her. Nanna referred to April as her manager, but Rebecca didn't think anyone managed her grandmother. April's job was somewhat vague. It seemed she did whatever was needed to keep Nanna free for writing. Apparently, she was talented in the kitchen as well. All in all, Rebecca thought April was a pretty handy sort to have around.

"Why don't you get a manager, Mom?" Rebecca said around another bite of cookie.

"Because I have you," said her mother sweetly.

"But that's the whole point," said Rebecca stubbornly. "You wouldn't need me so much if you had an April." She took another bite. "I could focus more on my studies."

Skeptical looks were followed by wide grins, chuckles, and then outright laughter. It seemed to be contagious, whatever it was. At least to her parents and grandmother.

"What? What's so funny?" Rebecca looked from one to another of them, frowning. She hadn't really been joking. Having someone like

April around seemed like an immensely good idea to her. She slid onto a barstool, fidgeted, slid off again. She helped herself to another cookie. Finally, the laughter trailed off. Her father was still grinning from ear to ear.

"You're a piece of work, Princess," he said. He tousled her hair gently. She frowned at him, pulling her head away.

"Lissa's at the doll shop?" asked Nanna. She patted a tissue to the corners of her eyes.

Maggie nodded, still smiling broadly. She dabbed at her eyes with the hem of her shirt. "Mrs. Mason's a bit eccentric, but they get on famously. And she has time to study—"

Whatever else Maggie might have said was interrupted by another round of laughter. When it settled down again, Maggie said, "She does love the dolls."

"Serendipity finding that job," Nanna said softly.

"Mmm." Maggie acknowledged. "More than we knew, apparently. There's an entirely different aspect I only just learned of this morning."

Nanna looked interested. She waited for Maggie to go on.

"The rock shop has expanded."

They'd been over all this at breakfast. Rebecca looked around. "Where's Inkjet?"

"Oh, around here somewhere," said Nanna. "He was up in the loft last time I saw him."

"Can I take my cookies up and look for him?"

Nanna nodded and handed Rebecca a napkin. Rebecca went up the stairs to the loft, looking around for the big black-and-white cat. The loft was really just an open area with two comfortable chairs flanking a low table stacked with books. Nanna said it was a waste of space, but Rebecca liked the high, open feeling of it. Inkjet had a favorite chair, but he was nowhere in sight at the moment. Rebecca went down the hallway. The door to a small room stood ajar.

This was her favorite spot, far more than any of the soaring spaces and breathtaking views in the rest of the house. The little room was tucked under the eaves. Nanna called it the aerie. Rebecca thought of it as her hidey-hole. As she stood in the doorway, she felt a part of herself sort of float away. It was like she was two people, yet linked. Was this Laney again?

Rebecca looked around the room. Soft throw rugs, their bright colors faded from many washings, were strewn across the floor. There was a bed tight against one wall, draped with a colorful spread and stacked with fat pillows. A stuffed chair and a small table were nestled at the foot of the bed. Opposite the bed, the ceiling sloped down to a wall of bookshelves. Rebecca let her eyes roam over its contents, lingering on well-loved stuffed animals and dolls that shared space with favorite childhood books.

She crossed the room, her fingers trailing along the edge of the bed, and stepped through a French door onto a little balcony. Spreading cottonwood limbs arched over the deck. *Tree house,* she thought. There was just room for two chairs and a little table. She was high above the world here. It felt hidden, but she could see out. She noticed new leaves budding on the cottonwoods. They shrouded the trees in a pale green mist. Rebecca leaned against the deck rail and ate her last pumpkin-pecan cookie. A feeling of contentment settled over her, and she sighed. This was perfect. Problems always seemed to just slip away when she was here.

Not that I have any problems, she thought quickly.

There's Jackson the Jerk, whispered Laney. *That could be a problem.*

And there it was. The source of that niggling unrest that had dogged her all weekend. She straightened abruptly, wrapping her arms around her middle. She went back into the room and sank into the comfy old chair, running her hands over fabric worn a little shabby with time. Jackson the Jerk. Throughout the weekend, she had done her best to outrun, to ignore, to deny, to will away thoughts of Jackson. Mostly it had worked. But now . . .

Thanks a lot, Laney, she thought.

Her two selves seemed to snap back together. She sprang to her feet. She closed the door onto the deck and locked it. She looked around for a long moment and then left the aerie, pulling the door closed behind her. She hurried back down the stairs. Her mother and grandmother were sitting on the deck, deep in discussion, heads inclined toward each other. Something about their body language suggested the conversation was serious; instinct told Rebecca she was the topic. She paused, hesitating to make her presence known. The voices drifted into the kitchen through the open French doors.

". . . discovering her abilities," Rebecca heard the tag end of her mother's statement.

"You haven't seen anything specific, though?" she heard Nanna say.

"No, nothing specific," said her mother. "It's more a sense I have."

"Well, you have to respect that," said Nanna.

"I do, Mom. She just seems too young."

"She's nearly fifteen. I was only twelve."

"A young fifteen," said her mother.

"We always feel that about our children, don't you think?"

"No, I don't." Maggie's voice was firm. "I don't feel that way about Lissa at all. She's always been mature beyond her years—such an old soul. She was never really a babe. But not Becka. She's more . . . tender. Innocent."

Nanna nodded. "Well, yes, I'd have to say you're right about that."

Rebecca stood still at the base of the stairs, her heart thumping in her chest. She felt a tingling sensation in her solar plexus, not unlike the feeling that accompanied one of her ideas. But this one didn't feel as good. She wanted to listen longer, but she was afraid of what she might hear.

"Mom! Nanna! Who hid the pumpkin-pecan cookies?" And Rebecca clattered loudly across the kitchen.

"On the counter, Becka," called Nanna.

"Oh, here they are!"

Rebecca didn't really feel like another cookie. Not now. But she took one anyway. She had to, didn't she? She carried it out to the deck. Both women had been sitting upright, leaning forward in their seats. As Rebecca approached, Nanna reached for a glass of wine and relaxed into her big glider. She gave it a push with one foot. The glides squeaked in protest.

"I really need to get that fixed," said Nanna.

Rebecca's mother sat in a deep wicker chair with her own glass of wine. She set the glass down and sank into the depths of the cushions, drawing up her long legs and tucking her feet under her. They both smiled at Rebecca. Just two ladies relaxing in the spring sunshine and enjoying the view. But Rebecca imagined she could see energy-laced colors swirling around them. She started. Where had that come from? She was relieved to see Inkjet appear around the corner of the house. He was so . . . normal! Inkjet meandered over to them and leaped gracefully onto the glider. He gave one shoulder a few quick strokes with his tongue, scratched an ear with a hind foot, and settled into Nanna's lap. A perfectly regular, ordinary occurrence. Something you see every day. The image of those weird, swirly energies faded away.

Nanna patted the seat next to her. Rebecca sat and relaxed against her grandmother. Nanna smoothed the hair from Rebecca's forehead in a gesture Rebecca had loved as long as she could remember. She leaned a little into Nanna's hand; no wonder cats loved to be petted! She stroked Inkjet's fur. His ears twitched and his eyes closed to slits. Purring, he nudged Rebecca's hand with his nose. She ran her fingers through the thick fur, taking comfort from its softness and warmth. She relaxed a little more. For the moment, things were all right. But something was going on. And tomorrow . . .

CHAPTER 8

The Story Comes to Life

May 6

MONDAY MORNING DAWNED cold and gray. A drizzly rain dampened the vivid displays of spring, which had been so bright and hopeful over the weekend. Beads of moisture clung to the bright flowers Maggie had carefully planted on Saturday, and their heads drooped beneath its weight. Rebecca felt their grief. She shrugged into a warm jacket and grabbed one strap of her knapsack as she rushed out the door after Lissa.

"Lissa! Can I ride with you?"

Lissa turned and nodded. "I'm going by the doll shop."

"I don't care. I don't want to walk in this miserable rain."

Lissa nodded once more, and Rebecca ran for the car. In truth, Rebecca hoped to avoid running into anyone, even her friends. She was feeling strangely detached again this morning, but there was a fragile sense of safety in it, and she didn't want that compromised. She yanked open the passenger door, tossed her backpack onto the floor, and slid in after it. The knapsack was light. It contained her homework, a water bottle, and a snack. No story folders, no notes.

"Thanks, Lissa." Rebecca sighed as she buckled her seat belt.

"No problem." Lissa carefully backed the car out of the driveway and turned down the wet, tree-lined street.

Lissa and Rebecca shared the same honey-golden hair, light complexion with a dusting of freckles, and startling blue eyes. Their likeness pretty much ended there. Tall and willowy, Lissa was a younger version of their mother. Nothing seemed to disturb Lissa. She took the daily dramas and aggravations of school in stride. She seemed to get along with everybody. There was an otherworldly quality about Lissa. Rebecca remembered her mother's comment of the previous afternoon. "Lissa is such an old soul." What did that mean exactly?

Rebecca envied Lissa's calm and easygoing nature. And her long legs. Okay, also her crystal jewelry. Lissa had a seemingly bottomless trove of crystal rings, pendants, earrings. Even in her funk, Rebecca noticed the deep-green stone around her sister's neck.

Rebecca wasn't flashy. Not that her sister's green stone was flashy. It wasn't. But she felt more comfortable with things that didn't draw attention. Except for shoes. Rebecca loved shoes, and especially heels. She was sure slipping her feet into a pair of heeled boots would have put her in a better mood this morning. Her father's notions were just plain weird. It wasn't fair. Other than things relating to shoes, Rebecca's nature was often guarded. She thought of herself as average. Sometimes she felt okay blending in with the crowd. There was a sense of safety in being anonymous. But other days, she wished for some characteristic that was more . . . memorable. She was a late bloomer. Not completely comfortable with her budding womanhood, she tended to keep its evidence hidden beneath loose shirts and jackets. Although she was capable of being an excellent student, there were times when she failed to see the point. She could be moody. This morning was one of those times. No fashion boots, no crystal stone. Wrapped in her own thoughts, she retreated into silence. She was quite comfortable there.

"You're pretty quiet this morning," Lissa observed. "Even for you."

"Huh?"

"Nothing. Just noting that you're quiet," said Lissa.

"Oh."

Lissa glanced over at Rebecca. "Something on your mind?"

"No, just thinking about something."

"Um, that's . . ." Lissa closed her mouth, thinking affectionately, *That's what I said, doofus.* She gave her sister a long look. Rebecca didn't seem to notice. They rode the rest of the way to the doll shop in silence, Rebecca absently twirling a lock of hair around one finger.

Rebecca waited in the car while Lissa dropped off . . . whatever she was dropping off. She stared impassively at the gardens surrounding the old house. Dripping in the light rain, the trees and shrubs seemed to be withdrawn into themselves, waiting. *Like me*, thought Rebecca. But she didn't know what she was waiting for.

At the school, Lissa let Rebecca out in front of the big, new building with its facade of towering windows and impressive overhanging beams and eaves. Her earlier sense of detachment persisted, leaving her feeling disconnected. She quickly climbed out of the car so Lissa could move along with traffic. Lissa would have a long walk from the student parking lot in the cold rain, and Rebecca was grateful to have been let out close to the entrance.

As she stepped onto the sidewalk, she took note of the line of vehicles moving onto the school grounds. Some of them turned into the staff parking lot. Most continued around the loop to the loading zone where students were dropped at the curb. From the corner of her eye, Rebecca noticed a big black car moving toward the staff parking lot. She felt she should recognize it, but she didn't. Once inside the staff area, cars moved smoothly into vacant spaces. She glanced again at the black car. She still had no inkling of who could be driving it. She became vaguely aware of a group of boys, animated and rowdy, cutting with their bikes through the traffic flow and moving in the direction of the docking racks by the front doors.

Rebecca moved into the flow of students heading for the sheltered main entrance. As she mounted the steps, she heard a grating crunch and a simultaneous yell. Her heart leaped in her chest. She whirled to see a bicycle protruding from beneath the bumper of the big black car. As she watched, frozen, the dreaded Mr. Hammond maneuvered his bulk from the car and waddled toward a blond boy who was extricating himself from beneath the twisted bike. The boy lurched to the curb where he sank to the concrete. Cradling one ankle in his hands, he rocked back and forth, howling in outrage.

Rebecca knew it was Jackson Middleton without knowing how she knew. Well, maybe she *did* know how she knew. Her heart was racing, and she could feel her blood pulsing loudly in her ears. The scene before her played out with heightened clarity, unfolding in slow motion to a known outcome. Other students were converging on the scene, but to Rebecca's ears, their excited voices seemed to come from far away. Two or three more teachers appeared and began herding the onlookers toward the building. A teacher knelt by the student on the curb—knelt by Jackson—and the yelling subsided. Another teacher was speaking with the Fat Man. The Fat Man was scowling and the teacher was gesturing wildly. Rebecca saw one of the teachers pull out a cell phone. She was calling the school nurse. Rebecca knew that.

As more students congregated at the scene, Rebecca turned on her heel and walked toward the school entrance. In her head, along with the thud-thudding, which she could still feel, she heard Laney say, *Jackson the Jerk. Serves him right.*

This did nothing to slow her racing heart or quiet her pounding pulse, but to all outward appearances, Rebecca was calm and poised. She observed the school nurse hurrying out the main doors and down the sidewalk, accompanied by both the principal and the vice principal.

Then she saw Alexa in the crush of students making their way into the building, and when AJ called out to her, Rebecca smiled broadly and waved back.

"AJ!"

"Hey, Becks! Cool weekend?" AJ clutched her jacket close. She grimaced as a gust of wind hit them. "Jeez, I hate winter," she muttered. "Thought it was over."

"You're just a beach bum wannabe," said Rebecca.

"For sure," said AJ. "I make no apologies."

Arms linked, Rebecca's face turned up to her taller friend, the girls strolled into the building in familiar intimacy. The scene playing out on the curb was forgotten. Or nearly so.

CHAPTER 9

The "Accident"

May 6

NEWS OF JACKSON'S accident—that's what it was, an accident—was already viral by the time first period began. A star athlete hit by a teacher's car! It didn't matter that he was only a freshman. Everyone knew Jackson had great potential for varsity. Not to mention he was one of the highest-profile (make that popular) students in the school. First-period algebra was chaos. Mr. Hammond and Jackson, of course, never showed. Neither did Josh Kenyon. Rebecca could only wonder where Josh was. Maybe he went with Jackson to . . . wherever Jackson went. Rebecca tried to keep her mind from the idea of "hospital." The calm, detached feeling of Laney in her head had retreated, leaving Rebecca feeling like she was high on something. A jagged, unpleasant high.

Rebecca sat hunched in her desk across the aisle from the two empty seats. She refused to look at them, but it took a monumental effort. Her heart was still thudding dully in her chest. It felt like an appropriate compliment to the commotion all around her. About ten minutes after the bell, the vice principal came in to take over the class. He passed out practice algebra problems, but no one pretended to work. Even the vice principal didn't seem interested in them. He was barely maintaining order. He commanded the class to take their seats, and everyone did. But even then, conversations continued about the accident.

An accident. And a totally weird coincidence! Rebecca took a deep breath, let it out. Again. It did nothing to calm her. That's what it had to be. An accident. A fluke. There could be absolutely no connection between her little story and Jackson's accident. Really! There simply was no other explanation. Anything else was too far out.

She bought that. Mostly.

Things had settled down a little by the end of algebra, but second period brought together whole new groups of students to talk about it. There was nothing new to tell, but that didn't stop everyone from rehashing it. Including Tyler.

"I was practically right there," said Tyler. "And I never knew it happened. Did you?"

Rebecca nodded.

"You actually saw it?"

Rebecca nodded again but made no comment.

"You didn't say anything."

Rebecca shrugged uncomfortably.

"Why didn't you say something? What happened? How *could* it happen!"

"I don't know, Ty," said Rebecca. She struggled to keep her face and voice calm. "It all happened so fast."

"What was Jackson doing there on his bike?" Tyler persisted.

"Who knows? Why does Jackson do anything?"

"You know him. You have classes with him."

"That doesn't make me an expert on Jackson's behavior patterns." Irritation lurked just beneath the surface of Rebecca's emotions.

"Why didn't Mr. Hammond stop?" Tyler was upset.

"Tyler, I don't know. I don't know any of this. Get a grip!"

Tyler looked remorseful. "Sorry, Becks." But she seemed incapable of letting it go. "I just don't understand how something like this could happen. Especially to an important player." She grabbed her ponytail with one hand, gripping it tightly.

"What difference does it make that Jackson is an athlete? Would no one care if he was just a dweeb?" Rebecca's voice rose enough that several students glanced over at them.

Tyler didn't seem to notice any of it. "I wonder how bad he's hurt. I hope not too bad. There's a big game coming up Friday."

"A game?" Rebecca couldn't believe her ears.

"A baseball game," said Tyler.

"No one follows baseball, Ty," said Rebecca.

"I do." Tyler's voice was stubborn.

Now irritation uncurled from the pit of Rebecca's stomach. She tried to tamp it down, but Tyler was like a pit bull or something; she just wouldn't let go. Typical Tyler, really. The accident—yeah, accident—was such a weird coincidence. She'd never be able to describe it to Tyler. Or anyone else.

Mr. Gonzales called for order in the class, and Rebecca gratefully pulled out her science book. The class went pretty much the way algebra had. The cheerleaders whispered—well, whispered was a little lightweight for their decibel levels—all through the period. At least Rebecca assumed that's what they were yammering about. She saw Carrie wiping her eyes. She couldn't be crying over Jackson, could she? This was getting weirder and weirder.

Tyler continued to badger her with questions on the way to English. Rebecca fought for calm. She wondered if she could get away from Ty. Maybe duck into the girls' room and not come back out. But Ty would follow her. In exasperation, she took Tyler by the elbow and pushed her to the side of the hallway.

"Look, Ty," she said, "I don't know any more than you do. So quit asking me!"

"But you saw it!"

"Tyler Erin! You're obsessing!" There were interested looks from passersby. She lowered her voice. "Let it go, Ty." Her voice was a fierce whisper. "I. Don't. Know. *Anything.*"

Tyler stared at Rebecca. Her face was a mask of troubled emotions. She looked like she might cry. She opened her mouth, and Rebecca raised her chin defiantly. Tyler closed her mouth.

"Okay, okay," said Ty. She sighed. "Okay."

English was the first two periods all over again. Jackson's chair at the study pod was glaringly empty. Clarity and Brittany Andersen talked of nothing else, and they made no effort to keep their voices down. Similar conversations could be heard all over the room. Mrs. Lindzer tolerated the talk. She seemed distracted.

Drama was a relief. It was always a different world. Sports didn't have much of an impact for "students of the arts." That's what Charles called them. "We're students of the arts," he said. Angela Thornton was in drama, though. Rebecca wondered if Angela would be obsessed with the accident. As captain of the freshman rally squad, it made a certain sense. But Angela was usually obsessed only with herself, and today seemed no different. Mr. Tilson never mentioned the accident. For all Rebecca could tell, he didn't even know about it. He was lecturing on some famous movie; she hadn't quite caught which one. Or what the point was. She didn't really care. But drama was over all too quickly, and it was time to go back out in the world where Jackson was all anyone could talk about.

Rebecca took her time gathering up her things. Charles nodded and smiled at her. It appeared he was staying in the classroom. Sometimes students hung out there for lunch. She had been tempted to stay on occasion, but the draw of being with her friends always won out. She thought about lingering to talk to Charles, but she didn't know what to say. With some reluctance, she headed for the cafeteria.

Her friends were already there. Tyler was talking, perched precariously on the front edge of her chair. Her whole body conveyed her agitation. The red ponytail was flicking frantically from side to side. Rebecca waved, but went through the deli line for a sandwich and a bottle of water before she joined them. As she approached the table, Tyler jumped to her feet.

"Becks was there," she said. "She can tell us."

"It's all we've heard about all morning," said AJ. "Is there anything new to tell?"

"She saw it," said Tyler. "You have to tell, Becks."

Not even hello first. Rebecca sighed and slid into a chair. "One time," she said to Tyler. "And then I'm done." She unwrapped her sandwich. She looked at it, wondering if she'd be able to swallow. "I didn't actually see it happen," she said at length. "I heard it."

"You didn't tell me that before," said Tyler. She looked accusingly at Rebecca.

Rebecca pointedly ignored her. "I had noticed the car for some reason. It felt like I should know who it belonged to. Which was weird."

This was already more than she wanted to say. She twisted the cap off her water bottle before she went on. "And I saw Jackson and Josh. And a couple cheerleaders. But I didn't pay any attention. Why would I?"

Rebecca took a little bite of her sandwich. Her throat was dry, and the sandwich did not want to go down. She chased it with a swallow of water. Her stomach knotted in protest.

Tyler leaned back in her chair and folded her thin arms across her chest. Almost immediately, she was perched on the front edge of the chair again, one hand tugging on her ponytail.

Rebecca continued. "I was walking up the sidewalk when I heard a sort of metal scrunch and a yell. I turned around and saw Jackson. I was pretty sure it was Jackson. His bike was sort of under the car. He sat down on the curb. He was making a lot of noise. It didn't seem like he was hurt all that badly. And Mr. Hammond got out of the car and went over to him. Some other teachers got there. I saw Tyler, and we went into the building. And that's it."

Rebecca looked around the table at her friends. Tyler was still agitated. The others looked barely interested.

"No one has talked about anything else all morning," said Zoe.

"And no one *knows* anything," said AJ. "It's all speculation. So can we please talk about something else?"

"Sure," said Sam. "I was thinking we should have a sleepover." She turned a brilliant smile on Rebecca. "At your house, preferably."

A wave of relief swept over Rebecca. She could have hugged Sam. Would have, but she was on the other side of the table.

"Maybe you could bring those little desserts from your sister's restaurant." AJ looked at Zoe as she spoke. "They're totally to die for."

It took a lot to break through AJ's typical reserve, but the desserts from Mile High Cuisine could do it.

Zoe nodded, dark eyes sparkling. "They are, aren't they. I can ask. When are we thinking?"

"Not this weekend," said Sam. "I'll be at Uncle Clint's. His favorite mare is about to foal." She stretched jean-clad legs to rest western boots on an empty chair.

Rebecca wondered about the horse that was lame. She wanted to ask Sam, but she'd wait till it was only the two of them.

"It was your idea!"

"I know," said Sam. "And it's a good one. Just not this weekend."

"The next one, then," said Rebecca. "It's perfect."

"D'you think your mom will agree?" asked AJ.

"I'm sure of it," said Rebecca. She glanced at Zoe with a look of satisfaction on her face. Zoe smiled back at her, nodding.

"How come?"

"Because my birthday is nearly here!" Rebecca and Zoe high-fived. "And Zoe's is right after!"

It was settled. They were all in. Except maybe Tyler. She sat quiet and remote, slender arms still hugged to her chest, feet tapping restlessly on the floor.

***

The rest of the day was nearly normal. Rebecca's government studies teacher lectured on some boring congressional vote from a hundred years ago. Rebecca actually took a few notes, but her mind was elsewhere. When the bell finally sounded, she hurried to meet Zoe in French class. Like drama, French was a little removed from everyday reality. Rebecca and Zoe sat at the back of the room and pushed their desks close. Heads together, they copied down practice sentences. Ms. Collins strolled up and down the aisles as she instructed the class in pronunciation. The class answered in fractured French. Ms. Collins came to a stop in front of Rebecca and Zoe where their desks blocked the aisle.

Rebecca glanced up, a sheepish smile on her face.

"We'll move back," she said.

"You're fine," said Ms. Collins. "Meilleurs amis pour toujours?"

Rebecca looked blankly at Ms. Collins, but Zoe answered smoothly. "Oui, Mlle. Collins. Best friends forever."

Ms. Collins looked surprised and pleased. Zoe tried not to look smug. Rebecca explained. "Her grandmother is Cajun."

"Acadian," corrected Zoe.

Dark eyebrows arched delicately over gray eyes. "Ah," said Ms. Collins. "I'd love to meet her sometime." She turned back up the aisle and continued with her lesson.

"Einstein," whispered Rebecca. Zoe just shrugged.

Last period and Home Room. Rebecca and Zoe waited for Sam at the door, and they all went in together. Students milled about.

"I wonder if Mr. Hammond will show." Zoe glanced around as she spoke.

The vice principal entered and walked with purpose to the front of the room. "May I have your attention please!"

The room quieted some. Curious faces turned toward the vice principal.

"Due to this morning's unfortunate accident, this class is dismissed," said the vice principal. "If you wish to stay and study or finish homework assignments, you may do so in the library. Please exit in an orderly manner. That is all."

Rebecca's heart hiccupped, and her mouth dropped open. So much for nearly normal.

"What are you going to do?" Rebecca looked from Zoe to Sam.

"The buses won't go for an hour," said Sam.

"I'm going to the library," said Zoe.

Rebecca nodded. She looked toward the windows where sunshine poured in. "It stopped raining," she said. "I think I'll walk home." She looked at Sam.

"I'll go with you," said Sam.

Sam and Rebecca made their way outside into the brilliant sunshine. The air smelled fresh and clean after the morning's drizzly rain, although it was still chilly.

"So which horse is lame?" Rebecca asked. "And what's going to happen?"

"Lissa told you?"

"No. She asked Mom if veterinary medicine used nontraditional methods of healing. At Dad's Sunday breakfast do."

"Oh. And?"

"Not so much, is what Mom said. But she also said she wasn't all that familiar with the veterinary side of alternative healing."

Sam sighed. "Lissa mentioned Reiki, whatever that is."

"So which horse, Sam?"

"The one due to foal this weekend," Sam said. "It's Uncle Clint's favorite mare. Mystery Magic. My aunt is pretty partial to her too, plus the foal, or she'd be dog meat already."

"OMG!" Rebecca was aghast. "Won't they need her to take care of the new baby?"

"Not if they can find another mare with milk," said Sam.

"You can do that?

"Sure. It's expensive, but yeah."

"How long till you'll know?"

Sam sighed. "I don't know," she said.

They were at the corner where they split up to head for their respective homes. Sam looked up the street toward Rebecca's house. Rebecca loved Sam like a part of herself, but she truly wanted to be alone after such a grueling day.

"I have to go, Sam," she said quietly.

"Wait!" Sam grabbed Rebecca's arm before she could turn to go.

Rebecca looked at Sam. Sam hesitated. The green eyes were anguished. It wasn't at all like Sam to be lost for words. "What, Sam?" she asked gently.

Sam chewed her lip for several seconds and then said in a rush, "I want to talk to your mom about that Reiki stuff."

Was that all? Rebecca was relieved. "Sure," she said.

"Before the mare foals," Sam added. There was determination in her voice. Whatever she had decided, there would be no convincing her otherwise.

Rebecca felt trapped between what she so badly wanted for herself and what her friend obviously needed. She tried to keep the resignation out of her voice. "Do you want to come up to the house now?"

Sam shook her head. "Tomorrow you think? After school. Will your mom be there?"

"I'll make sure," said Rebecca. "I'll tell her it's about the lame horse and the ..."

"Reiki," finished Sam.

"Yeah."

"Okay. Thanks!" Sam's face bloomed in a beautiful smile, but there was resolve in the green eyes. She hugged Rebecca and quickly released her. "See you tomorrow, Becks." And she turned and walked rapidly down the street, western boots clocking on the sidewalk. Rebecca watched her go for a moment before she, too, turned and headed for home.

CHAPTER 10

The Law of Correspondences

Still May 6!

REBECCA LET HERSELF into the house feeling tense and edgy. Running a hand through her hair, she followed the sound of low voices to her mother's office. Her mom was on a call. She looked up and smiled at Rebecca, pressing the Mute button.

"I'll be five minutes," she said. And then, "You're early."

"No Home Room," said Rebecca. Her mother raised her eyebrows.

"Tell you later," said Rebecca. "I have homework."

Her mother nodded and turned back to her computer. Rebecca felt disappointed that her mother was tied up, but also somewhat relieved. She wanted to tell her mom everything. About the accident, everyone's reaction, Tyler's obsession. She'd just tell what she knew, which wasn't much. But deep down, she knew she wouldn't tell at all.

Downstairs, her room was dim and quiet. She dropped her book bag on her desk chair. She looked around, the heel of one hand unconsciously massaging the tightness over her heart. Slits of light from the shutters made a pattern of bars across the carpet. The bed was a rumple of covers. The closet door stood open, her jams from the night before in a pile on the floor. Rebecca crossed to the windows and opened the louvres. The room was washed with indirect light; the dark and light pattern on the carpet reversed, except for one stuck louvre that still cast a broad band of shadow. Outside, Andy was jumping on his trampoline. Scoundrel was running around the trampoline barking frantically.

Rebecca sat on the window seat and watched them for a while. The scene was comforting in its familiarity. The tightness over her heart eased a bit. Smiling to herself, she stood up. The stuck louvre caught her attention, and she climbed onto the window seat to set it right. Good. That was better. She turned to step to the floor, and her foot came down on a stuffed animal. It shifted under her weight. Arms flailing for balance, Rebecca grabbed for the window ledge and caught ahold of . . . nothing. Falling, falling in slow motion, a long cry escaped her as she plummeted. There was a loud crash as she ploughed headlong into her chair. Her wrist smacked hard against the edge of the desk, and her wail was punctuated with a howl of real pain. The chair, her book bag, and Rebecca went down in a crumpled heap, knocking the wind from her. She slid across the carpet facedown, scoring a rug burn onto her cheek. She lay still for a moment, aware of the sound of feet pounding down the stairs. As her mother burst into her room, Rebecca rolled onto her side, drawing up her knees and cradling her left wrist against her chest. Tears leaked from the corners of her eyes.

CHAPTER 11

An Odd Little Group

May 7

SAM, ZOE, AND Rebecca sat together, the near-deafening babble of voices in the cafeteria punctuated by the clatter of lunch trays and the heavy clang of doors as students and staff came and went. Zoe sat small and precise, ankles crossed, her lunch laid out neatly in front of her. She was nibbling on a sandwich. Sam munched on an apple, her boots resting on an empty chair. Rebecca was slouched over the table, her right hand cradling her left arm. An air cast encased her arm from her hand nearly to her elbow. Her left cheekbone bore a raw abrasion shadowed by a midnight-purple bruise. She looked with little interest at the pandemonium around them. Her lunch sat untouched where it had been pushed to one side.

Sam looked around the group. She was smiling.

"What?" Zoe smiled back at Sam. "What are you thinking?"

"Just that we're . . . I don't know . . ." Sam brushed a speck from one boot, adjusted her jean legs, and inspected a brightly lacquered nail. She brought her gaze back to her friend's. "It's just pretty cool, the three of us together. We rock. You know?"

Zoe's wide smile reached to her eyes, making them glow. "We do, don't we," she said.

Rebecca looked at Sam but said nothing.

"Do you ever wonder what we'll look back on? After this—" Sam gestured around the noisy cafeteria—"is all over. Besides the smell of grease and barely washed bodies." Sam made a face. "I've worked with cowhands who smell better than some of the dudes around here."

Zoe and Rebecca laughed. Rebecca winced and put her fingers gingerly to her abraded cheek.

"Where are you going with this?" asked Zoe.

Sam shrugged. "I just wonder, when it's finally all over, what will stand out when we look back on it? Besides the three of us."

"Don't you mean the five of us?" said Rebecca carefully.

"No." Sam shook her head, and she didn't elaborate. "I think there will always be a connection between us." She looked pointedly at Rebecca, and then at Zoe. "Not so sure about the others." She tapped a glossy nail against her lower lip. "And I wonder what would break up the relentless boredom of high school."

"I thought you loved high school." Zoe took a bite of her sandwich and then laid it on her napkin.

"Why would you ever think that?" Sam regarded Zoe as if she'd never seen her before.

"Sam loves the ranch," said Rebecca. "And horses."

"And nothing else?" Zoe couldn't believe that.

"Well, possibly some other things," said Sam. "But school wouldn't be on the list. A hot date maybe. A Taylor Hunt movie. Sunday afternoon at your nanna's house." She looked at Rebecca.

Rebecca and Zoe laughed, and Sam grinned back at them.

Wherever the conversation was leading, it was interrupted by the arrival of Ty and AJ. Ty slid into a seat next to Rebecca, careful not to bump Rebecca's arm; she had heard the story in second period.

AJ dropped into the chair at the end of the table and tossed her bag and jacket on the floor. She stretched her legs and propped her feet on her bag. She looked around the table, her gaze coming back to Rebecca. One eyebrow arched quizzically. "Becks . . .?" she said.

"I fell off my window seat." Rebecca frowned and tucked her injured wrist in her lap.

"How'd that happen?"

"A stuffed bear threw me off."

Everyone laughed except AJ. Her calm gaze remained on Rebecca. She didn't say anything. The eyebrow was still up.

"Okay," said Rebecca, "I climbed on the window seat to fix a slat on the shutters. Then I stepped on a stuffed animal and lost my balance. It was just weird." She grimaced and then winced, her right hand going to her cheek.

Now both of AJ's eyebrows were raised. "And?"

"In a rather spectacular crash, I took out my desk chair, my laptop, and half my room on the way down. On landing, I surfed across the floor with my cheek on the carpet." Rebecca attempted a grin and winced again. The story was an exaggeration, for sure, but it played better than the plain truth.

"Is it broken?" AJ nodded toward the air cast.

"No. Well, barely." Rebecca tried to make light of it. "Teeny hairline fracture and bruising. Hurts like crazy when I move it, though, and 'stability will make it heal faster.' That's what the doctor said." She made a face. "So that's why the air cast."

"Wow!" AJ seemed at a loss for words. She continued to study Rebecca and then murmured. "You and Jackson . . ."

Rebecca's stomach lurched. She stared at AJ wide eyed. Zoe appeared not to have heard Alexa, but Tyler and Sam looked on with interest.

Sam opened her mouth, but before she could speak, Rebecca said in a rush, "I *love* your boots, AJ! Are they knockoffs?"

Rebecca didn't want to follow Alexa's thought. And she didn't want anyone else to either. It had crossed her mind that she and Jackson shared similar injuries. A wrist instead of an ankle. It was not an idea she wanted to pursue, and she had ruthlessly shoved the thought away.

"They're totally the bomb," Sam had no problem shifting gears.

"Yeah," said AJ. "Knockoffs."

Tyler sprang to her feet. "Look at these, guys!" She brought one foot to the edge of the table. She rotated her ankle back and forth, showing off a short boot with a high wedge heel.

"Wow! Cool."

"Jeez, you and AJ are tall enough without heels!"

"Do you think they make me look older?"

"No, just taller."

Tyler studied her foot, frowning. "I think they make me look older," she insisted.

"What color is that?" AJ pointed at the color on Sam's long nails.

"I'm going with 'midnight,'" said Sam. "The bottle was some goth garbage like 'darkness.'"

"Black is black."

"Pretty much."

"Hey, AJ, what happened to your red highlights?"

Alexa ran a hand through her hair, fingering blue extensions. "They were washing out," she said, shrugging. "Turned pink. I don't do *pink*. And I wanted something different. Sizzle has all these extensions, and it's way easier than highlights. I can change up every day if I want."

"I love Sizzle," said Rebecca. "They have a truly awesome Beatles T-shirt I'm sort of saving my money for." She looked at Sam. "You'd love it."

Sam's face lit up. "A new Beatles T-shirt?"

Rebecca nodded.

"*Sort* of saving for?" Zoe looked skeptical.

"Well, I'm also hoping there will be generous amounts of cash for my birthday. That would minimize the need to save."

The girls laughed. "You're hopeless, Becks," said Zoe.

"My dad found a Beatles CD from the Hollywood Bowl . . ."

Ty's voice was lost beneath a babble of voices and scraping chairs as a cluster of girls arrived at the next table. It was freshman rally squad leader Angela Thornton, surrounded by four other cheerleaders. Clarity Austin pulled out a chair for Angela, who seated herself with fluid grace. Carrie Coffman laughed at nothing discernible. Peyton Long and Brittany mimicked Angela. They settled into their chairs, waving and calling to a group of jocks across the room.

"Well, if it's not the freshman cheering section," murmured Zoe.

"The Ice Maiden and her booster club," said Rebecca.

"Monkey squad is more like it," AJ said calmly. This brought giggles, and she smiled.

It wasn't a rally squad day, but even so, the girls were similarly dressed. They might have plucked their outfits from the same rack at some couture teen fashion house. Smart designer bags hung casually from every shoulder, and heeled boots completed the fashion-stamp look. Angela's expertly cut hair fell smooth and perfect in the current hot trend. The pack mentality was reflected in the hairstyles of the other girls, with the exception of Peyton Long. She worshipped a different fashion god. Dyed a red found nowhere in nature, with dark blue undertones and pink highlights, Peyton's short hair curled around her face in a swirl of color.

"God, I *love* her hair!" AJ's eyes were riveted on Peyton.

"And Angie's boots," whispered Rebecca. In spite of herself, her gaze was drawn to the hot-fashion, heeled boots worn by Angela.

"Who's the new blonde?" Sam asked.

"That's Brittany Andersen," said Ty. "She's in English with us. And science." Ty looked at Rebecca, and Rebecca nodded.

"Kind of a bitch," said Rebecca. She frowned. "How'd she get to be a cheerleader? I thought you had to be here at the beginning of the semester for tryouts or something."

"Booster Club advisor picked her when Lindsey March moved away," said Tyler.

The noise at the next table subsided. Alexa dug for something in her book bag. Zoe and Tyler returned their attention to their lunches. Rebecca gave a little nod to Angela. For a long moment, no one spoke. Then Sam flashed Angela a sunny smile and waved.

"Hey, Angela!"

"Sally Jo!" cried Angela. She rose gracefully and crossed to their table.

"It's Sarah Ann," said Rebecca.

"What?" Angela glanced at Rebecca. "Oh, hi, Rebecca."

"Her name is Sarah Ann, not Sally Jo," Rebecca repeated clearly. Her deep-blue eyes held Angela's pale-blue ones in a level gaze.

Angela covered her mistake with a tinkling laugh. "Of course it is. My bad." She rushed on, "I'm just so excited about the competition I can't keep anything else in my head!"

The other cheerleaders were now clustered around Angela. Clarity smiled a friendly hello. Peyton nodded at everyone, fluffing her rainbow hair. Brittany acted as though she didn't see any of them. She elbowed her way next to Angie, pushing Carrie aside. Rebecca noted this with a cold detachment.

"What competition?" asked Sam.

Angela beamed. It even looked genuine. Expensively manicured nails flashed as she ran her hand over straight blonde hair and then readjusted the thin strap of the designer bag.

"It's just luck, really," said Angela. "All totally last-minute. I should have had my entry form in months ago, but I never thought about competing. It's a scholarship competition for Junior Miss Denver."

"It's a beauty pageant," said Brittany. "She has what she needs to win, for sure." Her voice was Tupelo honey. She smiled at Angela.

Rebecca read the lack of sincerity in Brittany's eyes. Was Brittany implying the Thornton money would guarantee Angela's success? She didn't know where that thought came from, but it felt accurate.

Angela ignored Brittany, if she even noticed. "A contestant dropped out, and my mom pulled some strings. It's really her thing more than mine." She waved a hand dismissively and smoothed her hair again. "I'm really doing all this to make *her* happy." She sighed. "Makes my life easier." *The burdens of life could be so exhausting,* that sigh seemed to say.

"I have to come up with wardrobe and talent right away," she continued. "It's already late for submitting to the governing board. I need makeup and styling professionals. I need a coach." Angela sighed again. The put-upon look didn't quite ring true. "It's a huge challenge, really. There's so much to prepare for. It's way beyond just anyone to pull it off in so short a time."

Angela's glance took in Brittany and swept past her. Her face was smooth, her smile relaxed. Rebecca noticed the tiny tick at the corner of Brittany's eye. Rebecca glanced at Zoe and bit her lips to keep from grinning. Zoe sucked on the inside of her cheek. Was trouble brewing on the monkey squad?

"Well, gotta go," Angela sang happily. She waved at no one in particular and glided away. Rebecca wondered how someone so cold could be so graceful. The four other cheerleaders fell in behind Angie. They moved back to their table like a single organism, seemingly independent appendages moving randomly but controlled by one central brain. Not a particularly large brain, at that.

Speechless, Rebecca and her friends watched them go.

Rebecca broke the silence. "Doesn't her dad own half of downtown Denver?"

Sam nodded. "Colorado Springs, for sure. And about a kazillion acres of ranchland. My uncle's spread butts up against one little sliver of his Springs Ranch."

"So she wins a scholarship," said Ty. "What would she study? Is there a major for rich and snooty?" The others laughed.

"Why would she even think we care?" asked Sam. "It's not like any of us is her Facebook friend."

"I think that's the point," said Rebecca. "I mean, that we *don't* care, but she *wishes* we did." She nibbled absently at her lunch.

The girls considered this quietly. Their eyes followed the cheerleaders, expressions thoughtful. Angela separated from her fan club and moved confidently toward the cafeteria doors. She smiled coolly in their direction as she walked past.

"She does have a great figure," said Ty. "And boobs." She cupped her minimalist breasts in her palms, looking from one to the other.

This broke them all up.

"We are what we are," said Zoe. "We shouldn't try to be like someone else. That's what Grand-mère always says."

"Not odd at all," said Rebecca. It had just popped out, and she couldn't get it back. She didn't move, was barely breathing. Maybe no one had heard her.

But they had.

There was silence around the table. Tyler was the first to speak. "What do you mean!" she demanded. She was perfectly still. So was the ponytail.

Rebecca briefly thought of trying to talk her way out of it. She sighed, giving up on the idea almost immediately. "I'm sorry, guys," she said. "It's something my dad said. He said we're an odd little group." There. It was out.

Tyler huffed but said nothing. Sam's face was curious but calm as she gazed at Rebecca. Zoe nibbled again on her sandwich.

"An odd little group." Alexa didn't look pissed. Curious, maybe.

Tyler was still glaring at Rebecca, but Zoe and Sam turned questioning looks at AJ.

"It's just part of the mystique," AJ said after a moment. She nodded to no one in particular.

Zoe considered this. After a moment she said, "And we are sort of an odd little group."

Tyler opened her mouth to speak. The ponytail bobbed. Her expression darkened again.

Zoe cut her off. "We are," she said. "Unusual maybe, rather than odd. On the surface, we have nothing in common. We're all different." Zoe looked around at them. "Most groups are cookie-cutter. Everyone is all the same. We're unusual," she said again.

"So what are you saying?" asked Sam. "That being different is what makes us alike?"

"That's kind of crazy," said Ty.

"I get what you mean," said AJ. "On the surface, it looks like the only things we have in common are Front Range and Becks." AJ looked at Rebecca. "You're the common denominator, kind of. But it's more than that."

Zoe nodded. "We don't try to be all alike. We all get to be who we are and still be friends. Becks and her stories. Sam and her horses."

"You and your brains." Rebecca chuckled.

Zoe nodded her acceptance. "It's okay that we're different. In fact, it's powerful."

"Like your grandmother," said Rebecca. "My mom said that too. That she's powerful and unapologetically herself."

"I think your mom is right," said Zoe. "Even if she's a crazy old bat sometimes."

"So we are who we are and no apologies?" AJ nodded her head. "I like that."

Zoe turned pensive. Her eyes were directed across the room, but Rebecca was pretty sure Zoe wasn't looking at the soft-serve ice cream machine. She was zoned out. She spoke quietly to no one in particular. "That's us," she said. "Inexplicable."

They just stared at her.

She looked around at the others. She nodded to no one in particular again. "I have to go."

"Go where?" Rebecca asked.

"To see a counselor about an advanced summer class," said Zoe.

"You're really going to do that?" Rebecca was dismayed.

"I may," Zoe said calmly.

"But I won't see you all summer if you do!"

"It's not the whole summer, and it's not all day," said Zoe. "I want a full resume when I apply to college. You know I want Boulder."

"That's years away!" Sam was offhand and clearly disinterested. Sam wasn't much interested in anything other than horses after high school graduation. Or in the present moment, for that matter.

"It's not." Zoe waved at them as she headed for the doors. "Voir-vous dans la classe Française." She looked back at Rebecca.

"*What* about French class?" Rebecca shook her head.

"I'll see you there!" Zoe called. And she was gone.

"Einstein," muttered Rebecca. She was still looking at the door where Zoe had disappeared. A summer without her was unthinkable. What would she do with herself? Especially with Sam at the ranch, where she was sure to be. Pushing back her own chair, she stood up. Protecting her injured wrist, she collected her book bag and jacket. "I have to go too," she said, and she hurried after Zoe.

"That's okay," Tyler called after Rebecca. "I'll get your stuff."

"What's with that?" Ty asked.

"You mean Becks?" said Sam. "She's sort of . . . sometimes she's . . ." Describing Rebecca was challenging. Sam's voice trailed off. She adjusted the legs of her jeans.

"It's like she's two people and you don't know which one you're talking to from one minute to the next," said Tyler.

"Well, she is a Gemini," said Sam. Her tone was matter-of-fact. "You know, the Twins."

"Yeah, I know the Twins." Tyler's expression suggested she didn't like them very much.

"I think there are more than two of her," said AJ. "If you get me."

"Yeah, I get you." Her jeans now falling smoothly over her boots, Sam straightened up. She pushed her tousled hair back from her face, the high gloss on the black-lacquered nails sparkling in the overhead light.

"Will you take my tray for me? I need to go too." Sam looked at Tyler, who nodded in resignation. Slinging her jacket over one shoulder, Sam hurried in the same direction Zoe and Rebecca had gone, boots clocking against the tile floor.

Alexa and Tyler watched Sam until she disappeared through the heavy doors.

"So it's just us dweebs," said Tyler. "The supreme trio leaves us to scrub the fireplace.'

"Don't even go there," said AJ. "You know that's not true."

Tyler opened her mouth, and AJ shook her head firmly. Tyler closed her mouth again, but her look was stubborn.

"Look, they've known each other since they were practically babies," said AJ. "There are always going to be places they share that we can't go. It doesn't make us less. In the friendship, I mean."

"Maybe so," Tyler said, but she didn't sound convinced.

"No one's making them hang out with us. They do it because they want to."

Tyler nodded. "Yeah, I guess," she said.

They collected what the other three had left behind. Depositing the trays and trash as they left the cafeteria, they walked out into the May sunshine shoulder to shoulder.

CHAPTER 12

A Matched Pair

May 7

REBECCA THREADED HER way through the maze of hallways to swap out her morning books for the ones she'd need in afternoon classes. At her locker, she knelt to open the little cubby and stared blankly into its depths. She absently cradled her wrapped wrist against her chest. Sighing, she pulled out her government studies book. What a boring class! *Uninteresting* didn't begin to cover it. The teacher couldn't be any less inspiring without being dead. Actually, dead, she might be more interesting.

When Rebecca got to class, there were clusters of students talking in low tones. Nothing new to that. Making her way to her desk, she caught snatches of conversation about Jackson's accident. When was this going to turn into old news? As she slipped into her seat, the girl in front of her turned around. Rebecca thought her name was Abbie. Or Andi. Though they sat next to each other every day, Rebecca barely knew her. Abbie-Andi seemed painfully shy and usually showed no inclination toward conversation. Which was fine with Rebecca.

Abbie-Andi smiled a tight little smile. "Do you . . ." She cleared her throat. "Have you heard anything about Jackson?" Her voice was barely more than a whisper.

"No." Rebecca shook her head.

"No one seems to know if he'll play again." Abbie-Andi looked like she might cry.

"I heard his leg was broken in three places," said another girl from across the aisle.

"I thought it was just a sprained shoulder." A pimply boy in front of Broken in Three Places chimed in.

"I heard he'll never walk again without a crutch."

Abbie-Andi's distress increased visibly. "Oh no!" she breathed.

"And Hammond might be arrested," said Sprained Shoulder.

"No, I heard he was just reprimanded," said Broken in Three Places. "But he should be. Arrested, I mean!"

This was crazy. Rebecca shook her head. "You can't listen to every rumor," she said. "They can't all be right. Probably none of them are."

"You know him really well, don't you?" Abbie-Andi's voice was a sigh.

"I have some classes with him," Rebecca agreed cautiously.

"I heard you and he were sort of . . ."

"Sort of what?" Rebecca stared hard at Abbie-Andi.

"I don't know. Close." The girl seemed to shrink into herself under Rebecca's challenging gaze.

Rebecca was considering whether to answer when the teacher clapped her hands for attention. Abbie-Andi turned toward the front of the class with another sigh.

Thank the gods, thought Rebecca.

They turned in homework and reviewed the next chapter. Rebecca's mind wandered. As the teacher droned on, Rebecca caught herself doodling "pageant" in her notebook. She looked at the word in surprise and then scratched through it. She pulled her book toward her and stared at the pages. Her thoughts were far from the structure of Congress. She doodled "B for Bitch," then "Accident," and then "Pageant/Ice Maiden." She scratched it all out and looked up at the clock, willing it to be two o'clock. It wasn't.

There was less talk of Jackson in French, but Rebecca wished only for the day to be over. She knew it would be a free-for-all when she and Zoe got to Home Room. Sure enough, it was. With a sinking heart, she looked around for Sam. Her wrist ached, her ribs hurt, and her cheek burned. She felt drained and exhausted. Sam had staked out three desks, and with a deep sigh, Rebecca eased herself into one of them. Zoe slid smoothly into the other. One of Jackson's best friends, a jock, of course, sprawled in a desk on the other side of Sam. B-something. Rebecca could never remember his name. There were two empty seats beside him. Jackson had not been in algebra or English. Rebecca was too tired to wonder if he would show up for Home Room. Probably not. Mr. Hammond was not in sight either.

Zoe and Sam talked in low tones to each other. Rebecca didn't join in. She leaned her chin heavily on her good hand and let her mind space out. Her eyelids were heavy. Her brain felt heavy too. She lowered her head to her arms and closed her eyes.

"There's Jackson! And Josh!" Excited voices echoed around the room.

Rebecca's head came up with a jerk. She looked toward the door to see Jackson hobbling into the room on crutches, Josh trailing after him carrying two backpacks. The vice principal was right behind them. He made his way to the front of the room.

No one cared about the vice principal. All eyes were on Jackson. His left leg and foot were encased in a cast that reached nearly to his knee. The cast looked like some sort of high-tech packing material and was fastened together on each side with something like Velcro. But what caught Rebecca's attention most was that it looked exactly like a larger version of the air cast on her left wrist. She tucked her arm in her lap.

Jackson's jean leg was cut off to accommodate the cast. Bruising darkened one eye, and an abrasion ran down one cheek, bright red. Someone clapped, and the room erupted in cheers and applause. Jackson grinned his lopsided grin as he hobbled toward B-something. There were some calls of "Go Saints!" and "QB1!"

Rebecca stared in spite of herself. She thought Jackson looked pale. Her brain fixated on a smattering of freckles across the tops of his cheeks. She had never noticed them before.

B-something scrambled to his feet and nudged his desk toward Jackson. "Jacks! Hey, man. Drop it here." His dark face was wreathed in a wide smile.

"Express!" Jackson leaned on one crutch to bump fists. He awkwardly maneuvered his tall frame into the seat, stretching the injured leg in front of him. He nodded at Josh. "Thanks, Telluride." He was still grinning, but he sighed heavily.

"Welcome back, Jackson."

"What's the damage, man?"

"Hey, QB1, heads up!" Someone lobbed a balled-up wad of paper across the room. Jackson reached up and plucked it from the air with one hand. There was more cheering.

"Ooh, can I sign your cast?" A perky little brunette Rebecca recognized as a member of the rally squad batted her eyes at Jackson.

"Oh, me too!"

"I'll carry your stuff for you," said another girl. "Or whatever you want."

There was no answering jive from Jackson. People were crowding around him. He pulled his backpack away from Josh, dropped it between his feet, and leaned over it. Rebecca had never seen him without a quick comeback. Her brain could barely process the phenomenon.

The vice principal called for quiet. "Find seats, everyone," he said. "Let the boy breathe. And let's try to get back in a normal groove. Jackson, good to see you."

Jackson nodded. Blake—that was it; B-something was Blake!—and Josh leaned in close to carry on a quiet conversation with him. Rebecca couldn't hear what they were saying. Her stomach churned, and she felt like she might be sick. She saw Zoe lean over and touch Jackson's arm. He turned to look at her. The usual reckless grin was missing. He looked tired and exposed.

Rebecca didn't want to see it. She had no frame of reference for this Jackson. She felt panicky. She needed to get out of the room. She whispered to Sam, "I'm going to the ladies'."

Sam looked at her in surprise. "You okay?" she asked.

Rebecca nodded. "Sure," she said. "Just gotta go. You know?"

Sam nodded back at her, and Rebecca got up and headed for the door. She slipped out into the hall and walked rapidly toward the girls' loo.

She hadn't been prepared to see Jackson looking so subdued. Vulnerable, almost. She didn't know what she had expected, but not that. In the ladies' room, she bent over a sink, leaning on her arms, her head down. She turned on the water, held her hands under the flow, and then pressed them to her hot cheeks. She stared into the mirror, barely recognizing the face looking back at her. Her eyes were large and dilated and underscored with dark smudges. She was pale, the freckles scattered across the tops of her cheeks and on her nose standing out in stark relief. The rug burn on her cheek was an angry smear of red and purple.

"Jeez, you're a sight," she said to her image. "You look worse than Jackson."

She heard voices coming and ducked into a stall. She didn't want to see anyone. Or be seen. She perched on the edge of the toilet and waited.

One of those voices was familiar. Angela. Rebecca listened.

"It's not the competition so much. That's mostly a real pain. But it could lead—" Flushing toilets drowned out the rest.

Running water, and then, ". . . just jealous."

"I just don't need it."

Hand dryers blasted. ". . . modeling if you win."

"Oh, I know I can win. And I don't need to show her anything." The voices moved off.

No shortage of confidence there! Rebecca stood up and peeked out the door. This was ridiculous. She might as well suck it up and go back to class.

The vice principal looked up when she came in, but he said nothing. Sam looked a question mark at her and mouthed, "You okay?"

Rebecca nodded.

Jackson glanced up at her and did a double take. "What happened to you? You get in front of Hammond's Beemer too?" He grinned. It wasn't his usual grin, but it wasn't bad.

Zoe looked from Jackson to Rebecca and then back at Jackson. Her eyes widened, and she blinked twice. "Wow," she said. "You two are really a matched pair."

Rebecca's stomach lurched. Her mouth opened, but no sound came out.

"Okay, people." The vice principal's voice came from the front of the room. "Let's use the remaining time for something other than chatter."

Gratefully, Rebecca pulled her algebra assignment out of her book bag and tried to focus on math problems. Sam slid down in her desk and stretched booted feet out in front of her. She picked idly at the black polish on one thumb. Zoe scooted her desk closer to Jackson's and carried on a low conversation with him. The vice principal didn't notice. Or didn't care.

Rebecca glanced repeatedly at the clock, sure the hands were stuck. When the bell finally rang, the girls collected bags and jackets and headed for the door. Jackson stayed where he was, flanked by his two jock buddies, and was soon surrounded by girls and curious classmates.

Once outside, Rebecca turned to Zoe. "What was that all about?"

"What?"

"All that cheek-to-cheek with Jackson the Jerk." Rebecca tried to keep her voice calm.

"Well, you know . . ." Zoe just shrugged.

"No," said Rebecca. "I don't know."

"He's not so bad sometimes, Becks," said Zoe. "And I wanted to know how serious it is." Zoe glanced at Rebecca, then at Sam, and then at Rebecca again. Rebecca's expression was dark.

"So how serious is it?" Rebecca asked.

Zoe's smile was beautiful. "Not that bad. He was lucky. It's really just a stress fracture. And there's a lot of bruising. He's in a tall integrity fracture walker boot."

Rebecca and Sam gaped at Zoe. "He's in a *what?*"

"It's an air boot," said Zoe. "My dad had one." She shrugged nonchalantly, as if this explained everything. "It's just like yours," she added to Rebecca. "He probably doesn't need the tall boot, but his doctor thought it was a good idea. With football season not that far off."

Rebecca fixed her friend with a long, unreadable look. Her stomach felt fluttery with agitation. "Ah, football season," she said. "You're such a fan."

Zoe returned Rebecca's challenging gaze with a bland look. She squared her small shoulders, however, and her dark eyes did not blink.

"And since when are you so concerned about Jackson the Jerk's football career?"

"I'm not," said Zoe. "But Jackson is. Supremely so."

Calm brown eyes held flashing blue ones. Neither girl spoke.

Sam watched them, her face troubled. She threaded her arms through Rebecca's and Zoe's, tugging them forward. "No one cares about Jackson's football career," she said a little too brightly. "But you can't be glad he got hurt. That would be too mean."

"Right." Rebecca made an enormous effort to sound casual. "That would be too mean."

CHAPTER 13

Reiki 911

May 7

REBECCA AND SAM let themselves into the house and dropped their stuff in the mudroom. They could hear the murmur of Maggie Coleson's voice coming from the office.

"Do you want a snack or something?" asked Rebecca.

Sam shook her head.

Rebecca's mom looked up with a smile when Rebecca and Sam stopped in her doorway. She gestured toward two comfortable-looking chairs opposite her desk, and the girls sat down.

"Becka. Sarah Ann." Maggie assessed them. "You two look like you've had a hard day," she said. "How are you feeling, Becka?"

"Really glad today's over." Rebecca cradled her casted arm in her good hand, leaning gratefully into the soft cushions of her chair.

Sam got right to the point. "We have a lame horse at the ranch," she said. "The vet thinks it might be a bruise, but it hasn't healed." Sam paused. "She's due to foal any time—plus, she's a favorite of Uncle Clint, or else . . ." Sam's voice cracked.

"It's the one Lissa told us about," Rebecca said. "They'd have already . . ." But she couldn't say it either.

"We've tried herbal wraps," said Sam. "There's an old woman—she's Cook's mother, actually, and she does a lot of . . ." Sam looked apologetically at Maggie and didn't finish.

"So you want to know about Reiki." Maggie could get right to the point as well.

Sam nodded.

"Well, I could talk about Reiki for hours," said Maggie, smiling. "There are thousands of practitioners, and literally hundreds of hospitals use it now. At its minimum, it reduces stress and anxiety. At its best, it produces miracles. Most of the time, it's somewhere between those two."

"But what is it?" asked Sam.

"Reiki is life force energy. Or God force energy. Ancient and indigenous societies all have a cultural definition for life force energy. Western culture does not. At least, not beyond 'with it, you are alive; without it, you're dead.'" She grimaced.

"How does it work?" asked Sam

"A very good question. Are you familiar with acupuncture?"

"Yeah!" Sam perked up. "My mom had it done. Aunt Jo wanted to try that, but she couldn't find anyone to do it on Magic."

Maggie nodded. "Reiki has some similarities to acupuncture," she said. "It's based on the premise that we are all vibrational beings. Light Beings, if you're a Yoda and *Star Wars* fan. Energy. Everything is just energy vibrating at different frequencies. I wouldn't say it's totally mainstream thinking yet, but the concept is supported by quantum physics and quantum biology. Dis-ease, dysfunction, pain—they are caused when the energies are out of balance. Or blocked. Acupuncture and Reiki seek to return the energies to proper balance and flow. When that happens, the body heals itself." Maggie paused to let the information sink in.

Sam was listening intently. "And it works the same for animals as for people?"

"Some practitioners think even better." Maggie looked at Rebecca, who had raised her eyebrows. Then to Sam again, she said, "People tend to have preset notions about what can work and what can't work, and they unconsciously block anything new or that they don't understand. Animals don't carry all that negative baggage. They are far more instinctive."

"So do you know anyone who does this . . . does Reiki . . . on animals?"

"Actually, I do."

Rebecca's eyebrows went a little higher.

"I've done some checking around," said Maggie.

Sam had that resolute look in her eyes. "Who can do this? Learn Reiki, I mean. And how would . . . can *anyone* do it?"

"Pretty much," said Maggie.

"How do you learn it?"

"You take a series of classes. There are typically three levels. At Level II, you're ready to start taking clients."

"Clients?"

"Practicing Reiki," said Maggie.

"I want to do it," said Sam. "How long do the classes take?"

Maggie looked surprised, but she didn't miss a beat. "Well, that depends on the Master Teacher," she said. "And the student's background. For someone with limited alternative healing knowledge, usually about eight to ten months. The actual classes for each level can be done in a day. Most teachers prefer to have at least a month between Level I and Level II classes. You can give Reiki with a Level II."

"So . . . you mean it would only be a month? Before I could do it?"

"Potentially, yes."

"Is it real expensive?" A note of doubt had crept into Sam's voice. "I have some money, but not like, you know, thousands of dollars."

"Not anymore," said Maggie. "Reiki classes used to be very expensive. But not anymore," she repeated.

Now Sam looked uncertain. She fidgeted in her chair and pushed her tousled blonde hair from her face with both hands. "Um . . ."

Maggie waited for Sam to go on.

Sam said finally. "Are the classes hard?"

Maggie smiled. "No, Sarah Ann. Not at all. And they aren't like typical school classes. Most of us involved with Reiki feel like the learning is a lifelong process. But it's more about learning to know yourself than it is about learning from books. And how to work with energy."

"Are you a Reiki practicer?"

"*Practitioner.* Yes. I hold Reiki Master certification in two methods of Reiki."

Rebecca gaped. "You *do*?"

Her mother shrugged. "I've been doing Reiki since before I began with alternative medicine. It's what led me there."

"Reiki is part of CAM?" Rebecca asked. She was still stunned.

"A very significant part," said her mother.

"Do you *do* it?" demanded Rebecca.

"I don't have a client list, per se," said Maggie. "But yes, I do it. Every day."

"How come I never knew this?" There was a sharp edge to Rebecca's tone.

"You know it now," said her mother.

"But . . ."

"The time wasn't appropriate before," said Maggie.

"Could you teach me?" Sam broke in eagerly.

"I could, technically," said Maggie. "But I think I'd be more inclined to connect you with just the right person. Other than me," she added with a smile.

"And you'd do that?"

"Of course!" Maggie considered for a moment. "In fact, I think April Lowry would be just the right teacher for you. If she has the time, that is."

Rebecca's jaw dropped again. "You mean Nanna's April? She does this too?"

Maggie laughed. "April is an exceedingly complex and talented woman, and those talents are . . . far-reaching." She looked levelly at Rebecca. "Nanna is a Reiki Master as well.

Rebecca just stared.

"I love April!" There was wonderment in Sam's voice. "I could be ready to do Reiki in a month?" She tapped a long blue nail against her lips. "This just might work out."

"A month, more or less, from your first class, yes." Maggie nodded.

Sam got abruptly to her feet. "Thanks so much, Mom C.! You may have just saved the life of an innocent horse." Sam's laugh was giddy.

She turned to Rebecca. "I have to go. I have some things to do."

Rebecca could only nod. This was all too much. Her mother, April, Nanna—all this Reiki stuff. And Sam. Jeez, Sam doing it. That was really . . . well, Rebecca wasn't sure what.

At the door Sam turned back. "If I can't get started right away for some reason, or if I don't finish in time, could you or April, or someone you know, work on Magic for me? For us," she corrected.

"In time?" Maggie raised her eyebrows.

"Yeah," said Sam, and her voice was hard. "While that foal still needs its mother."

"Of course," said Maggie. "We'll begin immediately."

"We?"

"There is a group of us . . . We have what we call a Reiki 911 Network. For just this sort of thing. Accidents, sick children, dogs with snake bite." Maggie's smile was soft. "Lame horses. I'll make some calls."

Sam stared hard at Maggie, and then she crossed the office and threw her arms around her neck. "OMG," she whispered. "You don't know what you've done for me." There were tears in Sam's eyes when she rushed from the office.

"Yes, I do," said Maggie Coleson softly. "Oh, yes, I do." The front door slammed shut. Rebecca and her mother looked at each other.

CHAPTER 14

The Fat Man Is Back

May 9

BY THURSDAY MORNING, Rebecca was feeling almost normal. Her sleep had been deep and dreamless. Most of the soreness caused by her tumble from the window seat was gone, except for her wrist, and that was less painful. She wondered if her mom had been "doing Reiki" on her, whatever that would entail, but she didn't ask. Her cheek was still tender, but the rug burn was fading. So was the bruise, which was turning a grisly yellow. She checked the patch of sky visible from her windows, and her spirits lifted at the sight of blue. The day felt promising. She hitched a ride to school with Lissa, not minding the detour past the doll shop. She and her sister made the long walk from student parking in comfortable silence, going their separate ways in the high, bright atrium just at first bell.

When she got to algebra class, Jackson was already at his desk. He was sprawled with his casted leg thrust into the aisle beside his desk, his crutches leaning against his knees. Josh's and Blake's desks were still empty.

As Rebecca slid into her seat, Jackson poked her desk with the end of one crutch.

"So, if you didn't get hit by Hammond's Beemer," he said, "you been in a fight?"

She turned to look at him. He grinned his FIGJAM grin, blue eyes teasing. Blond hair tumbled over his forehead, and he brushed it back in a familiar gesture. She had seen it a thousand times. The freckles across the tops of his cheeks had retreated with the return of his normal coloring. The bruise on his cheek was fading to a yellow similar to her own.

"No," she said at length. "I . . . um . . . had a little . . . fall."

"Must have been *some* fall."

"It was." She felt stupid saying she fell, but it was already out there. She changed gears, trying for lightness in her tone. "Not like being run over by Fat Mr. Hammond. Where is he anyway?"

"Got suspended for a couple days while the accident is being investigated," said Jackson. "My parents are letting him off easy. Not making trouble."

The word *accident* rang unnaturally in Rebecca's ears. *Yes, accident,* she said to herself. *That's what it was. What else* could *it have been?*

"Is that what you told them?" she asked carefully. "That it was an accident?"

"Well, yeah. It sort of was. Don't know what I was doing."

"You were trying to make time with a little blonde cheerleader." Rebecca smirked, but her heart was thumping.

Jackson looked surprised, then a little sheepish. "Could be," was all he said.

At that moment, the classroom door crashed open, and Rebecca looked up to see Josh and Blake surge into the room. "Fat Man's coming," said Blake. They dropped their books onto their desks and threw themselves into their seats just as Mr. Hammond appeared in the doorway. The room fell silent as he walked heavily to the front of the class. His briefcase thudded onto his desk. He opened it and withdrew a sheaf of papers. He was frowning.

"Quiz tomorrow," he said. There were mutters from the class. He dropped several sheets on the desk at the head of each row. "Pass these back."

That's it? thought Rebecca. *Just business as usual?* She felt his attitude was seriously lacking, weird even, but then he was weird. And she couldn't think what might have been better. What can you say after you've run over a student, even if it was the student's fault?

Josh and Blake immediately engaged Jackson in an unintelligible verbal exchange accompanied by fist pumps and shoving. Mr. Hammond glanced in their direction but said nothing. The boys opened their algebra books but continued with their horsing around.

Boys are so retarded! thought Rebecca.

Jackson balled up a piece of paper and lobbed it at the back of Blake's head. Blake retaliated by shooting a spit ball at Jackson. Mr. Hammond gave the boys another look, but still said nothing. The stub of a pencil flew across the aisle. Jackson ducked, and the missile bounced on Rebecca's desk, coming to rest in her lap. Mr. Hammond rapped his knuckles on the top of his desk. "We have some review to cover," he said. "So let's cut any monkey business." His flat stare fell directly on Rebecca as he spoke.

Rebecca's breath came in a surprised little gasp. Her mouth fell open. She stared back at Mr. Hammond in disbelief. Giving herself a hard mental shake, she snapped her mouth shut. She ducked her head and rummaged in her book bag to cover the flare of anger that heated her cheeks. She wasn't involved in any jock monkey business! She pulled her algebra notebook from her bag and slapped it onto the top of her desk.

I was not talking. I was not involved, she thought furiously. *Why does he have it in for me? And the jocks get away with anything!*

As though on cue, Blake threw the original wad of paper back at Jackson. He missed, and it ricocheted onto Rebecca's desk. She knocked it onto the floor, where it bounced up the aisle.

"Is there a problem, Ms. Coleson?" Mr. Hammond was strolling down the aisle in her direction. He bent his bulk to retrieve the wad of paper. He uncurled it, smoothing it against the large, rumpled shirt tenting his huge stomach. The paper was blank, except for a name penciled at the top. Jackson Middleton. Mr. Hammond dropped the paper onto Jackson's desk and waddled back toward the front of the room. Jackson and Blake sniggered at each other, wearing twin idiotic grins.

Rebecca's face was hot with anger and resentment. "You *so* got what you deserved when he ran over you!" she hissed at Jackson.

Jackson laughed out loud, earning another look from Mr. Hammond, but no reprimand. Furious, Rebecca hunched low in her seat, ducking her head down. Her thoughts were murderous. Fat Mr. Hammond was such a waste of life! Wouldn't she just love to see him get back some of what he handed out.

She could dream, but rules were all for adults, and the exceptions all favored athletes. Sighing deeply, she propped one elbow on her desk and leaned her cheek against her hand. She pushed her math book aside and pulled her notebook close. She doodled, "What goes around comes around." It was one of her father's favorite sayings. Her mind wandered over various scenarios where Mr. Hammond got what was coming to him. The jocks were still talking, Josh describing to Jackson a remarkable crash at his most recent fat-tire race. Rebecca listened idly.

"It was huge, man," said Josh. "The guy's wild. Always half crazy. He could be a real contender, but he has no discipline. You gotta have discipline, man. Same as any sport."

Rebecca doodled "crazy" and "no discipline."

"You shoulda seen 'im," she heard Josh say. "He was totally moving, but out of control. Completely off the track. He went flying over this little ridge and totally airborne into the parking lot. Seriously. He crashed onto some guy's Jeep. His bike was wrecked. You know those canvas bodies on old Jeeps? Took one whole side out. And the kid gets up and walks away." Josh chuckled. Jackson looked impressed.

Rebecca scribbled the rough shape of a Jeep. It wasn't very good.

"Who is he?" Jackson asked.

"Don't know 'im," said Josh. "But he goes to Centennial. Plays ball for the Cougars."

Jackson made a rude noise at the mention of the Cougars.

"Yeah," Josh agreed. "No discipline," he said again. "You goin' to the game Friday?"

"Nah." Jackson shook his head. "What's the point?"

Rebecca doodled a baseball next to the Jeep. She grimaced at the crude images. Better to stick with writing. Drawing was definitely not her medium.

"Where's your team spirit?" Josh chided Jackson.

"Screw it, Telluride," said Jackson. "We suck this year. Can't hit worth crap, except for An the Man." Jackson added, "He can always hit."

Josh made a sympathetic noise, but baseball wasn't one of his sports.

"No fun watching a bunch of chumps knockin' fouls out of the park."

"Unless they take out a windshield." Josh chortled. "Mess with somebody's ride."

Rebecca drew what was meant to be a baseball crashing through a windshield. She absently coiled a lock of hair around one finger. An idea was coming. She didn't know what it was yet, but she felt that little tingle.

CHAPTER 15

Three Bitches and a Puppy

May 10

SECOND BELL WAS sounding as Rebecca slipped into her chair in science Friday morning. Ty looked up with brown eyes shining. Her excitement was palpable. Rebecca was pretty sure it wasn't related to science class.

"Hey, Ty, what's up?"

"I'm going up to my dad's tonight," said Tyler.

"To Steamboat?"

"Yeah. I'm going on a shoot with him." Tyler bounced on her chair in her excitement. "But that's not the best part."

"Let's get right to it, people." Mr. Gonzales wasn't wasting any time.

"What's the best part?" Rebecca whispered. It must be good. Tyler was excitable, but she seemed jazzed even for her.

Gonzales was at their table. "I know you have other pressing matters to discuss." His voice dripped sarcasm, and he looked pointedly at Tyler and Rebecca. "But see if you can put it on hold and focus on science for fifty minutes."

Rebecca glanced at Ty. Tyler's head dipped, and she opened her notebook. Her knees jittered up and down, heels tapping lightly on the floor. Tyler could, and would, focus on science for fifty minutes, putting aside her good news. Whatever it was, it would have to wait. Rebecca grudgingly turned her attention to science as well.

At the end of class, Tyler hurriedly stuffed her things into her backpack. "Come on. I'll show you in English."

Rebecca hurried to keep up. At the study pod in English, Tyler pulled an envelope from a pocket in her book bag. "Dad came down last night, and he talked Mom into letting me have a puppy!" Ty was exuberant.

"A puppy! I'm so jealous!"

"We went and saw the litter. They gave us these." Tyler pulled several photos from the envelope and laid them on the table. A tiny bundle of curly black-and-white fur with drooping ears stared out of the first picture.

"Ooh, she's so darling!" Rebecca picked up a photo.

"Isn't she?" Tyler shuffled through the pictures. "I can't have her for at least a week because she's still too young."

Rebecca inspected another picture. A much larger version of the black-and-white puppy lay on its side, head resting on outstretched front paws. Five look-alike puppies tumbled every which way, tiny paws bracketing curly black-and-white heads. They burrowed against their mother as they nursed.

"The mother dog looks tired," said Rebecca.

"Bitch," corrected Ty.

"*Excuse me*?" Rebecca glared at Ty.

"No, no!" Ty laughed. "Not you! The mother dog is a bitch."

Rebecca was still glaring at her.

"Really, Becks. That's what they're called. I can't believe you don't know that."

"Well, I guess I do now." Rebecca laid the picture on the table. "So what kind of dog? I mean, the puppy. What is it? "

"Looks like a dog."

Rebecca whirled at the sound of Jackson's voice.

"You think so, Einstein?" she shot back.

Jackson laughed. "That's cute, Becka."

Jackson leaned on one crutch and ruffled her hair as he hobbled to his seat. Rebecca shook her head violently, but Jackson was already gone. Two girls from the next study pod immediately began flirting with him.

Ty tugged on Rebecca's arm. "She's a mixed breed," she said. "The bitch is part cocker spaniel. The sire is a mix too—part Cavalier King Charles. She's not going to get very big."

"How can you be sure?" asked Rebecca.

Tyler was distracted by the arrival of Brittany and Clarity, heads conspiratorially close. Brittany was whispering excitedly into Clarity's ear. They dropped their books onto the table.

"Cute puppy," said Clarity. "Is it yours?" Brittany glanced in Tyler's direction, but it was like she didn't even see her.

"She will be," said Ty with satisfaction. "In about a week." She slid several photos across the table for Clarity to admire.

"I love puppies," Clarity said.

Brittany pushed the pictures away. She pulled insistently on Clarity's arm.

"He said he'd call me!" Rebecca could easily hear Brittany's voice. "He goes to CSU!"

"I heard that part," said Clarity. "So he's a college man. Where'd you meet him again?"

"You're not listening!" hissed Brittany.

Sighing, Clarity turned and gave Brittany her full attention, the puppy photos abandoned. Rebecca leaned across the table to retrieve the pictures, listening to Brittany and Clarity's conversation. It wasn't difficult. Brittany didn't seem interested in keeping it private.

"At Dave and Buster's. My brother, Jordon—it was his birthday last week. Jordon knows him from CSU."

"When did he say he'd call?" asked Clarity.

"This weekend. I think he's going to ask me out!"

"Would your mom let you go out with a guy so much older? He must be eighteen or nineteen!"

A sly look appeared on Brittany's face. "Well, probably not if she knew about it."

The arrival of Mrs. Lindzer reduced the conversation to whispers below the range of Rebecca's hearing. Sighing, she opened her English book.

Rebecca slid the puppy pictures back to Tyler. "I can't wait till you get her," she whispered.

Tyler hugged Rebecca's arm. "Me, too," she whispered back.

Mrs. Lindzer laid a stack of papers in the center of each pod. "This is a little brain teaser for you," she said. "It's for extra credit."

There were sighs and groans around the room. "Come on, people," said Mrs. Lindzer. "This is middle-school level. I'm throwing you a bone for easy credit."

They settled in for the remainder of the hour. At period's end, Tyler gathered up her materials and shoved them into her knapsack with uncharacteristic haste.

"What's the rush?" asked Rebecca.

Tyler pushed back her chair and slung her book bag over one shoulder. "Gotta pee." She rolled her eyes and headed for the door.

Rebecca watched her go, feeling a mixture of amusement and forbearance. Tyler was, well, Tyler. It was best to take her as she was. As Rebecca picked up her English book to slip it into her book bag, two photos of the new puppy fell to the floor.

"Oh—" Rebecca glanced over her shoulder, knowing Ty was already gone. She picked up the photos and looked at the puppy again, smiling to herself. She was so adorable! Maybe there were still puppies available from this litter. What fun if she and Ty both had puppies!

I might as well ask for the moon, she thought, and her shoulders sagged. She was pretty sure her parents wouldn't agree to another animal. Especially given Scoundrel's habits. He was in trouble almost daily. There were so many rules! She could hear her father's voice in her head in his lecturing tone: *When you take responsibility for the privileges you already have, we'll consider additional privileges. It's a privilege to own a pet, and it's a big responsibility.* She'd heard that one enough times. Usually directed at Andy, but still. No, a puppy would be sweet, but Rebecca didn't think it was going to happen at their house. She slipped the pictures into her jacket pocket as she headed for drama.

Mr. Tilson was pretty unconventional; you could never be sure what was coming. She had selected drama as her freshman elective thinking it would be totally cool to dress up in character and pretend to be someone else. She loved the idea of, literally, wearing the cloak of a mystery persona.

But it hadn't worked out quite like she thought. Upperclass students usually got the good parts in productions, and that left bit parts and grunt work for the freshmen and sophomores. For the two major productions this year, Rebecca's choices had been to work on sets or write a thousand-word essay relating to the play or some other topic approved by Mr. Tilson. She had chosen to work on sets, and that had been fun. She and Angela had painted background scenes and props together. Rebecca had to admit the Ice Maiden could be okay when she wasn't surrounded by her silly, empty-headed friends.

Could was the operative word here. And not on this day.

Angela was already there when Rebecca arrived, and she had turned on the charm with a group of students clustered by the little stage at the back of the room. The now-familiar phrases floated to her ears. Charles glanced over at Rebecca and nodded. She nodded in return but didn't join the group.

Just more of the same, thought Rebecca. She listened for the capstone.

"Of course, there are scholarships involved. That's the real reason I'm bothering with this." Angela tossed this off with cool indifference.

"So you'll be appearing in a bathing suit?" Charles leered at Angela.

Angela laughed. It was a light, tinkling sound. "Certainly, for one event. Also, an evening gown. And business dress for—"

"The smaller the better, hey, Todd?" Charles interrupted Angela. He and Todd elbowed each other and sniggered loudly.

Angela drew herself up and raised her chin. "You have no idea of the level of professionalism and talent involved in a scholarship competition like this." Her tone was imperious. Head high and back straight, she turned and marched off. Todd and Charles followed her progress, their eyes glued to Angela's perfect size-six figure.

Angie headed straight for Rebecca. She slid into the desk in front of Rebecca and turned around to face her, smiling a tight little smile.

"Hi, Angie," Rebecca said. She smiled politely, but without enthusiasm. Without really meaning to, she added, "They were total jerks."

"They just have no clue," Angela muttered. "This is a really great opportunity for me," she said. "I know I can win. I mean, really. You just have to know who the other girls are!"

"Who are they?" asked Rebecca.

Angie didn't seem to hear. She fussed with her designer bag. After a moment, she continued, "There is so much pressure on me. Ordinary people have no idea how difficult it is and how much is expected of me."

Rebecca glanced at the big clock above Mr. Tilson's desk. "Why is—"

"The preparation is *so* intense."

Rebecca smiled woodenly. This wasn't really a conversation.

"You have no idea." Angela went on. "You all think this is just about looking good in a swimsuit, which I certainly do, and not falling off my high heels."

Keep this up, thought Rebecca, *and the* ordinary *people will be* rooting *for you to fall off your high heels.* Rebecca was still smiling but it felt tight. Probably any idiot could tell it was fake. She had been almost sorry for Angela when the boys acted so crudely, but her sympathy was pretty much gone.

At last, Mr. Tilson breezed into the room, clapping his hands and calling the class together. Rebecca sighed deeply and pulled her notebook out of her backpack. She was greatly relieved when Angela turned and faced forward in her seat.

***

Rebecca hurried into the cafeteria, looking around for her friends as she grabbed a tray. She could barely wait to fill them in on all the latest. She selected a sandwich from the self-serve deli, then added a big chocolate chip cookie and a small carton of orange juice to her tray. "That's a healthy lunch," she muttered under her breath. "Orange juice and"—she peered closely at the sandwich wrapper—"chicken."

As Rebecca made her way through the crowded cafeteria in search of an empty table, she looked around again for her friends. She saw Tyler and Alexa coming through the doors just as she found a table. She waved, and they joined her. Ty's boundless energy was barely contained as she bounced from one seat and then to another, finally perching on the edge of a chair to withdraw a misshapen sandwich and an envelope from her knapsack. Alexa dropped into her chair and let her book bag fall to the floor, her jacket on top of it. She stretched long legs to prop her feet on the whole mess. Rebecca noted that AJ's high-heeled sandals matched the frames of her glasses. Sam and Zoe appeared, Sam grinning and gesturing. Zoe's eyes widened at whatever Sam was saying. Rebecca felt a rush of warm emotion for her oldest friends. Sam shrugged out of her denim jacket, revealing a bright-red T-shirt with a running horse on the front.

Sam and Zoe had barely settled into their chairs when Sam jumped back up.

"Look, new boots," she exclaimed. Propping one foot on her chair, she tugged worn jeans high enough to show off a pair of dark-red western riding boots. "Look at the tooling. My uncle got them for me." She traced the sinuous curves and swirls of the intricate design with a long fingernail accented in glossy lacquer that matched her boots.

"Cool, Sam," said Rebecca approvingly.

"Are you really going to ride in those?" asked AJ.

"Jeez, Sam, how many pairs is that?" asked Ty.

Sam grinned. "Sure," she said, looking at AJ. She tugged the leg of her jeans back into place and dropped into her chair. "A few," she said to Ty.

Tyler bounced up, beaming happily. She pulled her puppy pictures from the envelope. "I'm getting a puppy," she announced.

"Oh, Ty, you left two pictures in English," said Rebecca. "They're in my jacket." Rebecca twisted around for her jacket, but only her book bag hung from the back of her chair. "Um . . . which is in my locker," she finished.

Ty just nodded as she proudly passed around her pictures. Lunches temporarily ignored, the girls exclaimed over the photos. Ty beamed.

"Actual pictures," said Sam. "Can't you take pictures with your phone?"

"Of course," replied Tyler. "I did. The owners had these."

All but Rebecca nodded. Her dad's rules, of course, didn't include cell phones for freshmen. Even though everyone else she knew had one, including some kids Andy's age.

"What are you going to name it?" asked AJ.

"Is it a boy or a girl?" queried Zoe.

"I don't know yet," said Ty. "It's a girl."

"Don't you mean bitch?" laughed Rebecca. Ty grinned back at her.

Passing the pictures—really, she'd already seen them—Rebecca said, "You should have heard Angela in drama." She took a bite of cookie.

"More pageant stuff?"

"Yeah. Charles, he's a senior, and another guy totally jived her about appearing in a bikini. They were pretty gross. Angela gave it right back. I was sort of glad she did."

"That total bitch ice maiden thing?"

"Most definitely," Rebecca nodded. "Mr. Tilson was late, and she kind of cornered me. I got this 'I'm so great and everyone else is so ordinary' bit."

Rebecca took another bite of cookie. "She's getting pretty irritating. She said how ordinary people couldn't do what she does, and how everyone thinks it's just about not falling off your high heels. Which, by then, I was sort of hoping she will do." Rebecca felt a little tingle in the pit of her stomach, and she rubbed a hand over her solar plexus.

Ty picked it up from there. "The new blonde . . . Brittany? She thinks some hot CSU guy—well, she thinks he's hot—is going to ask her out. She's going to sneak out with him without her mother knowing." Tyler looked at Rebecca for confirmation, and Rebecca nodded.

"Like she's some superhot number," said Rebecca.

"I heard about it in fourth period," said AJ. "First, she tells me the whole thing. And then she got really snotty."

"What do you mean?" asked Sam.

"You know, acting all superior. Like she's so hot and that I could never get a date because I'm a slob or a fashion nerd or something," said AJ. Her voice was flat. She didn't sound mad, exactly, or upset. But not indifferent either. Cold maybe.

"No way!"

"You're not a slob! You're just not a slave to stupid fads!"

"My god! Can't she *see* you?"

"You're gorgeous! She hasn't seen you giving swimming lessons," said Ty.

AJ fixed Tyler with a cool, level look. Rebecca thought AJ could pose as a goddess, with her great figure, honey-colored skin, and high cheekbones. But she knew better than to say it.

"Not all gorgeous girls are stupid," said Zoe. She seemed to read AJ's mind.

AJ nodded, but made no comment.

"What did she say exactly?" asked Rebecca.

"She said"—AJ made air quotes—"'I know you don't understand how totally the bomb this is. If you were ever going to get a date with a college man, you'd need to learn how to dress.' And she gave me this total put-down look."

AJ pushed her glasses up her nose. "You'd have to've been there," she said calmly.

"Maybe you'd only have to know how to put out," said Ty.

There were giggles. Rebecca didn't share the humor. A cold finger of anger curled in her belly. *Bitch*, she thought.

"It's no big deal," said AJ. She pulled a baggie from her book bag. She frowned at it, and then extracted a piece of . . . something brown and crumbly.

"Cookie anyone?"

There were no takers. Silence stretched out around the table.

"She's so sure she's going to get this date," said Rebecca at length. "Maybe she won't."

"What do you mean?" asked Zoe.

Rebecca chewed slowly on the last bite of her own cookie.

"Nothing," she said finally. "Just that the guy hasn't even called her yet."

***

As the teacher droned on about checks and balances in government, Rebecca doodled in her notebook. Not a story idea. Not exactly anyway. She wrote, "Judiciary Branch, Executive Branch, Legislative Branch, Branch of Broken Dates." A little smile played around the corners of her mouth. She added "Bitch," absently retracing the letters. The anger she had felt when Alexa told them about Brittany's put-down in fourth period stole over her again, and she slashed two thick lines beneath the word. Who did Brittany think she was?

Rebecca drew in a deep breath and straightened her shoulders. *It's not your fight*, she told herself. *Besides, AJ didn't seem to be steamed about it.* She crossed out her doodles. Brittany wasn't a friend of Rebecca's, but neither was she an adversary. She was just one of the empty-headed mimics appended to Angela. Angela was getting pretty hard to take too, but that wasn't part of this. *AJ is my friend, and friends stick together.* She wrote the words "Branch of Broken Dates" again. *They stand up for each other, don't they?* She wrote "stand up for each other," and then "stand her up." A little tickle teased the pit of her stomach. She studied what she had written and then slowly crossed it all out.

This was crazy. It wasn't like she could do anything anyway. She tore the page from her binder, folded it into a small square, and stuffed it in her book bag. She turned to a fresh page and looked up at the blackboard where the teacher was writing a list of . . . something. She wasn't sure what. Maybe she should be listening. She absently twirled a lock of hair as she stared at the blackboard, pen poised over paper. But her mind was somewhere else.

CHAPTER 16

Is Zoe a Little Cozy with Jackson?

May 13

REBECCA STOOD IN her closet surveying her options for school. She absently ran her hands through sleep-rumpled hair. If she'd done her laundry over the weekend, she'd have had more choices. Well, she hadn't. She padded in bare feet to her windows to check her patch of sky. It was a brilliant blue. She pulled out a sleeveless top with a deep neckline and a pair of cropped jeans. The top was last year's and a little snug. And it showed her firm, round breasts in the neckline. Last year, she had worn it layered over a bandeaux, and it had been plenty loose. She hugged herself, and the bit of bosom became a considerable amount. Lissa wore this type of top, but she was so slender there wasn't much to see, even with a plunging neckline. And Laney would do it! Rebecca studied her figure. She tried to imagine walking into algebra or Home Room with her boobs visible for all to see. Especially Jackson! That did it. She skimmed the top over her head.

She wished she had Laney's courage. Or Lissa's self-confidence. Or Sam's nonchalance. She swapped the top for a colored Tee. She slipped her feet into flat sandals, sighing at her dad's ridiculous rules. Rules could be such a bore.

She caught up with Sam and Zoe in front of the school. They lingered outside in the bright sunshine as long as they could, watching the stream of people flowing past. Angela went by them with a cool smile. Brittany and Clarity came up the steps, heads together. They passed within two feet of Rebecca and her friends, but Brittany ignored them completely. Clarity nodded at them, looking uncomfortable.

"She's getting really hard to take about that college boy," said Zoe.

"Yeah. The CSU idiot," said Sam.

"CSU idiot? What do you mean?" said Rebecca.

"Well, he'd pretty much have to be, wouldn't he?" Sam smirked.

They all laughed. "Oh, I'm so feeling that," said Rebecca.

"Has anyone seen him? Is he hot?"

"Don't know. Brittany's not exactly ugly. He could be."

"Yeah, hot. A hot ho." More giggles.

"She's probably just his flavor of the month."

"He hasn't asked her out yet," said Rebecca. "It's all she talks about in English. His name's Jason. It's Jason this and Jason said and Jason thinks. It's like she doesn't have a brain of her own."

"Why would you think she does?" asked Sam.

"Yeah, good point. She's still treating it like a slam dunk," said Rebecca. "That he'll ask her out."

Sam and Zoe nodded.

"There's Jackson!" Zoe waved enthusiastically at Jackson, who was getting out of an SUV, Travis right behind him. Jackson nodded back with his "Damn, I'm good, just ask me" grin. He limped in their direction. Travis followed with two packs.

"That's an odd pairing," said Sam under her breath. "What do you know about Travis?"

"Nothing. He's in our English pod. And French class. Cute. That's about it." Rebecca was thoughtful.

"He takes French?" Sam was surprised. And then, "I thought you liked blonds?"

Rebecca gave Sam a withering look but didn't reply. She and Sam headed for the doors, but Zoe hung back. Jackson stopped in front of her. Travis nodded at him. "Later, Jacks," he said. He handed off one pack before he walked away.

Rebecca turned back to look for Zoe, surprised to see her in earnest conversation with Jackson. Jackson looked discouraged. Zoe put a hand on his arm, and Jackson nodded. Rebecca couldn't hear the conversation; she watched the exchange with curiosity and something else. Something she couldn't put a name to. There was a little knot in her solar plexus. She put on her neutral expression. At least she hoped she did. She glanced at Sam, who seemed oblivious to the whole thing, and then back at Zoe and Jackson. They were walking toward Rebecca now, Zoe smiling up at him.

"Gotta go," said Jackson. He looked directly at Rebecca. "Hey, Becka. You're lookin' almost like you."

Involuntarily, Rebecca touched a hand to her face. The bruising was mostly gone, but her cheek still bore a fading pink blemish from the rug burn. Her left wrist was still in a cast.

"Yeah," was all she said.

First bell was sounding, and Jackson limped off. Rebecca stared after him for a long moment and then faced Zoe.

"WTF was that?" she demanded.

"What do you mean?" Zoe was offhand.

"You're sure cozy with Jackson. That's what I mean."

"I told you Friday. We talk sometimes, that's all." Zoe shrugged.

"You talk sometimes."

"Yeah, we talk sometimes. Lighten up, Becks. I see him around school, and we talk. He seems to like talking to someone who . . ." Zoe looked a little uncomfortable.

"Someone who . . . ?" Rebecca frowned.

"Someone who has a brain," said Zoe.

"As opposed to . . ."

"Not you, Becks," said Zoe. "We know *you* have a brain. I mean all the brain-dead ho's who throw themselves at him all the time."

"Come on." It was déjà vu. Sam linked her arms through theirs and tugged them forward. "Second bell is any minute. You don't want to be late in Hammond's class." She glanced at Rebecca.

That got Rebecca moving. A run-in with the Fat Man was the last thing she needed. The girls parted in the big atrium, and she hurried for her algebra class.

The exchange between Zoe and Jackson was still on her mind. Rebecca was beginning to wonder if her friend had a thing for Jackson, as difficult as that was to fathom. A nub of concern wedged itself into a corner of her brain and refused to budge for the remainder of the morning. In spite of that, classes went smoothly enough, although her teachers were pouring on homework in preparation for finals. At least that's what they all said. Rebecca thought there might be a sadistic element to it. Maybe it was part of getting a teaching credential. *How to legally torture your students into submission.*

Fourth period was a relief. There was a curveball, though.

Mr. Tilson was perched on the front edge of his desk when Rebecca walked in. There was a mischievous gleam in his eyes that made the skin on the back of her neck prickle. What were they in for today? She soon found out. Mr. Tilson didn't even wait for second bell.

"Okay, people!" he said with a wide grin. "Ms. Thornton is going to preview her talent skit for this weekend's competition. We will *objectively* critique her and coach her on technique and delivery in hopes of abetting her chances for success." He gestured toward Angela, arm outstretched, palm facing upward, much as he did when presenting his cast after a performance.

Angie looked a little uncomfortable, but she went to the front of the room. She took a minute to gather herself and then launched into a parody of dressing for Front Range weather, which changed faster than even she could change her outfits. In a three-minute skit, Angela managed to wear five different ensembles. Angela didn't have the real outfits—just a few pieces from the costume closet—but still, Rebecca was grudgingly impressed. Angela had an easy, natural ability, which felt at odds with Rebecca's opinion of her as the Ice Maiden. The class gave her an enthusiastic round of applause, and Angela smiled almost shyly, nodding her head in acknowledgment.

Rebecca relayed all this to her friends at lunch. They eyed Angela at the next table where she sat with the cheerleaders.

"I'm sick of the whole pageant thing," said Rebecca. "It's all she talks about. But she's a good body actor. She's just different somehow in drama."

"Maybe she likes playing a different role. You know, pretending to be someone else," said AJ.

"Maybe." Rebecca chewed one side of her lower lip. "That's part of why I took drama, actually," she said. She had never told this to anyone, not even Zoe or Sam. "To see what it would be like to be someone else. I thought it would be totally the bomb."

"I get that," said Ty. "Most of the time, I'd *love* to be someone else."

"Like you and Laney," said Sam.

Rebecca looked at Tyler and changed the subject. "When do you get the puppy?"

Tyler beamed. "This weekend," she said.

"So you won't be going up to your dad's?" asked Rebecca.

"No, he's coming down. Mom just loves that." Ty's tone left no room for interpretation. "Mom says he's just a kid who never grew up. She's been sort of hinting that letting me get the puppy was a bad idea. Dad's bad idea."

"What are you going to call her?" Sam asked. "The puppy, I mean."

"I'm thinking Anne Boleyn. I'm reading *The Other Boleyn Girl*, and it's really awesome. Plus, I just love the name."

"Anne Boleyn," Rebecca tried it out. "A lot of name for a little puppy."

"Little Brit," said AJ.

"Maybe . . ." Ty wasn't sure.

"Headless." Sam grinned.

"That's mean!" Tyler glared at Sam. One hand clutched the ponytail.

Sam propped her boots on an empty chair and crossed her ankles, at the same time running her fingers through her tousled blonde hair. She didn't have anything else to say about the puppy. And she didn't offer an apology.

CHAPTER 17

Dogs That Earn Their Living

May 13

AFTER FRENCH CLASS, Rebecca and Zoe found Sam waiting for them at the bottom of the stairs. They went into Home Room together. Every time Rebecca entered this room, she was reminded of the fight. It still felt like yesterday. There were times when she recalled her humiliation and embarrassment so vividly she felt almost sick. And that always brought her around to the little story, and the ensuing accident. She didn't want to think about any of it.

As if on cue, Josh and Blake strolled into the room, self-assurance radiating in their confident walks.

"Where's Jackson?" asked Zoe of no one in particular.

Rebecca wondered again if Zoe had a thing for Jackson. She shrugged. "Wherever he is, I'm sure he's causing trouble," she said.

"Why do you say that?"

"Because that's what he does." Rebecca scowled.

"Maybe he only causes trouble for you," said Sam.

Rebecca looked hard at Sam. Sam smiled sweetly back. Rebecca changed the subject. "You don't seem too enthused about Ty's puppy. I thought you liked dogs."

"Oh, I like dogs fine," said Sam. "Just not ridiculous little ankle biters."

Rebecca giggled. "How do you know Anne Boleyn will be an ankle biter?"

Sam frowned and picked at a red fingernail. "Little dogs are so worthless. I like dogs that earn their own living," she said.

"You mean like a nine-to-five job?"

Sam laughed. "No," she said. "Like guard dogs, or herding dogs. Seeing Eye dogs. That sort of dog. Dogs with some meaning."

Rebecca thought about Scoundrel. He was a big dog, but still totally worthless. Unless you factored in Andy's adoration. She didn't contradict Sam, but she wondered if that was meaning enough.

"So what happened with Magic?" asked Zoe. "Did she have her foal yet?"

Sam looked carefully at Zoe. "Um, yes, she did, actually." She glanced at Rebecca.

"And?" Zoe said.

"And what?" asked Sam.

"What is it? And is Magic okay?" Zoe looked puzzled.

"Oh! Yeah, Magic is good. The leg is actually better, though no one has the first clue why." Sam looked again at Rebecca, who wore a carefully neutral expression. Sam continued, "It's a filly. Uncle Clint is happy because he says mares are better tempered with riders, and ultimately, the filly will be a workhorse."

"No one gets to slack off at a dude ranch, I guess," said Zoe.

"No," said Sam. "Everyone, including animals, has a job to do. Especially the animals, actually. I think they work harder than some of the hands."

This was safe turf. Rebecca sighed inwardly. It was hard to keep secrets from Zoe, but Sam would tell about the Reiki when she was ready. Rebecca had to respect that.

"Mom is good with the sleepover," she said. "But now she wants it to be Memorial Day weekend. Then we can have it Sunday night." She looked around for agreement.

"I'm good with that," said Zoe.

"Then I can have Saturday at the ranch," said Sam.

"And if the weather's good, we can sleep out on the trampoline." Rebecca delivered the coup de gras.

"Totally the bomb." Sam grinned.

Zoe's eyes widened, and she blinked twice. "Sweet," was all she said.

CHAPTER 18

The Ice Maiden Wins

May 14

THE FOLLOWING DAY in drama, Mr. Tilson announced that Angela had taken first place in her initial competition. Her skit had received high marks for originality and delivery. "We're all pleased for Ms. Thorton's success," he said. "Let's give her a hand."

The class responded with applause and a few whistles. Angela rose from her seat and bowed gracefully to the class and then to Mr. Tilson. Mr. Tilson bowed formally to her in return.

"And we wish her well with her next level of competition," he said. Angela slid back into the seat next to Rebecca looking very pleased with herself.

"And I have some good news of my own." Mr. Tilson gestured at a thick stack of papers on his desk. "I have been asked to edit a manuscript for a friend of mine who directs Off-Broadway," he said. The more serious drama students gave him a standing ovation. White teeth flashed in his tan face.

"Thank you," he said, waving off the applause. "The deadline is pretty tight, so I'll be trusting you to pursue your individual theater interests quietly while I work. Consider it a boon that is yours for the losing." He looked around his class. "My one caveat," he added, "is that whatever you choose to do, you do it quietly and with a minimum of disturbance."

He settled himself at his desk, drawing the thick manuscript close.

Rebecca didn't know what to do with the bonus of free time. This was more laid back than usual, even for drama class. There would be no drama final to study for. The last production of the season was long over. She supposed she could study for another class, but that was a pretty boring idea. A handful of drama scholars made their way quietly to the small stage at the back of the room. An impromptu pantomime skit ensued. Rebecca watched for a while. It was lighthearted and cool, and she was tempted to participate, but shyness held her back. Plus, she wasn't really a fan of mime. A few students appeared to be actually studying for other classes. Two or three seniors slipped out of the room altogether. Some kids collected in small groups just hanging out for the hour. Charles and Todd were sitting alone together, and Rebecca thought about joining them.

Angela fiddled for a few moments with a fat binder labeled PAGEANT, and then she turned to Rebecca.

Rebecca smiled dutifully at her. "Congratulations," she whispered. "I thought your skit was really good."

Angela acknowledged her with a tight smile, but she looked preoccupied. "Now I have to figure out how to do it all over again," she said.

"For the next pageant?" Rebecca asked.

Angela dipped her chin down and back up. "Competition, yes. I don't know whether to change my talent or improve on this one," she said.

Rebecca nodded, barely interested.

"I need a new bathing suit," said Angela. "And a different evening gown. Well, an entirely new wardrobe would be best. Dad's having a fit about that. It's so unfair!"

Rebecca fidgeted in her seat. She mentally compared her own version of unfairness to Angela's. Angela fiddled again with the binder. "My tan is practically nonexistent this early in the season." She glanced at Rebecca.

"Tanning booths aren't safe. I could just ruin my skin. I'm thinking of changing my hairstyle. Something edgy that no one else is doing. I'm not really happy with the stylist Mom chose for the last competition. Or the makeup professional."

Rebecca bit her lips and said nothing.

"There's so much to think about."

"It doesn't sound like winning is all that much fun," said Rebecca.

Angela looked straight at her. "The next level demands a huge amount of work and commitment," she said. "And then school finals are coming up."

"I'm sure you'll do great," said Rebecca. "On all of it." She wasn't sure, and she honestly didn't care. What she cared about was this conversation being over. "I need to study for science," she said. She didn't really, but it couldn't hurt. She pulled her science text from her book bag and pointedly opened it on her desk.

Angela sighed dramatically. She ran a slender hand over perfectly styled hair and opened the pageant binder.

Rebecca couldn't get her mind on biology. She cradled her casted wrist and watched the clock. The hands didn't seem to move, but finally, the period bell rang. She grabbed her things and hurried for the cafeteria.

She was the last to arrive. "Hey," she said, grinning at her friends. "S'up?"

"Same ol' same ol'," said AJ. "Brittany's getting really intolerable with her CSU idiot stuff. I wanted to drown her last period."

"Wow!" That was pretty strong coming from AJ. Rebecca looked in surprise at her friend. AJ was sitting up straight, her shoulders squared and her feet on the floor. Her brows were drawn together in an uncharacteristic frown.

"Same thing in English," said Tyler. Rebecca nodded her agreement. "I went to the baseball game last Friday," Tyler went on. "Brittany and Angela got into it over something. I was too far away to hear what, but they were really going at it."

"Jeez, Brittany was her biggest fan," said Sam. "You guys are gonna love this." Sam stretched her legs and planted her booted feet on an empty chair. They looked at her in anticipation.

"Angela's getting pretty tired of hearing about Jason."

"*Angela's* tired . . ."

"I know, I know!" Sam leaned forward. "In Ms. Markham's English class, Angela told me Brittany just doesn't realize no one is interested in hearing about Jason. She said, and I quote, 'There's just no shutting her up.'"

"You've got to be kidding! There's no shutting Angela up about the pageant!"

"For real?"

"Yeah." Sam shrugged, her face wreathed in a wide smile. "It's pretty rich."

"Get this," said Rebecca. "Angela pinned me like a bug in drama. Now that she's won the first pageant, she's all in a twist about what to do for the second one. And her dad is giving her a hard time about the cost."

"NFW!"

"There's more," Rebecca said. "Angela is thinking about a new hairstyle. Something 'edgy' that no one else is doing."

That broke them all up. "That would last all of five minutes," said Zoe. "Every girl on the rally squad would be all over that."

"And half the girls in freshman class."

"Except Peyton," said AJ. "Her hair is awesome."

"Yeah, she's totally out of the water with her hair."

"Angela and Brittany are both impossible," said Sam. She squared her shoulders and sat up straighter. "Neither one of them gives a rip about anyone else."

"I think Brittany's the worst," said Rebecca. "There're these two senior guys in drama. "Charles, especially. He gives Angela a hard time practically every day about the swimsuit competition. She gives it right back to him. Pretty stuck-up, but not a *total* bitch. And Charles deserves it."

"You're not becoming a fan of the Ice Maiden, are you?" asked Zoe.

"No. But Charles is a jerk about it. And I sort of like to see Angela hold her own. You know, it's a 'women versus the world' thing.'"

"That's good," said Zoe. "I like it. Even if it's the Ice Maiden."

Rebecca glanced at the cheerleaders' table, a little frown on her face. "Angela's all about herself," she said, "but I think Brittany is plain mean."

CHAPTER 19

Things Get Really Interesting

May 16

REBECCA WALKED INTO drama class to find the room unusually quiet. Mr. Tilson was hunched intently over his script-editing project, scribbling furiously in the margins. Several students were focused on open textbooks, albeit not drama textbooks. Well, drama didn't exactly have textbooks, did it? The remainder were scattered in low-key groups talking quietly. The little stage was empty. Rebecca settled herself on its apron and slid her book bag off her shoulder. She had just pulled out her math homework when Angela glided into the room. She glanced around and then made her way toward Rebecca.

Angie sat on the apron next to Rebecca, drew her knees up to her chest, and clasped her slender arms around them. She didn't speak.

Rebecca sighed inwardly. "What's up, Angie?" she said.

"It's my dad," she said at length. "He's being a real jerk about my costs."

Rebecca stifled a laugh and schooled her face into a neutral expression. At least she hoped she did. "I thought your dad—"

"Yeah, I know," Angie interrupted. She shrugged, still hugging her knees. "But if it's not his thing, Dad goes on like a real Scrooge sometimes."

Rebecca couldn't think of anything to say to this.

"Mom's handling him." There was a pause. "But I get a little tired of hearing about it."

Rebecca bit her lower lip hard, nearly choking on the irony. When she could speak, she said carefully, "And he's not behind you on this?"

Angela sighed. "He went on and on about the wardrobe for my first skit," she continued. "He just doesn't get it. He wants me to do something that only requires one dress, or use the same talent for the next event."

"Is that not—"

Angela shook her head vehemently before Rebecca could finish her question.

"I thought your skit was really cute," said Rebecca. "You acted it out really great." She paused. "At least here in class. I didn't see the pageant. Competition, I mean."

"It's my strength. I need to play to it." Angela mused almost as if Rebecca weren't there. "My voice isn't bad. I could sing if I wasn't up against that Fort Collins girl. Her voice is practically operatic. She's had voice lessons since she was five."

Rebecca just nodded. There was no way to reply.

"I have a real advantage if Mr. Tilson coaches me again," Angela said. "I just need a really original idea." She stretched shapely legs, crossing them at the ankles, and leaned back on her arms. Rebecca glanced longingly at Angela's hot-fashion shoes and forced her gaze away.

Suddenly Rebecca sat up straight. She felt a tickle of anticipation in the pit of her stomach. An idea was taking form. She practically shivered with the energy of it.

Angela gave her a funny look. "What?"

"What if . . . what if you did a skit on selecting your outfits for the pageant?" Rebecca was excited. "It would be a spoof. You know, poking fun at the process. It's a little like the weather one, but you have such a perfect figure. Like you said, play to your strength."

Angela exhaled forcefully. "That would be a great way to set my dad off," she said. "Talk about cost!"

"Well . . ." Rebecca was thinking fast. It was a really good idea, she knew it. She was still feeling that creative tingle. She rubbed her palms together. "You could go to one of those places where rich people take clothes they only wore once or twice."

The words were out before Rebecca could stop herself. *Oh, great,* she thought. *Mrs. Thornton is probably one of those rich people.*

"You mean like *Goodwill?*" Angela was horrified.

"No, no . . ." Rebecca shook her head. "Consignment stores. Like The Morning After. Or Second and Queens. I've been there with a friend of my mom's. They have real good stuff. Designer names."

Rebecca was still thinking. "You could pick your outfits to be sort of 'out there.' A little exaggerated. To reinforce the idea of it being a spoof."

Carefully arched blonde eyebrows, subtly highlighted with pencil, climbed toward white-blonde hair as Angela gazed down her slender nose at Rebecca.

"And," Rebecca plunged on, "you could make it a point for the environment. You know, reduce, reuse, recycle. And then give them away after . . ." Rebecca's voice trailed off.

Seconds dragged out as the two girls stared at each other.

When Angela at last spoke, her voice was flat. "I don't think so, Rebecca. This is all out of your league." And she stood up and moved away.

Rebecca sat in stunned silence as she watched Angela float across the room and slide gracefully into a vacant seat. She felt a warm flush creep up her face. Anger and indignation began a slow simmer in her gut. It was a great idea; she knew it was! *Why did I even listen to you carrying on about your rich-girl troubles!* Rebecca thought. *I hope you do fall off your high heels.*

CHAPTER 20

One Bitch Bites Back

May 16

REBECCA WAS STILL seething as she made her way to the cafeteria. Zoe and Sam were already there, lunches spread before them—Sam's haphazardly and Zoe's neat and precise. Rebecca slumped heavily into a chair next to her friends.

"Not eating today?" asked Zoe.

"No." Rebecca propped her elbows on the table and leaned her chin on her hands. "Yes." She shook her head. "I mean, I'm eating in a minute." She glanced over at the next table. "Oh, Lord." She sighed, dropped her head onto the table, and covered it with her arms.

Zoe and Sam shared a concerned look. "Becks, what's up?"

Rebecca raised her head and pointed to the next table. Brittany was on her cell phone, and Clarity was leaning in close to hear the conversation. Angela managed to appear both bored and put upon at the same time. From the look of rapture on Brittany's face, Rebecca guessed she had either been named freshman homecoming queen—and it was the wrong time of year for that—or the caller was the CSU idiot.

"Being around those two these days is like being constantly exposed to high-tension wires," Rebecca muttered.

Sam's look was a query. Zoe held back a smile. "What would that be like exactly?"

"You know, feeling sort of strung out. Or wired up. Like escape is crucial, but you're already trapped in an energy vortex. Or something." Rebecca shrugged. "Between the pageant and the CSU idiot, they're both impossible."

"They've always been impossible," said Zoe. She was matter-of-fact.

Just then, angry voices broke out at the next table. Angela's chair scraped against the floor as she sprang to her feet. Clarity huddled in her seat looking like she wished she could disappear.

"You are *so* self-centered. You don't think about anyone but yourself!" Angela's voice carried even though it was pitched low.

"Me!" Brittany's voice was not pitched low. It was a shriek. *"Me!"* She bolted to her feet, shoving her chair so hard it tipped backward with a crash. "All we've heard about for weeks is your precious *pageant*. You'd think you were Miss Universe already or something. You used to be fun to be around, but now you're just a conceited bore."

"And you think the rest of us give a rat for every single word of Jason's?" Angela's tone dripped contempt.

"Oh, that's really *rich*, Angie! I don't *even* tell you every word Jason says."

"You act like he's a movie star or something. He's just some guy from CSU. And he hasn't even asked you out yet!"

"Well, he has now!" Brittany was triumphant.

"Great! Now we'll never hear the end of it," said Angela with a sneer. "It's just a *date*, for God's sake. Haven't you ever been out on a date before?" Angela slung her designer bag over one shoulder and headed for the exit. Her very body seemed to radiate condescension for Brittany. Rebecca knew what that felt like.

Clarity looked trapped. Her head swiveled from Angela to Brittany and back. For a long moment, she remained where she was. Then she jumped to her feet, threw her own designer bag over one shoulder in a movement that exactly mimicked Angela's, and headed after her at a run.

Brittany stood by her overturned chair, hands planted on her hips, glaring at Clarity's retreating back. Her angry gaze fell on the three girls at the next table, and, unaccountably, she swooped down on them. Rebecca and Zoe averted their eyes and instinctively shrank down into their chairs. Sam pasted a sickly smile on her face and looked up at Brittany.

"Brit, s'up?"

"What an arrogant, conceited bitch!" spat Brittany. "We've heard nothing from Miss Junior Rich Bitch for weeks except how she's going to win every pageant—my bad, *competition*." Her voice oozed sarcasm. "And go on to be queen of America or something. She thinks she's so perfect!"

Rebecca tried not to roll her eyes and to keep her face impassive. Sam stared glassy eyed. Zoe studied her hands.

"You couldn't possibly understand," Brittany continued. "You're just a bunch of misfits. And you!" She rounded furiously on Rebecca. "Don't think I don't know what you're thinking." Her voice was a snarl. "Little miss cutesy sweet pants. You think you're something because some lame *high school* football player has a crush on you. *I* have a date with a *college* man!"

"Wha—" Rebecca's mouth dropped open. She felt like she'd been sucker punched. She was too stunned to utter a word. It didn't matter anyway. Brittany turned on her heel and stormed out of the cafeteria. Three sets of wide, astonished eyes followed her progress until the heavy door closed behind her with a reverberating clang. For a long moment, they continued to stare at the door.

"Wow, that was . . ." Sam trailed off.

"Yeah," murmured Zoe.

Rebecca was still staring at the door where Brittany had disappeared. Zoe nudged her. "Becks?"

Rebecca shook her head. Three quick little shakes. Astonishment gave way to anger, which was replaced by a calculating look.

"Becks?" Zoe said again. She put a tentative hand on Rebecca's arm.

"Where does she get off?" Rebecca muttered under her breath.

"She's just jealous," said Sam.

"And mad at Angela," said Zoe. "Just ignore it."

"She's toxic," said Rebecca. "And totally full of herself." Her voice was cold. "Not to mention full of shit. She needs to be brought down." Rebecca gathered up her things in stony silence and left the cafeteria. Sam and Zoe exchanged glances as they watched her go.

***

Rebecca was out of sorts for the balance of the day. A cold detachment had overridden her initial anger and astonishment. She felt sort of disconnected from herself. And a little numb. In Home Room, she was quiet and remote, and Sam and Zoe left her alone.

Rebecca tried to work, but she found it difficult to concentrate. Where were her notes from government class? Rummaging in her book bag, she came across a carefully folded piece of paper. She pulled it out and held it in her hand. She stared at it, a little tingle starting up in the pit of her stomach. She unfolded the paper and smoothed it out. She read the words "Judiciary Branch, Executive Branch, Legislative Branch, Branch of Broken Dates" and "stood her up." Just words. But that little tingle was stronger. She carefully folded the paper and returned it to her book bag.

***

Rebecca trudged up the tree-lined street toward home, replaying the incidents of the day. Angela had been arrogant and snotty. For sure. So what else was new? But Brittany! Brittany had been vicious to the extreme. And for no reason. A cold knot of anger burned in the pit of Rebecca's stomach. But she had . . . not a plan, exactly, but an idea, and it came with a sense of curiosity and anticipation. She was aware of her emotions but felt somehow detached from them. Like they belonged to someone else, and she was just watching. How could that be? Who was this cool Rebecca Jean? She found her a little frightening. But at the same time, she wanted to know her better.

She used the keypad to unlock the "people door" so she could let herself in through the mudroom. Her mother didn't like anyone tracking dirt in through the front entrance. It irritated Rebecca that the pretty double front doors with their leaded glass and tall, narrow sidelight windows were reserved for guests. Wasn't the family good enough? When she had her own house, she would come and go by the front door every day! She'd walk the dog through the front door. She'd take the garbage out through the front door if she felt like it! Frowning, she dumped her backpack on the mudroom bench and went into the front hallway.

Something delightful was baking. The enticing scent transported her to long-ago times. She felt suddenly dipped in a magical childhood elixir. The day's tribulations simply fell away, and she dropped back into herself. It was a good self. She found her mother busy in the kitchen, racks of freshly baked cookies arranged neatly on the island.

"Wow, are those for us?" A smile lit her face.

"Some." Her mom smiled back at her.

Rebecca slipped onto a stool at the island. "I can have some of these?"

"A couple. Don't spoil your dinner."

Rebecca reached for a cookie. She took a big bite.

"Did you have a good day?"

"Not especially," said Rebecca.

"Not Jackson again."

"No." Rebecca took another bite. "Mmm. Good, Mom."

"If not Jackson, then what?" Her mom opened the oven and pulled out two sheets of cookies. She placed them on cooling racks and slid two more pans into the oven.

Rebecca didn't answer. She helped herself to another cookie. It was warm and soft, but also chewy. There were gooey bits of melted chocolate and crunchy nuts.

"Mmm. Great, Mom!" she said again.

Maggie looked closely at her daughter. "You're okay, then?"

Rebecca helped herself to another cookie. "Sure. These are *really* good. Who gets the rest of them?"

"They're for Andy's school picnic. It's not for two weeks, but I have a four-day conference in Telluride, and I won't have time to bake. I'm going to freeze them."

A part of Rebecca's mind idly registered that her birthday was in two weeks. "But you'll be here on my birthday."

"I'm sorry, sweetie." Her mother looked at her apologetically.

The cookie-induced upgrade in Rebecca's good humor hit an error code. It tried to reboot her from her mellow mood. A part of her resisted; another part stepped back to observe. She folded her arms across her chest, one hand cradling her casted wrist.

Her mom paused, holding a pan of cookies. "Your birthday's on a school night," she said. "And we're having both the family party at

Nanna's and your sleepover on Memorial Day weekend. You and I can have a little shopping event or something after school is out."

"Are you trying to buy me off?" Rebecca's attitude thawed a little.

"Would that be possible, do you think?"

"Mmm." Rebecca grinned lopsidedly at her mother as she reached for another cookie. Her mom just nodded. Part of her was still floating away.

"Did I tell you Tyler got a puppy? She is *so* adorable!"

"Nice try, Rebecca Jean," said her mom firmly. "Don't even ask."

"Yeah, that's what I thought." She sighed. "Well, I have finals to study for." She took one more cookie, and both Rebeccas headed for the stairs.

A considering look played across Maggie's face as she watched Rebecca go, but she bit back any further questions. Thick carpet muffled Rebecca's footsteps as she bounded down the stairs. Maggie heard the door to Rebecca's suite close with a solid thud.

Something was going on with Becka, of that she was certain. For a long moment, she stood gazing toward the stairs where her younger daughter had disappeared, the tray of cookies held forgotten in her mitted hand.

CHAPTER 21

Branch of Broken Dates

May 16

REBECCA CLOSED HER bedroom door and stood still in the cool dimness of her room. She did not switch on the light. The shutters were still closed from last night. Rebecca's hasty departures each morning rarely left time for little details, like opening the shutters. Or making the bed, for that matter. Her gaze fell on the rumpled pile of jams, sheets, and covers littering her bed. She yanked them into some sort or order, stuffing her pajamas under a pillow. The situation was only marginally improved. She eyed her computer. She realized she had left her book bag in the mudroom. She would get it later.

Right now she had an idea. She was going to conduct a little experiment. To write a couple paragraphs and see what happened.

Rebecca moved to her desk. She could feel that little tingle in the pit of her stomach. She was definitely out of herself now, the one self dispassionately observing the other. She rubbed her palms together and settled both hands on the keyboard, where her fingers tapped a rapid, weightless staccato. Feather light, too soft to depress the keys. After a long moment, she typed in Branch of Broken Dates.

Rebecca closed her eyes. She summoned the episode in the cafeteria to her mind, focusing her attention on Brittany's angry face and harsh, hurtful words. She felt the knot of anger in her solar plexus grow, along with a sense of . . . energy? Of power. This frightened her a little, but she forced herself to stay with it. And then she began to type.

> Brittany spared no lengths getting ready for her date
> with Jason. She had touched up the highlights in her dark

blonde hair. She had tweezed her eyebrows, shaved her legs, and applied lotion so they were soft and smooth. She had applied her makeup with the greatest care, including the new eyeliner she had nicked from her mother's bathroom. She had misted on expensive scent, also "borrowed" from her mother. She had debated endlessly over what to wear to please Jason. She wanted to appear grown-up and sophisticated, seductive but not a ho. And she did not want to give the impression she was trying too hard.

Now at last she was ready. She settled down in the living room to wait. From here, she would be able to see a car pulling into the drive. She would take her time answering the door. "Oh, you're early," she might say. "I'm not quite ready. Can you give me a minute?" But of course, she was ready. She was perfect. She sat carefully on the sofa so as not to wrinkle her outfit. It was 7:35 p.m. Jason was due in ten minutes. She watched the clock move with aggravating slowness toward the quarter hour, impatience and anticipation building. This would so show up Angela and her stupid pageant.

At last it was time!

But no car appeared in the drive. Brittany waited. The clock read 8:00. She got up and walked to the front window to peer out at the street. She opened her little bag and pulled out a lip gloss to refresh her lips. She waited. The clock ticked quietly on the mantle. It read 8:15. And then 8:30. Brittany felt like she had a heavy stone lodged in her chest. Still she waited, moving restlessly from sofa to window, going upstairs and coming back down, pacing around the room. Time dragged on. Maybe she should call Jason. But he always called her; she didn't have his number. It was in her cell phone, which she had stupidly left in her bag, and the bag was in her locker at school. She thought about calling her brother but dropped the idea as far too humiliating. Tired of pacing, she slumped onto the sofa. She sat there, unmoving, for what seemed like hours.

At 10:30, Brittany admitted to herself that Jason wasn't coming. She was almost too stiff to stand. He had broken their date. Worse, he had stood her up! She was too disappointed to be mad. She would be mad later. Right now, she just wished she could die. How could she ever admit this to the other girls?

Rebecca's fingers paused on the keys. She sat perfectly still, her head tilted slightly. That seemed to be all. It was more than she had written for Jackson's accident. She would call the stories Events. Not that she planned to write any more. This was just a curiosity, and it wasn't going to work anyway. Brittany would go on her date and then run on endlessly about it until the whole rest of the world was sick to death of hearing it. Who was she kidding? The whole rest of the world was *already* sick of hearing it!

Rebecca studied what she had written, nodding her head as she read the few paragraphs. It was satisfying, even if it didn't work. And how could it? She closed her laptop and went upstairs for her book bag. With a little effort, she could ace her finals. She felt good. Brittany was a bitch, but it didn't really affect Rebecca. The world was really pretty okay.

CHAPTER 22

"Headless" Comes Home

May 17

REBECCA SLIPPED INTO her chair next to Tyler in English. She had missed the first two periods because she was getting her air cast off. Tyler was beside herself with excitement. Anne Boleyn was finally coming home. Ty pulled up a video of the new puppy on her iPhone. Anne Boleyn was adorable. Rebecca was smitten.

"Do you think I could come over tonight and see her?" asked Rebecca. "If I can get Lissa to drop me off?"

"That would be totally the bomb!" said Tyler. "I know you'll love her. Even Mom thinks she's pretty sweet. The girls are going to love her too. I just know it." Tyler had no doubts.

All but Sam, thought Rebecca, but she nodded in agreement. "Here comes Mrs. Lindzer. You'd better put that away."

Tyler quickly tucked the phone into her jacket.

At lunch, Tyler passed the phone around so everyone could watch the video clips. With the exception of Sam, who at least tried to act enthusiastic, they were all hooked. The puppy was too cute. Tyler could talk of nothing else. "Becks is coming over tonight to see her," she said.

"If I can get a ride," Rebecca amended Ty's statement.

"Zut!" Zoe muttered. "I'm babysitting tonight."

"Can't you get out of it?" Ty's brown eyes pleaded.

"I have no idea," said Zoe. "But I have no intention of screwing up this job."

"What about you guys?" Tyler looked from Sam to AJ. She bounced on the edge of her chair, and the red ponytail danced.

"I have a swim lesson this evening," said AJ. "Six-year-old brat, but it pays." Her nod to Zoe communicated understanding. Cash was cash, and you did what you could to get some. She extended her long legs and crossed her ankles.

Tyler was still on point. She looked hopefully at Sam.

"Um, I'm going down to the ranch this weekend," said Sam.

"Can't you go tomorrow?" Tyler implored.

"I have to go when my ride goes," said Sam.

Rebecca knew Sam was taking her Level I Reiki class this weekend. Sam would be with April all day Saturday. She had made Rebecca swear she would not to mention it to anyone. Not to *anyone*. Rebecca glanced at Sam. Sam looked levelly back, green eyes holding blue ones.

"Maybe you could bring her to the sleepover," said Zoe. "And we could meet her then."

"Oh, that would rock!" Tyler bounced in her chair.

"That would be great," said Rebecca. "Except we have a big cat and a bigger, stupid dog. Anne Boleyn could be—"

"Headless," said Sam. She tapped a lacquered nail against her lips.

Tyler gasped. She opened her mouth and closed it again. She reached for the red ponytail and gripped it tightly, a horrified expression on her face.

"Sam, that was pretty tight," said Zoe.

"Sorry," said Sam, but she didn't sound all that sorry.

"Are you bringing those little desserts from Mile High to the sleepover?" AJ asked Zoe.

Zoe nodded. "For sure."

"The bomb," said AJ.

Their attention was diverted from delectable sweets to the noisy arrival of several cheerleaders at the next table. Angela and Brittany were both missing from the group.

"Where's the Ice Maiden and the Bitch?" Rebecca wondered aloud.

"Not together, I'd bet on that."

"Brittany's big date isn't for a week," said AJ. "I may have to drown her before then."

Rebecca listened to her friends but had nothing to add. She absently cradled her left wrist, which was now wrapped in an Ace bandage. She thought about the paragraphs filed on her computer. Branch of Broken Dates. What would happen? She felt a little tingle of anticipation along with a glimmer of guilt. But her most prevalent emotion was curiosity. These were not things she could share with the others.

CHAPTER 23

Reiki, Rumors, and the Doll Shop

May 19

S UNDAY-MORNING BREAKFAST WAS French toast and little pastry puffs stuffed with raspberries and a creamy light filling, plus sausages and fresh fruit. Rebecca loved it all, but she was dreading the week's high/week's low routine. The week had been a roller coaster of ups and downs, most of which she couldn't share at the breakfast table. Tyler had brought the new puppy home, but that wasn't Rebecca's news, so she didn't think it would be accepted as a high point for her. Angela and Brittany had both been irritating and downright insulting, but she didn't want to talk about it. Writing the Branch of Broken Dates Event was sort of a high, in that she felt powerful and elated when she did it. But she certainly couldn't tell that around the breakfast table! Her air cast was off, but it felt like a pretty pitiful high to her, and it was associated with the Jackson the Jerk story in her mind, even though it couldn't have anything to do with the little story. Her sleepover was only a week away; maybe she could use that. She sighed inwardly. If only her dad was less set in his ways . . .

"Sarah Ann did Reiki I with April this weekend?" Lissa looked at her mom. "Did you talk to April or Nanna last night? How did it go?"

"I haven't spoken with either of them," said Maggie. "It's exciting, though."

"Why?" asked Rebecca. "Why is it exciting for you when someone else takes the class?"

"It's always exciting when someone new comes into the alternative healing fold, and for me, especially so when it's a young person," replied her mother. "I love seeing young people with such open minds."

"I'm not sure she's open-minded," said Rebecca. "More just desperate."

Maggie smiled. "You'd be surprised how many fervent champions of Reiki began with desperation," she said. "They've tried everything else, and nothing works. And then they come to energy healing, and an entirely new world opens up."

"Has Sam said anything to you?" Maggie's expression was carefully neutral.

"No. I haven't seen her or heard from her." Rebecca knew she sounded petulant. She looked down at her plate and pushed her French toast around in its bath of syrup.

Jack frowned and opened his mouth, but Maggie caught his eye and shook her head. "Don't," she said quietly.

"What's new at the rock shop?" she asked Lissa.

Remodeling, restructuring, expanding inventory, and methods of getting the word out about The Center's new image—Lissa was full of details. Rebecca was grateful. Focused on her own troubles, she only half-listened to her sister.

"How's the job pitch coming?" asked Jack.

Lissa leaned back in her chair, smiling with satisfaction. "I have planted a seed, and I am nurturing it," she said. "There is a rumor going around that Mrs. Mason is going to hire someone to promote The Center's unique combination of services."

"And that someone would be you?" said her father.

"It is my intention that it be me," said Lissa. She sounded very sure of herself. "At least me in the store and social media. Maybe someone else outside. Since I'm not eighteen yet."

Rebecca wondered again how it would feel to be so confident and self-assured.

"I might have an idea for that someone outside," said Maggie.

"You?" Lissa asked.

"No, I'm pretty slammed," said Maggie. "Someone who wants to make a job change."

Lissa now looked pointedly at Rebecca. "I would need help in the doll shop."

"You mean . . ." Rebecca was suddenly all ears.

"Yes, I mean you," said Lissa. "Mrs. Mason has to approve it, but I have proposed that you work part-time in the shop over the summer. Starting right after school is out."

"Wow!" Rebecca couldn't think of anything else to say.

"You do want to do it, don't you?" asked Maggie.

"Yeah, I just never thought . . . how much will it pay?" Rebecca asked.

Lissa laughed. "You get right to the point," she said. "Minimum wage, which just went up in Colorado."

"Minimum?" Rebecca frowned. *Minimum* didn't sound promising.

"It's compared to the zero dollars you have now," said Lissa. "Oh, and you have an interview with Mrs. Mason after Memorial Day weekend. I don't know the exact day yet."

Rebecca was thinking about what she could do with that kind of money.

"I'm sure you'll want to save a good portion of that," her father said dryly.

"Of course, Dad." Butter wouldn't melt in her mouth. "How will I get there?"

"With me," said Lissa. "No problem."

Andy had been silent so far. "I taught Scoundrel a new trick," he said.

Rebecca tuned it out. No question now of the high point of her week. She smiled to herself in satisfaction.

CHAPTER 24

Triumph in Algebra Class

May 20

MONDAY MORNING DAWNED bright and clear, no surprise in a state that boasted three hundred sunny days a year. Rebecca felt decidedly unsunny. Her sleep had been fitful and filled with restless dreams. She couldn't quite remember any of them, except the weird "box" dream, and not much of that. She had put something new in the box, which had made it bulge alarmingly. She was left with a hangover of unease. She felt tired and wrung out. Thankfully, there were only five more days before the long weekend.

Rebecca stood in her closet frowning. She sighed and pulled on a pair of distressed jeans and a plain top. She slipped a pair of dull, flat sandals on her feet, scowled at them, collected her book bag, and trudged upstairs. Andy was at the table, a stack of pancakes in front of him. Her mom was taking bacon off the griddle and laying it on a paper-towel-covered plate. It smelled good, but Rebecca wasn't hungry. She poured herself a glass of orange juice and took a banana out of the big fruit bowl on the counter. She pulled out her chair and sat dispiritedly, propping her elbows on the table. Her mom stirred cream into her coffee. Andy prattled about things only a seven-year-old would find interesting. It grated on Rebecca's already-raw nerves. Nibbling on a strip of bacon, she tried to ignore him.

"Mom, how many more days of school do I have?" Andy asked around a bite of bacon.

"Nine more days," said Maggie. "All this week, and four next week."

"And how long am I off for the summer?"

"Two months and a little bit more."

"How much more?"

"A little more, Andy. Another couple weeks."

"Summer's gonna be great," said Andy. "I'm gonna see Jimmy every day. Am I gonna see Jimmy every day, Mom?" Andy besieged his mother with big blue eyes.

"Not every day, no."

"Jimmy teaches me riddles. His brother teaches him. Do you want to hear one, Mom?"

Maggie glanced at the clock and shook her head. "Save it for me, Andy. I'm to be on a conference call in ten minutes. Hustle up with your breakfast. It's almost time for your bus."

"I'll tell Becka." Andy turned to Rebecca, his eyes shining with expectation. "Becka, listen, I learned this riddle from Jimmy . . ."

Rebecca could stand no more. "Can't you be quiet for one single second!" she demanded. "Do you have to go on and on about stupid nothings!"

Andy's face registered disbelief, then shock, and then it crumpled. His shoulders slumped, and he ducked his head, tears not far away.

"Rebecca! That was completely uncalled for," chided her mother.

"But it's true! He never shuts up!" Rebecca defended herself hotly.

"What goes around comes around, Rebecca. So think carefully before you put something out there." Her mother spoke gently, but her displeasure was clear.

"What*ever*!"

Rebecca shoved her chair back and sprang to her feet. There was nowhere to go. Angry and frustrated, she stormed into the pantry and pulled the door closed behind her. Her breath was ragged. The familiar scent of spices and dried herbs and the indefinable pantry smell was soothing. She took a deep breath and let it out slowly. When she thought she could hold it together, she went back to the kitchen. Andy had disappeared. Her mother was leaning against the sink, her coffee cup in her hand. Rebecca glanced in her mother's direction but refused to make eye contact.

"Becka," her mother said softly.

Rebecca looked at her defiantly.

"I know something's bothering you." Maggie placed her coffee cup on the counter, crossed the kitchen to her daughter, and gently pulled her into her arms.

Rebecca resisted for a moment and then leaned into her mother's safe embrace. She was tempted to spill out everything—Jackson, Brittany, the stories, her fears, her excitement and the guilt it created, all her worries. But something held her back.

The defiance had gone out of her, leaving her feeling tired and jangled again, like she was wearing all her nerve endings outside her skin. She wished she could stay safe in her mother's arms all day and not have to go to school and deal with . . . anything. But the longer she stayed, the harder it would be to go. Her tone dejected, she said, "I have to go, Mom. I'll be late for school." She pulled back, still not meeting her mother's eyes.

Rebecca gathered her book bag and walked out the door. She didn't look back. Her mother could only watch her go.

"No more stories," Rebecca muttered to herself as she left the house. "That's what's screwing everything up."

Events, you mean, whispered Laney in her head. *You mean Events, don't you? You can't throw the stories away. You'd be throwing me away.*

No, I couldn't throw you away, thought Rebecca. *Even if I tried.*

Starting the day with Mr. Hammond and the jocks was the last thing she needed. But for that, there was no escape.

Rebecca surveyed the room from the doorway. The jocks were nowhere in sight, but she'd need to be on her guard. She took a deep breath and then exhaled. Straightening her shoulders, she walked to her desk.

She wished for the thousandth time that Mr. Hammond was as relaxed about seating in algebra as he was in Home Room. She'd be able to avoid proximity to Jackson if that were the case. And think of the devil, there he was. His crutches and the tall air boot were gone, replaced by what looked like a shorter version of the same thing. He moved pretty well in it. He sprawled into his seat across the aisle from Rebecca. Her right hand involuntarily cradled her left wrist. It was still tender, even with the Ace bandage. Josh barreled into the room and threw himself into the seat in front of Jackson. Blake was right behind him.

"Jacks, whaddya know?" Josh punched Jackson on the arm.

"Hey, Telluride. Not much, man." Jackson grinned back.

"There's a news flash." Rebecca muttered it beneath her breath, but Jackson heard.

He looked across the aisle at her, still grinning. "Ow, brutal!" He clutched both hands to his chest. "You're wreckin' my heart, darlin'."

Rebecca's mood ticked up a tiny notch in spite of herself. Jackson's teasing could be irritating, but sometimes it was infectious. With mock gravity, she said, "You have a heart?"

Josh turned in his seat, his face alight with the prospect of live sport. "Yeah, man," he said. "You have a heart?"

Rebecca glanced at Josh, and he winked at her.

Jackson looked from Rebecca to Josh. He shifted in his seat. Rebecca put on her best innocent face and smiled sweetly back at him. Josh smirked wickedly. Jackson took a breath and opened his mouth.

The classroom door flew open. Mr. Hammond lumbered into the room, his beady eyes going immediately to the three of them. He headed in their direction, plodding up the aisle between their desks. Rebecca averted her gaze and ducked her head, instinctively flinching away. Hammond tapped Jackson's desk with two fingers as he went by. Pointing at the injured ankle, he said, "Taking care of that, Middleton?"

"Yeah, I guess." Jackson slouched casually, legs extended. He crossed his casted ankle over the other one.

Mr. Hammond labored up the aisle. He dropped his briefcase onto his desk with a solid thud and lowered himself heavily into his chair. Breathing hard, he opened the briefcase and began extracting papers.

Josh took advantage of Mr. Hammond's preoccupation to punch Jackson again. "You're wreckin' my heart, darlin'," he drawled in a perfect mimic of Jackson.

Jackson grinned crookedly back at Josh. He brushed the hair from his eyes.

"You got a thing for our Becka?" Josh continued in a honeyed tone. "Sure she has one for you, Jacks."

It was a taunt, and Rebecca knew it. *Don't do it,* she silently chided herself. In Rebecca's head, Laney's voice echoed, *Don't do it.*

But she did. She drew herself up straight and fixed Josh with a level gaze. "You must be smoking something," she said in an even tone. "Or maybe its brain damage. One too many fat-tire plunges down a mountainside?"

Jackson laughed and winked at her conspiratorially. He nudged Josh's chair with his good foot. "Yeah, brain damage."

"Brain damage . . ." Josh twitched in his seat, crossing his eyes and lolling his tongue from one side of his mouth. "It's brain damage!" He wrapped his arms around his head and cackled a high-pitched, demented laugh. "Jacks, give us something! We're havin' a seizure!"

Jackson laughed aloud, and Rebecca couldn't help but join in.

"The brain damage . . . I know things. I see things," Josh intoned. He cackled again, still clutching his head in both hands and rocking back and forth in his chair. "She loves ya, Jacks. She's got it bad, man. Bad. I can see it!"

This was a little embarrassing. Rebecca leaned out of her seat to stretch across the aisle toward Josh. She rapped him hard with her open palm. "Not even in your dreams," she said. "You're demented!"

Other students were now watching with interest. Catcalls came from two other jocks across the room, egging them on.

"Hey, Jacks!"

"Way to go, Telluride!"

"Take 'im down, blondie!"

Rebecca sensed more than saw the approach of Mr. Hammond as he sidled quietly down the aisle. Not for the first time she wondered how he could sometimes move so quietly. Like a stalker. She drew quickly back into her seat and turned to face forward, sitting up straight. Still smiling broadly, she looked pointedly down at her desk. But too late. Her eyes fell on Mr. Hammond's scuffed shoes and wide pant legs.

"*Ms.* Coleson." Mr. Hammond's voice was frosty.

A flurry of thoughts raced through Rebecca's head.

Laney's voice whispered softly, *Warned you . . .*

Her own feelings were not so soft. *Not this again!* She sighed deeply, thinking, *I'll take the fall for this. Even though it wasn't just me.*

Sure you will, so don't fight it. That was Laney again. She "felt" defiant. *Not letting them know how you feel is the best defense. Sometimes the only defense.* It was Laney's voice, but the words of advice had been Alexa's.

Mr. Hammond's bulk blocked Josh from her view, but a sideways glance informed her that Jackson was watching her. Was the expression on his face resignation?

Not this time. Rebecca took a deep breath. She reached for a carefully neutral expression; she was pretty sure she had it. "Yes, Mr. Hammond?" Her voice was polite. Beneath her desk, out of Mr. Hammond's sight, her hands were clenched tightly in her lap, fingernails digging into her palms.

"Explain yourself!" Had there been just the slightest hesitation before Mr. Hammond pounced?

She turned wide blue eyes up to his scowling face but didn't meet his eyes. She couldn't quite make herself do that. Instead, she stared at his chin, noticing a stubble of beard he had missed shaving. She held on to her impassive expression. Her heart was beating so loudly she was sure the whole class could hear it.

"Explain what, Mr. Hammond?" From the corner of her eye, she saw Jackson break into a broad smile.

A flicker of surprise flashed across Mr. Hammond's face and was quickly replaced by the former scowl. "This disruption, Ms. Coleson. Something at which you seem to excel."

Rebecca didn't think about what she said next. The honeyed words just flowed out of her mouth. "I did take part in it," she said sweetly. "I apologize, Mr. Hammond. It was thoughtless of me." Her knuckles were white under the desk, but her face was smooth.

Mr. Hammond took an involuntary step backward, bringing Josh into Rebecca's line of sight. Josh was watching her curiously. Mr. Hammond opened his mouth and closed it again, looking both confused and furious. Jackson laughed outright. The class was silent.

"It was Kenyon," Jackson said smoothly. "He went a little ape."

"Me!" Josh stared in disbelief. "*Me!*" His voice cracked. "It was you, you maggot!"

Rebecca dropped her gaze, ducking her head and chewing her lips to contain a broad smile. She could still see both boys. Josh punched Jackson again, incredulity plain on his face. Jackson was grinning his FIGJAM grin. Mr. Hammond seemed to be temporarily lost for words.

"Naw, it was . . ."

Mr. Hammond's angry voice cut across Jackson's. "*That's enough!*" His glare traveled from Rebecca to Jackson and then to Josh. He expelled his breath in a great huff. Rebecca sensed he was fighting to maintain a semblance of control, and she willed herself to be invisible.

"That's enough," Mr. Hammond repeated, this time more calmly. "You boys would benefit from a little self-discipline. On the playing field and off."

Mr. Hammond directed a stern look at his two jocks. He glowered again at Rebecca. He opened his mouth, clearly about to say something further to her, but again he snapped it shut. Still frowning, he walked back up the aisle, his tread once more heavy and labored.

"Turn to appendix A in your text," he growled at the class. "This section will be included in your final, so listen up!"

Students glanced at each other in surprise. The appendix sections were normally considered optional. Students could do the work for extra credit, but it was never included in the tests. Mr. Hammond was breaking long-held protocols.

Rebecca watched him, feeling giddy with astonishment. She stole a glance at Jackson. He looked steadily back at her. The corners of his mouth twitched up. He nodded his head ever so slightly. He brushed the hair from his eyes. Then he pulled out his algebra book and actually opened it.

Jackson's response to her was interesting. But Mr. Hammond's was mind-blowing. *He's just a bully*, she thought. *A bully and a coward!* She pulled her algebra book and notes from her backpack and placed them thoughtfully on her desk, still wondering at Mr. Hammond's surprising reaction.

Maybe one more, she thought. *One more Event to bring that fat bully down.* A little thrill of expectancy danced up her spine. She heard Laney murmur something that sounded like, *Careful as you go, girl,* but she paid the voice no heed.

Mr. Hammond scowled through the entire period, piling on homework. His excess produced groans and muttering from the class. Josh and Jackson shared looks of dismay. Rebecca remained quiet. *He's taking it out on everyone else,* she thought. *What a loser!* This thought was followed by, *Definitely one more. Just one more.*

The class passed with surprising speed. At the bell, she shrugged the straps of her book bag over one shoulder and headed for the exit. Jackson fell in beside her. Weird, for sure. Beyond that, Rebecca wasn't sure how she felt about it. Unaccountably pleased, but also uncomfortable. She unconsciously reached to tug her jacket closer around her before she realized she wasn't wearing one. Feeling awkward, she gripped the straps of her book bag with both hands, which did nothing to diminish her unease.

"Hey, Becka."

"Hey."

Jackson looked like he might say more, but he didn't. He flashed a grin at her before limping down the hall. Had that been a look of approval on Jackson's face? Rebecca wasn't sure, and it didn't really matter. What mattered was that she had maintained her calm and refused to give the Fat Man the satisfaction of getting the best of her. Well, at least the illusion of calm. Scared out of her mind? For sure. But only she knew. Algebra class had provided her with a great deal to think about, very little of it having to do with mathematical equations.

***

Rebecca tried to focus during her next two classes, but it was hard. She kept replaying the scene with Mr. Hammond, and the amazing outcome. And Jackson . . . what was that all about? He had seemed genuinely pleased when she stood up to the Fat Man. Why would he even care? It was a mystery. She was tempted to tell Tyler about all of it, but she didn't. She wanted to keep it to herself until she figured it out.

Mrs. Lindzer was piling on assignments, all in preparation for fast-approaching finals, or so she said, and all due in two days. Rebecca needed to pay attention, but her thoughts were whirling. She savored again her coup in algebra and smiled to herself. Alexa's advice for dealing with jerks was worth perfecting. But she wanted more. Mr. Hammond deserved to be taken down, and Rebecca wanted to be the one to do it. Also, she wanted to test out this new . . . ability. How reliable was it?

You're taking a lot for granted, whispered Laney in her head. *What makes you think it will work?*

Rebecca ignored the voice. She felt the now-familiar exhilaration mixed with prickly guilt. Was there a word for that? There should be. It was all a muddle. Mrs. Lindzer's voice droned on, a distant buzz in Rebecca's ears.

At last the bell sounded. With a little start, Rebecca realized she had hardly heard a word Mrs. Lindzer had said.

"Ty, can I see your notes?" Rebecca begged. "I'll get them back to you at the end of school."

Tyler looked questioningly at Rebecca.

"I sort of spaced in class. Please . . ."

Ty hesitated and then slid her carefully written notes over to Rebecca.

"Thanks, Ty. You're the best!" Rebecca scooped up the pages and filed them carefully in the front pocket of her binder.

Tyler slipped her knapsack on. "Don't lose them, Becks." And she was gone.

CHAPTER 25

Suspicions

May 20

R EBECCA WALKED INTO the drama classroom with two senior girls, her early-morning funk nearly gone. The room was already mostly filled with students. The senior girls joined a group on the little stage. Rebecca looked around for a seat, somewhat reluctantly sliding into the desk across the aisle from Angela. Angela was thumbing through the big pageant binder. When she noticed Rebecca, Angela slapped the binder shut and turned it facedown on her desk. Glancing at Rebecca, she flashed a brilliant smile.

"Rebecca!" Angela's voice was falsely cheerful. The pale-blue eyes looked uneasy.

"Angie, hey." Rebecca couldn't think of anything else to say. She smiled woodenly back. "Um . . ." Her eyes fell on the binder, and she grasped at the first thought to enter her head. "How's your skit for your next . . . um, competition . . . going?" she asked.

"My skit?" Angela fidgeted in her seat, suddenly looking nervous. Her hands moved to the binder, and she adjusted it on the desktop, long fingers curling protectively around the top edge. "Um, good. Really good. Why do you ask?"

"No reason." Rebecca thought Angie was acting totally weird. She couldn't think of anything else to say.

Angie fidgeted with the pageant binder again and shifted in her seat.

Mr. Tilson blew into the room, the thick manuscript tucked under one arm. Conversation in the room fell to a murmur.

A brilliant smile split his tanned handsome face. With no preamble at all, he said, "So, shall we give Angela a critique on her upcoming competition burlesque?" He nodded expectantly in Angela's direction, gesturing toward her with his free arm, his hand outstretched as though to present a diva to an appreciative audience.

There was a sharp intake of breath from Angela. Rebecca thought she looked like a rabbit caught in headlights. She cleared her throat and opened her mouth, but no sound came out. She swallowed. Finally, she managed to say, "Uh . . . I think I'm good, Mr. Tilson."

"Rubbish!" exclaimed Mr. Tilson. "We'll be gentle with you. Won't we, class?"

There were a few titters and half-hearted murmurs of consent from the class. A number of heads turned curiously in Angela's direction.

Mr. Tilson's hand was still extended toward Angela, his face expectant. "Your next event is imminent, is it not?"

Angela nodded dumbly. Her face was nearly the color of her white-blonde hair. Rebecca was watching her closely now. She didn't know this mute, hesitant Angela.

Unexpectedly, Angela sprang to her feet. "I . . . I'm not feeling so good." Her voice was breathless. She certainly didn't look like she felt good. Clutching the pageant binder tightly to her chest, she bolted for the door.

Heads turned to follow her hasty exit. Mr. Tilson took two steps in the direction of the door through which Angela had fled, his hand still outstretched. He looked both surprised and irritated. At length, he dropped his hand, straightened his shoulders, and turned back to the class.

"Well," he said. He glanced once more at the door. "In lieu of a final . . ."

This drew a chorus of groans. Mr. Tilson waited for the room to grow quiet again and then continued, "In lieu of a final, we will have a verbal critique of the year's theatrical productions. Discussion will include the method of selection for production material, the rehearsal process, and acceptable criteria for grading students not actually performing in a given play. The level of success for performers is judged by me, and also by the reaction of the audience. Audiences can be obtuse and thickheaded, influenced by a latent mob mentality. I could harbor unknown agendas." He grinned wickedly. "We will address any questions, concerns, or aspirations you wish to express. What would you have done differently this year, and why? What types of performances would you like to see next year, and why? What are your personal goals for drama? I expect an energetic dialogue involving each and every one of you." He looked pointedly at a group of seniors who were giving him less than their full attention.

"Including seniors," he said, pausing for dramatic effect. "Nothing is a done deal yet." His inference was clear. It wasn't too late to mess up a good grade.

"I expect you to give this serious attention. It would be an excellent idea to commit your thoughts and ideas to paper or PowerPoint to aid you during our discussion. Anyone who wishes to turn in a 'Talking Points' for consideration of extra credit may do so."

Mr. Tilson looked expectantly around the room. "Any questions? No? Okay then. You can use this hour to formulate your discussion points."

His movements brisk, he crossed to his desk and sat. He opened the bulky script, bending immediately to his task. Abruptly, he looked up again.

"Oh, Ms. Coleson . . ."

Rebecca's heart skipped a beat and then seemed to drop to her stomach. "Yes?" Her voice was steady, in contrast to her racing heart.

"You're a friend of Ms. Thornton's, are you not?"

"I . . . um . . ."

Mr. Tilson didn't wait for an answer. "Would you be so kind as to advise her of my expectations for this class relative to a final." It was not a request.

Rebecca nodded. "Sure."

White teeth flashed in the tan face once more. "That's all," he said and turned his attention to the manuscript before him.

Rebecca looked thoughtfully at the chair Angela had just abandoned. Why was Angela suddenly so closemouthed about the pageant? She had said Mr. Tilson's coaching for her first skit had helped her. What had happened since? *Could it have something to do with me?* she wondered. On the surface that seemed preposterous. An instinct born in the same deep place that sparked Rebecca's story inspirations was niggling away at her. Angela was hiding something. But what?

***

At lunch Rebecca waited for Sam to say something about the Reiki class. But Sam was completely mum on the subject. Rebecca didn't share the weird scenario from drama. She had only vague, unformed suspicions, and she didn't know how to describe them. The talk was mostly about Brittany and Angela, and in truth, she was tired of hearing it.

Later, Rebecca waited for an opportunity in Home Room to ask Sam about the Reiki, but it didn't happen. People were pretty much quiet and working on studies. It seemed the whole school was feeling pressure. Was it looming finals? Was the moon out of sync or something? Rebecca didn't know where that thought came from. It was unsettling, though, and she tried to get the image out of her head . . . of the moon in a wobbly orbit or drifting away from Earth. Jeez, all these weird thoughts. Was she going psycho?

Ty and AJ caught up with them after Home Room, and Rebecca handed over Ty's English notes. Ty took the notes and rushed off, eager to get home to Ann Boleyn. Sam mumbled something about the new filly, but it didn't make sense that she would be going to the ranch on a Monday night. It all sounded very vague. AJ caught a ride with her brother. Zoe said she had a special-credit assignment and was going to work in the library for a while.

Rebecca found herself standing on the wide steps in front of the school by herself. And really, she didn't mind all that much. She let her mind come back to the amazing scene in algebra that morning, and all the disquieting questions just floated away. With a small smile playing at the edges of her mouth, she set out on the walk home.

CHAPTER 26

The Lost Puppy

May 20

REBECCA WAS STRUGGLING with her English assignment. If only Mrs. Lindzer had asked them to just *write* something! But no, she wanted all these sentences broken down and structured properly. And what else? Rebecca hadn't been listening at all in class; her mind had been busy with thoughts of the incredible scene that had played out in algebra. Mrs. Lindzer had stressed the importance of this assignment—the last regularly graded assignment before finals. Rebecca should have paid closer attention. She had made a photocopy of Ty's carefully written notes, and it was spread before her, but she still couldn't make heads or tails of this last group of problems.

Rebecca pushed her binder away in frustration. What to do? For a moment, she continued to sit at her desk, drumming her fingers in agitation. Her dad had strict rules about—well, everything, really, but especially about phone calls on school nights. But what if she needed to make a phone call in order to *finish* her homework? Rebecca frowned in irritation. Stupid rules. This was where texting would be so handy!

Rebecca shoved back her chair and ran up the stairs. Her father was in his big recliner, a book on his lap. His eyes were closed, his head nodding forward onto his chest. *Some way to read a book*, thought Rebecca.

Without ceremony, she gave his arm a rough shake.

"Dad, where's Mom?"

Her father's head jerked up, and his eyes flew open. The book slipped from his hands and landed with a thud on the carpet. He stared at his daughter, eyes glassy. "Errgh . . . um . . ." He cleared his throat. He said groggily, "Upstairs. Getting Andy down."

"Dad, I'm stuck on my English homework. I need to call Tyler. Just a couple quick questions for her. No other talking, I promise."

"You know the rule, Princess." Her father leveraged himself out of his chair. He picked up his book and set it on the table beside his recliner.

Rebecca had anticipated this. She sometimes wondered if strict enforcement of rules was just a way to avoid making tough decisions. "Daaad!" She wrung her hands and put on her best pleading face. "It's almost finals! Mrs. Lindzer said this assignment is *crucial*!" She might be overselling just a little, but if it helped her case . . . "Just for two minutes tops!"

"Maybe I can help you," he said.

Rebecca fixed her father with a level gaze, the expression on her face sliding into neutral. There was a telling pause before she said, "Sure, Dad." Her eyes never wavered from her father's. "Come on downstairs and give it a shot."

Jack Coleson regarded his daughter. He thought she was trying not to laugh. She wasn't smirking; her face was smooth. It wasn't that. It was just something he felt in his gut. A random thought flitted through his mind. *If I could get that face down, it would be great for negotiations with clients.* Becka was unquestionably a master at it.

The silence stretched out. Rebecca gestured. *Well?* It was unspoken but clear. Her eyebrows arched over the carefully neutral blue eyes. She still said nothing.

Jack gave it up. "Okay, you got me," he laughed. "Call Tyler. But keep it short."

Rebecca's face came alive. She stretched on tiptoe to throw her arms around her father. "Thanks, Dad! I will."

Jack yawned again, sighed deeply, and headed wearily upstairs. "Good night, Princess," he called over his shoulder.

"'Night, Dad!"

Rebecca snatched the kitchen phone off its base and hit speed dial for Tyler. It rang for what seemed a long time. Finally, Rebecca heard

Mrs. Lane on the other end of the line. Her voice sounded . . . different. Odd. Maybe strained.

"Hi, Mrs. Lane," she said in her best grown-up voice. "It's Rebecca Jean. I was wondering if I could talk to Tyler for just a second. I have a question about our English assignment. Otherwise, I'd never call so late."

"Oh, dear," sighed Mrs. Lane. "I don't think Tyler can talk."

"I only need a minute."

Mrs. Lane didn't respond immediately. When she spoke again, her voice was definitely strained. Rebecca thought she might be crying. "We're having a bit of a problem here."

"Is Ty all right?" A little knot was forming in the pit of Rebecca's stomach. "Is Ty okay?" she asked again.

"Anne Boleyn is missing, and Tyler is pretty upset about it."

"Missing!" Rebecca was at a loss for words. How could such a thing happen? Tyler wouldn't be merely upset. She would be utterly wrecked!

Mrs. Lane spilled a sorry tale. The puppy out of sight for just an instant. An exhaustive search of the backyard. The hole beneath the fence. They had searched the street. They had canvassed the neighbors. They had talked to Mrs. Lamont twice. The old lady had a cat; she sometimes put a kibbles dish outside. Had she seen Anne Boleyn? All to no avail.

Rebecca listened with her heart in her throat. When Mrs. Lane fell silent, she sat down hard on a kitchen chair. "Oh my God!" she whispered.

"I'll tell Tyler you called," she heard Mrs. Lane say. And the line went dead.

Rebecca sat motionless, staring at the phone in her hand. She felt numb. Poor Tyler. This was beyond awful. Anne Boleyn was so little. She was just a baby still. She'd be helpless outside overnight. She'd be cold and alone—She would *not* let her mind go there! But what could she do? Tears leaked from her eyes and ran down her cheeks. She brushed them away impatiently. She crossed to the French doors, staring unseeing out at the twilit patio. What *could* she do?

She could do *nothing*—that's what she could do. Absolutely nothing. Rebecca thought about sneaking out and running over to Tyler's house. It was quite a way, but she had walked it a thousand times. But what would it gain, besides getting herself in deep doo-doo? Rebecca's sense of helplessness was a heavy weight in her heart. It contracted her chest. It turned her breathing shallow and irregular. It was horrid to be so powerless.

Tinker appeared at the door and meowed to be let in. She stretched up on her back feet, her front paws on the glass. Rebecca opened the door absently, and Tinker sidled inside.

"Where've you been, Trouble?" Rebecca addressed her cat distractedly, closing the door behind her. "Stealing cat food from the Jeffersons' garage again? You're going to get—"

Rebecca paused with one hand on the doorknob, the phone still gripped in the other hand. An idea was coming, she could feel it. Garage. Something about a garage.

What if . . . Just a soft sigh. Rebecca went very still. "What if . . . ?" She whispered the words aloud. She waited, letting her mind settle so the idea could come as it would.

What if you wrote *Anne Boleyn home?* That was Laney.

CHAPTER 27

A Benevolent Effort

May 20

REBECCA DIDN'T WAIT to see if Laney had more to say. She didn't need to. The solution had emerged fully grown in her head. She tossed the phone on the table and raced to the stairs, clattering down them at full speed. She tore into her room, shoving the door closed behind her. Breathing hard, she stared down at her computer. For a long moment, she stood frozen. She had intended to stop writing Events. Did this count? If it was for something good? She wasn't sure. And it might not work anyway. That didn't bear thinking about. It had worked once already. The second story hadn't "matured" yet; Brittany's date wasn't till Friday night. Rebecca drew a deep, shuddering breath, swiped the tears from her face, and sat down at her computer. She didn't know how this would go, but she had to try.

Rebecca slashed the mouse across its pad and clicked on her word processing app. A blank page appeared before her. She took another deep breath and paused to gather herself. This had to be just right. Her fingers continued to lightly noodle the keys. "Okay," she breathed. Her hands went still on the keyboard. And then, slowly and deliberately, she began to type.

> Anne Boleyn was excited to be outside. She sat for a moment, tongue lolling, her little sides panting in and out. She trotted across the patio to lap a cool drink from a puddle. She squatted and marked, looking around for praise from her pack mom. Not there.

Full of curiosity, she followed her nose to the edge of the patio, onto the lawn, and into the shrub hedge. There were all sorts of fascinating scents here. She snuffled along, still following her nose. Coming to a barrier, she turned and followed alongside it. She poked her nose into a depression, and it opened into a small hole. Interesting smells! She put her head through it. By wriggling on her belly, she could just get her whole self through.

She could smell her own scent here and there. She crossed some grass and found herself on a hard, smooth surface. A huge opening gaped in front of her. It smelled strange, but at the same time familiar. She trotted in. There were bits of food on the floor. It made her hungry. She sniffed carefully. It smelled a lot like her own food. She ate one bite. It was good. She ate another. Her nose led her to a big bag smelling of the same thing. A sudden loud convulsion erupted overhead, immediately followed by a deafening clatter and shuddering vibrations. She yelped and dashed into a corner behind some boxes. The light was dimming. The clattering and burring stopped with a loud thud, and then it was quiet. And dark, except for slivers of light framing the big opening where Anne Boleyn had entered.

Rebecca paused and stretched. This was getting pretty long. Was it too long? She didn't think so. She had to build up to a certain conviction—a conviction that Anne Boleyn would be found safe and unharmed. Anything else was just unthinkable. She drew in a long breath and let it out slowly. She closed her eyes and refocused her mind.

Anne Boleyn huddled behind the boxes while her eyes adjusted to the dark. When she could see in the dimness, she nosed around her hiding place. There were some old blankets. They smelled like cat. Anne Boleyn knew cat, because one sometimes came around the pack mom's den. This was not the same cat, but the smell didn't alarm her. Fatigue dropped over Anne Boleyn like a shroud. She turned in a small circle, turned again, and settled into the blankets.

RAINIE YORK

Curling herself into a tight little ball, she sighed deeply and tucked her nose under her tail. She was asleep almost instantly.

Anne Boleyn woke much later. Her hiding place was completely dark now. Night sounds came to her, unfamiliar and unsettling. She whimpered, settling deeper into her nest of blankets. She buried her nose beneath her tail again, but her eyes remained open, and every little sound made her jump. She thought with longing of the bag of food. She could still smell it. But she was too frightened to leave her hiding space. Exhausted, hungry, and scared, she finally drifted again into sleep.

When Anne Boleyn awakened the next time, slivers of light lessened the darkness. She sat up, disoriented. She was hungry and thirsty. She raised her nose and sniffed, testing the air. She edged out of her hiding place, piddled on the floor, and followed her nose back to the big bag of food. She was sniffing around its base when a door suddenly opened and a broad shaft of light fell on the floor. Illuminated by the light, a large body stood in the opening. Frightened again, Anne Boleyn scurried back to her hiding place.

"Heavens!" a voice said. "What are you doing in here?"

Steps shuffled across the floor toward Anne Boleyn's hiding place. She cowered behind the boxes, shrinking against the wall behind her. There was nowhere to go. A hand reached in and plucked her out. She was lifted high and held in the air for what seemed a long time. The grip that held her was firm but not harsh; it smelled like a pack mom. Not her own pack mom, but not bad.

Anne Boleyn looked up into the face of the figure holding her. The face was kind, but Anne Boleyn was still frightened. She felt like she might widdle again.

"Come along, dearie," the voice said. "Let's take you home."

Rebecca sat staring at her computer screen. That was all. It was done. She felt tears leaking from her eyes again. Hope. She had to hope.

She named the file Found Puppy and saved it to her Events folder. She clicked out of the word processing application and closed her laptop. She gathered up her homework, the last English problems still unsolved, and carefully put everything in her backpack. She brushed her teeth and ran a brush through her hair. A scratching at her door caught her attention. Tinker wanted to be let in.

Rebecca opened the door for her. Tinker trotted through, and Rebecca closed it again. Tinker jumped onto the bed. Rebecca skimmed out of her jeans and shirt, leaving them in a pile on the floor. She slipped into jams. She slid between the sheets, plumped her pillow, and laid her head on it. She pulled the big orange cat into her arms.

"Tinks," she said softly.

Tinker responded with a rumbling purr and rubbed the side of her face against Rebecca's cheek. Rebecca buried her face in the warm fur. Tinker kneaded the pillow with her front paws, eyes closed to slits in contentment. Rebecca sighed deeply. Her heart was still beating rapidly. It was going to be a long night. She knew she would never sleep. Never in a million years.

But she did.

CHAPTER 28

Did It Work?

May 21

REBECCA WOKE FROM a heavy sleep feeling disoriented. Tinker was curled in the curve of her body, a warm ball. A glance at her little clock told her it was early. No need to get up yet, but she knew it would be useless trying to get back to sleep. She stretched carefully, trying not to disturb Tinker. She yawned, checked her windows. Her little sliver of sky was a dull gray. Rebecca gently stroked Tinker's soft fur, thinking absently about what she might wear if the weather was truly bad. Four more days, and then the long weekend. She stretched again, moving Tinker out of her nest, and swung her feet over the edge of the bed. Her book bag sat on the desk next to her laptop, ready to go.

OMG! The puppy! Her stomach plummeted to her feet.

The events of the night before came rushing back to her. She stumbled to her desk and gingerly opened her laptop, going immediately to the new story. Standing in bare feet and rumpled jams, she read quickly through the Event. When she was finished, she stared at the computer screen for a long moment.

She needed to know if Anne Boleyn was home. Wouldn't it be great to have an iPhone! Stupid rules! She ran through other possibilities while she hastily performed her morning routine. She dressed without caring what she wore. She came up with no solution except to wait until school and talk to Tyler. If the puppy was still missing, would Ty even be in school? Rebecca doubted it.

Lissa was talking with their mother when Rebecca got to the kitchen. She had an armload of stuff, and her purse was slung over one shoulder. Clearly, she was ready to leave.

"Can I ride with you?" Rebecca asked.

"I need to go right now," said Lissa.

"I'm ready. Let's go."

"Becka, what about breakfast?" said Maggie.

"I'll grab something at school," said Rebecca. "At the deli." She gave her mother a quick hug and headed after her sister.

"Rebecca Jean—"

"I'll eat fruit or something healthy, I promise," called Rebecca. She grabbed an old jacket from its hook in the mudroom and dashed after Lissa.

Rebecca hurried across the driveway, shivering in the gray chill. She slid hastily into Lissa's car and pulled the door shut. She dropped her book bag on the floor at her feet. Lissa glanced at her and then turned to study her younger sister.

"What gives, Becka?" she said. Her voice was soft but firm.

Rebecca stared straight ahead, shoulders tense and hands clasped tightly in her lap.

"Just spit it out," said Lissa.

Rebecca looked at her sister for a long moment, and then she turned her head to look out the window. Lissa waited quietly.

Rebecca sighed and looked back at Lissa. No way could she tell her sister about the stories. No way. "It's Ty." She took a deep breath. The truth and nothing but the truth. Just not the whole truth. That would be the ticket.

"Anne Boleyn was missing last night. Ty's new puppy." As Rebecca spoke these words, the damn inside her broke, and her words came out in a rush. "I called to ask Ty about our English assignment, and her mom was totally upset and told me about the puppy and that Ty couldn't talk, and I can't even imagine how wrecked she must be. I wanted to *do* something! I felt so helpless, and I hate that! I thought I'd never be able to sleep, but I did. I just want to get to school and catch up with Ty and see if she's all right. But I don't have a class with her until second period, and I don't know how I'll even find her."

Rebecca felt tears lurking behind her lashes and dabbed the bottom of her sweater beneath her eyes. "It probably sounds silly to you," she went on, "but that puppy means everything to Ty. Her dad got it for her. If she hasn't come home, I mean I *hope* she's come home. Probably she's come home." An inner voice warned to go cautiously there. "But what if she hasn't?"

Lissa didn't say anything. The car rolled with stealthy quiet down the street, coasting to a gentle stop at the corner. Rebecca stared straight ahead, biting her lower lip. Neither girl spoke. At the next intersection, Lissa turned onto the cross street. She turned again, driving at a steady speed down the street. Not in the direction of the doll shop.

"Well, let's just go check on Tyler and Anne Boleyn, then," Lissa said.

Rebecca's breath caught. "What about the doll shop?"

"It's not that important," said Lissa. She reached across the car and touched the backs of her fingers to Rebecca's cheek.

Rebecca caught her sister's hand in her own and squeezed hard. Trying not to wince, Lissa tugged her hand free to turn onto another street. It would have been a long walk in the dark, but in only a few minutes, Lissa pulled up at the curb in front of Ty's house. Rebecca couldn't move; she could only stare at the front door.

"You'll have to go and ring the bell," said Lissa. "If you want to find out."

Her movements wooden, Rebecca got out of the car and made her way up the driveway. It wasn't just the morning chill that made her shiver. She pulled the jacket closer about her body. At the front door, she raised her hand to the bell, her index finger extended toward the button. Her hand did not want to move. Rebecca took a deep breath, steeled herself, and pushed the bell.

She heard sounds from inside. The *ding-dong* of the bell. The baby was crying. Mrs. Lane called out, "Tyler, get the door!" There were muffled footfalls. The door opened. Tyler stood there in her bathrobe. Her dark-red hair was a tangled mess. Her eyes were swollen and her face splotched from crying. But in her arms was a small ball of black-and-white fluff. She looked at Rebecca, and her face broke into a huge smile. She held the puppy tightly to her chest.

"Mrs. Lamont brought her home this morning," said Ty. "She got locked in the garage last night."

CHAPTER 29

Suspicions Mount

May 23

REBECCA FELT SO wired these days she thought her eyes might explode. Or something equally gross. She pitched emotionally between the incredible highs of her successful face-off with Mr. Hammond and the Found Puppy story, and the accumulating heaviness of the other Events. Sometimes she actually believed she was writing things into being, however difficult a concept that might be. Her instinct told her it was true. Her left brain told her she was certifiable. There didn't seem to be a middle ground.

She had also jumped on Andy for no real reason. She got in trouble for that, so maybe it evened out. There was Sam still not talking to her about Reiki. And Angela hiding something from her. Maybe she was just paranoid. On the plus side, there was the way Jackson had looked at her when she stood up to the Fat Man. She didn't need or want Jackson's approval—that was a certainty. At least she told herself it was. But that didn't mean she couldn't feel good about it. Walking with him out of class felt pretty good too. Sort of a thumb in the Fat Man's eye. Even though it was totally weird.

And that was just her. The whole school felt sort of . . . it was hard to describe. Maybe like the common energies were overcharged or something. That was a bizarre thought all by itself. And WTH did it mean, anyway!

Rebecca sighed. One more day after this one, and she could leave all this behind for the long weekend. It would be a busy three days, too busy to think about school stuff. She walked into the cafeteria holding that thought. She was the last to arrive. She pulled out a chair and lowered herself into it with a sigh.

"I'm so ready for the long weekend," she said. "Summer, in fact. I'm totally over school."

Sam looked at her and nodded vigorously. "That's what I was saying before," she said. "That high school is such a bore."

"High school doesn't bore me," said Rebecca. "It's more like it's burned me out."

"What do you mean?" asked Zoe.

Rebecca frowned. "It's not any one thing," she said. "It's a lot of stuff." She set a banana and a little bag of cheese puffs on the table in front of her. Around a bite of fruit, she said, "Does anyone think Angela is acting funny?"

"Funny how?" Sam asked. She ran blue-lacquered nails through her tousled hair.

"She always acts funny," said Zoe.

"No, she always acts stuck-up and superior," said AJ. She sat up a little straighter and pushed her glasses up her nose. "Funny how, Becks?"

"Like she's hiding something."

"What do you mean?" asked Ty. She turned to look at Rebecca.

"I haven't figured that out," said Rebecca. She ripped open her snack bag and munched on a cheese puff. "But I'm getting a tingle." Rebecca placed one hand over her solar plexus.

The girls nodded. They all knew about Rebecca's tingles. Rebecca ate another cheese puff. "It has something to do with the pageant, though. I'm sure of it."

"I never see her carrying books, but she has that big binder," said Zoe. "And she keeps it closer than jam on toast." Zoe nibbled on an apple.

"She does!" Ty was suddenly attentive. The ponytail bounced as she sat up straight. "She never lets go of it."

"I've noticed that too." AJ nodded.

"Really?" Rebecca looked around the table. "Then it's not just me. I'm not, like, being paranoid?"

"No." Zoe was matter-of-fact. "She has it now."

She nodded in the direction of the next table where Angela sat, the monkey squad clustered around her. All heads swiveled to take in the rally squad table. All eyes fastened on Angela. And the big binder.

The binder lay on the table in front of Angela. Both of her arms rested on it, and her fingers curled protectively around its top edge. Her small Hobo bag lay beside the binder, ignored. The cheerleaders were pointing at someone and giggling, but Angela looked distracted.

"What are you thinking?" AJ looked casually at Rebecca. Heads swung back to their own table, eyes going first to AJ and then to Rebecca.

"I don't know yet," said Rebecca calmly. "The weirdest thing happened in drama the other day." She told her friends how Angela had bolted like a scared rabbit when Mr. Tilson suggested she preview her next pageant skit.

"She loved doing it for the first pageant," Rebecca added. "Even when Mr. Tilson and the seniors critiqued her, she loved it. You could tell. She had everyone's attention all to herself. And she told me it helped her. She was hoping Mr. Tilson would do it again. She told me that." Rebecca paused. "She's acting . . . I don't know, just creepy. It's not like Her Imperial Flaming Highness is shy or something." Rebecca's voice trailed off, and she gazed fixedly in Angela's direction. "And it's almost like she's avoiding me. That's a totally wacko thought. It's not like we're friends or something." Rebecca ran a hand through her hair. "I don't know," she said. "I haven't figured it out yet." She twirled a long lock absently around one finger.

"She's just being stuck-up," said Ty.

"And why do you care about her pageant, anyway?" This was from Sam.

"There's one other thing." Rebecca bit her lip, glancing around the table at her friends. She cleared her throat. She nibbled on a cheese puff.

"What?"

"Well . . . I sort of gave her an idea for her second skit," said Rebecca.

The other girls just looked at her and waited.

"She was going on and on about how her dad's pitching a fit about costs."

"Are you kidding!"

"The rich bitch? No way!"

"Yeah, I know," said Rebecca. "And I had one of those little tingly feelings, you know? I just spilled it to her."

The others were silent.

"It was a good idea. But she slammed me hard. She said . . . she said I was way out of my league and strutted off with her nose in the air. Like I was beneath her or something." Rebecca paused and then continued, "And the funny thing is, she's been acting weird ever since. And I think whatever it is, it's in the binder."

"Maybe you can get your hands on it," said Sam.

"But how?" Ty was frowning in concentration.

"Some sort of distraction in drama class maybe." Zoe was thinking out loud. "If she left it somewhere. Like on that little stage."

Rebecca's thoughts were running in the same vein, but she was skeptical. "It'll never happen," she said. To no one in particular, she said, "You're right. She never lets go of it."

The girls fell silent. Sam took a bite of sandwich and chewed thoughtfully. Rebecca ate another cheese puff, still twirling the lock of hair with one finger. AJ sipped on a soda, nudging red-framed glasses up her nose. Zoe finished her apple and replaced her lunch things neatly in her backpack. Ty's forehead was furrowed in concentration, one hand gripping her ponytail, but she came up with no solution. None of them did.

CHAPTER 30

The Mysteries of Reiki

May 23

A FTERNOON CLASSES WERE uneventful. Students were allowed to review for upcoming finals—a huge relief from the piles of homework that had been heaped on in the preceding days. Zoe didn't need to study French, so she worked quietly helping Rebecca. After class, as they filed down the stairs with the crush of other students, Zoe announced she wouldn't be in Home Room.

"Grand-mère is leaving tonight," she said. "I want to see her before she goes to the airport. Home Room is pretty much a waste anyway. No one seems to give a rip, and the jocks all just fart around. Especially since Jackson's accident."

"Yeah, it's worse than usual," agreed Rebecca. She thought, *Maybe I can finally talk to Sam.*

At the bottom of the stairs, Zoe flashed Rebecca a huge smile and disappeared into the melee. Rebecca glanced around for Sam and saw her coming down the hall. Rebecca felt an edge of concern. She couldn't define it; she barely recognized that it was there. Sam's face broke into a smile, and her eyes sparkled, but there was reserve there too. What was going on with Sam?

Jackson and Josh didn't show for Home Room, and the other jocks were more subdued without them. Mr. Hammond was his usual nasty, glaring self, but His Fatness settled behind his desk and left the class pretty much to their own devices.

Rebecca wondered how to bring up the subject of the Reiki. She had no idea. "I've hardly seen you all week," she said instead.

"Yeah." Sam didn't elaborate. She tapped a long nail against her lips. She was frowning. Rebecca's heart skipped. This was bad.

"Sam . . .?" Rebecca's voice was barely audible. No wonder—her throat was so tight!

Sam looked directly at Rebecca. Her face was serious. She opened her mouth and then closed it. Then she blurted out, "You really have to take Reiki."

Rebecca stared at Sam in amazement. Her own mouth dropped open. No sound came out.

"It's the only way I can ever talk to you about it," Sam said.

"Why!" A flare of anger turned her voice cold. "Is there some ritual of secrecy or something?"

"No! It's nothing like that!" Sam put a hand on Rebecca's arm and scooted her desk closer. "It's just that I can't tell you what it felt like. I mean, I can try." She smiled and her eyes danced. "But you'd need to've been there . . ."

"So what did you do?" asked Rebecca.

"Nothing all that special, really," said Sam. "At least not at first. We learned about this Japanese guy who was given the secrets of Reiki on a sacred mountain. And how it was passed down. It's called lineage, and that part was kind of boring. And there's a symbol we had to memorize. I had to draw it till I got it right. And a bunch of stuff about healing. How we aren't really the healers, because all healing comes from the thing being healed. We're just channeling the energy. Sort of like we're a straw. And then the symbol was imprinted to us or something."

Sam paused, and her face was filled with wonderment. "But the energy—" She shook her head. "You can actually feel it, Becks. In your hands. At least I did. My palms got hot and tingled like crazy. It's like my whole body was . . ." She shook her head again. "More alive or something," she finished.

Rebecca didn't know this Sam. There was a new dimension to her. She felt a stab of fear. What if Sam was never the same again? What if *they* were never the same again?

Sam went on. "And, Becks, I did it. I did Reiki on Magic. And she's better!"

"Yeah, Mom was going to do it too," Rebecca said. "Her Reiki 911 thing. Remember?"

Sam looked crestfallen. "So it wasn't me?"

"I don't have any idea," said Rebecca. She was being mean, and she knew it, but she felt powerless to stop. "And didn't Mom say you have to do the second class before you can do it on someone . . . something else?"

Sam looked sheepish. "Yeah, she did," she said. "And so did April. But the stuff she gave me to read covered all the levels, not just the first one." Sam seemed to be weighing what she was about to say. "I sort of read ahead."

Rebecca didn't know what was more amazing. That Sam studied on her own, or that she was so psyched up about the Reiki.

"You read ahead?"

"Yeah, I did." Sam was unapologetic. "I had to. The ranch foreman had been trying to talk Uncle Clint into putting Magic down as soon as the foal weans. He's a mean son of a bitch!" Sam's voice was venomous. "So I read ahead, and I practiced Reiki on myself, like we're supposed to. And now I'm doing it on Magic." There. It was out.

Sam rushed on. "And I can't describe how it feels, or how it makes *me* feel. Sort of like I've been . . . I don't know, only half plugged in, and suddenly I'm . . . like I have a new battery or something. Not that I run on batteries." Sam giggled, and it sounded like the old Sam. "I know it all sounds stupid. I can't describe this," she said again.

Rebecca felt a sudden rush of loathing for Reiki. For the indefinable thing that had put such a distance between her and her best friend.

Sam seemed to read her thoughts. "That's why you have to take it too," she said. Her eyes implored. "You just have to. So you'll understand." Sam hesitated. Could she even say this? "Because, Becks, I can't go back to the way I was before, and I don't think I want to." Sam sat back in her chair, looking intently at her friend. "So you see," she said again, "you just have to."

"Wow." Rebecca tried to think of something else to say, but her mind was a void. "Wow." She ran both hands through her hair. She grabbed a fistful in a tight clench.

"And, Becks," Sam said quietly, "*think* what it could do for your stories."

"What do you mean?"

"We talked about the ways people know things. Other than the usual senses, you know?"

Rebecca didn't know, but she didn't say so.

"How sometimes you just know something, or you see a picture in your head, or you feel something. Feel energy." Sam looked at Rebecca, and Rebecca stared back, her face neutral.

"April called it the clairs," Sam continued. "There are five of them. The only one I'd ever heard of is clairvoyant, but I didn't really know what it meant. You can see things in your mind's eye. You know?"

Suddenly Rebecca did know. She looked in stunned amazement at Sam. "OMG," she finally whispered. "That's how Nanna does it!"

"Does what?" Sam was puzzled.

"Nanna always says she writes the best when it just flows. Like she's not really doing it herself. It just comes to her. I always thought that was kind of weird, but I sort of got it too. Because of the tingles, you know?"

Sam did know. She nodded.

"So Reiki could make me more . . . could help me . . ." Rebecca didn't know how to phrase it.

But Sam understood. "Yeah," she said quietly. "April said that."

Rebecca looked at Sam with raised eyebrows.

"No, not you specifically," Sam said. "April said the more you do Reiki, the more intuitive you become."

"Intuitive?"

Sam nodded. "Like a sixth sense. You know, psychic. You just know things. But it's not really another sense—it's an added dimension to the five we already have." Sam shook her head. She didn't know where that description came from. It just sort of flowed out of her mouth. But it felt right.

Rebecca's expression clearly said *How?* although she never spoke aloud.

"Because," said Sam, "it's all energy. Everything is energy, and you can learn to read it. And even more, you can learn to use it."

CHAPTER 31

The Long Weekend:
A Perfect Saturday

May 25

F INALLY! IT WAS Memorial Day weekend. Rebecca was relieved to put the last three, torturous weeks behind her. The weekend was going to be packed. There would hardly be time for everything, and, she fervently hoped, no time to think about all the weird things going on. There was the family party at Nanna's tonight and preparations to be made for that; the sleepover tomorrow night and more preparations, although it was meant to be kept simple. There was to be a cake and different kinds of popcorn—her personal favorite was cheddar cheese—and the girls would watch movies all night. It looked like the weather was in their favor for sleeping out on Andy's trampoline. Monday seemed far away, and Tuesday . . . not even on the radar. No homework, no finals to think about, no Jackson, no Angela, no Fat Mr. Hammond.

Rebecca flew through her chores Saturday morning. She was unfailingly patient with Andy and Scoundrel. It wasn't easy. The big slobbering mutt followed Andy around like they were joined by some invisible leash. Where there was one, there was the other, always in her way. But she managed to maintain her calm.

She helped her dad wash his pickup truck. She loved the time with her dad, but she was also secretly hoping he'd be moved to reward her with a little cash. She was not disappointed. Her dad slipped her a twenty when they were done, along with a big, sweaty hug. Rebecca was thrilled. Twenty dollars! She couldn't think how the day could get much better. And there was, of course, the question of what she would get her for her birthday.

Afternoon found Rebecca and her mother in the kitchen, baking two cakes. One was to take to Nanna's. The other was for tomorrow night with the girls.

"What's for dinner at Nanna's?" asked Rebecca.

"I think spareribs on the grill," said her mom. "Those little cheese biscuits you like. Probably grilled veggies too. You like grilled carrots— it makes them so sweet."

"Mmm," Rebecca thought her mom might be overselling a little on the carrots.

"Andy has plans with Jimmy Norton," her mother went on. "Marcy Norton is picking him up right after dinner. I said okay to that. I didn't think you'd mind."

"No, I don't mind," said Rebecca. "So it'll be just the grown-ups after dinner."

"Yes, just the grown-ups." Maggie's face was carefully impassive.

"In a year, I'll be driving," said Rebecca. That should tweak her mother!

"Gods!" Her mother covered her face with her hands and shuddered. It was a little overdone, and Rebecca laughed.

"I'll do the frosting if you have other things to do," said Rebecca.

"You just want the frosting bowls all to yourself."

Rebecca laughed again and did a little dance step. "Is Pappa going to be there tonight?"

"Yes, he is," said her mom.

Cool. Pappa might slip her some extra cash too.

"What's Nanna getting me for my birthday?"

"I haven't the first clue," said her mom.

"You and Nanna talk about everything," said Rebecca. "I know she told you what she's getting me. She probably asked you what I want."

"Think you have it all figured out, don't you?" Her mother dodged the question.

"So what's she getting me?" Rebecca persisted.

"I have absolutely no intention of telling you."

"Then you do know!" exclaimed Rebecca.

"We talked about it. Nanna will do what she wants. She's perfectly capable of coming up with something clever on her own." Maggie lips were, apparently, sealed.

"Money would be good," said Rebecca.

"Rebecca Jean!"

"Whaaat?" Rebecca dodged as her mother took a swat at her rear. She raised her shoulders in an exaggerated shrug, feigning innocence.

Maggie Coleson shook her head as she put the cakes in the oven. "Okay, that's taken care of." She wiped her hands on a towel and smoothed them over her hair. Rebecca watched the gesture she had seen a thousand times. She appraised her mom, noting the dark-gold hair pulled into a loose ponytail. Unruly wisps had escaped, curling around her face and at her neckline. She had a smudge of flour on one cheek. She wore a pair of faded jeans, the knees threadbare and the hems frayed, topped by an old Styx T-shirt. Rebecca thought her mom looked kind of a mess, but even so, she was still one of the prettiest moms she knew. Her mother caught Rebecca's look.

"What?"

"Nothing," said Rebecca. "Can I walk up to Zoe's? The cakes won't be cool for a while."

"Are you through with your chores?"

"Yes, Mother."

"And you're wearing that to Nanna's?"

Rebecca looked down at her clothes. She was pretty much a mess too. "No, I'll change when I get back . . . if I can go to Zoe's?"

"Well, okay. You be back here by four, with or without Zoe. We leave for Nanna's at five sharp."

"Okay." Rebecca hugged her mother and danced out the back door.

Maggie watched Rebecca bound across the backyard, hair flying, skipping from stone to stone along the path through the flowerbed. Earbuds were tucked in her ears. She paused at the top of the path to dance to the beat, her body language expressing pure joy and abandon. Then she clambered up the back fence and dropped from sight on the other side.

Maggie's heart contracted. *Fifteen*, she thought. *May the goddess give me strength.*

***

Rebecca and Zoe returned in plenty of time for Rebecca to change and for the girls to frost the cakes before leaving for Nanna's. There was a red velvet cake, which they covered with white icing. This was for Rebecca's sleepover. The cake to take to Nanna's was vanilla bean with buttercream frosting. Zoe was whipping in fresh strawberries to give the frosting a pretty pink color, and because she and Rebecca both loved strawberries. The girls worked from recipes Zoe had printed from the Internet, liberally sampling as they went. Rebecca scooped big gobs of frosting onto the cakes, and Zoe knifed them into artful shapes and textures. Putting a last swirl on the red velvet cake and several fresh strawberries on the vanilla bean cake, Zoe nodded appreciatively and licked the frosting off her knife. Rebecca ran one finger around the inside of a bowl and stuck it in her mouth.

"Oogh," she said. "I think I've had enough." With a grimace, she set the bowl in the sink.

"We should clean up this mess," said Zoe.

Maggie was passing by the kitchen with a load of laundry in her arms. Setting the basket on the table, she came up behind Zoe and put her arms around her.

"I'll do the kitchen," said Maggie. "You two have done a nice job." She looked at both cakes, nodding approvingly.

"You're the best, Mom!" Rebecca planted a buttercream kiss on her mother's cheek.

"Really, we don't mind doing it," said Zoe.

Rebecca glared at her friend. "Zoe Lynne Bodie!" she hissed. Zoe gazed calmly back at her, dark eyes widening. Rebecca sighed. "Okay, okay, we'll do it."

Her mother kissed the top of her head. "That's great," she said. "I can get cleaned up a bit before your father gets back from his errands." She disappeared up the stairs, the basket of laundry on her hip.

By the time Rebecca and Zoe finished their cleanup, Maggie had returned. Her hair was brushed back from her face and fell in thick waves to her shoulders. She had applied a little makeup and was wearing fresh jeans and a pretty top with little sparklies woven into the fabric.

Rebecca eyed her mother. "That's new!" she said.

"It's only sort of new," said her mom.

"How come I haven't seen it before?"

"I've had it hidden away." Her mother chuckled. "So I could wear it first."

Rebecca fingered the fabric. "Can I wear it tomorrow night? For my party?"

"Probably not."

"Mom . . ."

"All right, girls." Her mother changed the subject. "Good job. Thank you."

At that moment, Jack Coleson walked purposefully into the kitchen.

"Here, Jack." Maggie handed a cake to her husband. "In the truck, girls."

Jack looked at the cake in his hands. He seemed to be wondering why he was holding it. The question unresolved, he hollered up the stairs. "Andy!"

"Coming, Dad!" Andy bounded down the stairs, Scoundrel at his heels. They blasted into the kitchen at warp speed. Rebecca and her father dodged the pair of them.

"Put the dog in the backyard, son," said Jack. He held the cake precariously at shoulder level. Rebecca thought he looked a little panicky. That was a new idea relative to her father.

Andy opened the French doors and stepped aside. Scoundrel hurdled past him to the patio, beside himself with anticipation. Or maybe he was just beside himself on general principles. Scoundrel was a mystery. Andy quickly closed the doors. Scoundrel skidded to a stop, looking over his shoulder in surprise. He bounded back to the doors and stood there, his head tilted to one side, one ear cocked up and his tongue lolling out, looking hopeful.

"Too bad he can't go," said Andy sadly.

"Not a chance," said Jack. Balancing the cake in one hand, he checked the lock on the French doors before herding everyone toward the garage. Rebecca's mother hurried back down the stairs.

"Let's everybody move!" commanded her dad.

Everyone did.

***

Evening was falling over the Front Range. The Rockies loomed dark on the horizon, massive peaks backlit by a soft purple sky fading to turquoise. Dinner was over. Nanna was putting out cake plates and forks when April appeared in the doorway. Gray braids were wound around her head, held in place with brightly decorated hairpins. Some of them had dangles on the end—the sun and moon, crystal orbs, a Celtic symbol. She and Nanna exchanged glances that seemed to convey an entire conversation, and April moved smoothly to help.

Rebecca watched this silent interplay. *They don't even have to talk,* she thought. *They know what the other wants without saying a thing.*

Rebecca reached toward one of the cakes to scoop a dab of frosting onto her finger. *Maybe it's that clairs thing,* whispered Laney. Rebecca's hand froze.

"We have vanilla bean cake with strawberries," said Nanna. "And sour cream pumpkin." She dropped a kiss on the top of Rebecca's head.

Rebecca's brain seemed to be split into factions, one focused on pumpkin cake and one on the clairs. She looked at Nanna but didn't really see her. *Shut up, Laney,* she said to the voice in her head.

"Can we have both?" asked Andy.

"Certainly," said Nanna.

"Oh boy!"

"And you, Jimmy? Do you want some of both cakes?"

Jimmy shook his head. "Just the one with the strawberries, please," he said. "But ice cream. I can have ice cream too?"

"Of course, you can," said Nanna.

April and Nanna cut the cakes and scooped on ice cream, and Maggie passed the plates around. There were murmurs of appreciation as everyone dug in, and then the only sound was the clinking of forks on plates. The plates were empty in no time.

Rising smoothly together, April and Nanna cleared the plates away, and Maggie placed presents in front of Rebecca.

Rebecca looked at the stack of brightly wrapped packages, her eyes bright with anticipation.

"Start with mine!" Andy bounced on his seat. "It's the red one."

"Okay," said Rebecca.

She pulled the red package out of the stack and ripped off the wrapping. Inside was a little book about cats. Rebecca thumbed through it, chuckling at the graphics, which pleased Andy immensely.

"D'you like it?" he said eagerly.

"I do, Andy," said Rebecca. "I love it. Thank you." She hugged Andy and ruffled his hair. Andy squirmed away, glancing at Jimmy, but his expression was one of satisfaction.

Zoe fished her present out of the stack and handed it to Rebecca. Inside was a book by Sarah Addison Allen, one of Rebecca's favorite authors.

"Awesome!" she said. "I didn't know this one was out yet. Thanks, Zoe!" Rebecca scanned the jacket for a hint of the story line. "Have you read it?"

"I thought about reading yours," laughed Zoe. "But I didn't. So no, I haven't read it."

Rebecca raised her hand, and Zoe signed her back, her small face flushed with pleasure.

Lissa handed Rebecca the next present. "I hope you like it," she said.

Rebecca tore off the wrappings and opened the box. Nestled in layers of tissue was a wide leather bracelet inset with a blue crystal. She lifted the bracelet from its nest and ran her fingers over the surface of the stone. It was engraved with intricate shapes, almost too subtle to see. She looked quizzically at her sister.

"It's supposed to calm the mind and sharpen focus, both at the same time. And also stimulate creativity," said Lissa. "It's celestite. And the shapes are sacred geometry. Ancient, but also mathematical."

"Cool," said Andy. "It matches your eyes."

"Is it magic?" asked Jimmy.

"Magic?" Lissa laughed. "Well, I guess that depends on how you look at it."

"That stuff isn't very scientific, is it?" asked Rebecca.

"You mean that crystals have specific properties?" said Lissa. "That stuff?"

"I guess that's what I mean," said Rebecca. She looked dubiously at the bracelet.

"There is considerable study of the properties of stones," said April. "Just not anything that's admitted to by the scientific mainstream. Yet." April frowned when she said this.

She gently removed the bracelet from Rebecca's hands, holding it almost reverently. "I like the leather with the delicate stone," she said. "An interesting balance of yin and yang."

April turned the bracelet in her hands, studying the shapes. "The symbols are another thing altogether. They're based on Pythagorean geometry and tie into the fundamental laws of the universe. The supposed relationship between geometric laws and quantum mechanical laws."

"I read about that!" Zoe perched on the edge of her chair in her excitement. "A lot of Gothic cathedrals were built using sacred geometrical proportions."

"Yes." April smiled. "Symbolic and sacred meanings are ascribed to certain geometric shapes and proportions. Ancient symbols carry a great deal of power in their energetic signatures." She handed the bracelet back to Rebecca.

"How do you know all this?" Rebecca held the bracelet tentatively.

"There's much you don't know about our April," said Nanna fondly. "She is widely read and extraordinarily knowledgeable on a great variety of topics. Including quantum physics."

"And Reiki too?" Rebecca hadn't meant to say that. It had just popped out. "You're not for real!" Her amazement was genuine.

Zoe looked confused. "Quantum physics and . . . But I thought you were Wiccan . . ." She closed her mouth, looking embarrassed.

"Wiccan?" April shook her head. "A Druid, actually."

"Seriously?" Zoe considered that. "A Druid . . ."

"You'd be surprised how much ancient beliefs overlap with quantum science." April chuckled.

"What's Druid?" asked Jimmy.

"It means she's a witch," said Andy. He was matter-of-fact.

Rebecca glanced sharply at Andy. "How do you know that?"

"Hey, I'm not stupid," said Andy. "And I hear stuff."

"More than we thought, apparently," said Maggie. She looked both pleased and a bit alarmed, if that was possible. "I wonder what else you know," she murmured.

"So are you a witch?" Jimmy demanded loudly.

"Your mother just drove up," said April, diverting the subject from witchery. "Why don't you go gather up your things."

Jimmy looked about to protest, and Nanna cut him off. "I'll wrap up some cake for you, boys," she said. "Andy, give me a hug, and then don't keep Mrs. Norton waiting."

Rebecca looked from the bracelet to April and back at the bracelet. She didn't know what to think about the wrist piece. She liked it well enough. Maybe that was all that mattered. She slipped it on her wrist and fastened the clasp. The weight of it felt comforting. Weird, but true. "Thanks, Lissa," she said. "It's really great. And why do I think it's going to grow on me?"

Lissa was delighted. "Oh, I hope so," she said. She beamed at Rebecca.

Her mother thrust a white gift bag into Rebecca's hands. A bag Rebecca hadn't seen in the pile of presents. The subtle Apple logo was embossed on its side. Rebecca's breath caught. She pulled a slim box, exquisitely wrapped, from the nest of tissues inside the bag. "This is so pretty," said Rebecca. She glanced at her mother, who had stepped back and was leaning against her dad. Rebecca couldn't read either of their expressions. She ripped the ribbons off and tore away the paper. A small white box. Another Apple logo.

"Ohmigod! A new iPod?" The little box was surprisingly heavy.

"Open it, Princess," said her father.

Rebecca did. The box did not hold an iPod. Inside was an iPhone. She stared at it, her heart racing and tears beginning to spill from her eyes. She looked from one parent to the other. When she could finally move, she jumped to her feet and threw her arms around her parents.

"I don't know what to say." Rebecca's voice was choked.

Maggie hugged her daughter hard and then gently pushed her away. "You could start by thanking your father," she said. "And then open the rest."

Rebecca did. Her father hugged her fiercely back. "Dad . . ."

"It's okay, Princess," he said. "I know."

Rebecca thought her father's eyes were glistening. He *couldn't* be tearing up! Could he? She'd have to think about that later.

There was one package remaining. It was a beautiful box wrapped elegantly in Nordstrom's signature paper. Rebecca held her breath as she gently removed the wrapping to reveal a shoebox. With shaking fingers, she lifted the lid and folded aside the tissue.

"Heels . . ." She lifted one shoe from its nest of tissue. "Ohmigod!" The shoe was a strappy sandal, each strap a different color. The heel wasn't as high as most of Alexa's, but they were real heels! It was almost more than she could get her brain around. She looked at her mother, and then at her grandmother.

Hugging the sandal to her chest, Rebecca moved slowly around the table to Nanna and leaned against her, hugging her tightly. Over Rebecca's head, her mother and grandmother exchanged knowing, satisfied glances. Rebecca sneaked a look at her father; his face registered a jumble of emotions. She couldn't decipher the mix, but she thought resignation was one of them.

"Thank you, Nanna! These are perfect! They'll go with everything!" Rebecca glanced at her grandfather. "Thank you too, Pappa. You're the best."

Pappa smiled his satisfied-bear smile and handed Rebecca a slim envelope. It contained a gift certificate to her favorite store at the mall. There was a matching slender envelope with Zoe's name on it.

"I've been apprised that your birthday is just around the corner," said Pappa.

Nanna hugged Zoe. "And you're like one of our own."

"Thank you very much, Mr. and Mrs. Hawthorne." Zoe was faultlessly proper, but her voice shook. She shared an excited look with Rebecca.

Nanna and Maggie tidied up the island, putting presents and tissue back in bags and boxes and stacking everything neatly. Rebecca packed the iPhone carefully back in its white box and tucked it into the white gift bag.

Lissa got to her feet. "I'm meeting James in half an hour," she said. "I'll see you at home later." At the door, she called over her shoulder. "Happy birthday, Becka."

"Thanks, Lissa. And thanks for the bracelet." Rebecca fingered the leather strap.

Lissa just nodded. Her smile was indecipherable.

"Can we have a fire out on the deck?" asked Rebecca.

"That's a great idea," said Nanna. "Pierce, would you mind getting it going for us?"

"Sure," said Pappa. He ran a finger around the edge of one of the cake plates. Licking the frosting from his finger, he headed out to the big deck, followed by Jack.

"Do you want coffee?" Nanna called after them.

"Not me, thanks," said Pappa.

Jack shook his head.

"Thank you for the gift certificate, Pappa. It's the best," Rebecca called after him. "I can't wait to buy an outfit to go with my new shoes. I think I'll put them on now!"

"The bomb," said Zoe, and the girls dove into the pile of presents that had been so recently and neatly stacked.

"Coffee, sweetie?" Nanna asked her daughter. "Or a magic bullet?"

Rebecca's mom laughed. "Oh, definitely a magic bullet!" she said.

Nanna laughed too. "Magic bullet" was their nickname for an after-dinner beverage. Rebecca had noticed it wasn't strictly limited to after dinner, and she wasn't sure what went into it. It seemed the actual ingredients could vary. This evening, Nanna pulled a big pitcher out of the fridge and set it on the island. She placed four crystal mugs beside the pitcher and filled them half full of ice.

"My raspberry lemonade," she said to Maggie, who nodded. Nanna filled the mugs with the dark-pink liquid, dropped two raspberries in each mug, placed a long straw in two of them, and handed them to Rebecca and Zoe. Into the remaining two mugs she poured a generous splash of clear liquid from a tall frosted bottle. She swirled the contents. The two women sipped as they moved toward the deck. The girls followed after them, Rebecca tottering alarmingly in her new heeled sandals.

Pappa had the fire going nicely. He and Jack were leaning comfortably against the deck railing watching the flames. The wood popped and snapped, throwing sparks against the fine mesh screen covering the firepit.

"I have cookies, if anyone is interested," said Nanna, savoring another sip of her magic bullet.

Zoe and Rebecca shook their heads. "I'm stuffed," said Rebecca.

Maggie shook her head no.

Jack looked interested. "What kind?" he asked.

"Jack, you can't be serious!" Maggie stared at her husband. Nanna just smiled.

"Let's check it out," said Pappa.

The two men disappeared into the house. Rebecca could hear the low timbre of their voices coming from the kitchen. It made her feel warm and protected, and so happy she thought she might cry. She couldn't imagine her family without her father and Pappa. Ty's father lived hours away, isolated from her by miles and miles of mountain roads. Sam's father was—well, creepy. And AJ hadn't seen her father since she was little. Rebecca thought she might cry for that too. Zoe's family was cool, but often over the top to the point of being kind of crazy. Her dad was really quiet. Well, no wonder. Rebecca liked the solid sense of safety in her family. In spite of all the stupid rules.

The spring night was crisp, and Maggie and Nanna pulled chairs close to the fire ring and settled comfortably into the thick cushions. Maggie pulled up her long legs and tucked her feet beneath her. Nanna stretched out her legs, her feet close to the fire. Laughing and grunting with the exertion, Zoe and Rebecca dragged Nanna's glider closer to the warmth.

"Here, right here!"

"No, over a bit."

"I want it close to the fire."

"Not *too* close!"

"You can have the cold end."

"Okay, okay. That's perfect!"

Rebecca and Zoe collapsed giggling onto the cushions. Rebecca stretched out her legs and draped them in Zoe's lap. She turned her feet this way and that to admire the new sandals. Zoe curled against her cushions with one foot tucked up, the other brushing the deck, pushing the glider into gentle motion. The glides squealed softly in protest.

"I really need to get that fixed," said Nanna.

Rebecca smiled to herself. She didn't know how the day could have been better. She was so contented she felt like purring. No sooner had the thought popped into her head than Inkjet appeared around the corner of the house. He moved with feline grace across the deck and sat in front of the glider. He looked from Rebecca to Zoe.

"I know," Rebecca said to the big black-and-white cat. "Nanna's supposed to be here." Rebecca patted her lap. Inkjet raised his nose to test the air and seemed to consider. At length, he sprang lightly onto the glider and settled himself comfortably on Rebecca's outstretched legs. Rebecca ran her hand down his back, her fingers caressing the thick fur.

"Vous êtes un bon chaton." Zoe nuzzled Inkjet and stroked the top of his head. Inkjet pushed his head against her hand in pleasure. He stretched luxuriously, sighed deeply, and settled into a rumbling purr.

"He's hardly a kitten," said Rebecca. When Zoe looked up at her, she said, "Yeah, I listen sometimes too. Like in French class."

Rebecca and Zoe lapsed into companionable silence. Rebecca watched the flames leap and retreat, the firelight playing across her face. She coiled a lock of hair around one finger. Her eyes were bright with satisfaction. Zoe's small, pale face, framed by her mass of sable hair, was faerie-like in the glow of dancing flames. Her expression was quiet and thoughtful. Rebecca relaxed deeper into the glider, leaning her head against the back cushion and closing her eyes. She could hear the breeze sighing softly through the pine trees and feel its cool breath on her skin. She was grateful for the warmth from the fire. The glider's soft squeal at every push of Zoe's foot, Inkjet's loud purring and his solid weight on her legs, the hiss and snap of the fire, the murmur of her mother's and grandmother's voices in quiet conversation—it was all just so perfect. Rebecca sighed in contentment.

"I've started a new book." Nanna's voice came to Rebecca's ears.

"Not much of a break between projects this time."

"Mmm . . . when the spirit moves," said Nanna.

"That's so cool!" Zoe sat up straighter. "Is it another Ellie Lawrence?" Nanna wrote young adult books under this pen name, and Zoe had read all of them. So had Rebecca.

"It is," said Nanna.

"What's it about?" asked Zoe eagerly.

Rebecca's eyes were open now, and she was regarding her grandmother carefully. There was a little tingling sensation in the pit of her stomach.

"I've been wanting to write this story for a long time," said Nanna. "Just for fun. It's about a young woman who discovers quite by accident that she has, shall we say, special gifts. Originally, I thought the book would be fantasy. Magical. But now . . ." Nanna glanced at her daughter, and Rebecca saw her mother nod her head almost imperceptibly, "there have been so many discoveries in quantum science it's hard to tell science and magic apart."

"Totally the bomb!" said Zoe. Her eyes were shining. "What sort of gifts?"

Rebecca was suddenly alert. The little tingling sensation had intensified to more like a buzz. Involuntarily, she held her breath. She sat up straight, pulling her knees to her chest and wrapping her arms around them. Forcefully removed from his comfortable spot, Inkjet jumped off the glider, landing on the deck with a solid thump. He looked accusingly at Rebecca.

"I haven't really worked that out yet," said Nanna. "But it will involve the power of mind and tapping into energy."

"Energy?" Zoe was fascinated.

"Energy. Magic. The quantum field," said Nanna. "It's all around us. It's what we are."

Zoe considered the idea. "So this special gift . . ."

Rebecca didn't want to hear any more. This was too much like all the bizarre goings on she had wanted to *not* think about for three days! She bolted to her feet. "Let's go check out those cookies!" she said. "And then we'll go up to the hidey-hole. Come on, Zoe!"

Her voice sounded a little too loud in her ears. She pulled Zoe to her feet. Zoe looked surprised but made no objection. Tugging her friend behind her, Rebecca hurried toward the kitchen, wobbling somewhat unsteadily in her new shoes. Once in the house, she kicked off the heeled sandals and ran for the stairs to the loft, any idea of cookies discarded. Zoe followed more slowly, looking over her shoulder apologetically to Rebecca's mother and grandmother before she disappeared up the stairs.

Nanna and Maggie shared a long look.

"I guess you're right," said Nanna. "She just isn't ready."

"No, but maybe she needs to be," said Maggie. "That was an interesting reaction."

"Mmm." Nanna's gaze was on the fire. She sipped her magic bullet.

CHAPTER 32

Lost and Found

May 26

REBECCA WOKE SUNDAY morning with a delicious sense of both satisfaction and excitement. The patch of sky through the shrub hedge was a brilliant blue. The leaves on the shrubs were still, though that could change in a heartbeat. It looked like they'd be able to sleep out on the trampoline. The little party the night before at Nanna's had been awesome. Rebecca couldn't wait to wear the new heels. The weekend didn't present any logical opportunity for that, so school on Tuesday might be the soonest she would wear them. She suddenly wished it was Tuesday already.

Laughing to herself, Rebecca threw back her covers and swung her feet over the edge of her bed. Tinker emerged from the pile of covers, and Rebecca scratched her chin. No, she didn't really wish it was Tuesday. There was too much cool stuff happening between now and then.

She padded in her bare feet to her desk, where she had left her birthday treasures. She looked again at the gift certificate from Pappa, excited that Zoe had an identical one so they could shop together. She set the new book from Zoe on a shelf next to previous works by the author. She pulled the heeled sandals from the tissue in their box and slipped them on her feet. They didn't do much for her jams, but they'd be great with a pair of jeans and a lacy top, or a swingy skirt. Almost anything, really. She picked up the little book Andy had given her and thumbed through the pages, smiling again at the drawings and funny captions. Next was the celestite bracelet from Lissa. She slipped the leather on her wrist. She hadn't noticed the night before, but there were intricate carvings even on the clasp. She turned her wrist this way and that to catch the light on the crystal.

She had been saving the best for last. The iPhone. Not the latest model, but a good one. Or so her father had said. Were there bad models? She doubted it. She picked up the signature gift bag and ran her fingers over the subtle silver-on-white design. She pulled out the tissue paper and then the box inside. She took a deep breath of anticipation and opened the box.

It was empty.

Rebecca's heart plummeted, and her mouth went instantly dry. Holding her breath, she felt beneath the remaining tissues in the gift bag. Nothing. She dumped the papers and warranty booklet onto her desk. She held the bag upside down and shook it. A pair of earbuds fell out, but nothing else. She flipped on her overhead light and peered into the bag. It was empty. She took every piece of packing out of the iPhone box, knowing full well the phone could not be there.

She sat down hard on her desk chair. Her hands found their way into her tousled hair and fisted wads of tawny silk. Her heart thudded loudly in her chest.

"Okay, okay. Think!" she muttered under her breath.

She sat motionless for a moment and then sprang to her feet. She lined up the gift bags and boxes on her desk. One by one, she searched methodically through them. And then, frantically, again. How could this be? She remembered placing the iPhone carefully back in its beautiful box after everyone had admired it. Its slimness. The sexy weight of it. The neat protective cover. She looked once more through every shred of paper, wrapping, boxes, gift bags. She checked her purse, even though she was certain she had put the iPhone back in its box and the box in the Apple gift bag. She checked the pockets of the jeans she had worn to Nanna's, knowing the phone was not there. Someone must have taken it, but who? And why? She sank back into her chair, the white Apple bag dangling from one hand.

"Becka, breakfast!" Her mother's voice floated down the stairs.

She'd never be able to eat. But she should, since she would probably be homeless when she told her folks the iPhone was missing. How could this have happened?

"Rebecca!"

"I'm coming," she muttered. And then louder, "I'm coming!"

Rebecca started up the stairs. Her legs felt like lead weights. Her heart thudded. Her mouth was too dry to swallow. It was difficult just to pull air into her lungs. At the kitchen, she stopped, one hand going involuntarily to her hair. She didn't notice the delicious aromas and bright sunshine.

Lissa and Andy were already at the table, their backs toward her. Neither looked up. Her father was at his place. He glanced up at her and smiled.

"Well, you're a sight," he said, and he winked at her.

Her mother took one look at Rebecca, and her heart lurched. She had been stirring cream into her coffee, and her hand froze over the cup. She took in the pajamas and the new sandals, the leather wristband with the blue stone, the rumpled hair. The Apple gift bag dangling from a listless hand. But mostly, she noticed the ashen color of Rebecca's face and the feeling of desperation flowing off her.

"What on earth—" The spoon dropped into her cup and coffee splattered onto the counter. Maggie didn't notice. "Becka, what's wrong?"

There had been no time to plan an explanation, and anyway, she wasn't very good at subterfuge. Rebecca wondered briefly what she could possibly say. And then she just said it. "I can't find my new iPhone." Her voice was a croak.

"Your iPhone?" Her mother didn't seem to understand.

"My new phone," Rebecca wailed. "I've looked everywhere a thousand times, and it's not here! I can't find it!"

"Your iPhone?" Her father cleared his throat.

Was there a bloody echo in here? Rebecca looked from her mother to her father. She was waiting for the explosion and then the long lecture about responsibility and privileges. She was dead meat. She'd be grounded until she graduated from high school. Longer, except by then, she'd be eighteen. And all they could do was stutter and stare.

Her father reached into the pocket of his shirt and pulled out a small object. He placed it on the table. "I have your phone, Princess," he said.

Rebecca was speechless. She looked uncomprehendingly at her father, at the phone, and back at her father.

"Jack?" Maggie's one word was a loaded gun.

Jack looked both alarmed and a little sheepish. He shifted in his chair under the penetrating gaze of his wife. "I was going to take it down to Apple to get it set up this morning. Then I thought they wouldn't be open so early on a Sunday, and that it would be better for Rebecca to come with me." He shrugged helplessly, looking from his wife to his daughter. "To get a little tutorial," he finished lamely.

"Oh my God!" Rebecca was rooted to the floor. She thought her feet might actually be growing into the polished wood.

"And you didn't tell her?" Maggie's voice was calm, but Jack imagined the sound of the hammer being pulled back on that loaded gun.

"I didn't think Becka would . . ." Jack looked contrite. He held the phone out toward Rebecca. "I was trying to help. I guess I just didn't think, Princess," he said. "I'm sorry."

Rebecca moved woodenly toward her father and took the phone. She felt so many emotions she thought she might actually explode. Relief was huge. But also disappointment. Did her father not give her enough credit to even *talk* to her about the phone? *Her* phone! Her stomach knotted suddenly; she thought she might throw up.

"No harm done," said her father a little too brightly. "Let's enjoy our breakfast while it's nice and hot."

"Breakfast?" Rebecca just stared at her father. "I could not possibly—" Her voice was raw. Her stomach clenched again, and she turned and fled down the stairs, the iPhone grasped tightly in one hand, the gift bag fluttering wildly from the other.

Jack looked like he might be about to say something, but one look at Maggie convinced him otherwise. She threw him a withering look and followed her daughter down the stairs.

CHAPTER 33

The Sleepover

May 26 Late Afternoon

WHILE ALL MIGHT not be forgiven, and certainly not forgotten, Rebecca and her father had at least come to workable terms. A small (not very likable) part of her brain whispered that she could get a lot of mileage out of the iPhone episode, but when she saw the misery on her father's face, the thought made her feel small and mean. With party preparations minimal, Rebecca had agreed to go to the Apple store with her father and get the phone programmed. She knew some basics from watching her friends and occasionally using one of their phones, but the wide range of available functions was mind-boggling. She'd be lucky to figure out how to answer a call or send a text!

Zoe had come over early to help and to hang out. With the simple party measures under control, she and Rebecca fixed Andy's supper while Rebecca's parents ran errands.

"Can I have some cake?" Andy asked.

"No."

"Why not?"

"Because it's for my party, and it hasn't been cut yet. You can have some tomorrow."

"You'll eat it all tonight." Andy was bereft.

"No, we won't," said Rebecca.

"Can I watch movies with you?"

"No," Rebecca said flatly.

"What're you gonna watch?" Andy persisted.

"Andrew, if you promise to leave us alone, I'll, um . . . feed Scoundrel for you tonight. No! Tomorrow night. The party and all tonight . . ."

Andy's face smoothed into an acceptable seven-year-old version of Rebecca's infamous neutral expression. Zoe watched this transformation with fascination.

Rebecca looked at Andy appraisingly. "Okay, two nights," she said.

Andy looked steadily back at Rebecca. He didn't answer.

"And I'll let you have one of those little desserts Zoe's sister makes."

One corner of Andy's mouth twitched. Just a tiny twitch. Rebecca saw it and knew she was being played. Well, she already knew that. The twitch was just confirmation.

"Take it or leave it, sport," she said.

"Take it," said Andy. Looking very satisfied, he left them.

The girls loaded Andy's supper dishes into the dishwasher and washed up the two pots. They laid out the paper plates and napkins, along with plastic forks and cups. They opened big bags of popcorn—cheddar, caramel, and plain butter and salted—and dumped them into large bowls, sampling as they worked. They retrieved sleeping bags, flashlights, and air mattresses from storage.

"When Dad gets back, we'll ask him to blow these up with his air gizmo thing," said Rebecca.

"Efficient," said Zoe.

A blast like a gunshot shattered the afternoon quiet. The girls jumped involuntarily, staring at each other with wide, startled eyes. From the backyard came frantic barking. Arms linked, they moved toward the front door and opened it. AJ and Tyler were climbing down from Tom's old pickup.

Rebecca and Zoe met them on the porch and helped them with their gear. From the corner of her eye, Rebecca saw Tom's pickup heading back down the street. It backfired again as it disappeared around the corner. She had last seen Tom and his battered truck on the afternoon of her humiliating fight with Jackson—the episode that had triggered the first Event. That line of thought reminded her that last night was to have been Brittany's date with the CSU idiot. She didn't want to think about those things tonight. She shoved them into her mental box.

"We'll take all this stuff out to the tramp," she said, piling blankets and sleeping bags into Zoe's arms. To AJ and Ty, she said, "You can take your other stuff down to my room." AJ and Ty nodded and followed directions. Rebecca filled her own arms with pillows and more quilts.

"Where'd I put those flashlights?" she muttered.

"You don't need them," said Zoe. "There are lights on our phones."

"Oh," said Rebecca. "Really?"

"Really," said Zoe. "I'll show you."

"Well, just in case." Rebecca held on to the flashlights.

They headed for the backyard. Rebecca climbed into the trampoline and Zoe handed in all their gear. Rebecca stacked it neatly along one edge against the safety net. They would spread everything out after Sam arrived and the air mattresses were in place. They heard Rebecca's parents pull into the driveway, and Rebecca dashed out to intercept her father.

"Dad, can you blow up our mattresses for us? With your air thingy?"

"Sure, Princess," said her dad. He took a big bag of dog food from his truck and headed into the garage.

"Right away, Dad! That way, we'll know if any of them are going to leak."

Jack wearily dropped the dog food on his workbench. He retraced his steps to the pickup and pulled out some grocery bags.

"Daaad!"

"Rebecca Jean, five minutes won't make or break your party. Take a deep breath." He frowned at his daughter. Then, "Is that Sarah Ann?"

Sam was coming up the street burdened with a shoulder tote and a rolled sleeping bag. Rebecca met her in the driveway and took the sleeping bag.

"Dad!"

"You bring the air mattresses to me," said Jack. Was that a hint of irritation in his voice? "My air thingy, as you call it, doesn't travel lightly."

"Okay, Dad! We're on the way!" Rebecca practically danced into the house, Sam's sleeping bag tucked under one arm, Sam following.

The girls reappeared in a string, out the front door, down the sidewalk, and into the garage, each dragging a limp air mattress. Jack shuddered inwardly, wondering how many new holes this treatment would precipitate. Holes he would be called on to stop up and repair.

Miraculously, once filled with air, none of the mattresses seemed to leak. The girls danced back into the house the way they had come and out to the trampoline. This show was about to hit the road!

***

Dirty Dancing ended for the second time, and the credits rolled. Accompanied by the awesome soundtrack, Jennifer Grey and Patrick Swayze danced, danced, danced behind the crawl. In the Coleson family room, no one moved. The room was littered with wrapping paper, pizza boxes, popcorn bowls, and cake plates with only crumbs and smears of frosting remaining. The girls were sprawled in various semi-comatose positions.

"I don't think I can move," groaned Sam.

"Me neither!"

"I'm wiped, but wide awake. I don't think I'll ever sleep."

"Nothing to do with too much sugar."

"Ya think?"

"I'm not changing into jams to sleep outside," Tyler said around a huge yawn. "If I'm to be attacked by wild animals or a madman, I want to be fully clothed."

"Stop! Don't even say that!"

"We could get Scoundrel and let him sleep with us," suggested AJ.

"He'd bark and wake up the whole neighborhood," said Rebecca.

"At least we'd be awake before we had our heads chopped off," said Ty.

"So are we going out?" asked Zoe.

"I just have to switch off the TV and lights," said Rebecca. She did this, and they tiptoed outside, crept across the patio, and hurried over the lawn to the trampoline. Whispered exclamations broke the late-night stillness.

"We have to keep it down!"

"Shhh . . ."

"That's my foot!"

"Where's my pillow?"

Rebecca reached for the zipper tab on the safety net, pulling it firmly down to the floor of the trampoline. It was only netting. Even so, it felt somehow safer that way. They had arranged the sleeping bags like spokes, all piled high with extra quilts and blankets, pillows at the center. Legs crisscrossed, quilts wrapped around their shoulders, they formed a circle facing inward.

Ty waited until everyone was settled, and then she dug into her pillowcase and pulled out a small square box.

"I have something," she said.

"Not another present," said Rebecca.

"Sort of," said Ty. "But for everyone."

"Why?"

"Because we're so awesome," said Ty.

Tyler removed the lid from the little box and peeled back layers of tissue. She laid a small pendant on her pillow. Digging in the tissue, she uncovered four more pieces. In the light of her smartphone, they watched Ty lay out the pendants, each one a horse and each one different—a mare with her head turned to nuzzle a new foal, a rearing stallion, a bucking bronco. There was a mare in full gallop, and last, a small herd, also running.

Sam added the light from her iPhone. She gasped. "OMG!" She put one hand over her heart. "They're horses."

"Not just horses," said Ty. "Wild mustangs." Ty fastened the herd pendant around her own neck.

"But why?" asked Rebecca. "You already gave me a nice chain."

"The chain is for this," said Ty. She handed the galloping-mare pendant to Rebecca. "I want you to have this one." She gestured to the other three girls. "You guys pick which one you want."

"Why?" Rebecca asked again.

"My dad has this friend. Okay, they're more than friends. She makes jewelry. This is old inventory. She doesn't do this style anymore. I was looking at stuff she was going to just give away, and she said I could have these. They're sort of a set she did."

Sam reached for the rearing stallion. Ty and Zoe looked at each other. "The mare and foal?" Zoe murmured. AJ nodded and handed the mare to Zoe, taking the bronco her herself.

"How much did she sell these for?" asked Sam.

"I don't know," said Ty. "These are all pewter. Her new stuff is silver and pretty expensive. Luna says—that's her name, Luna LoveStar—"

"Luna LoveStar?"

"That's a weird name."

"Who would name their kid Luna?"

"No one," said Ty. "It's a made-up name. She made it up. You can laugh, but you should price LoveStar Creations. That's her business name. No one's laughing about that."

Ty went on. "Each mustang is different. And that's like us," she said. "Different and unique. Luna says we should celebrate our differences and not apologize for them. We aren't friends because we only feel safe with others exactly like ourselves. It's because we choose to be. Luna says that's really powerful."

They considered this quietly. Their faces glowed in the light of the two smartphones.

"I can feel the power, I swear." Sam cradled the stallion in the palm of her hand. "It's making my palm tingle."

"Luna seems to know a lot about us," said AJ.

Ty just shrugged. "Mmm. Some," she said.

"You'll tell . . . Luna . . . that we love them?" said Rebecca. She slipped her pendant onto the chain Ty had given her and fastened it around her neck.

"Yeah, sure."

They admired the pendants in the light of the smartphones until Zoe, suddenly shivering, dove into her sleeping bag. "I'm freezing," she said.

"Me too!" Rebecca and Sam agreed in unison. They clambered into their bags. Tyler slipped under her own covers, and AJ followed suit.

Snuggled in, the girls lay on their stomachs, chins propped on hands or resting on forearms, pillows clutched to their chests. They fingered their pendants, adjusted their zippers, plumped their pillows. No one spoke.

Rebecca said into the silence, "I might be getting a job at the doll shop."

"No way!

"That's so cool! When?"

"What's Lissa going to do?"

"It's not for sure yet," said Rebecca. "I have to meet old Mrs. Mason. Lissa's going to be working at the rock shop."

"The rock shop? Doing what?"

"Well, it's not just a rock shop anymore. Turns out Mrs. Mason owns it, too, and she's making it into a really cool alternative health center. Mom's pretty impressed. And Lissa's going to be . . . well, I'm not sure what she's going to be doing, but she's totally psyched about it. She sort of made up the job she wants and then pitched it to Mrs. Mason."

"It probably didn't hurt that she's been playing with dolls with the old lady forever."

"Yeah. Tough job."

"Well, I'd do it." Zoe's voice was muffled by her pillow.

"You'd be perfect for the job," said Sam. "You still have all your My Twin dolls. And all those outfits April used to sew for you."

Rebecca smiled, her face soft at the memory. "You used to slap our hands away when we wanted to dress those dolls."

"You both had your own," said Zoe.

Tyler glanced at Alexa. AJ shook her head. They hadn't been in the group long enough to have shared doll memories. *Let it go*, said the look on AJ's face. Tyler chewed on her lower lip.

The girls fell silent again. Their eyelids were growing heavy. Rebecca yawned and snuggled into her pillow.

AJ stretched and rolled onto her back. "Look at the moon!"

Ty didn't move, but the other girls rolled over to gaze up at the night sky. A sliver of moon hung suspended among countless stars, a wispy thread of cloud floating across its face.

"Wow!"

"It's so beautiful . . ."

"It's like magic!"

"Maybe we'll see shooting stars!"

A light breeze played through the big maple tree, causing the new leaves to rustle and whisper. A few houses away, a dog barked. In the distance, another dog answered. The night fell silent again. Rebecca closed her eyes and drew in a deep breath.

AJ's voice broke the stillness. She addressed the vastness of space. "The CSU idiot stood Brittany up."

CHAPTER 34

The Tale of Brittany and the CSU Idiot

May 27 (Technically)

REBECCA'S EYES FLEW open. She lay motionless on her back. Her heart thudded dully in her chest. There was absolute silence. After a long moment, Zoe rolled back onto her stomach to look at AJ in the dimness. Sam and Rebecca did as well.

"What did you say, AJ?" whispered Rebecca.

AJ was still contemplating the stars. At length, she rolled over. She doubled up her pillow and rested her chin on her crossed arms.

"I said the CSU idiot stood Brittany up."

"How do you *know* that!" Rebecca demanded in a fierce whisper.

AJ had their undivided attention. "I was at Sizzle yesterday afternoon. Remember those new hair extensions I wanted? Well, I got them. I was in a fitting room, and I overheard a conversation from next door."

"You were trying on hair extensions?" Giggles followed Tyler's question.

"No," said AJ patiently. "I was trying on tops."

"How do you know it was Brittany?"

"Just let AJ tell it!"

"Thank you, Zoe. Yes, if you'll all just be quiet, I'll tell you."

AJ fussed with her sleeping bag, adjusting the zipper. She plumped her pillow and hit it with her fist. The other girls watched impatiently, eyes glimmering in the moonlight.

"I saw her come in," AJ said. "I was paying for my extensions. She didn't see me. It was lame, I guess, but I wasn't up for any of her put-downs, so I sort of hid in a dressing room. I wasn't even thinking that Friday night was supposed to be the big event."

Rebecca winced inwardly at AJ's use of the word "event."

AJ continued, "I grabbed a couple tops so I'd have an excuse to go in the dressing room. Brittany was with a girl I didn't know. Not from Front Range, I don't think. Brittany called her Tiffy. I don't know a Tiffy, do you?"

Heads shook in unison. No one knew a Tiffy.

"They both had a bunch of stuff, and they went into the other fitting room. There's only the two there."

Heads nodded. They all knew. Sizzle offered just the two small fitting rooms, which shared a thin wall.

"I could hear them talking. Not about anything in particular. And I wasn't paying any attention. Just hiding. Then I heard the other girl, Tiffy, ask how the big date went." AJ paused, fiddling again with the zipper on her sleeping bag.

The girls waited with collective breaths held. The night breeze brushed across cheeks and noses that were chilly to the touch. Finally, AJ went on. "At first, Brittany didn't answer. She kept talking about the jeans she was trying on and about getting her hair fashion dyed, if only Peyton didn't have hers dyed in a rainbow already."

"She said rainbow?" asked Zoe.

"No. I said it," said AJ. "Anyway, Tiffy asked her again. 'How did your hot date with Jason go? Did your mom find out?'"

AJ relayed the rest of the tale as she had heard it unfold, sitting silently in the stuffy little fitting room adjacent to Brittany's, T-shirts forgotten in her lap.

***

"Come on, Britt, tell it!" Tiffy tugged at Brittany's arm.

Brittany jerked her arm away. "Give it up, Tiffy!" Then she sank onto the bench. "Oh, what's the point? He stood me up, all right? The freaking jerk freaking stood me up!" Brittany's voice broke as she struggled to hold back tears of anger and mortification.

"No way! He didn't!"

"He did, Tiff! Would I make it up!" Brittany sniffled.

"What happened?" Tiff was aghast.

"I have no idea. Everyone else was gone. I was ready early and waiting for him. I was perfect. Perfect! I took two hours getting ready. My hair was perfect. My makeup was perfect. My dress was perfect! I had—"

"You were perfect," Tiffy said with sarcasm. "What did you wear?"

"Oh, for God's sake, it doesn't matter now!" Brittany spat out the words.

A muffled "Sorry" came from Tiffy, along with the clatter of hangers. Was she still trying things on? AJ wondered.

Brittany blew her nose before she continued. "I filched Mom's eyeliner. It goes on with a real fine line, and smooth. Not like the cheap stuff. And she just got some totally sexy new perfume. I sort of borrowed some of that."

"How do you borrow perfume? It's not like you can give it back—"

A sharp slap accompanied by a gasp came from next door, and AJ covered her mouth with one hand to stifle a giggle.

"Just shut up, you moron!"

AJ knew that tone, had personally been the target of that biting condescension.

"I was waiting for him. I had it all planned out—how I'd take my time getting to the door. Act surprised to see him early. Well, he wasn't early. He wasn't even late. He just freaking never came! Never called. I waited forever. I couldn't think what to do. I finally just gave it up and went to bed."

"You didn't try to call him?" asked Tiffy.

"No. I might have. But I forgot my cell phone. I left my bag in my locker. I was thinking about *seeing* him, not calling him. I don't know his number. I have it in my cell. But he always calls me. I've never called him. And anyway, what would I say?"

"Maybe he called your cell. In your locker." Tiffy wasn't coming across as the brightest bulb in the box, but this was a valid comment.

"Maybe."

"Maybe he was in a wreck or something." Tiffy's voice sounded hopeful. Brittany's voice was flat. "I don't think so."

"Why not? He could've been," insisted Tiffy.

"No." Brittany was emphatic. There was a pause. Next door, AJ heard more rustling, shuffling feet, hangers clacking together again, and a deep sigh. She almost felt sorry for Brittany. Almost.

"This morning I asked Jordon, just casually, how Jason was doing. He said 'Good, I guess. Saw him last night.'"

Tiffy gasped. "Oh my God! He stood you up and then hung out with your brother!"

"No, Tiffy!" Brittany was losing patience. "They didn't 'hang out' together. Jordon just ran into Jason at some CSU deal."

"How do you know that?"

"Because Jordon said so, stupid!"

Silence stretched out in the next dressing room. Eventually, Tiffy said, "You don't have to be mean, Britt. It's not my fault Jason stood you up."

"Sorry, Tiffy. I'm pretty upset, as I'm sure even you can imagine."

Tiffy overlooked this last slight. "So what are you going to do?"

"I'm not going to do anything. What *can* I do? I don't know how I'm ever going to live this down. I may have made . . . sort of a big deal out of it to . . . some of the girls at school."

"You mean you were a real bitch bragging about dating a college guy?" Tiffy's tone was sweeter than Tupelo honey.

"I wouldn't talk if I were you." Brittany's voice was hard. Cold.

AJ still sat motionless, not daring to move, barely daring to breathe. There was another long silence, eventually broken by the sound of the door opening. The two girls moved away. AJ cracked open her door and peeked out. She could just make out the two girls moving through the racks and looking at clothes. They did not return to the fitting room. AJ did not leave hers.

***

In the circle of friends in the trampoline, no one moved. All eyes were fixed on AJ.

"I sat there for ages," AJ said. "I was afraid to leave the fitting room for fear of running into them. If they saw me come out . . ." AJ didn't finish the thought. "Finally, one of the store girls knocked on the door to see if I was all right. All I had was the two T-shirts. How long could I take trying on two T-shirts? I had to come out."

"And they were gone?" Sam whispered.

"Yeah. I got out of there and out of the mall as fast as I could." AJ fell silent.

"So maybe the CSU idiot isn't such an idiot after all." Tyler's voice was low.

Laughter erupted around the circle, quickly muffled as the girls buried their faces in pillows or burrowed deeper into their sleeping bags.

"How come you're just telling us this now?" asked Zoe.

"I just forgot," said AJ in a matter-of-fact tone.

"You forgot? How could you forget?" Tyler demanded.

"How could I forget?" AJ pondered this. "I don't know," she said. "Maybe because I don't care that much what Brittany does."

"Mmm."

"Oh."

And then silence.

"Becks, how'd you know?" Sam asked in a low voice.

"Know what?" Rebecca's heart was still beating rapidly. She was grateful for the dark. No one would be able to read her face. She didn't think she'd be able to pull off her neutral expression.

"Know he'd stand her up!"

"How could I know that?" Rebecca's heart lurched in her chest and then resumed its rapid beating.

"You said it," insisted Sam. "That day in the cafeteria."

Zoe spoke into the dark. "She said it wasn't a done deal because he hadn't called yet. Not that he'd stand her up."

Rebecca silently thanked Zoe's awesome memory and desire for exactitude in all things. She made no comment.

"Oh, yeah," said Sam.

The sliver of moon had moved across the sky and was now only partially visible through the leaves of the big maple. Conversation did not resume. Sam's head slumped onto her pillow, and her eyes closed. AJ piled on extra quilts and stretched out in her sleeping bag. Zoe curled into a ball, only the top of her head visible, and barely so, the jet hair appearing as a denser smudge amid shadows. Rebecca snugged deeper into her own sleeping bag and closed her eyes. She heard the steady breathing of her friends, one of them snoring softly. Far off, a coyote howled. A chorus of *yip-yip-yips* answered—a wild, primal sound that brought goose flesh to Rebecca's arms and a tingling sensation to the back of her neck. She was glad she had pulled the zipper closure on the safety net fully down.

Three times now. Three times she had written a little story, and it had come to pass. Once might have been a fluke. Two times stretched the limit of her belief that it could have been chance, especially since there were so many details that matched up. But three times . . . Something was going on. It was frightening. But it was somehow exhilarating at the same time.

CHAPTER 35

Little Lies

May 28

TUESDAY MORNING DAWNED bright, but windy and cold. As excited as Rebecca had been to wear the new strappy sandals to school, she realized her enthusiasm didn't extend to wobbling through the day with freezing cold feet. And the wobbling was another thing. She feared she would look like a total dork until she learned to walk confidently in the heels. She wasn't up to it this morning. She needed practice.

The iPhone was a different matter. Even though the use of a phone of any kind was forbidden in all classes at Front Range and could result in it being confiscated, Rebecca's parents had grudgingly admitted there was no use having the phone for emergency situations if Rebecca was not allowed to have it with her. Quite a lengthy lecture from her father had accompanied this conversation, with ominous warnings about responsibility, loss, breakage, theft, and a host of other dire potentials. Rebecca had glued what she hoped was an attentive look on her face and nodded and smiled at her father, all the while trying to keep her eyes from rolling backward into her head and hoping her face wouldn't crack into a million pieces from the strain of it. She loved the iPhone and had no intention of treating it with anything but the utmost care.

She pulled on a pair of old jeans and a warm top. She took the new pendant from its nest of tissue paper and fastened it carefully around her neck, liking the pleasing weight of it against her skin. She tucked the iPhone into a back pocket of her jeans and twisted so she could admire it in the mirror. It felt satisfyingly solid and substantial in her pocket. But more than that, *she* felt more substantial with the little device there. She patted it with one hand. Then she pulled the phone out of her pocket and placed it in an inside pouch deep in her book bag. It wasn't her father's lecture that caused her to do this, although that lecture was echoing in her head. She saw kids every hour of every day with their phones sticking out of a pocket, and it always seemed like an unnecessary risk. She remembered too clearly her feelings of panic and despair on Sunday morning when she had thought the iPhone lost.

She gave herself a little shake to ward off her edginess and slipped her feet into the plain flats she hated so much. Well, maybe not as much as she let on. This morning, they felt safe and comfortable. There was no reason she would particularly need comfort and safety today. None at all. It had been an awesome weekend, beyond even her hopes and expectations. The iPhone, the sandals, the sleepover, the pendants—they were all spectacular. It was just looming finals that had her on edge.

And maybe seeing Brittany in English, whispered Laney.

She thought about telling Laney to shut up. Was just thinking it the same as telling her? Rebecca didn't know; it was a murky area. But Laney could have a point, and anyway, it was useless to argue with her. Laney was in her own head, and deep down, Rebecca admitted that Sam was right—she and Laney were really one and the same. Two disparate aspects of the same, but still the same. To argue with her would surely be a sign of some sort of schizoid behavior, and she felt schizoid enough being the architect of the Events. Which led right back to Brittany. Rebecca sighed and headed up the stairs. She wanted to catch Lissa for a ride to school.

That turned out to be a good decision. The wind was really fierce, and its bitter bite had both Rebecca and Lissa clutching their jackets as they ran for the car.

"Wow!" Lissa shivered. "You lucked out with your sleepover Sunday."

"Yeah." Rebecca smiled in memory of the perfect night. "It was pretty sweet."

Lissa started the Prius, which came to life with a whisper and sat silently waiting for piloting instructions. Lissa backed the car carefully out of the driveway. It shuddered as a gust of wind hit from the side.

Small, new leaves torn from waving branches whirled and eddied in the street. Rebecca shivered.

"So your interview with Mrs. Mason is tomorrow after school. You good with that?" Lissa glanced at Rebecca.

"Interview? I thought I only had to meet her." Rebecca felt a little twinge of alarm. "I've never been interviewed before. What do I do?"

"Don't worry," said Lissa. "It's pretty much yours to lose. Mrs. Mason is really a sweet little old lady. Just be yourself."

Which self? wondered Rebecca. Aloud she said, "I thought she was sort of crazy."

"Jeez, Becka! You and Andy! Where do you two get those ideas?"

"I don't know—from you, do you think?" Rebecca didn't even try to keep the sarcasm from her tone.

"Okay, okay." Lissa exhaled forcefully. "Maybe it's my fault. But she's a rich old lady who can do pretty much what she wants, and what she wants is to dress and sell beautiful dolls to collectors and fund an alternative healing center. If that makes her demented, I hope I'm that crazy my whole life!"

Rebecca looked at Lissa, surprised by the passion behind her words. "You really like her, don't you?"

"I do. And I respect her," said Lissa.

"So what do I do?" Rebecca asked again.

"You answer her questions honestly, and you be polite. Other than that, you let your instincts guide you. You'll know what to do."

"I don't think my instincts are all that good," said Rebecca.

"That's bull!" Lissa laughed. "Then let Laney do the talking."

Rebecca's mouth dropped open. How did Lissa know about Laney?

"Don't worry, I think she's totally cool, and I'm glad you have your stories and your alter ego," said Lissa. "Just go with it."

They were pulling into the school parking lot. Lissa stopped at the drop zone at the front entrance. "I'll meet you right here after school tomorrow," she said.

Rebecca nodded and scurried for the front doors to get out of the vicious wind.

After the glorious three days off, it was jolting to come back to classes and prep for finals. Algebra was quiet and intense as students struggled with the extra work Mr. Hammond had dumped on them the previous week. Even the jocks were low-key. The hands on the clock crawled around the hour, but finally, it was over. Rebecca gratefully headed out to meet Tyler.

She wrinkled her nose at the disgusting, if familiar, smell of the science classroom and slipped into a chair next to Ty. Ty was already deep in concentration, but she looked up from her notes with a brilliant smile, the ponytail dancing. Ty's pendant hung from its chain inside her top. She pulled it out and fingered the running mustangs, making eye contact with Rebecca before tucking it back under her sweater. Rebecca didn't pull hers out, but her fingers lingered against it where it rested over her heart. She loved the running mare and thought all the pendants were the bomb, but she wondered if Ty was trying a little too hard. Too hard to . . . Rebecca wasn't sure. Be one of them, maybe?

Science was as intense as algebra had been, and there was no mention of AJ's astounding news at the sleepover. Rebecca actually focused on her review notes.

"Jeez, I'm glad that's over," said Ty as they filed out of the room.

"I wonder what's gonna be up in English." Rebecca was thinking about Brittany, but Tyler just shrugged.

"Probably just more of the same," she said. "I'll be glad when this year is O-V-E-R!"

Rebecca nodded. Curiosity vied with mild anxiety as she slid into her place at the study pod. Clarity and Travis were already there, but there was no sign of Brittany. Jackson arrived as the bell sounded, hardly limping at all in his short air boot. Rebecca's right hand wrapped involuntarily around her injured wrist, now free of both the cast and the Ace bandage. She massaged the wrist gently, trying not to look at Brittany's empty chair.

Clarity leaned forward, her elbows on the table. Her posture exposed more than a little of her breasts, round and firm. There was a small beauty spot on the left breast. For some reason, Rebecca wondered if the beauty spot was real or fake.

"Jackson." Clarity's voice was whispery. She looked at him from behind half-lowered lashes. "You poor thing," she purred. "How's your foot?"

Rebecca studied Clarity. Her behavior upheld Rebecca's theory that most girls were brain-dead when it came to boys, and pretty much *all* girls were brain-dead where Jackson was concerned. Jackson looked back at Clarity, his expression bland. He brushed the hair from his forehead in the so-familiar gesture. His body language was relaxed to the point of boredom. As if to say, *This is too easy.*

He didn't bother to correct Clarity on the location of his injury. "I'm good," he said.

Despite her better judgment, Rebecca drawled, "It's the brain damage we worry about." No wonder she was always getting into trouble!

Jackson sat up a little straighter, and his attention shifted to Rebecca. He regarded her with interest. And something else: it looked like glee. Rebecca had a flash of understanding. Jackson liked a challenge! Zoe had said it without actually saying it. That Jackson liked to talk to a girl with a brain—one who gave back as good as she got. This would take some thinking about.

Her look was a dare, and he was about to make a retort—Rebecca could feel it as much as see it—but at that moment, both Mrs. Lindzer and Brittany arrived at the study pod. Brittany took her seat, her eyes cast down and her face sullen.

"Glad you could make it," said Mrs. Lindzer dryly. She dropped a stack of papers in the middle of the table. Ty reached for them and began passing them around.

Brittany muttered something unintelligible.

Mrs. Lindzer moved on, and Clarity's flirtation with Jackson was forgotten. She turned to Brittany and asked in an excited stage whisper, "So how did the hot date go?"

Tyler and Rebecca glanced at each other in surprise. Clarity didn't know! This could be good. Rebecca felt almost sorry for Brittany, but curiosity overrode pity.

Brittany didn't answer.

"Spill the tea, Britt." Clarity nudged her. "Did Jason live up to his reputation?"

"Not quite," Brittany mumbled. She pointedly turned away from Clarity, unseeing eyes fixed on the pages Tyler had passed around the table.

"What do you mean?" Clarity nudged Brittany again. Her smile was more of a leer. "Spill it, Britt. Tell me he's as good as you thought."

Brittany whirled on Clarity. "He's a jerk, okay!" she hissed.

Clarity recoiled with a startled gasp, her hand flying to her mouth.

Brittany got ahold of herself with huge effort. She straightened in her chair and smoothed her hair. She put a hand on Clarity's arm. In a calmer voice, she went on, "I found out what a jerk he is." Her voice was ragged. "So I didn't go out with him. That's all there is to tell."

"That can't be all there is to tell!" wailed Clarity. She tugged on Brittany's arm.

"Ladies!" Mrs. Lindzer's voice came from the front of the room. "Could you save the drama for later?"

Rebecca glanced sideways at Tyler. Ty looked surprised, but also distressed. Rebecca's own emotions were mixed. Brittany's anger and her lie were a cover for her humiliation. But she had so earned it! She had been smug, arrogant, and a complete bitch for weeks, flaunting her relationship with "a college man." She had been demeaning to Alexa. She had turned toxic on Rebecca in the cafeteria for no reason, attacking her viciously.

She really deserved this, Rebecca thought. But it wasn't as satisfying as she had expected it would be.

At lunchtime, Rebecca was the last to arrive. She dropped her books on the table and pulled out a chair, looking around at her friends. It was too quiet. No one moved or spoke, except Zoe, who raised her hand to Rebecca.

"What's up?" Rebecca asked, signing back. "Did somebody die?"

Zoe took a little bite of apple. No one else moved or spoke.

"Come on, guys, what gives?" Rebecca looked around the group.

"Finals." Sam sat up straighter and ran both hands through her tousled hair. "They really piled it on today." She sighed. "In every class."

"Yeah." Ty looked dejected. "It's not the work so much," she said. She leaned her chin in the palm of one hand. The ponytail twitched and then stilled. "I get the work done," she went on. "I know the stuff. But when it comes to the test—it's like my brain freezes up or something."

There were sympathetic nods. Zoe spoke encouragingly. "That's just mind over matter," she said.

"It's not that easy, Zoe." Ty stared defiantly at Zoe.

Zoe smiled apologetically. "I didn't mean it was easy," she said. "But you could—"

"Get hypnotized!" Sam broke in. She leaned into the table. "My uncle wanted to have it done on my cousin because he wouldn't ride horses! Loved them, but wouldn't ride. Not too good on a working dude ranch. You should see him now. He's amazing."

The table fell silent once again. Tyler remained in her slumped position, looking dejected. The ponytail hung motionless, as though it, too, was depressed.

"Who saw Brittany today?" Sam was staring over at the rally squad table.

"We did," Rebecca said cautiously, looking at Tyler. Ty nodded.

"Me too," AJ said. "She was pretty surly." AJ's tone was dry. "I wanted to ask her who Tiffany is, but I didn't know how to bring it up." She pushed her glasses up her nose.

"She really slammed Clarity in English," said Ty. "She lied about it. Said she found out Jason is a jerk so she didn't go out with him."

Rebecca wanted to change the subject. She could share her flash of understanding about Jackson, but she decided against it. She might tell Zoe later, just so Zoe would know she understood. But not right now. She leaned forward, elbows on the table, nodding as her friends talked, one finger absently twisting a lock of honey-blonde hair.

CHAPTER 36

Trouble Is Brewing

May 28

"I HAVE TO see my college counselor today." Zoe was tucking her lunch things neatly back into her book bag as she spoke. "We're going to review my options for precollege summer classes." She pushed back her chair. "And then I'm going to clean out my locker."

"Summer classes!" Rebecca was dismayed.

Zoe looked at Rebecca, her small features set in determination. "I want Boulder," she said. "It's a top-ranked school for quantum science. It's in-state for me. I will do what it takes." She slipped her book bag over one shoulder and headed for the cafeteria doors.

Rebecca watched Zoe walk away. She understood. Really, she did. Besides, if Zoe didn't go to Boulder, she might end up . . . who knew where! It was impossible to know how things would unfold in the future, but Boulder might be the lesser of the evils. Right now . . . well, it didn't bear thinking about. She sighed with resignation and pushed back her chair.

"Me too," she said. "I was going to do it next week but . . ." She headed after Zoe.

"What's Becks going to do?" Ty was clearly puzzled.

"Clean out her locker?" AJ shook her head. "I don't think she meant Boulder."

"That girl!" mused Ty. "She's at least three different people."

"At least," Sam agreed softly. "And one of them is witchy. Or something."

When Rebecca caught up with Zoe, she fell into step beside her. They walked together without speaking. At the counseling offices, Zoe turned to Rebecca, her hand on the doorknob. "I'll see you later, then," she said.

"I thought you were going to clean out your locker," Rebecca said.

"I have to do this first," said Zoe. She disappeared through the frosted glass door, and it closed with a soft click.

Rebecca stared at the door, her friend's figure wavy and distorted through the opaque glass. After a long moment, she turned and headed up the hallway.

Rebecca had intended to clean out her locker next week. Probably on the last day of school. Why rush into these things? Now she stood in front of it, wondering if it was such a hot idea after all.

She stared at the offending lower unit and sighed. She spun the combination lock, yanked open the door, and settled to her knees to peer inside. She hated being on the bottom. Pulling everything out onto the floor, she began picking through the general mess, sorting things into two heaps—one to keep and one to pitch. There was the missing library book she had hunted for so fruitlessly, finally paying the full lost-book fine. There were notes for assignments long completed. Programs for the drama productions over the past year. A crumpled folder held information about freshman orientation. That was a useless bit! She investigated the contents of a brown paper bag and thrust it quickly away from her nose. Eeeew! Was that part of a sandwich? She didn't want to know. With her face screwed into a grimace, she scooped up the pitch pile and deposited it in the nearest trash can.

She came back to inspect the locker, settling to her knees again to get a better look. There was one more thing, stuffed onto the shelf at the top of the locker. Rebecca gingerly pulled the crumpled mass free from its hiding place. Her lost jacket! She had looked all over for this jacket, tearing her closet apart one Saturday. Her mom had been plenty annoyed about it, for sure. She gave the jacket a good shake and slipped it on, letting the soft fabric settle around her. She tried to smooth out some of the wrinkles, not very successfully, and thrust her hands into the pockets.

"Ow!" She yanked her hand out and pressed a finger against her mouth, tasting blood. Cautiously investigating the pocket, she pulled out two flat squares of stiff, glossy paper. What looked like two pictures were stuck together with some unknown and disgusting substance, the corners sturdy enough to have cut her finger. She carefully peeled the pictures apart and found herself staring at . . . she wasn't quite sure. She turned the photos this way and that. Ty's new puppy!

Anne Boleyn and her litter mates had been tiny, eyes barely open, when these pictures were taken. Sucking on her cut finger, Rebecca smiled at the memory. Ty had brought the photos to school and excitedly shown them to Rebecca in English. These two had been left behind when Ty rushed off after class. It seemed like years ago, instead of just a few weeks.

She took off the jacket and carefully folded it into her book bag. She slid the photos into a small outside pocket with her pens and pencils. She put what she needed for her afternoon classes in her bag and stacked the remaining lot neatly in the locker. She tucked the library book under one arm. She would drop it off on her way to government studies. Maybe she'd get most of her money back. That idea was hugely appealing.

***

Government studies was, as usual, boring. Rebecca forced herself to pay attention in case she missed something critical for the final next week, but her mind kept wandering. She thought about Angela's recent weird behavior in drama. Rebecca mulled over ideas to get her hands on that pageant binder. She pulled her mind back to the present with difficulty, stifling a yawn as the teacher came down the aisle passing out review notes.

"I'm making it easy for you," she said. "Know this, and you'll do well on your final."

Rebecca glanced at the page and nodded to herself in satisfaction. It was a lot, but knowing what to expect certainly saved a ton of wasted study time. The bell finally signaled the end of class, and she stuffed everything into her backpack and headed for French. After that, only three more Home Rooms before the end of school. There would be no Home Room next week. Finals week.

After French, Rebecca and Zoe walked together to Home Room, neither of them talking. They scanned the room for Sam. There were several open seats toward the front of the room, closer than Rebecca wanted to be to the Fat Man. And Jackson was there. She didn't feel any particular animosity toward Jackson at the moment. That was weird in itself. She was still awed by the face-off in algebra the previous week. She wasn't exactly looking for an opportunity to practice her newly discovered skill with Mr. Hammond. Well, "skill" was a bit overreaching; onetime lucky was hardly a honed skill. Just staying under the radar seemed the best plan. The safest thing to do would be to spend this hour preparing for her algebra final.

"Becka, park it here." Jackson grinned at her and nudged a desk with one foot. He nodded at Zoe. Josh barreled into the room and flung himself into an empty desk next to Jackson just as Sam appeared in the doorway. Rebecca glanced at Zoe, and the girls dropped into chairs on the other side of Jackson. Sam took the last empty seat just as Mr. Hammond lumbered into the room.

Jackson and Josh had their heads together as they turned pages in a battered notebook. Jackson was hunched over the notebook, almost like he was trying to hide it.

"That one, man," said Josh. He pointed. Rebecca couldn't quite make it out.

"You're sure?"

"Yeah. It's rad."

Jackson carefully tore the page out, folded it in fours, and handed it to Josh.

"Thanks, Jacks. This'll be sweet." Josh tucked the paper in his pocket.

Rebecca talked quietly with Sam and Zoe until Mr. Hammond cleared his throat and glowered at them. Nothing for the jocks sitting next to them. Rebecca stole a surreptitious look at her friends. Zoe just shrugged. Sam mouthed *Total loser* with a look that said, *What're you gonna do?*

Nothing, thought Rebecca. *That's what I'm gonna do. That's all I can do.* But it burned. She fished in her book bag for her algebra book. She saw the iPhone nestled safely in its pouch and ran her fingers over the exposed lip of its case. She smiled to herself.

Rebecca dropped the book on her desk with a solid thud and fished in the outside pocket for a pencil. Something was hanging things up. Irritated, she gave it a yank. Her pens and pencils, and something else, came flying out and landed across the aisle at Jackson's feet. Ty's pictures. They had reglued themselves together, along with everything else in the pocket. She leaned over to retrieve them. Jackson looked down at the little heap by his feet. He nudged it with his toe, and then reached for it just as Rebecca did. Their hands touched, and she yanked hers back. Jackson picked them up.

"What's this?" Jackson pulled the pens and pencils loose and handed them to her. He pried the pictures apart, holding one in each hand. He turned them this way and that, studying them with mock seriousness. Josh leaned over Jackson's shoulder.

"Looks like pieces of lint," Josh said.

Rebecca held out her hand. "Just let me have them, Jackson," she said.

"More like fuzzy socks," said Jackson. "You took pictures of your socks?" And he flashed his FIGJAM grin at her. Josh grinned, as well, and thumped Jackson on the arm.

Irritation flared. She was way too close to Mr. Hammond's desk. He wasn't there now, but he couldn't be far away. Lurking. Stalking. Laney's voice whispered softly, *Don't let them see you're mad,* and tapered off into silence. Rebecca made a huge effort to hide her annoyance. She looked at Jackson with what she hoped was a haughty smile. An Angela smile.

"They're not socks!" she said. "Are you blind? It's a puppy."

"Naw." Josh reached for the photos. "Pieces of lint." He grabbed the pictures from Jackson and held them at arm's length.

"Sock lint!" he exclaimed in triumph. "That's it!"

Jackson's gaze met Rebecca's for a moment, and then he turned toward Josh. Josh held the photos out of reach, and they scuffled. This was unbelievable. Feigned calmness was well and good, but she wanted the pictures back! Rebecca was about to launch herself at the two jocks when a niggling sensation in the pit of her stomach stopped her.

"I'll take those."

Mr. Hammond had crept silently up the aisle behind them. Again! As her heart sank, Rebecca couldn't help but marvel at the Fat Man's amazing stealth. It was truly remarkable. He held his hand out, and Josh dropped the photos without protest into the pudgy palm.

"It's every day with you three, isn't it." It was not a question.

Mr. Hammond scowled at Rebecca and then at the boys. He glanced at the photos.

"To whom do these belong?"

Josh and Jackson had fallen strangely quiet, not looking at each other or her, sliding down in their chairs. Laney's voice murmured softly, *Just let it go.* From the corner of her eye, Rebecca saw Jackson open his mouth. He closed it without speaking.

No way, Rebecca said silently to Laney. Aloud, she said, "They're mine."

Mr. Hammond turned his piggy gaze on her. Rebecca clinched her hands in her lap beneath her desk and looked up at him. She couldn't quite make herself meet his eyes. She found herself looking instead at the multiple chins pouring over the top of his shirt collar.

"Not anymore," said Mr. Hammond. He glared at no one in particular and waddled around his desk to his chair. He wasn't quiet now. Each graceless step seemed to reverberate through the classroom and echo in Rebecca's head. How did he do it? How did he manage to come up on them so silently?

Rebecca felt the so-familiar mixture of anger and frustration settle heavily over her. She looked toward Sam and Zoe. The expression on Sam's face was quietly observant. Zoe's dark eyes held clear sympathy. Rebecca's gaze shifted from Zoe to Jackson. She glared at him accusingly. He shrugged his shoulders and pushed the hair off his forehead. There was no idiot grin; the blue eyes held an unfamiliar expression. Could it be remorse?

Laney was whispering something again, but Rebecca didn't want to hear it. She didn't want to hear any of it. And she didn't want Jackson to suddenly grow a new image. It was too confusing. Scowling at no one in particular, she shook her head, settled herself in her chair facing straight forward, and opened her algebra book.

The girls worked quietly for the duration of Home Room. Rebecca kept her attention on her math book, studiously ignoring Jackson and Josh and occasionally sneaking a glance at the Fat Man. When the period ended, the room came alive with the sound of books closing, papers rustling, and chairs scraping. There was little conversation.

Josh sprang to his feet. "Gotta go, Jacks," he said. "Training for the Full Tilt. He punched Jackson on the arm and headed for the door.

Jackson took his time getting to his feet. He stood a little off balance, favoring the mending ankle.

"Hey," he said to Rebecca.

She glanced in his direction and then turned her attention to her knapsack, willing her face smooth and her expression bland.

Jackson shifted his weight unconsciously to the other foot and then back to the good ankle. "I can get the pictures back for you."

Rebecca looked coolly at him. "Teacher's pet," she said.

Surprise flickered across Jackson's face, and something else that passed too quickly for Rebecca to name. The idiot grin appeared. "If sock lint is that important to you," he countered.

"Don't bother," Rebecca said. "I can get them myself."

The idiot grin slipped a little. There was a little pause before Jackson dipped his chin, the briefest of nods. He tucked his book under one arm. "See ya, Becka," he said, and he turned and walked away. He wasn't limping at all.

Rebecca slipped her pack over one shoulder and walked to the back of the room where Zoe and Sam were waiting. "I'm getting Ty's pictures back," she announced to them. To their questioning looks, she said, "The ones Mr. Hammond took."

"Jeez, Becks." Sam looked uneasy. Zoe touched Rebecca's arm, but she said nothing.

Before her courage could fade, Rebecca marched up to Mr. Hammond's desk. The big man looked up at her, his face impassive. Rebecca felt her insides settle. She mentally braced herself and looked directly at him, struggling to school her own face into a neutral expression.

"May I have my pictures back?" There was the tiniest pause before she added, "Please."

Mr. Hammond looked at Rebecca, eyes glittering with malice. He leaned back in his chair. The springs protested loudly. He picked up the pictures, but his gaze remained fixed on Rebecca. She could feel her heart hammering, and her palms were sweaty.

"I don't think so, *Ms.* Coleson." Mr. Hammond sat forward again, the springs protesting once more. He held the photos between the thumb and forefinger of each hand and deliberately ripped them into two pieces. His eyes never left her face as he ripped them again before dropping them into his waste can.

Rebecca bit her lower lip. She knew her face was no longer neutral. She could barely believe what she had just witnessed. She felt fury smoking up from her belly. She glared at Mr. Hammond for long seconds. His fleshy cheeks cracked in a smile, displaying uneven teeth, but there was no smile in his eyes. The look there was mean and challenging. Rebecca turned on her heel and fled down the aisle.

Zoe and Sam were waiting at the door for her.

"What happened?"

"What pictures, Becks?"

"Did you get them?"

Rebecca waved off their questions, her lips pressed into a thin line. Too furious to speak, she pushed through the throng of students filling the wide hall and out the big front doors. Zoe and Sam followed her. AJ was waiting for them. She looked at Rebecca's face and then questioningly from Zoe to Sam.

"We don't know exactly," said Zoe to AJ's unasked question. "But it involves the Fat Man, of course." They followed Rebecca out into the sunshine.

Rebecca stopped at the bottom of the broad steps to wait. She forced herself to take a deep breath. Her face was stony.

"Becks?" AJ put an arm around Rebecca's shoulders. Zoe laid her hand on Rebecca's arm. Sam shifted from one booted foot to the other, her face troubled.

"Ty's pictures," Rebecca began.

They nodded and waited.

"Remember the pictures she showed us that day? Of the puppies, before she could even take Anne Boleyn home?"

More nods. Rebecca spilled the entire story. How the pictures had been in the pocket of her lost jacket. How she had found the jacket in the back of her locker. How she had stuffed them into a pocket in her book bag and they had fallen out when she was looking for a pencil. How first Jackson had grabbed them, and then Josh. And finally, His Fatness.

"Sock lint," said Rebecca. Her friends looked at her, mystified. Rebecca didn't explain.

"Mr. Hammond took them," she said. Her voice was hard. "I went up to him after class to ask for them back. Politely. I said please."

Heads bobbed encouragement.

"He just stared at me," said Rebecca. "With a really mean look. He said, and I quote, 'I don't think so, *Ms.* Coleson.' And he tore them up and dropped them in the trash."

Three sets of disbelieving eyes stared at Rebecca. It might have been funny if it had been someone else. Someone else the object of Fat Mr. Hammond's malice. Someone else with three pairs of eyes staring at her dumfounded, mouths hanging open in total synchrony. But it wasn't. No one spoke. Even AJ's normal coolness was shaken by this news.

Rebecca nodded her head emphatically. "He tore up Ty's pictures and threw them in the trash," she repeated.

"He can't do that!" Zoe was indignant.

"He did!" Rebecca snapped. "He already did."

"What are you going to do?" asked AJ quietly.

Sam watched Rebecca, but she said nothing. Her usual cheerful smile was missing.

"Do? What can I *do*? It's done!" She grasped a handful of hair in one hand in a very Ty-like gesture. "He's toxic," she said. "And he has it in for me. Why?"

"I think he hates girls," said Zoe. "He probably hates his mother too."

"If he even *has* a mother," said Sam.

AJ and Zoe giggled and then glanced quickly at Rebecca. Amusement flickered briefly in Rebecca's eyes, but the smoldering anger quickly returned.

AJ guided them away from the swarm of students still spilling out of the school, Rebecca at her side. Sam and Zoe followed. They walked in silence, avoiding as best they could the throngs of students. Rebecca was deep in thought, her face intent.

"What would set him off?" Rebecca muttered. She spoke more to herself than to her friends. "I mean really tear him up. What does he really love?"

"You mean more than the jocks?" Sam tried to ease the tense mood.

"He does seem to love the jocks," agreed Zoe.

"I don't know what he feels for the jocks," said AJ. "But I don't think it's love. I don't think he's capable of love."

"Not for anything warm and breathing anyway," said Sam.

Rebecca was still musing out loud. "Yeah, you're right," she said to no one in particular. She stopped abruptly and whirled around. Sam collided with her. AJ slowed and Zoe walked into her. Arms pinwheeled and feet did little dances as the girls fought to save their balance and separate from the pileup. Rebecca righted herself first and looked in triumph at her friends.

"More than the jocks," she said again. "And not something warm and breathing."

Uncomprehending, they stared at her.

Rebecca huffed in exasperation. "Come on," she prompted. "He's a fat, lazy slob, but he parks at the edge of the parking lot. He makes the jocks clean and polish it when they screw up. It must have killed him when he ran over Jackson, and not because he was worried about him."

AJ was the first to get it. A little gasp from Zoe indicated she had caught on too. AJ and Zoe looked at each other and then at Rebecca.

"His car!" the two girls said in unison.

"His car," Rebecca said flatly. A little smile played around the corners of her mouth, but her eyes were far from smiling as she turned and headed up the street. AJ, Sam, and Zoe watched in silence for several heartbeats before hurrying after her.

Sam was the first to catch up. She caught Rebecca by the arm and dragged her to a stop. "What are you going to do?" Sam repeated AJ's question.

"Do?" Rebecca laughed. It was a brittle sound. "I'm going to go home, fall facedown on my bed, and, hopefully, wake up just in time to graduate," she said. She pulled her arm free and glared at Sam. "What on earth could I possibly *do*?"

Rebecca turned on her heel and walked away. Sam, Alexa, and Zoe stared after her.

CHAPTER 37

Birthday Bribery

May 29

REBECCA TRUDGED UP the stairs and into the kitchen, the strap of her backpack in one hand, the pack bumping along behind her. She had told her friends the day before, after the disaster with Fat Mr. Hammond, that she was going to go home and fall on her face. She had done pretty much that, dropping into a heavy sleep lasting until supper. Dinner had been catch-as-catch-can, with her mother working late in the office on a project. Lissa had been at the doll shop. Her dad had fixed something for Andy, and the two of them had eaten by the time Rebecca came upstairs. She had foraged for herself and returned to her room.

She had tried to study—had, in fact, completed her algebra assignments. That had been no small task. She had wondered briefly how Jackson and Josh were faring, given Mr. Hammond's pitiless homework levels, and quickly decided she didn't care, especially in the face of Jackson's abandonment of her in Home Room. *That's not fair,* Laney had whispered. Rebecca didn't care. She had tackled her English homework, which was tedious and boring. She had not finished it. She had looked closely at her government studies review sheet and decided she was in good shape there. And she had been in bed early. But sleep had been elusive and restless when it finally came. She felt like she had plowed fields all night, or some other manually exhausting task. And her brain felt like mush. Again.

It was Wednesday. Would this week never end?

As Rebecca came into the kitchen, she was greeted by the sight of her mother leaning against the counter, stirring cream into her coffee.

Maggie looked up and smiled. On the island sat an oversized lone cupcake with one candle, and several colorful envelopes.

"Happy birthday, Rebecca Jean," said her mom warmly. She set her coffee cup on the counter, crossed the kitchen to meet Rebecca, and pulled her into a big hug.

Rebecca leaned into her mother's embrace. She felt warmed and protected. She had actually forgotten today was her birthday in the aftermath of all the weekend excitement. The week before finals was a rotten time to be born. Growing up was no picnic. Some days she wished she could have stayed a little girl, never having to leave the safety of her mother's arms.

"What are the envelopes?" she asked, her face snuggled against her mother's neck. She smelled the familiar, slightly citrusy scent of her mother's shampoo.

"Acknowledgments of your birthday from far-flung relatives," said her mom.

"Cool," said Rebecca, but she didn't move. "Do I get the cupcake for breakfast?" she asked hopefully.

"I don't see why not," said her mother.

"Seriously?" Rebecca pulled back to look at her mother.

"Sure. You only turn fifteen once." Maggie said.

Rebecca's surprise and pleasure was quickly deflated when her gaze fell on a suitcase sitting beside the bottom step of the stairs, a neatly-folded linen jacket lying across the bag.

"Oh." Rebecca sighed. "That's right. You're leaving today." She appraised her mother thoughtfully. "So you're just bribing me."

"Well, yes," agreed Maggie. "So make the most of it, would be my advice."

Rebecca couldn't help but smile. Not only had she forgotten her mother was going to Telluride for a conference, she had forgotten her own birthday. Her brain really *was* mush!

"Nanna's picking Andy up at school, and he'll spend two nights with her," said Maggie. "I know you and Lissa will be fine. Your dad will be home early."

"When do you get back?"

"Sunday noonish."

Maggie sipped her coffee, and Rebecca sniffed at the cupcake. She took a tentative bite and set the sweet back on the counter.

"Josh rides in fat-tire races at Telluride," Rebecca said. At her mother's questioning look, she added, "Josh Kenyon. The guys call him Telluride. Because of the bike races. He's a friend of Jackson's." The usual venom reserved for references to Jackson was missing from her voice.

"Are you and Jackson becoming . . . a little more friendly?" inquired Maggie.

"I'd say that's a bit over the top," said Rebecca. "Mostly, I think it's more that I'm learning how to sort of handle him. At least sometimes."

Maggie looked at Rebecca, feeling a tug at her heart. This child was such a complex set of contradictions—one moment seeming so innocent and vulnerable, the next so grown-up.

"That sounds like a topic for a girls' day," said her mom. She put her hands on Rebecca's shoulders and looked into her eyes. "I promised you after I got back, we'd have a shopping day. Something special. Let's get finals out of the way, and then do something big, just you and me."

"Bigger than shopping?"

"Bigger than shopping. Why don't you think about it while I'm gone. I will too. We'll decide later." Maggie hugged Rebecca fiercely. "Now I have to go. It's a long drive."

"Where's Andy?"

"Your dad took him for breakfast and is dropping him off at school."

"More bribery?"

"I like to think of it more as a distraction," said Maggie.

"Lissa's gone already?"

Maggie nodded.

Rebecca sighed. "So it's just me this morning."

"Just you, Becka," said her mother softly. "And you'll do fine. Just remember to go out through the garage. Everything else is locked up."

"I know, Mom. I've done it a thousand times." Rebecca sighed.

A wave of remorse washed over Maggie. How could she just leave for four days when this child needed her? No, not a child anymore.

Words tumbled through Maggie's head. In the end, all she said was, "I love you, Princess."

"Me too, Mom. It's cool. Go on."

There was nothing else to do, so Maggie picked up her jacket and headed for the door. Rebecca followed her to the door and watched as her mother loaded her things into her car.

Her hand on the car door, Maggie turned and looked at Rebecca. "Things have a way of working out," she said. "Even when life seems really confusing. When there are things happening that you don't quite understand."

Rebecca smiled a sad little smile. "And this is one of those times?" she said.

Maggie's heart tugged at her again. "Isn't it?"

"Yeah. I guess it is. I'll be okay, Mom. Don't worry."

"I know you will, Becka," Maggie said.

Rebecca watched as her mom folded herself into the car, drawing long legs in and pulling the door shut. She fastened her seatbelt, checked the mirrors, started the engine. Slipped the car into reverse. Her foot on the brake pedal, she looked up and smiled at Rebecca and then waved her a kiss.

Rebecca waved back. She couldn't see that her mother's eyes were bright with unshed tears. She watched the car easing out of the garage and down the driveway into the street. Rebecca stood where she was as the big door lumbered down and settled with a thud onto the concrete. Just like old Mrs. Lamont's door had done, trapping little Anne Boleyn inside, alone and frightened.

Rebecca walked back into the kitchen. The house was very quiet and felt strangely empty. She glanced through the cards on the island, noting return addresses. She stacked the envelopes neatly and looked at the cupcake. She picked it up and took another bite. A cupcake for breakfast. It reminded her of one of her favorite movies, where the witches give their nieces chocolate brownies for breakfast. It would be fun to be a witch. To be able to make things happen. Magical things.

You mean like writing a story and it happens? That sort of magical thing? The voice was Laney's, and it brought Rebecca up sharply. She put the cupcake down and stared hard at it.

"It's all about energy," her grandmother had said. What did Nanna know? Could she shed some light on all these strange events? Rebecca mulled over that idea. It was pretty scary, but it no longer seemed totally ridiculous.

Rebecca stood perfectly still and closed her eyes. She opened her senses to the house around her. Did she actually hear, or just imagine on some level, the sounds of laughter, the voices of her parents, Andy calling for Scoundrel? The murmur of her mother's voice in the office. Lissa watching her favorite dance show. Her father's country music, her mother's classic rock. Scoundrel snoring in his bed, Tinker at the French doors demanding to be let in. Suddenly the house didn't feel so empty. It was filled with the energy of all the people she loved best, and who loved her regardless of her imperfections. She felt warmed and heartened. She could still hear Tinker at the French doors. Maybe things weren't so bad.

Rebecca took a deep breath. Smiling to herself she opened her eyes. Tinker really *was* at the French doors, and she was demanding to be let in!

Rebecca laughed. "So you're real after all," she said. She opened the door, and Tinker slipped inside, winding herself around Rebecca's ankles. Rebecca picked her up and nuzzled her face in the soft fur. "I'll give you a treat," she said. "Just because you're you. And then I have to go to school and face . . . events."

Rebecca put Tinker on the floor. She filled Tinker's bowl with a generous helping of her favorite kibbles. She swung her book bag over her shoulder and looked around the warm and inviting kitchen, well ordered and spotless just as her mother liked it, the neatly stacked birthday cards and the cupcake making a splash of bright color on the counter. She walked resolutely to the mudroom. She paused, turned, and came back to the kitchen. She picked up the cupcake and took another bite. She put the rest in a storage container and tucked it into her book bag. She let herself out of the house, checking to see that the door was securely locked. She was smiling to herself as she walked down the street and toward school.

CHAPTER 38

The Binder

May 29

WHEN REBECCA SLID into her seat in algebra, Josh and Jackson were already there. She thought they looked a little glassy eyed. Mr. Hammond demanded assignments be turned in, and a chorus of sighs and groans accompanied the rustling of pages as homework was passed forward. Rebecca couldn't look at the Fat Man. She could feel a dull sensation in the pit of her stomach, but she wasn't sure if it was anger or an idea. Perhaps some of both. Her thoughts kept returning to her musings of the day before. *What does he love most?*

His car. But how did that knowledge help her? The class dragged on, everyone quiet under the pressure of Mr. Hammond's unjust demands. At the end of the period Jackson and Josh barreled for the door ahead of everyone else. Rebecca gathered her things and joined the crush filing out. His car. The hairs on the back of her neck prickled, and she sneaked a peak over her shoulder at Mr. Hammond. His piggy little eyes were square on her, and she could feel the venom in his stare. Her stomach clenched involuntarily, and she jerked her head straight. Her heart was racing.

Damn! she thought. *He really does hate me*! She felt a sudden urge to turn and flip him off. That would just about do it! *He's gonna get me. Somehow. Unless I get him first.*

Rebecca hurried down the hall toward her science class. Mr. Hammond receded in her mind as she thought of the big cupcake in her backpack. Ty was already at their table. Rebecca dropped the backpack onto her chair and rummaged inside it for the cupcake. Smiling in triumph, she plopped it unceremoniously on the table in front of Ty. It was now a little misshapen, but no matter. She produced two napkins and plastic forks.

"For me? You shouldn't have . . ." Ty smiled back at her.

"I didn't exactly," said Rebecca. "This is my breakfast. Want to share it with me?"

"Your breakfast! Since when does your mom let you eat cake for breakfast?"

"Since she had to leave on business this morning. Guilt can be a powerful motivator." Rebecca's smile was sly.

"Jeez," said Ty. "Your mom leaving, finals next week. What a great time to have a birthday."

"Yeah, I'm all over that one," said Rebecca. "Let's eat this quick in case we have to do something repulsive in class today. It's bad enough that it smells funky in here."

The girls dug into the cupcake. It was down to crumbs before the bell rang.

"Mmm." Rebecca licked the last bit of frosting off her fork. "That should be enough sugar to get me through English."

"Yum. Thanks." Ty licked her fingers and nodded.

Science class was all review, with no disgusting experiments, and the morning proceeded uneventfully.

Mrs. Lindzer allowed students to work on finals review during the class period. The two girls worked quietly together, occasionally comparing notes on a problem. Brittany was in no better mood than she had been on Tuesday, and Clarity had taken the chair where Jackson usually sat at the end of the pod. Jackson breezed in just after the bell, not limping at all. He looked at Clarity, frowned, but then slipped into the chair opposite Rebecca and Tyler. He shared a glance with Travis, who, as usual, looked calm and unruffled. Jackson was still wearing the slightly dazed expression he had worn in algebra. The pod—in fact the entire class—was quiet throughout the hour.

"I'll see you at lunch," said Rebecca at the end of class.

Ty nodded. "Yep. See ya, Becks!" And she was gone.

Rebecca watched the red ponytail until it disappeared into the crowd, and then she turned and ran in the opposite direction.

RAINIE YORK

Rebecca hurried into the drama classroom just before the final bell. Most of the seats were full, and there were students perched on the apron of the little stage. Rebecca slipped into an open desk. Angela was across the aisle and forward one seat, the big pageant binder resting on her desk. She was sitting sideways in her chair, talking to the boy in front of Rebecca. Chas sat directly behind Angela. He nodded and winked. Rebecca smiled back. Angela gave no outward sign that she had even seen Rebecca . . . how could she not have? She swiveled forward in her seat and cradled the big pageant binder to her chest.

Mr. Tilson was already at his desk. The fat script he had been editing was nowhere in sight. Instead, conspicuous on his desk, were two hats. As the bell sounded, he pushed back his chair and strode around his desk rubbing his hands together, teeth flashing white in his tan face. He perched on the edge of his desk, one leg swinging.

"So," he said, "we're going to have some fun today."

The class waited. Expressions were mixed. Apprehension. Mild interest. Expectation.

"I assume you're all working on your discussion points." Mr. Tilson looked around the room, still smiling broadly. "No? Saving it for the last moment, are we?"

There were uneasy murmurs, and desks creaked as some students shifted nervously in their seats. Angela brushed a hand over perfectly cut blonde hair, uncrossed and then recrossed slender legs. She glanced over her shoulder at Rebecca. Rebecca had passed the discussion points assignment criteria to her as requested by Mr. Tilson. The Ice Maiden had acted bored and disinterested. "I've got it covered," she had said tersely and had turned and walked away. Rebecca had thought, *And many thanks to you too, bitch!*

"We're going to do a little miming," Mr. Tilson continued. "It's good experience for body acting, if you need a reason for today's activity." His smile widened. "But the real reason is that I find it tremendously amusing to watch."

There was wary laughter from the class.

"You won't be graded," Mr. Tilson went on. "But participation is not optional." His smile was now more of a Cheshire grin. "I will draw a name from this hat." He picked up one of the hats and held it aloft. It was a bowler with a red feather stuck jauntily into the band. Rebecca remembered seeing it in the costume closet.

"Each participant will draw a challenge from this hat." Mr. Tilson held up the second hat, this one a western ten-gallon. "You will then mime your challenge." He paused, still grinning. It was an impish grin.

"You must draw blind," he continued. "You may exchange your challenge if you don't like it, but you will still be drawing blind. You may do this twice. Then you must choose from among your draws. Each participant will have two minutes. I strongly suggest you use some of that time to prepare yourself."

There were groans and murmurs of protest. Every student in class knew two minutes onstage could feel like two years, especially if you didn't know what you were doing. The prep time, however, would evaporate in what felt like a nanosecond.

"Observers—you," Mr. Tilson gestured around the room at his students, "will call out when you think you know what a mime is portraying."

"This is just charades," someone called from the back of the room.

"Quite like," said Mr. Tilson. He looked around the room. "Any questions? No? Then let's have some fun."

The first name out of the hat—could it be coincidence?—was a senior with enviable acting skills. He would be a difficult act to follow, but his performance might provide inspiration to those less . . . enthusiastic . . . about miming. Rebecca fell into this category. She didn't like mimes, and she thought her body acting was weak. Still, if no one was to be graded . . .

The senior drew a slip of paper, studied it, and got right to it. His mime was identified with time to spare. He bowed and returned to his seat amid appreciative applause. The next name drawn belonged to a sophomore whom Rebecca had never actually seen perform. However, he was comfortable in his own skin, a great comic, and easily made people laugh. Perhaps every day was just an act to him. His mime was never identified, but the class was engulfed in laughter before his attempts were over. He returned to his seat, grinning widely. One by one, students were called to the front of the class, and the spirit of the performances was fun and lighthearted. Animated cheers and whistles greeted any performer whose mime was identified.

Rebecca held her breath each time Mr. Tilson pulled a name out of the bowler hat, but she was enjoying herself. Chas was called up, his mime was identified at the last second, and he came back to his seat, grinning and bowing to a round of clapping. Mr. Tilson reached again into the bowler.

"It's our own beauty queen, Ms. Angela Thornton," announced Mr. Tilson.

Angela stiffened. She remained frozen in her seat with the pageant binder clutched against her chest. Mr. Tilson looked at her expectantly. Rebecca wondered if Angela would bolt again. Chas was still standing in the aisle. He draped a long arm around Angela's shoulders.

"Come, come," said Chas in his best Mr. Tilson voice. He extricated the binder from Angela's arms, placed it on her desk, and pulled her to her feet. Laney suddenly came on full alert in Rebecca's head. Rebecca's heart pounded with anticipation. She had an idea, and she didn't need Laney to spell it out!

Angela was still rooted to the floor, her anxious gaze going from Mr. Tilson to her binder. Chas gave her a little push, and Angela began to move, almost stumbling, toward the front of the room. She glanced back at the binder, now sitting vulnerably on her desk, but Chas gave her another little shove. Reluctantly, Angela moved forward again.

Rebecca seized the moment.

"Chas!" she whispered urgently. "Change seats with me!" She had one chance at this. She was out of her seat and sliding into Charles's empty desk before he could protest. He looked at her curiously but didn't object. He perched on Rebecca's desk, arms folded across his chest, and turned his attention to the front of the room.

Rebecca stretched over the front of the desk and snagged the pageant binder, pulling it onto her lap and sliding low in the seat in one smooth movement. She prayed the students in front of her would block her from Angela's view. She glanced toward the front of the room. Angela's back was to the class as she reached into the ten-gallon for a slip of paper.

Her heart thudding in her ears, Rebecca opened the binder. It was carefully tabbed in a flowery hand. She scanned the headings. They meant nothing to her. They were just dates! She flipped to the first date tab. Subheadings marched neatly down the edge of the page. Judging categories? This made more sense. Rebecca skimmed quickly over headings for entry requirements, business dress, swimsuit, interview, judges' panel. Talent! Rebecca's heart leaped. She thumbed to that section and scanned the page. It was a description of Angela's first skit.

Rebecca stole a glance toward the front of the room. Apparently, Angela had been unhappy with her first draw. Holding a slip of paper in one hand, she was again reaching into the ten-gallon hat. Rebecca had a minuscule reprieve. She flipped back to the main headings, trying to make sense of the dates. The second date was more than a week away, on the weekend following finals. Angela's next pageant? Rebecca flipped to the section and selected the "Talent" heading. The page was blank. Just a plastic page protector, empty. Puzzled, Rebecca turned to the next page. On the left side, arrayed inside the plastic, were colorful cutouts of assorted wardrobe items ranging from swimwear to formal. The right-hand page was titled "Dressing for the Pageant: A Humorous Look at Selecting Attire for a Scholarship Competition." Rebecca's heart seemed to stop. She could barely breathe. The description that followed was exactly as she had suggested it to Angela. There was even a notation in parentheses about diving for treasure at The Morning After! Disbelief was followed by a cold, mounting fury.

Laughter and applause caused Rebecca to look up. Angela was smiling happily. Her mime was finished; someone had guessed it. Could the Ice Maiden act, or had Angela just gotten lucky? Either way, Rebecca's time was up. She snapped the binder shut and leaned forward to return it to Angela's desk. She slid out of the seat and all but pushed Charles back into it, slipping into her own desk as Angela started down the aisle. Angela's smile faded. She looked with suspicion at them. Rebecca stared back at Angela, her face a neutral mask. At least she hoped it was. Her heart was racing. She could feel a warm flush in her cheeks. Angela seated herself and placed both hands on the binder. She opened the cover, thumbed through the divider pages. Closed the binder and rested her arms on it, her fingers curled around the top edge. She glanced over her shoulder at Rebecca again. Rebecca stared back at her, expressionless.

At lunch Rebecca was distracted and withdrawn. After initial attempts to jolly her out of her mood, the other girls let her be. Rebecca was relieved.

After French, Rebecca traipsed down the stairs with Zoe, her mind racing. At the girls' loo, she tugged on Zoe's arm. "You go ahead," she said and ducked into the bathroom. She closed herself in a stall and waited until the corridor was quiet. Holding her breath, she slipped out of the lavatory and hurried down the hall. Away from Home Room. They couldn't do anything to her this late in the school year, could they? And besides, wasn't Home Room supposed to be optional? She wasn't sure, but it didn't matter. Pausing at the entrance, she glanced over her shoulder. What was she expecting to see? Mr. Hammond or the vice principal coming for her with handcuffs? She chuckled to herself at the image, but it was a dark sound, more like a soft growl. She stepped into the warm sunshine of the late May day. There were a surprising number of students around, but no one paid her the slightest attention. She hurried toward home, her thoughts tumbling back and forth between Angela and Fat Mr. Hammond. A little niggling in the pit of her stomach pulled at her. She was forgetting something . . . but what? Well, she'd figure that out later.

She was going home to an empty house. This was unusual since her mother worked from home. Rebecca normally didn't like being alone at the house. Like this morning, it seemed somehow less welcoming when there was no one else there. Now it felt like an opportunity, and she was excited. She had made a decision and was eager to get on with it.

She let herself into the house and dropped her backpack on the bench in the mudroom. She glanced at the birthday cards lying on the counter. There were a few crumbs from the lone cupcake. She smashed the crumbs onto her finger and licked them off. Dry. She made a face. She foraged for a snack. With no one around, she'd have whatever she wanted. She tapped one finger against her lips as she studied the contents of the pantry. Hmm. What *did* she want? Surely there was something delicious and forbidden in here. She found a carefully hidden, vacuum-sealed canister of Nanna's chocolate cookies. Rebecca wrinkled her nose. Maybe there were some of the pumpkin-pecan . . . A search of the pantry left her disappointed. She settled on a bag of cheddar popcorn left over from her party. Could that have only been four nights ago? She took a bottle of water and the popcorn and headed for her room. She hesitated at the top of the stairs, glancing back at the birthday cards. No, that could wait. This . . . other . . . was tugging at her.

CHAPTER 39

Double Hitter

May 29

R EBECCA JEAN PULLED her bedroom door closed behind her. The latch snicked softly into place. Walking lightly on the balls of her feet, she moved across the room to her desk. To her computer. Now that she had decided to do this, she was feeling a sort of guilty glee; knowing what she was about to do could get her into trouble. Probably *big* trouble. But no one would ever believe it, not in a million years, so how could she get caught? And besides, it might not even work.

No. Deep down, she knew it would work. She set her water and popcorn carefully on the desk beside her keyboard. More trouble if her parents knew she was eating in her bedroom. Rules, rules, rules. Sometimes it seemed there was no end to the rules, and they were all so meaningless! She sat down in her chair and rolled close to the desk. She felt a sense of power and a tingling anticipation as she opened her Events folder and scanned the list of files: The Jerk, Branch of Broken Dates, Found Puppy.

Rebecca hesitated, busying herself with straightening her desktop, eating a couple bites of popcorn, taking a sip of water. She was stalling, and she knew it. She took a deep breath and reached for the mouse, her fingers hovering just above it. Her left hand found its way into her hair and twirled a lock around one finger, around and around. She settled her right hand over the mouse, her fingers curling around the small device, and clicked the left button to open a new file. She titled it Louisville Slugger.

She closed her eyes, took another deep breath, letting it out slowly, and focused her mind as she had taught herself to do. "Sometimes you're the Louisville slugger / Sometimes you're the ball." She unconsciously sang a bit of the Dire Straits song, toneless and under her breath. "Sometimes you're the windshield / Sometimes you're the bug." The pads of her fingers tingled. She rubbed her hands together and returned them to the keyboard. "Sometimes it all comes together baby / Sometimes you're going lose it all." She opened her eyes and stared fixedly at the monitor, but her attention was on something else, something removed, something . . . far away.

"Today," she said aloud to the empty room, "I am the Louisville slugger." And she began to type.

> Mr. Hammond reluctantly parked his prized BMW in a faculty spot close to the bleachers. Most teachers enjoyed the perk of close-in parking for sports events, but he didn't like the risk of picking up door dings. Most teachers didn't have gorgeous cars, so it hardly mattered if the doors got dinged. But he was late.
>
> Mr. Hammond didn't want to be at this baseball game at all. School was out; high school sports were over till the start of football practice. This was a post-season exhibition game with a Saints' rival, not even a very good one, set up by the two head coaches who apparently had no life outside of baseball. Mr. Hammond was regretting his commitment to stand in for another teacher to oversee the concession stand. To make matters worse, the Saints' star player was on the injured list. The irony was not lost on Mr. Hammond that the star player was out because he himself had run him over.
>
> Mr. Hammond pried his bulk out of the car, closed the door, and pressed his remote to lock it. The car beeped pleasingly back at him. He used his shirtsleeve to remove a smudge on the doorframe and ran his hand lovingly over the front fender that had been damaged by Jackson's bike. There was no sign of the accident. He had been concerned about matching the paint exactly, but the repair was flawless. Black paint gleamed in the sun. He smiled in smug satisfaction as

he walked toward the entrance, glancing over his shoulder to admire the big car one more time.

Later, with the concessions running smoothly, Mr. Hammond was able to watch the game. The Saints were on a roll, cleaning up on the visiting team, and Mr. Hammond wondered why they hadn't played this well during the regular season. Anson Nolan was at bat, but he seemed only half interested. No wonder, given the score. The pitcher was struggling. Anson was toying with him, swinging early and hitting foul balls repeatedly into the third-base stands.

"Wait for the pitch," Mr. Hammond muttered under his breath.

As if he had heard Mr. Hammond's thoughts, Anson stepped out of the box, wriggled his body in some bizarre gyrations, took a practice swing. He stepped back into the box. He waited for the next pitch. The pitcher pulled from somewhere deep to send a sizzling fastball over the plate. Anson was caught by surprise. He made a heroic swing, but he was late. Foul again, but this time over the first-base bleachers. The stands grew quiet, and necks craned as the ball climbed up and up and back over the bleachers, and then begin its way down, leisurely, lazily, as if in slow motion. This ball was going clear to the parking lot! And then it was no longer in slow motion. The ball sailed past the stands and hurled downward. There was a dull crunch, followed by a nearly simultaneous shattering crash.

A man standing next to Mr. Hammond turned to him, grinning. "There goes some unlucky bugger's windshield," he said.

Mr. Hammond's stomach lurched. He turned and lumbered toward the entrance, his pulse drumming in his ears. He was nearly running, panting in loud gasps by the time he reached his car. Horrified, he stood looking at his precious BMW. There was a huge dent in the hood, and the windshield was shattered, glass littered everywhere inside the car. Tears of helpless rage and frustration ran down Mr. Hammond's pudgy face.

Rebecca stopped typing. She took a deep breath and sat back in her chair. She read over the paragraphs she had written. She sipped her water and munched on cheddar popcorn, her eyes distant and dreamy. She shook her head. *Where does this come from?* she asked herself.

She read on. She smiled in satisfaction when she reached the end where Mr. Hammond stood alone, furious and powerless, crying over his precious car.

"Are you feelin' that?" she said half aloud.

She nodded to herself and hit Save, still staring at the screen. She took a deep breath. Another. Her movements slow and deliberate, she opened another new file and began to type.

> Angela was supremely confident as she waited to parade onto the stage for the bathing suit competition. Her performance had been so far flawless. There had been several bloopers by other contestants, making her look that much better. The girl with the operatic voice had badly missed a note; her confidence had been shaken and the rest of her performance had been stiff. One girl had suffered from wardrobe problems and been forced to hold her dress together on the runway. Another contestant had dropped her prop. Interview answers had been lame. It was really Angela's to lose.
>
> She teetered just a bit on her high heels. She glanced down to admire them. What a find she had made, snagging them for five dollars at that secondhand shop. They were really very high, but she adored them. And they made her legs look longer, more elegant.
>
> The swimsuit competition was very well done, Angela thought, especially for a pageant of this level. A koi pond, complete with waterfall, fish, and lush greenery, had been set up on the stage. The girls appeared from behind the waterfall and were to stroll past the pond before making their swing down the runway.
>
> It was her turn. Nerves made her teeter again on the heels. She ran her hands over her perfectly styled blonde

hair, tugged at the bottom of her swimsuit. She took a deep breath to compose herself.

She stepped into the lights. Moving perfectly in the heels, she walked with unhurried strides. Smiling graciously at the judges, she made her promenade past the waterfall. She could feel a cool mist on her legs. As she strolled past the pond, she waved at the audience. It was a nice touch, totally spontaneous. The audience loved it. No way could she lose this.

And then she made a misstep. It was tiny, but just enough. Her stride broke. She was a little off balance. Her foot slipped off the edge of one heel. She lurched forward with her other foot. The heel skidded on the smooth floor. She staggered, dangerously close to the edge of the pond. She tried to right herself, almost had it, but couldn't quite capture her balance in the ridiculously high heels. Arms flailing, she plunged into the koi pond.

Rebecca reread the story, her eyes still distant. She wondered again where it all came from—the koi pond, the problems of the other contestants, the wave for the audience. But it felt right. And she had been eerily accurate with the other Events. She sat perfectly still, her head tilted as if listening to a far-off voice.

Nothing more. She nodded to herself.

"Okay. That should do it." She named the file High Heels and saved it. She closed her laptop and went upstairs.

CHAPTER 40

What Goes Around Comes Around

May 29

A S THE HIGH of her trance-like state wore off, Rebecca was left feeling restless and kind of prickly. She wandered through the kitchen, the family room, her mother's office. Silent and empty without her mother, the office filled her with a piercing loneliness. She went back to the kitchen and stood looking at the pile of birthday cards. There was no sense of excitement or wonder, but she decided to look at the cards, methodically slitting each envelope and inspecting its contents. They all contained money. Rebecca counted the crisp bills and checks, totaling them up in her head. Added to the gift certificate from Pappa and the twenty dollars for helping her dad wash his truck—well, she was loaded!

Even so, her spirits lifted only a little.

She retrieved her book bag from the mudroom and plopped it unceremoniously on a kitchen chair. She pulled out her notes from morning classes, wondering what she had missed after lunch. The muffled buzz of her iPhone, still on Mute from classes, made her jump, and she dug into the deep inner pocket of the bag to retrieve it. It was Lissa.

"Hey, Lissa," said Rebecca.

"Where are you!" Lissa's voice was angry.

"I'm at home," said Rebecca. "Where *would* I be?"

Her voice tight, enunciating carefully, Lissa said, "You are *supposed* to be at the drop zone, where I am to pick you up and take you to your interview."

Rebecca's heart plummeted to the pit of her stomach. "OMG!" She gasped for air, and her head rang. "OMG! I totally forgot! I came home early—"

"You came home early," Lissa repeated in a flat, disbelieving voice. "And now you are impossibly late for your interview. I have been looking for you for thirty minutes!"

"I forgot . . . I was . . . today has been . . . I forgot." There was nothing she could say, and her voice trailed off.

"I thought you wanted this job," said Lissa.

"I do!" wailed Rebecca. "I really do!"

"Well, it's probably moot now, because we can't possibly get you there in time," snapped her sister. "I'll just have to call Mrs. Mason and make excuses for you. What should I tell her? Run over by a bus? Detained for fighting in the cafeteria? Abducted by aliens?" Lissa's voice dripped with sarcasm.

"Lissa . . ."

"Well, it needs to be good," said her sister. "Don't move. Let me call her and then call you back. Don't. Move!" And the line went dead.

Rebecca dropped heavily into a chair and rested her head on her arms. What a mess! Where had it even begun? With her mom going away on her birthday. With that bucket of lard, Mr. Hammond. With Angela's pageant binder.

No. The voice was a soft whisper, barely discernible.

Rebecca's head came up slowly, her mind going very still. She stood up carefully, paced once around the island, and came back to the table. Perhaps it had begun with her writing Branch of Broken Dates. She didn't want to entertain this thought, but there it was. Not even asking permission to come in—just suddenly there.

No. Earlier. That was Laney's voice. Coming from inside her own head.

Rebecca clutched the back of the chair with both hands for support. She thought about the Jackson the Jerk Event. She heard Zoe's voice saying, *You're a matched pair.* Because she had fallen in her room. Her mind balked at the concept and raced on to Ann Boleyn going missing and the Found Puppy story. This brought no relief, however. There was the lost-and-then-found iPhone. She couldn't have had anything to do with the lost part of either of those. Could she? The found, though . . . Brittany going ballistic and the story that followed. AJ telling them of Brittany's broken date, complete with specific and damning details, as the girls listened wide eyed on the trampoline, surrounded by darkness and night sounds, the moon riding silently across the star-filled sky.

A disconnected memory floated through Rebecca's mind. She heard Nanna saying, "Well, it's the Law of Correspondences." Her mom and Nanna talking about some unknown set of events. "What we put out there certainly does come back around." Her mom laughing. The clink of glassware.

The Law of Correspondences, the Law of Correspondences. What goes around comes around. The words echoed through her head, repeating, repeating.

Rebecca wrapped her arms around her middle as though she had been sucker-punched. She sank heavily into a chair, nearly missing the seat. She had pretty much come to accept that she was making things happen by writing her little stories. But it had never occurred to her that she might have been also setting herself up for balancing reactions.

"Just coincidence," she said aloud. The sound of her own voice startled her.

Of course! None of this could be real. It was just too bizarre.

Sam's voice as she described Reiki. "It's all just energy. You can learn to read it. You can even learn to use it."

Nanna's voice after her party, talking about her new book. "It's about energy . . . about a girl who learns how to manipulate it with her mind for her own purposes."

But that's just a book. It's fiction!

Your fiction is based on real life, said Laney softly.

"Based on, not the same as," said Rebecca. Now she was talking out loud to the voice in her head, alone, in an empty house. She was certifiable!

Her phone bleeped its merry incoming call tune, and Rebecca jumped. Lissa again. She grabbed for the phone.

"Lissa . . ."

"You are incredibly lucky," said Lissa without preamble.

"I am?"

"Unfortunately, Mrs. Mason *isn't* so lucky," said Lissa.

"What do you mean?"

"Her granddaughter is ill, and Miss A. is going to Savannah for a few days. She's leaving tonight. She made her apologies." Lissa's voice dripped with the irony of it. "We'll just have to reschedule when she gets back."

"This can't be real," whispered Rebecca.

"Well, it is. So you have a reprieve. I'm not sure you deserve it, under the circumstances, but there it is. Happy birthday. Oh, and Dad's on his way home and he wants to take us both out to dinner. To celebrate your birthday," said Lissa.

"I don't think—"

"*Don't* think," Lissa cut in. "Just go with the flow. We'll leave all this out with Dad." And her phone cut off.

Rebecca sat at the table with her phone in her hand, staring at the wallpaper—a picture of Tinker and Scoundrel in a rare pose of friendliness—her eyes glassy and her head swimming.

This was too much! At least she hadn't done anything to make poor Mrs. Mason's granddaughter sick. She didn't even know her. She wasn't sure how all this stuff was connected, but she *was* sure none of it had anything to do with Mrs. Mason. Wasn't she? Was she really sure about *anything* these days? And the other stuff . . . She'd just have to put it out of her mind till later. She couldn't think about it now and get through a birthday dinner with her father. That's what she had to focus on, because she was pretty sure if she didn't, she'd choke on anything she tried to swallow.

***

Jack Coleson arrived home earlier than usual. Andy was at Nanna's. Lissa wasn't home yet. Jack looked around the cold kitchen and cocked his head as if listening for something.

"It's good we're going out," he said. "Let's go someplace nice. Since it's your birthday. Nice, but not too slow."

Rebecca nodded. Her head was still spinning. She knew Lissa was furious with her, but even so, she wished her sister would get home. She didn't know how she'd keep up a facade of normalcy with her father by herself.

"You and Lissa decide," said Rebecca. Her father opened his mouth to speak, and Rebecca shook her head. "To surprise me," she said. She smiled at her father, and he seemed to accept it, but the smile felt brittle on her face.

"Lissa's on the way. I'm going down to . . . partify . . . a little." And she made her escape.

Her father nodded absently. Rebecca turned back at the top of the stairs to look at him. He seemed lost and somehow . . . diminished. She had a sudden insight. Her father was the tough guy who seemed to make all the rules and set the standards, but it was her mother's gentle strength that guided the household and held things together. She felt another pang of loneliness and a heightened level of respect for her mother, along with a sudden rush of sympathy for her father. Without her mother—well, there was no thinking about such a thing! Her mother would be back in a couple days, and everything would return to normal. She could think about it then.

You're getting a lot of stuff in that box, whispered Laney as Rebecca hurried down the stairs.

"What box?" Rebecca spoke under her breath. This was getting to be a habit—this talking out loud to the voice in her head. She could be an inch away from completely bonkers. In light of all that was going on, however, it seemed the least of Rebecca's worries.

The box with all the stuff in it that you're not thinking about, said Laney.

Rebecca went into her bedroom and closed the door behind her. "I just need to get through dinner tonight," she said. "So get off my case!"

Laney had no response. Rebecca stood in the center of the room, her head tilted to one side, waiting for a reply. Huh. Could Laney be silenced that easily? How would that work exactly? The thought made

Rebecca giggle, and that little giggle lightened her mood immeasurably. She rotated her shoulders in an exaggerated fashion as if shrugging out of a heavy coat. She crossed to her closet. When she came out, she was wearing the little blue sweater and the white jacket her mother had bought her what seemed like years ago and a pair of white jeans. The new strappy sandals dangled from the fingers of one hand. She would focus on the fact that her mother had bought the sweater and jacket for her. And leave that disastrous day in Home Room "in the box." She waited for Laney to comment. When no reply came, Rebecca nodded to herself. She slipped the sandals on her feet and stood in front of her mirror, evaluating the effect. Not too bad. She was a little unsteady on her feet still, but she'd be sitting down most of the evening. Besides, she had to practice wearing the heels *sometime*. She ran a brush quickly through her hair, tossed it onto her bed, and headed for the door.

She could hear Lissa and her father talking as she came up the stairs. On the top step, she stopped and took a deep breath. She pasted a smile on her face and breezed into the kitchen.

***

The evening had passed fairly smoothly, but Rebecca was exhausted from the effort of acting normal, whatever that was. It had at least kept her mind off all the other stuff. Lissa had shown pity and rallied to keep the evening light and upbeat, telling funny stories about some of Mrs. Mason's doll clients and talking about all the new crystals arriving almost daily at The Center. How beautiful they were, how they all "felt" unique. Some made her palms tingle like Reiki. Rebecca had wondered if Lissa did Reiki too—was she the only one who didn't?—but didn't have the energy to pursue the idea out loud while also keeping her carefully constructed facade in place. There had been cheesecake at the end. And finally, they had gone home to a dark and empty house.

"Mom always thinks to leave a light on," said Rebecca sadly.

"Your mother thinks of a lot of things," said her father.

They all walked silently into the kitchen, where Tinker sat unperturbed on the island, her fuzzy butt parked on the pile of birthday cards.

"Yeah, she does." Lissa hugged their father, patting him on the back. "Couple more days," she said. She kissed him on the cheek. "'Night, Dad."

Rebecca hugged her father too, laying her cheek against his chest. "Thanks for dinner," she said. "It was the bomb."

"Really?" He seemed surprised. "You seemed . . . I thought you were a little . . . maybe missing your mom. So not a bad birthday?"

"Really, Dad. It was great."

"I'm glad, Princess," he said. He hugged her back hard. "So fifteen's pretty good?"

"Oh, yeah! Totally the best." The brittle smile. "But I still have finals in a couple days."

"Of course. Do your homework," said her father.

"You going to bed?"

"No, I'm going to call your mother first. Then probably read."

There didn't seem to be a response to this, so Rebecca just nodded. She grabbed her book bag and headed for the stairs.

"Come on, Tinks. 'Night, Dad."

"Goodnight, Princess." He smiled brightly.

Rebecca heard the hollowness in her father's voice. And with this came another insight. Were her father's rules because he worried what could happen to the rest of them? Was it an attempt to keep everyone safe? She had always assumed grown-ups were in complete control, but what if they weren't? Were they pretty much powerless, just ricocheting through life, bouncing off walls and into one another in random fashion? It was not a comforting thought.

All this had to go in the box. For sure! Rebecca wanted nothing in the world so much as to fall into bed and never think about anything again. If this day had been typical of being fifteen, she thought the best thing to do would be to just shoot herself. And do it now.

CHAPTER 41

A New View of Life as We Know It

May 30

REBECCA AWOKE THE next morning with Tinker curled behind her knees. She rolled onto her back and stretched luxuriously. Tinker protested, but then curled again next to her side. Rebecca stroked the silky head and was rewarded with a deep, rumbling purr. She turned her head to check the piece of sky visible through her high window. Clear and bright. The shrubbery was still. It looked like the beginning of a good day. But something didn't feel quite right.

And then, piece by piece, the previous day came back to her. She let the memories come without fighting them. Her mom leaving for four days, and on her birthday! Sharing the big cupcake with Ty in science class. The pageant binder in drama, confirming Angela's duplicity. Fat Mr. Hammond tearing up Ty's pictures. That had been the day before yesterday, but it played out with yesterday's Event marathon. Ditching Home Room. (Today would reveal any repercussions from that little act of rebellion.) Missing her appointment with Mrs. Mason. And at last, the torturous dinner with her father and Lissa to celebrate her birthday. Quite a load to be reviewing so early in the day!

But there was more. Rebecca lay motionless in bed except for the hand that absently stroked Tinker's head, her eyes directed toward the patch of blue sky but not focused on it. There was something else she had . . . done? Discovered? Ah . . . the connection between happenings in her own life and the stories. Tit for tat. What goes around comes around. Rebecca curled onto her side with a big sigh. And that wasn't all. Her insights about her father, and potentially all grown-ups. Was it all just a charade? Day number two of being fifteen, and already it sucked. She closed her eyes, wishing there were Rewind and Replay buttons for life so the last two days could be miraculously transformed, or erased. Maybe the last month would be better.

A spark of defiance ignited in Rebecca's gut. She threw back her covers and jumped out of bed.

"I don't think so!" she said to herself aloud. "Today I am going to have fun with my friends and pretend deepest respect for Fat Mr. Hammond, which will make him crazy. Smile sweetly at Angela, which will make *her* crazy. It's almost the weekend. Maybe Zoe and I should go down to the ranch to see Sam. Because that is certainly where she will be. And I will think about *nothing* else!"

More stuff in that box? This from Laney.

"Ah, so you are still around." Rebecca yanked her covers straight. Almost. "Yes, it's pretty damn full, and I don't care. Not today."

There was something from Laney. Not quite spoken. But Rebecca got the gist. Laney was, after all, in Rebecca's own head. "I'll figure it out later. Maybe after finals." Rebecca threw off her jams and headed for the shower.

Rebecca dressed in cropped jeans and a light sweater top. She fastened the mustang pendant around her neck. She would wear the strappy sandals. She slipped them on and admired the effect in her mirror. It would be an easy, breezy day. She was determined that it be so.

And it pretty much was. Everything was review in classes. Rebecca wasn't worried about the upcoming tests. Testing was easy for her, and she often thought it was preferable to the dreary chore of homework. She felt kind of bad for Ty, who was so psyched out by tests. When Rebecca walked into science and spotted Tyler, she put one hand to the pendant around her neck. Ty nodded and did the same. Science passed uneventfully, and the girls left the lab side by side.

"Aren't you kind of tall?" Ty asked as they headed for English.

"Yeah. It's my birthday heels." Rebecca balanced on one foot, hanging on to Tyler's shoulder, so she could extend the other one for inspection.

"Totally the bomb! I love them! Expensive?"

"From my grandmother, so probably," said Rebecca.

In drama, Mr. Tilson left them alone, and most students used the time as a free study period. Angela was not in class, which was curious. There would be no torturing of the Ice Maiden by pretending sweetness and amity.

At lunch, she showed off her shoes; Sam and AJ hadn't seen them yet. The shoes were the bomb. Becks looked tall and sophisticated. It was very satisfying. Sam was wearing the new tooled red boots, and Rebecca danced a little quick step with her, heels tapping lightly on the tile floor and Sam's boots clocking a deeper accompaniment.

Rebecca had yet to tell her friends she had seen the pageant binder. Now that she had written High Heels, she was reluctant to do so. She pushed both of the new Events out of her mind. Into that bulging box. It helped to remind herself that both Angela and Fat Mr. Hammond more than deserved what was coming. It did nothing, however, to diminish her concern about potential fallout. For herself, personally. And that little insight from yesterday afternoon about balancing actions. No. Best to keep it all under wraps for now.

It was pretty hard to *not* think about Louisville Slugger when she was in the Fat Man's presence. Then she didn't care what the balancing action, if that's what you wanted to call it, turned out to be. It would be worth it. She'd just ride it out. Pick herself up, dust herself off. Find someone to reattach missing limbs if necessary.

In Home Room, she sat with Zoe and Sam on the opposite side of the class from Jackson and Josh, which at least minimized the risk of getting into a fracas with them and becoming a live sacrifice to His Fatness. He was still in an evil mood. Well, when wasn't he? It certainly did nothing to stimulate Rebecca toward feelings of remorse.

The girls talked quietly, keeping their heads low. Rebecca occasionally scanned the other side of the room. Jackson and Josh seemed to be studying. There was no surreal glow about them; they were just two ordinary boys. In spite of all the fights and tormenting, she grudgingly admitted there had been fun too. This thought surprised her. Was Jackson behaving differently? Was she? Had her act of vengeance somehow evened the scales? That didn't feel quite right. All these thoughts were making her edgy. And it wasn't just Jackson the Jerk—there were five of them now, counting Found Puppy. Who was she becoming? How was all this going to settle out?

Nope. Rebecca shook her head. Not going down that road!

Sam nudged Rebecca with one elbow. "Did you tell Ty about the pictures?" she whispered.

Rebecca shook her head. "I haven't remembered to. And anyway, she has 'Headless,' and a phone full of shots. She doesn't need two more pictures." She and Sam locked eyes and burst into giggles. Rebecca loved Ann Boleyn, but the nickname for the puppy was too hilarious.

Mr. Hammond was now roaming the room and coming their way. The girls bent their heads over their books trying to stifle their giggles. Rebecca kept track of Mr. Hammond's progress out of the corner of her eye. He lumbered heavily down the next aisle and returned to his desk. She sighed inwardly.

When the bell finally signaled the end of the period, the three girls made their way out of Home Room in silence. AJ was waiting for them at the wide front doors, her book bag hanging from one hand, the other fingering a blue extension in her light-brown hair. They walked into the bright May sunshine together. Tom was waiting, and AJ hurried to the beat-up truck. They watched her slide into the old pickup, swing long legs in after her, and pull the door shut, the hinges creaking loudly. She rolled down the window and waved at them.

"I need to catch the bus," said Sam after a moment. "So I can do my chores at home and then get a ride down to the ranch." She answered Rebecca's unspoken question: "I'll be back for school tomorrow. You guys coming?" she added.

"I am," said Zoe. "I have a babysitting gig tonight that starts early."

"You go ahead," Rebecca said. "I think I'll walk."

Zoe and Sam looked at her in surprise.

"You want to walk?"

"Yeah. No one's home, so I'm in no rush."

"I'll walk with you," said Zoe. Sam looked at Zoe in exasperation.

Rebecca shook her head. "Thanks, Zolly," she said. "You don't want to be late for your job. And . . . I want to sort of . . . think about some stuff." Sam was giving her a speculative look. Rebecca was becoming all too familiar with that considering gaze.

"You're sure?"

"Really, I'm sure." She smiled brightly at her friends.

"Okay, then. Tomorrow, Becks." Zoe hugged her.

Rebecca was touched. Zoe didn't question her; she was just always there. Rebecca almost changed her mind about walking by herself. But she didn't. She hugged Zoe back. "Bye, Zolly. Bye, Sam."

Sam and Zoe ran for the loading area where yellow buses were lined up next to the curb. Rebecca watched them go. They both turned to wave as they clambered onto their bus. The doors accordioned shut, and the bus pulled away from the curb almost immediately.

Rebecca had gone only a few steps when she saw Jackson hurrying toward the bus loading area. He made a rude gesture at a retreating bus as it pulled onto the street. It was unusual for Jackson to be by himself, and Rebecca thought he looked a little lost.

"Don't go all soft in the brain," she muttered to herself. "He's still Jackson the Jerk."

Jackson turned, saw her watching him, and grinned his lopsided grin. He headed in her direction. Rebecca didn't want to talk to Jackson. She started up the sidewalk toward home, but he caught up easily and fell into step alongside her. She glanced warily at him. Jackson didn't speak. He simply ambled along beside her. It made her nervous. She couldn't think of anything to say. The silence weighed heavily.

"You never ride the bus." Lame! She cringed inwardly. "Get your bike run over again?" The words just popped out of her mouth.

Jackson looked at her sharply and then shrugged. "Nah, Josh had a ride and wouldn't wait for me, the maggot. Hammond made me stay late."

"How come?"

"He seems to be worried about my algebra grade."

"Oh," she said. And then, "Are *you*?"

"Nah. Well, not much." Jackson glanced at her. The grin had slipped a little.

"You're his star jock. I thought you could do no wrong."

Jackson shrugged again. "He doesn't like to be crossed. I think I pissed him off."

"How? By throwing yourself under his car and making him look bad?" Rebecca giggled.

"Cute, Becka." Jackson didn't sound mad. Mad would have been easier to deal with.

Rebecca regretted her smart-ass words. Sort of. "Sorry," she muttered. "I couldn't resist."

"Pretty brutal," he said. "Smart, but brutal."

"No favors from the Fat Man, so it's all up to you?"

"Guess so."

"And?"

"And I'm not a brainiac like you."

"Jeez, I'm not a brainiac," Rebecca grumbled.

They were at the street, cars streaming by with a green light. They waited for the light to turn. "Okay, that's not what I meant exactly." Jackson shoved his hands in his pockets. "It's not like you're a nerd or something."

"You think I'm a *nerd*?" Rebecca whirled to glare at him.

He took one step back, looking cornered. "I said you're *not* a nerd!" he said defensively. He pushed the blond hair out of his eyes. The grin was gone; Jackson looked serious. Rebecca was not familiar with this expression on Jackson's face.

"What I mean is, it's all so easy for you," he said.

"Is that what you think?"

Jackson didn't flinch. His jaw was set. "Yeah," he said. "That's what I think." The light turned, and he stepped into the crossing.

Rebecca stared after him, her mouth pulled down in a frown. Then she followed him. "Do you know the word *study*?" she demanded.

"Yeah, I do." Now he sounded annoyed. "You think just because I play ball I'm stupid or something. Did it ever occur to you that I might play ball *and* have a brain?"

"No." Rebecca shook her head.

"Or that without a sports scholarship maybe I won't get into college? And if I don't get into college, I'm stuck with—" Jackson caught himself.

He looked grim. "So if I'm injured, or don't have grades, I'm pretty much screwed." He looked like he might say more, but he closed his mouth firmly. He'd already said too much.

Rebecca shook her head again. She felt a sharp stab of guilt at his reference to injury.

"That's what I thought," muttered Jackson.

I always figured you were lazy, Rebecca thought, but she clamped her mouth shut before the words could blurt out. She didn't actually know what to think, and she didn't know this Jackson Middleton. She couldn't remember ever hearing him string two meaningful sentences together. It pushed the limits of her perception of him. They walked along in silence, Jackson looking irritated, Rebecca with a puzzled frown on her face.

They reached another intersection. Jackson barely glanced in either direction before trotting into the street against the light. Rebecca hesitated and carefully looked both ways. She saw no approaching cars, so she hurried after him, her heart fluttering at the risk.

"Did it ever occur to *you* this is why you got run over?" Rebecca felt mean, but it was too late to get her words back.

Irritation blossomed into quick anger in Jackson's eyes. Just as suddenly, the anger was replaced with his FIGJAM smirk. "You're on a real roll today, aren't you?"

The sudden change of attitude caught Rebecca off guard. She huffed wordlessly.

"You're cute when you're mad, Becka," he said softly.

Rebecca's eyes widened in surprise, and Jackson's grin broadened. He studied her for a moment. If he came to any conclusion, it wasn't apparent on his face. He set off up the street again.

Rebecca watched him go. Laney's voice in her head cautioned, *Let him go.* Rebecca considered it, but then she followed Jackson, trotting to catch up, her book bag slapping uncomfortably against her back. The strappy heels slowed her down, not to mention they were beginning to hurt her feet.

"Jackson . . ." She was a little out of breath. She thought he moved pretty fast for an injured gimp. "So you're telling me you do study and finish homework assignments. Turn them in. All that stuff?"

Jackson didn't even glance at her. "Yeah," he said. "Counter to popular belief."

It *was* counter to popular belief. At least it was counter to her belief. She found this idea difficult to process. Did Jackson increase his pace? Rebecca was nearly jogging to keep up. She wished she was wearing flat, comfortable shoes.

Without warning, he whirled to face her. "You ever hear of No Pass No Play?" he demanded.

Rebecca rammed right into him. Her book bag slipped off one shoulder. She struggled not to fall in the strappy heels. For a moment, they were a tangle of scrabbling arms and shifting feet. Jackson was the first to get his balance, and he stepped back, one hand on her shoulder to steady her. She brushed at her jeans and straightened the little sweater. He dropped his hand to his side. They stared at each other.

"Sure, but—"

"But what? You think I just kiss up to all my teachers?"

"Well, um . . ."

Jackson wasn't grinning now. "I study, and I do homework," he said. There was an edge to his voice. "Tests freak me out, okay?" He looked suddenly exposed, and then uncomfortable. And then his face closed.

Rebecca stared up at him, speechless. A charged silence stretched between them. She fought for a neutral expression. She wasn't sure she got it. Jackson was watching her. One side of his mouth twitched up. Still, his eyes didn't exactly smile. She didn't know what to call the look in them. He stared at her for what seemed a long time before turning to head up the street again. Without looking back, he broke into a long-legged jog that rapidly put distance between them. He wasn't limping at all. Rebecca stood rooted to the ground, watching him go.

***

Rebecca walked slowly toward home, mulling over this new information. She didn't quite know what to do with it. She remembered Jackson's look in Home Room after Fat Mr. Hammond had confiscated Ty's pictures. Had that look been apologetic? And he had offered to get the pictures back. She had been angry with both Jackson and Mr. Hammond and had rebuffed him out of hand. What was the fleeting expression she had seen on his face before the usual idiot grin appeared? She didn't know. She thought about the morning in algebra class. Jackson had seemed genuinely pleased when she stood up to Mr. Hammond. Well, stood up to him might be a little strong, but she had managed to keep her anger hidden. Who was this Jackson Middleton? On these occasions—okay, rare occasions—he had acted decidedly *un*jerk-like. It was puzzling. He had walked beside her leaving algebra class that day. That was more than weird. It was almost freaky. Unless it was just coincidence. She just didn't know.

He had said, "Tests freak me out, okay?" It was the same with Tyler. Ty worked really hard in her classes, often to have a decent grade destroyed by a bad test. Rebecca just couldn't get her head around the concept of Jackson studying. She had always assumed he simply didn't care, or that he was lazy. He was always so flippant about—well, everything. Except sports.

Could it be a cover?

This idea caught her up short. Jackson was like an irritating rash. He took nothing seriously. But could it all be a cover? And if so, a cover for what? That he worried about getting into college? About grades? About being injured? Her breath came quick and shallow, and not from the walk up her street.

Rebecca let herself into the empty house. It was too quiet. She dropped her backpack in the mudroom and pulled off the new sandals with a sigh of relief. She padded in bare feet to the kitchen. Looking for a snack, she found herself standing in the pantry. The familiar spice-and-herbs smell was comforting. She looked around without really seeing the contents of the shelves. She wasn't actually hungry, but she had the munchies. She felt . . . like her skin didn't quite fit or something. What if she had been reading Jackson wrong? She was stabbed with a sudden pang of anxiety. Her father frequently reminded her, "What goes around comes around." Just the other morning, her mother had chided her with, "Think carefully what you put out there."

Rebecca sucked her breath in. She'd been throwing a lot of people under the bus lately. So to speak. She laughed out loud at the irony, and in the empty house, it sounded a little wild to her ears. Was this how bad karma got racked up? What was karma anyway?

This was giving her a headache. Rebecca left the pantry and pulled open the freezer door, wondering if you could undo bad karma with good deeds. How would that work? Would it balance out the scales, or just leave you always looking over your shoulder wondering what was going to hit you next? She rummaged through the contents of the freezer and, amazingly, found a little bag of April's pumpkin-pecan cookies. She took the cookies out of the freezer and laid them on a napkin. She found a bottle of water, and, with the cookies in one hand and the water bottle clutched under her arm, she wandered downstairs.

CHAPTER 42

Can You Balance the Scales?

May 30

REBECCA POWERED UP her laptop. She checked for e-mails. No pings. She took a bite of cookie. Still frozen. She opened her Events folder and read through her first story. It made her feel mean, even in light of the scuffle with Jackson that had triggered this Event. She reached for a place of distance and detachment. She couldn't get there. Her fingers noodled the keyboard. One hand found its way into her hair, and she twirled a lock around one finger. She ran the mouse pointer over the titles of her other Event stories but left them unopened. She tried another bite of cookie. It was still pretty cold, but she ate it anyway, not really tasting it.

Not sure where she was going with it, she opened a new file. Her hand rested on the mouse, the index finger tapping a restless rhythm. She tilted her head as if listening to something far off, her eyes distant and unfocused. She unconsciously settled into her chair, her body relaxing. Her hands moved to the keyboard. She began to type.

> Jackson pushed the books aside. It was Sunday night, and he had been cramming for finals. He was frustrated. He knew this stuff. He really did. But it wouldn't matter how well he knew it if he froze up during the test. Like he always did. Maybe he could get hypnotized or something. He'd heard of such things. That testing poorly could be all in your head. Well, it was a little late for that.
>
> Jackson really loved sports, and he was amazingly good at them. He needed a sports scholarship to go to college, and he needed decent grades to stay on the teams. The more he

thought about it, the more he worried about it. The more he worried, the bigger the block during a test. His brain just turned to stone. Studying didn't change that.

Jackson flung himself on his bed. He grabbed a pillow and jammed it over his face. "Fuuuuck!" he yelled into it. He threw the pillow across the room. He lay spread-eagle on his bed staring at the ceiling. His mind wandered, and without realizing he was sinking, he drifted to sleep. And he dreamed.

In his dream, Jackson was sitting for a test. Anxiety roiled in his gut. The test sheets were spread on a table in front of him. Panicky, he filled in answers without thinking, checked boxes at random. He didn't even know the subject! A proctor in a long black coat came and collected his papers. He glanced at the pages, made a few quick marks with a red pen, and handed them back to Jackson.

Jackson looked down at the red mark across the top of the paper. It read 61%. No surprise. And not good enough.

The process repeated itself several times with similar results. "Screw it," he thought. "Whatever happens, happens. I'll figure it out later." And with that, he relaxed.

Another set of papers appeared before him. With resignation, he pulled them closer. At least the panic was gone. Again, the proctor collected them. The test came back almost immediately with the red mark at the top. Jackson read 73%.

In the dream, he found himself reaching for the next test as he handed one in. Each score came back better than the one before. He realized he knew what he was doing—he knew the subjects, and he knew the answers. He didn't have to guess. The proctor collected each exam and almost immediately handed it back. A score of 85%. One of 94%. Then 99%. The scenario changed little. Sometimes the proctor was a woman, sometimes the man in the long coat, which was now white. Once, the score was 106%! How could that be?

This is easy, thought Jackson. *No sweat.*

The dream dissolved into a different scene. He was running laps around an athletic field, the track streaming by beneath his trainers. He felt really good. He looked up at the scoreboard and saw "University of . . ." He couldn't quite make out the name of the college. The dream faded away, and Jackson lay in a deep sleep.

When he woke in the morning, he felt elated, but he didn't know why. He sat up and rubbed his hands over his face. He was still in yesterday's clothes! Then he remembered the dreams.

Creepy, he thought.

But the sense of relaxed well-being stayed with him. Not thinking about the dream, tests, or much of anything, Jackson got ready for school. He felt strangely detached from it all. Yeah, he felt pretty damn good!

Rebecca sat at her computer with her head tilted, eyes far off. Her hands dropped into her lap. Was that it, then? She thought so. She reread the piece and saved it to a file called Dreamweaver. She could hear sounds upstairs. Someone was home. She reached for the mouse to click out of her word processing program, but then she paused. Laney was whispering something: *Ty freaks out at tests too.*

Rebecca gasped. Of course! Why hadn't she thought of this? If it could work for Jackson, it could work for Ty! If it worked at all.

She pulled her chair closer to the desk. Her hands poised on the keys, she closed her eyes and listened for that far-off voice. And she began to type.

The Event that unfolded was short and to the point. Tyler's father was into all sorts of bizarre stuff, like meditation and crystals and rain dances and deep breathing. She "wrote" Mr. Lane into town for the weekend, and he taught Ty a technique to relax her mind. Rebecca thought it was really about confidence; she knew Tyler understood her stuff and was, in fact, pretty smart. Maybe not as smart as Zoe, but still. She finished it with a stunned Tyler showing her grades slip to all of them after finals. Rebecca closed her eyes again, listening for that far-off voice. That seemed to be all. She named the new Event Colorado

High for Ty. Now that was weird! But that's what had popped into her head, and that's how she did this stuff.

Nodding to herself in satisfaction, Rebecca closed the program. She ran upstairs to find her father starting dinner. Andy and Scoundrel were racing back and forth across the backyard. Tinker was sitting at the French doors looking impatient. Lissa came in through the mudroom calling out hello. It was all so normal. Reassuringly so. She missed her mother, but the rest of her family were all together. This was comforting. The world was okay. Rebecca felt lighthearted and good.

CHAPTER 43

The Law of Unintended Consequences

June 5

ALGEBRA FINAL FELL on Wednesday afternoon—the last final for Rebecca. It was almost over. Students were free to go as soon as they turned in their tests. Mr. Hammond announced he would be scoring exams as they arrived on his desk, and anyone who wanted to stick around for their test grade was welcome to do so, as long as they created no disturbance. The better students were the first ones to turn in their exams and, in general, the most interested in their grade. They tended to linger.

Rebecca found the exam questions mostly easy. Mr. Hammond had thrown in a couple surprises, but she was able to figure them out. She liked the neatness of math. It was not subjective. There were no shades of gray. If only real life could be like that! She turned in her exam and moved quietly to the back of the room to wait. She was in no particular hurry to know how she'd done—she was pretty confident in her score—but her father would want to know all her grades the second he walked in the door after work. It would be easier all around if she could tell him.

She doodled Laney ideas in a notebook while she waited. *I've missed you, Laney*, she thought to herself. What with her birthday and the sleepover, not to mention preparing for finals and writing so many Events, there had been no time for Laney stories. In truth, Rebecca was a little afraid to write a new Laney story, for fear this strange power she had discovered would bleed into it with unforeseen results.

Surprisingly, Jackson turned in his test soon after Rebecca. He made his way to the back of the room and settled into a desk across from her. She looked at him in surprise. Jackson shrugged. She wasn't sure if he looked uneasy or expectant. The Dreamweaver story was sharp in her mind. Jackson pulled a battered notebook from a back pocket, stretched out his long legs, and began to draw what looked to Rebecca like . . . what? Giant lizards? She craned her neck to get a better look, but Jackson tucked the notebook behind one arm. She glanced at him, but he ignored her. Odd.

At the end of the exam period, Mr. Hammond called for the last of the tests. The remaining students handed in their work and hastily departed. That left just those waiting for their grades. Mr. Hammond lumbered to his feet and made his way heavily toward them. He handed each student a slip of paper on which was written a grade. He made a few terse comments, such as, "Good job," or "Nice."

He stopped between Rebecca and Jackson. Without looking at her, Mr. Hammond shoved the grade slip at her. The paper fluttered and drifted toward the floor. Rebecca snatched it and pinned it on the desktop beneath her hand. She looked at her hand for a moment and then gingerly spread her fingers apart. She saw her name and a small, grudging "A" written in Mr. Hammond's sloppy hand. Rebecca smiled, her fingers moving back together over the slip of paper.

With measured movements, Mr. Hammond placed the last grade slip facedown on Jackson's desk. Jackson sat up straight and pulled in his legs. He made no move to touch it. Mr. Hammond studied Jackson for a long moment and then turned over the paper. In red ink was written "87%." Rebecca ducked her head to hide a big grin. Jackson simply stared at it.

"We have before us something of an anomaly, it would seem," said Mr. Hammond. His voice was flat, his expression unfriendly. "Our ace athlete appears to have become an ace student overnight." No one moved or spoke. Mr. Hammond continued, "Are we not just a little curious how this transpired?"

Jackson glanced up at Mr. Hammond and back down at the paper. He said nothing. Rebecca's breath caught. Anger curled in the pit of her stomach, and she felt Laney, restless in her head.

"Well?" Mr. Hammond demanded.

"Well, what?" Jackson looked genuinely at a loss.

"Would you care to explain how you accomplished this?"

Jackson shifted in his seat. "I studied," he said. He brushed the hair from his eyes.

"You studied." Mr. Hammond crossed his hands over his huge stomach, disbelief clear on his face.

"Yeah." Jackson nodded, still looking puzzled, but also a little annoyed.

"Only that?" Mr. Hammond leaned toward Jackson, his voice menacing. "No . . . backup plan?"

"Backup?" Jackson glanced up at Mr. Hammond in bewilderment. Piggy, accusing eyes stared down at him. And then he got it. Understanding bloomed on his face. He sat up straighter and squared his shoulders. He locked eyes with Mr. Hammond.

After a moment that stretched out in time, Jackson leaned back in his desk. He folded his arms across his chest. He grinned the FIGJAM grin, insolent and challenging. It didn't reach his eyes. "I did about a hundred practice equations," he said. "And then I braided my hair and got a good night's sleep." His eyes never flickered under Mr. Hammond's stare.

There were snickers from the few students who remained.

"You did practice equations," said Mr. Hammond. "That would be a first, wouldn't it?" His tone was openly accusatory now.

Rebecca's mouth dropped open. Where was Mr. Hammond going with this? He couldn't be suggesting Jackson had cheated, could he? Not one of his star athletes. Not one of his precious jocks! But what had Jackson said after school last week?

"He doesn't like to be crossed. I think I pissed him off." Rebecca had made a smart remark at the time, but she had also crossed Mr. Hammond and had personally experienced his petty revenge. She remembered all too clearly his mean, beady eyes as he tore up Ty's pictures and dropped them into his waste bin. This was not petty, however. Neither was it what she had meant to happen when she wrote Dreamweaver. This was her fault.

Rebecca looked over at Jackson. The FIGJAM grin was gone. His jaw was set. This was going to go badly. Laney whispered urgently in Rebecca's head. *The hypnosis,* said Laney. *It was in the dream.*

Rebecca didn't take time to think. There *was* no time to think. "It must be the hypnosis," she said smoothly. She didn't dare look directly at either of them.

"The what?" Mr. Hammond shifted his ugly glare from Jackson to her.

"The hypnosis." Rebecca sneaked a glance at Jackson.

Jackson stared at her, openmouthed. Mr. Hammond glowered at her in fury. The scattered group of nerds watched her curiously. Sheesh, she felt like she was onstage half naked under a spotlight. Laney whispered in her head, *He'll go with you. Just do it.*

Rebecca put on her best innocent face. "You said you might do it," she said, beaming at Jackson. "Hypnosis. You were certain it would work." Her heart was thumping, but she smiled sweetly up at Mr. Hammond. "Looks like it did."

"Yeah." Jackson looked baffled. Even so, he said, "Looks like it did."

"You're telling me you underwent hypnosis?" Mr. Hammond turned back to Jackson, his voice scornful.

Jackson tipped his head, neither yes nor no. His eyes slid back to Rebecca.

"It has a good track record for helping to remove blocks," said Rebecca. "Like with testing." This came out of nowhere. Now Rebecca's face mirrored the surprise on Jackson's. Well, she'd be as surprised as the next person to learn Jackson had performed well on an algebra test, wouldn't she? She wasn't pretending; she actually *was* surprised, in spite of her Event.

Mr. Hammond whirled toward Rebecca again, his face a mask of anger. Her stomach turned over even as she raised guileless blue eyes to meet his furious ones. "And what is this to you?" he demanded.

Rebecca stared back at Mr. Hammond. There were no whispers coming from Laney now, or anywhere else for that matter. She opened her mouth, but nothing came out. She closed it again. She could hear Mr. Hammond's heavy breathing. The wall clock clicked as the hand jumped to the next minute. Outside, a horn honked. Muffled laughter drifted in from the hallway.

Jackson unfolded from his desk and got to his feet, his mouth pulled into a grin. Or maybe a grimace. He palmed the grade slip and tucked it into the battered notebook, which he stuffed in a back pocket in his jeans. Jostling Mr. Hammond as he did so, he reached down and snagged Rebecca's backpack. "You coming?" he said to her.

Rebecca scrambled to her feet, not looking at Mr. Hammond. Side by side, she and Jackson walked toward the door. Mr. Hammond stared after them in mute fury. Jackson was limping badly. Was it a not-so-subtle reminder to Mr. Hammond? That he had gotten off easy a month ago? Rebecca wondered. Jackson had seemed as good as new last week.

They stepped into the corridor, and the algebra room door closed behind them. Rebecca exhaled deeply. Jackson stood up straighter.

"That was going to shit in a hurry," he muttered. "Time for a defensive play."

Rebecca looked up at him.

"Sometimes it's better to drop back and run a new plan," he said.

Rebecca assumed this was football jargon, about which she knew less than nothing. But it made sense to her in a general sort of way. They walked in silence down the nearly empty hall, the limp now nowhere in evidence. Once or twice, Jackson started to speak, and then didn't. As they passed the alcove housing school trophies, he took her by the arm and steered her into it. The very one she and AJ had stood in, Rebecca wordless with fury and frustration after she had wrestled with Jackson for her notes. Now, again, Jackson and his two best buddies grinned out at her, the freshman football team arrayed behind them.

"Okay, Rebecca, what gives?" Jackson's voice was soft, but there was a knife edge to it.

"What do you mean?" Rebecca struggled for an innocent face.

Jackson backed her up to the trophy case, one hand on her shoulder, pressing her against the glass. He looked confused, but at the same time, the blue eyes were intense.

"That whole hypnosis thing back there. What was that about?"

Rebecca tried to dodge the question with one of her own. "Did you get hypnotized?"

"No! I had a d—" Jackson shook his head. The pressure against her shoulder increased. His eyes held hers. "That's not the point," he said.

"What is the point exactly?" Rebecca tried for a calm voice, but it wobbled just a bit. Her heart was thumping wildly. She wondered if Jackson could feel it.

"The point is . . ." He took a deep breath and exhaled. He tried again. "The point is . . ."

"You said you might," said Rebecca gamely. Jackson shook his head again, his eyes still holding hers. She couldn't look away. She thought those eyes might laser right through her skull and short out her brain.

"Didn't you? Last week, walking home. You said you freaked out at tests. You said you might . . ." Rebecca's voice trailed off.

"I don't think so." Jackson's tone left little room for debate.

"Maybe it was Tyler. She freaks out at tests too. Her dad . . ." Rebecca fell silent under the weight of Jackson's gaze. She struggled to gather herself. "Well, I think the point is that you *did* do well on your test." Rebecca smiled hopefully at him. That wobbled a bit too. "How *did* you do that?"

Jackson released her, his arm dropping to his side. He looked a little sheepish. "You'd never believe me if I told you."

"I might."

Jackson looked down at her for a long time. He was trying to read her; she felt like one of those people you sometimes heard about who said they'd been hijacked by aliens and subjected to some sort of extraterrestrial brain scan. Indecision, bafflement, frustration, uncertainty—all these emotions played across Jackson's face.

"I know you didn't cheat, Jackson," she said softly.

"I didn't!"

"I know."

"I had a dream," he blurted out.

"A dream." She chewed her lower lip.

"Yeah, a dream." The look on his face dared her to make something of it. He paced a tight circle in front of her. He pushed the blond hair from his eyes. He raised one hand and gestured at nothing in particular. He stood in front of her again, close. Hesitant. "I dreamed I was taking a bunch of tests. That I didn't care."

It was a short version, but no matter. Rebecca waited for him to go on.

"And I relaxed. I dreamed it was easy. I woke up thinking finals would be no big deal. And they weren't." Jackson's expression slid from puzzlement to amazement. "They weren't," he said again.

"Wow . . ."

"I did practice equations," he said. "Not last night, but I always do them. If it wasn't for the tests—"

Rebecca nodded. "Wow." Another brilliant response.

"And if you say one thing to anyone, I swear, I'll . . . you'll . . . it'll be—" Jackson sputtered to a halt, but his threatening look said it all.

Rebecca shook her head. "Nothing. Not a word. It'd be stupid. No one would believe me." She was babbling. She clamped her mouth shut.

Jackson scowled down at her. "I'm serious, Rebecca."

She nodded vigorously. "No, I know! You said you were smart *and* a ball player! You said you study. No one would guess."

"Just no flapping the gums." Jackson leaned even closer. His eyes bored into hers. He pressed his hand against her shoulder again.

Rebecca shook her head again. "Not a word. Not to anyone. Not ever." Still babbling. And still she couldn't pull her eyes away.

Jackson's face was only inches from hers. She felt the pressure of his hand on her shoulder. Her head was against the glass of the trophy case. He was leaning in, almost as if he was going to kiss her. The thought was ludicrous. It made her panicky and, at the same time, curious. Her heart was still racing.

But Jackson didn't kiss her. So quietly she barely heard him, he said, "Not . . . one . . . word." His breath was soft against her face. It smelled of peppermint.

Rebecca nodded her head emphatically. She was beginning to feel like a little bobbin' doll on the dashboard of some redneck's ancient and rusting pickup. "Absolutely not. Not one word." Was she disappointed that he hadn't kissed her? Oh, good God, what could she be thinking!

"Can I go now?" she asked weakly.

Jackson stepped back, nodding. "Who's stopping you?"

He handed her knapsack to her. She grasped one strap, letting the pack sink to the floor at her feet. Eyes still locked, neither of them moved. What would it feel like to be hypnotized? Like this? Unable to move or think? Or to be kissed by Jackson? Would that be pretty much like being hypnotized?

Get a grip! she chided herself. Laney was practically throwing sparks with a flood of contradictory emotions. It made Rebecca's brain spin. Shaking her head, she slipped the backpack onto one shoulder, still without breaking eye contact. She waited a moment longer.

Jackson took another step back. Rebecca pulled her eyes from his with effort and stepped around him. She walked to the big front doors without looking back, trying not to hurry. Her heart continued to race. Her shoulder felt warm with the remembered weight of Jackson's hand. She unconsciously brushed her fingers across the spot, as if to scrub away not only the sensation of his touch but the entire episode, beginning in the algebra classroom and ending in the corridor in front of the trophy case.

Confused emotions bombarded her. She was happy for Jackson over the test results. She wasn't sure, but it sounded like he'd done okay in all his classes. "I woke up thinking finals would be no big deal. And they weren't," he had said. She was stunned that she had thought he was going to kiss her. Where on earth had that come from! Even more so, that she might have let him. She was scared because this Event had nearly backfired in a horrible way. Under everything else, that fear burned with a bright intensity. She was worried about the path she was on, not in the least because she was enjoying it so much. Just how twisted was she? Her stomach roiled; she thought she might throw up.

At the front doors, she turned and looked back. Jackson was still standing in front of the trophy case. She nodded at him, unconsciously rubbing a throbbing temple.

"I'm glad you did okay on your test, Jackson," she said.

Jackson's face was shadowed. She couldn't see his eyes. But she thought he might have nodded, just the smallest of nods. Rebecca stepped through the doors and into the hot June sunshine.

CHAPTER 44

The Last Day of School

June 6

THE LAST DAY of school was a short one, and strange. The seniors were already gone, and the school felt half empty. There wasn't much to do; Rebecca turned in texts and materials, which she thought could have been done on an earlier day. It was really a waste to be there at all.

She caught up with her friends in a prearranged meeting in the cafeteria. It was nearly deserted. The clang of the heavy doors echoed through the empty space even louder than usual. The kitchens were closed, the deli cases barren, the vending machines empty. The smell of last week's grease hung in the air. Rebecca wrinkled her nose in distaste. Zoe was leaning back casually in a chair. A little smile played around the corners of her mouth, and she looked satisfied and relaxed. Sam sat on the table, her boots planted on a chair. She and AJ were comparing eGrades when Rebecca joined them at the table. Rebecca's grades were good. Okay, English and science could have been better— only Bs. She still had an A minus average for the year, but her father would undoubtedly deliver a lecture. Zoe, of course, would have straight A's. Sam had made no secret of the fact she would be happy with a C average.

Only Tyler was missing.

Rebecca felt a knot of tension in the pit of her stomach. How had Ty done? Jackson's algebra grade had been great. Was it too much to hope that Ty had also done well?

"So how'd you do?" Zoe smiled at Sam. "We don't have to ask how Becks did."

Rebecca nodded in acknowledgment. She combed her fingers through her hair and briefly twirled a honey-blonde lock.

Sam tapped a long nail against her lips. "Straight C plus," she said. "Except for a B in science." Her smile was radiant.

Rebecca's jaw dropped. There was a moment of shocked silence before anyone was able to respond to this astonishing news.

"That's so the bomb!!"

"Way to go, Sam!"

"How'd you do it?"

Sam shrugged. "Science isn't so bad." She slid off the table and propped her elbows on it. "I need to know some stuff for ranch work." She looked around at them; they weren't getting it. "For the horses, you know. So I don't sound like a dumb blonde when I talk to a cowboy or Uncle Clint. I just tell myself it's for the horses, and it's almost easy."

Now there were nods.

"Plus, Mom told me I have to have a C average, or I can't work the ranch this summer."

Ah. Now it made sense. There could have been no more compelling motive for Sam. Rebecca felt a little twinge of guilt. She could have given Sam a nudge with an Event too. It just never occurred to her. Well, it had turned out okay, hadn't it?

Taking a lot for granted, aren't you? Laney's voice was a whisper in Rebecca's mind.

The cafeteria doors clattered open. Tyler walked woodenly toward them. She looked dazed. She clutched a crumpled piece of paper in one hand. Her eGrades.

Rebecca's heart sank. The girls watched silently as Ty made her way to the table and sank into a chair between AJ and Sam. She didn't speak. No one did.

"Ty?" AJ broke the silence. She placed a hesitant hand on Tyler's arm. "Are you okay?"

Ty nodded, still without speaking.

Rebecca stared at Ty, her heart thudding in her chest.

"Are those your grades?" Zoe asked gently.

Another nod.

"Are they . . ." AJ seemed unsettled.

Tyler opened her hand and let the crumpled paper fall to the table. No one moved. After a long moment, AJ reached for it. She held it tentatively, as if it might somehow be dangerous. Her eyes met Tyler's. Without looking at the slip, AJ extended her arm toward Zoe. Zoe took it uncertainly. She looked down at the grade slip. Her eyes widened, and she blinked twice. A smile spread slowly across her face. She slapped the paper down on the table with her open palm and leaned over to catch Ty in a fierce hug.

"These are amazing!" she said excitedly. "You did great, Ty. Really great!"

This extraordinary behavior from Zoe seemed to shock Tyler out of her daze. A radiant smile bloomed on her face, and the ponytail swayed as she hugged Zoe back.

"They're good," exclaimed Tyler. "My grades are good. Can you believe it?"

"You didn't freeze up," Rebecca said softly. Her heart was still thudding.

"I didn't," said Ty emphatically.

"That's so great! How'd that happen?" Zoe asked.

"My dad showed up last Friday night," Ty said. "Mom wasn't too happy about it, I can tell you!" Heads nodded around the table.

Ty beamed at her friends. "You know all the wacko stuff he's into," she went on. "He showed me this really cool meditation technique. You write down the results you want and then sort of project yourself into them in the future, celebrating like it's already done. The good feelings, the relief. Whatever. I don't get how it works, but it did. Something did. Dad made me practice all weekend."

Zoe nodded in agreement. "There's a line of thought that suggests, if we quiet the left side of the brain, like with meditation, we can tap into a subtle level of intelligence." She seemed oblivious that her friends were gaping. Except Sam. Sam's face wore a quiet, thoughtful expression.

"And there is solid evidence in quantum physics," Zoe continued, "that our thoughts affect things." She looked so pleased you'd have thought she had discovered this scientific evidence herself.

"Okay, Einstein," muttered Rebecca.

"You can look it up," Zoe said. "I'm just saying. It's about energy."

Tyler sprang to her feet. She swayed and pirouetted in an exultant dance, her arms waving above her head, her face the picture of delight. The ponytail was going crazy.

"I don't know about your energies," she sang. "I just know I did it! I did it!" The little dance came to an abrupt halt, and Ty regarded them with fists planted on her hips. "And d'you know the best part?" she demanded. She didn't wait for an answer.

"I can do it again!" Throwing her arms in the air once more, her enthusiasm carrying her around the table, she caroled, "I CAN DO IT AGAIN!"

Rebecca felt both satisfaction and happiness for Ty, but her pleasure was tainted by a touch of apprehension. Only two Events to go. And good or bad, the karma was piling up. If there was such a thing as karma. Who knew for sure? Still, to see Ty so happy was worth it.

CHAPTER 45

Summer

June 12

REBECCA AND ZOE spread their towels on lounge chairs beneath a huge umbrella and dropped their totes on the grass. Sunglasses hid their eyes. Rebecca's hair was pulled into a smooth ponytail, although wayward tendrils had escaped and wisped about her face. Zoe's mass of dark waves was only marginally controlled by a colorful bandana. They waved at AJ, who was perched in the lifeguard tower surveying the big pool. AJ didn't wave back. She was wearing wraparound sunglasses, and her hair was stuffed under a ratty straw hat. Her bathing suit was lifeguard regulation, as were her red-and-white shorts. Her long legs were tucked to one side of her chair, and she leaned forward, elbows on the armrests, a whistle hanging on a thin leather cord around her neck. Her gaze was vigilant as she scanned the pool, watching for danger or unsafe behavior. When AJ's head turned in their direction, Rebecca and Zoe waved again. AJ gave them the briefest of nods.

"She'll be off in a little while," Zoe said, seeming to read Rebecca's mind. "You know it's not personal." Rebecca nodded. She took a long pull of cool water from her water bottle.

School was over. They had survived freshman year. The promise of summer stretched before them. Zoe would have her summer course. But for Rebecca, no more homework. No more noxious science experiments. No more boring English assignments. Best of all, no more Fat Mr. Hammond. Just two glorious months of liberty. Maybe her father would even lighten up a bit on the rules. In view of her remarkable maturity.

But then, maybe not.

No job, either. That bit big time. Mrs. Mason was still in Savannah. Lissa reported that the granddaughter was recovering, but for the time being, Rebecca's job was on hold. There was nothing for it except to wait and try to enjoy her leisure. At least she hadn't blown it completely when she forgot her interview.

After her Telluride conference, Rebecca's mom had suggested they go to Disneyland as soon as school let out. To make up for being gone on Rebecca's birthday. Rebecca hadn't thought of anything she wanted to do, so she readily agreed. Mother and daughter on a special adventure would be cool. No little kid rides, no meltdowns brought on by overstimulation, no early bedtimes. It had been glorious, not in the least part because it was such a sudden and complete remove from school. They had enjoyed the rides but also gone to a couple shows. They had lingered over coffee before hitting the parks in the morning and had relished quiet dinners in exotic restaurants. Just two girls, doing whatever they felt like doing, whenever they felt like doing it. Sometimes she had felt like her mother was watching her, almost like she was waiting for something. Once or twice, Rebecca had been close to confiding everything. But she didn't want to spoil the magic of the trip, so she had not, instead keeping it firmly pushed into that increasingly crowded box where she stuffed everything she didn't want to think about. She and her mom had returned just two days ago, and already, the trip seemed like ages past. School, out only a week, felt like part of a separate lifetime.

The girls closed their eyes against the glare coming off the water, a comfortable silence stretching between them. A jet droned overhead. The sound of happy voices floated to them from the shallow end of the pool. It was hot, but not nuclear. Still, the shade of the big umbrella was welcome. The canvas overhead fluttered gently in a light breeze. The smell of the pool, the slightly musty canvas, hot dry air, fresh terry towels, suntan lotion, popcorn from the concession stand—these were the scents of summer days and easy freedom with her friends.

But only for the moment. Zoe's course would begin in a few days. AJ would be lifeguarding most of the time. Sam was usually at the ranch, and Ty was in Steamboat for the summer. The prospect of summer all by herself had Rebecca wondering if all the leisure and freedom might be too much of a good thing. She really needed the doll shop job.

She sighed deeply and glanced at Zoe.

Zoe flashed her a quick smile. "Summer's great," she said. She had pulled a paperback from her tote, but it lay unopened beside her.

That remained to be seen. "Yeah." Rebecca sighed again.

Rebecca's thoughts drifted. The warm air and the light breeze caressing her skin lulled her into a languorous state where sounds became muted. From that soft and hazy place, she could think about the day of her algebra exam.

After finals, the trip with her mother had come up so fast there hadn't been time to think about much of anything. And the trip itself had been sufficiently enchanting to keep her mind engaged. Now, though, she could cautiously pull that event out of the box and look at it.

Twice now, she and Jackson had faced off in a . . . call it a close encounter. It didn't mean anything. It couldn't. She was drawn back to it because it was interesting and she was curious. Really, that was all. From that perspective, she replayed Jackson grabbing her book bag and saying, "You coming?" Leaving the classroom together under Mr. Hammond's furious glare. That in itself was more than sweet. Walking down the corridor side by side with Jackson and him steering her into the alcove that housed the trophy case. The pressure of his hand on her shoulder as he leaned in demanding an explanation. Feeling caught in the intensity of his gaze, trapped like a deer in headlights. Some of the emotional load had faded, but even so, thinking about it made her feel sort of giddy and light-headed.

Having inside information about Jackson wasn't quite so heady. It was a mixed bag, at best. There was a feeling of power in it, but also apprehension. She wasn't really comfortable knowing his secrets. She didn't want to get too close to him; he was way too high profile for that. It occurred to her that he was more complex than the popular girls thought. The ones who were constantly throwing themselves at him. But then, they didn't think about much of anything, did they? At least anything outside their limited set of desires. She remembered Jackson's lack of interest in Clarity when she practically popped her boobs out of her top at him in English. How the prospect of a challenge seemed to fire him up. Zoe had said Jackson liked to talk to a girl with brains.

Rebecca glanced at Zoe, half afraid she would be watching her and reading her thoughts. But Zoe was engrossed in her book. Reassured, Rebecca adjusted the back of her chaise and went back to her musing.

Jackson definitely responded to her verbal jousting. Josh had called her hard-to-get. She wasn't playing hard-to-get. That suggested she wanted to be gotten. She had to admit it was fun sometimes to tweak Jackson, but it was exhausting trying to keep it up. Better to keep her distance. She sighed. Unraveling the mysteries of Jackson Middleton was way beyond her. She put it back in the box.

The way Dreamweaver had run off its tracks was another thing entirely. She didn't want to think about it at all, but there it was—right in her face. She opened her eyes and sat up. She was relieved to see AJ coming toward them. Dreamweaver could be put aside once more.

"I'm going to grab something at the stand," said AJ. "You want anything?"

They did. Rebecca and Zoe got to their feet and followed AJ to the concession stand.

CHAPTER 46

Poor, Poor Pitiful Me

June 21

ANOTHER WEEK WITH no job, and summer had begun to lose its appeal. Rebecca was restless and bored. Bored didn't really cover it, actually, but she was at a loss to define what did. She was not writing. She had sat down to try a couple times, but nothing had come. She missed Laney's courage and irreverence, her flippant joie de vivre. And she missed the thrill of slipping into the zone and letting a story take her where it would. But she was afraid.

Sam was at the ranch full-time. No surprise there. Zoe's summer class had started, and she was also doing a little tutoring. Rebecca couldn't fault Zoe for wanting to come by some cash. Or Sam, either. It was just that with no job of her own, she missed her best friends even more. It didn't seem fair. Ty was, by all accounts, thriving in the wilds of Steamboat Springs. She had not been down the mountain at all since the beginning of summer. AJ worked most afternoons at the pool, and Rebecca had fallen into the habit of hanging around waiting for AJ to come off the lifeguard tower. It was lame, she knew.

Today, however, was a rare day. Zoe was free. They had met up with AJ before she went on duty. Once AJ was on the guard tower, Rebecca and Zoe had spent the afternoon in easy camaraderie. Occasionally, they would dip into the pool for a cooldown. It was good.

Rebecca wore a new two-piece swimsuit. She had checked herself out in her mirror before pulling on running shorts—not that she ran, mind you—and a T-shirt. Alone in her room, she had admired the round breasts exposed by the halter top. As long as it was just the girls, she could be daring. Laney had sniggered, saying it wasn't daring if there was no risk.

Rebecca had ignored her.

She adjusted the big umbrella and let herself sink contentedly into her lounger, her mind still and quiet for a change. Zoe was reading or dozing, it was impossible to tell which with oversized sunglasses hiding her face.

The sound of the pool gate slamming and rowdy voices disrupted her peace. Annoyed at the intrusion, she opened her eyes to see Jackson, Josh, and Anson making their way toward the pool. They were boisterous and noisy, punching each other and clowning around. The boys were all in flip-flops and swim trunks, faded towels slung over their shoulders. Jackson's ankle was bare. A baseball cap was jammed backward over his blond hair, the bill pulled down on his neck. Josh wore a T-shirt declaring him Fat Tire Fatastic. Like AJ, he was wearing wraparound sunglasses and the guard-reg, red-and-white shorts.

Rebecca sat up, suddenly self-conscious, and irritated that she felt that way. She dropped her sunglasses over her eyes, pulled her T-shirt from her tote, and yanked it over her head. She drew her legs up and hugged her knees. Zoe looked up from her book and glanced at the boys.

Rebecca watched as Anson made a graceful dive into the water. He popped up halfway down the pool, flinging back his head, water flying from dark hair. Jackson pulled his T-shirt over his head, exposing a hard, flat abdomen rippled with lean muscle. Rebecca watched him closely from the safety of her sunglasses. Was that a tattoo on his side? It looked like a small lizard. Or maybe a dragon. She couldn't be sure; it was on the side away from her. Jackson dropped his towel and baseball cap carelessly on his chair, kicked off his flip-flops, and followed Anson into the pool. A polo ball appeared from somewhere, and an impromptu game sprang up.

Rebecca shifted her gaze to AJ, who was coming down from the guard tower. Josh climbed swiftly up to replace her, settling his tight, wiry frame into the chair and assuming the classic lifeguard attitude, arms resting on the sides of the chair, leaning slightly forward, body tense with vigilance. Did lifeguard training include instruction in that watchful pose? Rebecca's eyes followed AJ as she crossed the grass toward her and Zoe.

AJ was a sight! Tall, bronze skin glistening. High cheekbones, straight nose. She was subtly toned from her swimming, and she had a really great figure. Rebecca was secretly in awe. Angela was pretty and sleek, but AJ was stunning. The ratty hat and careless hair only accentuated her classic beauty. The sun was behind her, and a nimbus of light surrounded her. Only backlighting from the burning Colorado sun, but she could have been a mythical goddess. Rebecca was mesmerized. Had she never really seen AJ before? She couldn't help but smile.

AJ stopped in front of Rebecca. She pulled off the worn straw hat and shook out her hair. Wild streaks of color were woven into the brown hair that fell in no particular style to her shoulders. Her nose was peeling from sunburn. None of these things diminished her beauty.

Whistles and catcalls caused AJ to frown. She pulled an oversized T-shirt from her tote and slipped it over her head, much as Rebecca had done. Her movements, however, were casual to the point of indifference.

"Hey," she said.

"Hey, AJ. Wow. You look great!" Zoe's admiration showed on her face.

AJ shrugged, dragged another chaise close and arranged herself on it.

"God, AJ, you should be the one in a beauty contest, not Angela." Rebecca knew as she spoke that her comment would not be welcomed by AJ, but she couldn't help herself.

AJ turned hazel eyes on Rebecca. "That's *so* not who I am," she said flatly.

"I know, I know." Rebecca was apologetic. "But, jeez, AJ . . ." She twirled a lock of hair as she studied her friend. "You're a bunch of things, most of them totally the bomb. And none of them are about being drop-dead gorgeous. But that doesn't mean you *aren't*. Drop-dead gorgeous, I mean," she added.

Zoe looked thoughtful. AJ's closest friends knew her mother used her beauty to get what she wanted, to the exclusion of any other means.

And also that AJ held her mother in disdain for it. There was a long history of issues between AJ and her mother, but that was a big one.

"She's right, you know," Zoe said. "Your mom isn't a twit because she's beautiful. She's a twit because that's all she knows how to be."

And there it was. Out in the open for anyone to hear. AJ turned her steady gaze from Rebecca to Zoe. The friction in the air practically hummed.

Rebecca was holding her breath, so she guessed it wasn't really hours before anyone spoke, even though it felt like it. Eventually, it was AJ who broke the tension. She turned her attention to her tote, pulling out a paperback book and a pair of glasses with blue frames.

"You're right," she said. Her voice was resigned. "And I know that. I just want to be known for something else. That's all people see most of the time. The superficial, I mean."

"Do you get that it's their dumb droidness? Nothing you can do about dumb droids." Zoe's tone was matter-of-fact.

"Yeah," sighed AJ. "I do. Some of the time. I just want to be seen for, you know, more of who I really am." She settled her glasses on her face and shifted in her chair. "If only I had some idea who that is."

"Well, who does?" said Rebecca.

"You do," said AJ. "Zoe is all about college. Sam has her horses. You've got your writing. And that you love to hate Jackson." AJ glanced at the pool where the boys were clowning around.

Rebecca let the Jackson remark slide. She might have consoled AJ by telling them she wasn't writing, but then she'd have to explain why. Instead, she said, "Is that why you hide behind . . . um—" She broke off.

"Being such a mess?" AJ laughed.

"No, I . . . what I meant . . ." Rebecca looked sheepish.

AJ laughed again. "No," she said. "I am pretty much a mess most of the time. I've done it on purpose most of my life, and you know why." She looked from one to the other, and both girls nodded. AJ went on. "I was at Aunt Tillie's last weekend. You know, in Santa Monica."

"Cool!"

"How come? Just vacation?"

"No, more than that. Tom had an interview at UCLA. Anyway, Aunt Tillie, she pretty much says whatever she thinks. She said maybe it was time I quit hiding behind my mother's issues and took advantage of my own strengths."

Zoe's eyes widened. Rebecca nodded. She couldn't think of anything to say.

"Yeah. I told you. Says what she thinks."

"What do you think?" Zoe asked carefully.

"I think she might be right," said AJ. "I think she's kind of psychic. Plus, all that attitude takes a lot of energy to maintain."

"Wow." Rebecca was still speechless.

"Psychic?" Zoe asked.

"Or something like it," AJ said. "She's a massage therapist, and since my uncle died last winter, she's been expanding into other stuff. The place where she works . . ." AJ looked at Rebecca. "It's kind of like your sister's rock shop," she said.

"Cool. Sounds like a California thing," said Rebecca.

"Maybe." AJ shrugged. "She said I should come out for the summer. Being close to the beach would be totally the bomb, but I kind of need the money." She inclined her head toward the lifeguard tower and abruptly changed the subject. "Anyone hear from the rest?"

It took Rebecca a moment to shift gears. "Sam's all about the ranch," she said. "Ty's loving Steamboat. Who would've guessed! Her dad has taken her on a couple photo shoots. Apparently she has a 'facility for nature photography.' That's what Luna said."

"Luna the jewelry-artist girlfriend?" said Zoe. "LoveStar Luna?"

"Yep. That one." Rebecca continued, "Her dad's also letting her help him with his river rafting trips. For pay." Rebecca's voice conveyed her envy. "Travis Scott and some other people went up and rafted three days in a row. Ty was really weird about it."

"Weird how?"

"Well, like maybe she likes him or something."

"He's cute," said Zoe. "Dark and mysterious. And smart. What's not to like?"

Rebecca shrugged.

"Not everyone has forsworn all but beautiful blond boys," said Zoe. She looked pointedly at Rebecca.

AJ laughed. Zoe smirked. Rebecca glared.

"Sam hasn't been up?"

Rebecca shook her head. She knew Sam's next Reiki class was coming up. Sam would be home for that, but they wouldn't see much of her. Rebecca was still sworn to secrecy about the Reiki, so there was little she could add.

"And Zoe already started her precollege courses." Rebecca tried to keep the note of accusation out of her voice, but she wasn't sure she succeeded.

AJ abruptly got to her feet. "I'm getting something to drink," she said. "Either of you want something?"

"I do," said Zoe. She clambered out of her chair.

Rebecca shook her head. Stretching her legs back out on her chaise, she watched AJ and Zoe walk away. She took another long drink of water. It was warm, and she made a face. Settling into her lounge chair, she sighed deeply and closed her eyes. It seemed like everyone was doing exactly what they wanted for the summer. No one else seemed to be lost and flailing. Her job hadn't materialized. She wasn't writing. She barely saw her friends; they didn't seem to need her anymore. She knew she was being unreasonable, but the feeling cut deeply regardless. What was wrong with her?

Cold water dripping onto her bare legs made Rebecca gasp. Her eyes flew open. Jackson stood over her. He shook his head and sent water flying at her again. Rebecca yanked her legs up and scrubbed at them with her towel.

"Jeez, Jackson!"

Jackson dropped into AJ's chaise. He stretched out and linked his fingers behind his head. Rebecca couldn't help but notice his lean, fit body. He did have a tattoo! She dragged her eyes away, directing her gaze to his left ankle where she could see a faint scar.

"Summer good, Becka?" he asked lazily.

"It's okay." She hoped for casual and offhand, but she wasn't sure she got it. Her eyes wanted to go back to that tattoo.

"You here a lot?"

"Some," was all she said.

"AJ looks really hot," remarked Jackson.

A swift stab of something cold and unfriendly sliced through Rebecca's chest. She wrapped her arms around her legs. Her reactions concerning Jackson were always such a muddle. Was he merely commenting on a fact? It *was* a fact: AJ looked fabulous. Why did it bother her that he noticed? *Did* it bother her? Her thoughts were scattered.

Don't let them see when they get to you. Those had been AJ's words. Rebecca tried to school her face into an impassive expression. She reached for a feeling of detachment. She pushed her sunglasses to the top of her head and fixed Jackson with innocent eyes. She smiled at him, sweet and cool at the same time. "So, are you still on the team?" she asked. "Ankle okay? Don't have to repeat freshman year?"

"Ow, brutal!" Jackson laughed, clutching both hands to his heart and pulling a face of mock pain. It didn't mean anything. Rebecca had seen it before. This was well-known turf.

"Mr. Hammond not threatening to bust you for cheating?"

Jackson looked at her in surprise. Almost immediately, his expression slipped into the familiar FIGJAM grin. *That was mean*, she said to herself. *Now who's being a jerk?* She dropped her own eyes in discomfort, waiting for Jackson to retaliate with a smart remark.

"You're in my chair." AJ and Zoe had returned. AJ looked coolly at Jackson.

"He was just leaving," said Rebecca.

Jackson unfolded his long frame from the chaise. He half bowed to AJ and made an exaggerated gesture toward the chair, flashing his lopsided grin. AJ was unmoved. Jackson nodded at Zoe, still grinning, and she smiled up at him. As he sauntered past Rebecca's chaise, he ruffled her hair. She wrenched her head away, but he was already gone, his laughter floating behind him.

"What was that all about?" asked Zoe.

"Nothing," said Rebecca, perhaps a trifle too quickly. "It was just Jackson doing what he does best—being a jerk." She pulled her sunglasses back down over her eyes.

Zoe gave Rebecca a long look but said nothing. AJ seated herself in her chaise and stretched her legs. She adjusted the back and settled into the recliner with a sigh.

"Here, Becks," she said in a neutral voice. "I brought you something." And she tossed a bag of cheese puffs onto Rebecca's lap.

"Thanks," said Rebecca. She tore the bag open and extracted a bright orange puff. Behind the sunglasses, her eyes followed Jackson as he made a neat, tight dive into the pool.

CHAPTER 47

Do You Know This Girl?

June 21

REBECCA WAS HELPING her mom clean up after supper, which had been a trial. Her mother had tried to draw her out about her afternoon with her friends. She should have been exuberant after being with Zoe and AJ. But all the exciting things happening for her friends left her feeling frustrated and left out. Was she doing something wrong? Were the stories doing this to her? Was it her fault? She couldn't explain it, and she certainly couldn't talk about it.

She methodically placed dishes in the dishwasher. Along with everything else, she missed feeling relaxed and open with her mom. At least as much as she missed her writing.

You need a trusted perspective on all this. Laney's voice was soft in her head.

Yeah, but how do I even start that conversation? "Hey, Mom, guess what I can do?"

You just have to start. Laney wasn't being very helpful.

Maybe if her dad wasn't right there in the family room, she could do it. Maybe she and her mom could go out somewhere.

"Mom, do you think—"

"Becka, do you know this girl?"

Her father's voice interrupted Rebecca. He was sitting in his favorite chair with a book in his lap. But he had the remote in one hand and was watching the TV with interest.

"What girl?" Rebecca sighed and glanced at her mother. She went to stand beside her father's chair.

"Hold on. Let me back up." Jack twiddled with the remote. "I recorded this show a while back. I don't know why this news piece got picked up."

"Because you don't know how to record, Dad," said Rebecca with affection.

Her father grunted but didn't respond. The picture on the TV, which had been racing backward, came to a halt to reveal a pair of talking-head newscasters.

"And in the local news, one of our crews caught this amazing scene on tape last night. This is a truly remarkable demonstration of pluck and courage."

The camera cut to a stage setup of a tropical scene, complete with potted palms and a pond. Rebecca's breath caught. She could feel her heart thudding in her ears. She heard the announcer's voice as if from a great distance, and not a word of it registered in her brain. A long-legged brunette in a skimpy swimsuit and high heels was strolling past the pond and onto a runway. Another girl appeared from behind the palm trees. Her slender figure was nicely accented by a one-piece swimsuit. She was wearing impossibly high-heeled shoes. Her white-blonde hair hung perfectly to just above her shoulders. She smiled graciously at the judges and gave a little wave to the audience.

Angela.

Rebecca couldn't breathe. She steadied herself with a hand on the back of her father's chair. She pressed the heel of her other hand against her chest. Angela came abreast of the pond. Still smiling, she made a little stumble. She tried to save her balance, *almost* had it, but couldn't regain her footing. She teetered precariously on the ridiculously high heels, and then, arms pinwheeling, plunged into the koi pond. Water flew in all directions. One shoe sailed through the air to land at the base of a potted palm.

Rebecca gasped, her hand flying to her mouth. Her father laughed. Her mother had come to stand beside Rebecca. "That poor girl," she murmured. "Do you know her, Becka?"

Rebecca nodded wordlessly. Her eyes were riveted on the television. She barely heard the announcer over the thunder of blood drumming in her ears. She watched in horrified fascination as Angela plummeted into the water, and then in amazement as the Ice Maiden got to her feet in the pond. She pulled off the remaining shoe and hurled it after the other one. She stepped out of the pond. She was wet, but the pond was shallow, and the white-blonde hair was mostly dry, if somewhat ruffled. Angela smoothed it with both hands. She gave herself a little shake, pasted a brilliant smile on her face, and proceeded toward the runway. Barefoot and soaked, walking on the balls of her feet like a dancer, beads of water trickling down her bare skin, she made her promenade to the end of the runway. The audience loved it. A few people clapped; there were some whistles. And then the entire auditorium was on its feet clapping and cheering. Angela's smile relaxed as she made her way back up the runway. She waved to the audience on each side, water droplets flying, and the applause became thunderous. The next girl was coming down the runway, stepping carefully around the wet footprints left by Angela. Another contestant made her appearance on stage from behind the waterfall, cautiously avoiding puddled water alongside the koi pond. The girl who had preceded Angela was just disappearing behind the palms. But all eyes were glued on Angela.

"We weren't able to talk to Ms. Thornton following the pageant," the announcer was saying to her fellow newscaster.

The other talking head nodded, smiling. She said, "Apparently Ms. Thornton placed next to last. I can't imagine another contestant topping that for disaster. A no-show maybe . . ."

"What fortitude," said the first announcer. "And of other interest locally . . ."

Rebecca didn't hear any more. "Oh my God!" she breathed. She turned wide eyes to her mother. Maggie looked carefully at her daughter, instinct bringing the hairs on the back of her neck to attention. Her father was chuckling.

Maggie turned on him. "Jack, that's cruel," she said. "What if that had been Rebecca?"

"I don't think we'll see Rebecca in that sort of contest," he said, still grinning broadly. "Not that she couldn't. But if it *was* our Becka, it would be different."

"How can you say that!" Maggie was becoming angry. "You're being totally insensitive. And what an obnoxious double standard!"

Grateful for the conflict distracting her parents, Rebecca escaped. She hurried down the stairs to her room and closed the door quietly behind her. She flung herself on her bed and buried her face in a pillow. Her heart was still pounding.

There was now only one Event left to play out. She had no doubt how it would go. And she had no idea what she should do about this incredible ability.

***

Rebecca didn't sleep well that night. She lay awake for hours, watching shadows cast by a three-quarter moon move across the patio. The brightly colored flowers in her mother's big pots were washed to soft shades of gray in the moonlight. When she finally slipped into a restless sleep, it was troubled by dreams. She couldn't remember them in the morning, but she felt edgy and off center. She couldn't get the images out of her mind of Angela plunging into the pool, followed by her courageous walk, barefoot and dripping, down the runway. Angela had exhibited a lot more spirit than Rebecca had expected. Maybe she wasn't just a spoiled rich girl.

Rebecca wondered if she had misjudged Angela too. If Jackson could be a smart athlete, maybe Angela wasn't just a twit. It was all so baffling, especially in light of Angela's typically cold behavior and superior attitude. Was that a cover, like Jackson's irreverence? *Was* Jackson's irreverence a cover? Rebecca didn't have any idea. But it didn't explain Angela stealing Rebecca's idea for her pageant skit! Should she have just let that go? Didn't Angela have to balance the karmic scales too? Rebecca thought maybe so. Maybe it would have been better to have left Angela to flounder in her own cauldron of fortune, or misfortune. The thought of balancing providence, as always, made Rebecca uneasy. She paced her room. Where would this all end?

She slumped into the chair in front of her desk and dropped her head onto her arms. She sat that way for what seemed a long time. A loud banging at her window made her raise her head. There, framed in the window, were Andy and Scoundrel, one grinning and making a ridiculous face, the other slobbering happily. Rebecca stared at them. After a long moment, she got to her feet, went to the window, and closed the shutters.

"Hey!" She could still hear Andy's voice, muffled by the closed shutters. She ignored it. The banging resumed, but it didn't take Andy long to grow bored with this line of entertainment.

Rebecca went back to her desk and sat down. She powered up her laptop and stared at the blinking cursor. Without really thinking, she began to type.

One final Event. She promised herself this would be the last. She had made this promise before, but this time she really meant it. As a result of her extraordinary performance after falling into the koi pond at the regional semifinal pageant, Angela would be contacted by a local modeling agency. There would be training and some local shoots for area retailers. It could lead to much bigger things. Rebecca didn't know if the pageant had been the regional semifinals or if there was any sort of local modeling agency. Her fingers seemed to move across the keys on their own.

When she was finished, she titled the piece Modeling, saved it, and closed her laptop. Feeling a little lighter, she dressed and went upstairs.

CHAPTER 48

Some Good News

June 23

REBECCA OPENED HER eyes to look at her nightstand clock. Not there. For a moment, she was confused. Then she remembered. She had retired it in favor of her iPhone. Sometimes she felt bad about that. The little clock had served her well for longer than she could remember and had been replaced simply because of newer technology. It didn't seem fair. But then, the world rarely seemed fair.

She was groggy with sleep. But she had heard the special tone she had set up for text messages. Hadn't she? She rolled onto her side to reach her phone, dislodging Tinker from her place against her side. The big orange cat protested and resettled herself heavily against Rebecca's thigh. Rebecca smoothed the silky fur with one hand and snagged the iPhone with the other. She noted that it was daylight outside, but the sun wasn't on her shutters yet. The iPhone said it was only 5:17. Irritation flared. Who could be texting her before sunrise! Maybe it had been her imagination. Or a dream.

But no, there was a new text, and it was from Sam! A surge of elation raced through Rebecca. She sat up and crisscrossed her legs, forcing Tinker to vacate her newly claimed spot. The cat regarded Rebecca with an annoyed expression and curled up again at the foot of the bed, her tail wrapped around her body, the twitching tip clearly conveying her lack of amusement. Rebecca opened the text.

Sam had written: "Sorry its so early. Have 2 work. Sunrise ride. Late already. Coming home Fri morning and 4 weeknd. HAVE to C U! SO much 2 tell!"

"OMG!" Rebecca breathed the words half aloud. She addressed Tinker at the foot of the bed. "Sam's coming home!" Rebecca ran both hands through her sleep-rumpled hair. "This is so great!" Tinker opened one eye a narrow slit. The tip of her tail still twitched.

Wide awake, Rebecca slid out of bed. But now what? The sun wasn't even up yet! No one would be up for ages. It was Sunday, wasn't it? The days all seemed to slide together with no school. She double-checked her phone. Sunday.

Her father's Sunday-morning breakfast routine was on hiatus for the summer. Rebecca half hoped it would be on hiatus permanently. The week's high and low thing had gotten too stressful, what with all her Events and wondering when the karmic shoe was going to drop. Laney had "suggested" that Rebecca clean up her act, but Rebecca feared the horse was out of the barn on that one. Today the traditional Sunday afternoon with Nanna and Pappa was on, though. Even Lissa would be there. It had been suspended since Rebecca's birthday because Nanna had been away a lot with book-signing commitments.

She thought about going back to bed. That was an attractive thought, especially given the time; but she wasn't just wide awake, she was wired. She could read, maybe. She had taken the new Sarah Addison Allen book to the pool a couple times, but she hadn't really gotten into it yet. She found the book and picked it up, running one hand over the smooth cover. Not so long ago, she had imagined herself writing books like these. And like the ones Nanna wrote.

You could write, murmured Laney.

"No!" A quick little shake of her head.

But could she? Could she tap into that nameless place the Events came from, but with a simple story as the goal? Some pretty scary things had come from that nameless place! And she had honed accessing it writing Events, not Laney stories. Could she write and *not* tap into that place? What would happen if she *did* write something? Would it manifest in her life? Could she *intend* that it not? Could she just refuse to write something she wouldn't want to happen to her?

"Maybe it wouldn't be about me," she said half aloud.

It's always about you, whispered Laney. *Because I'm you, remember?*

"What if I don't write about you?"

You always write about me. The voice felt . . . petulant.

But I don't have to, thought Rebecca. *I can write about anything!*

Laney was silent.

Rebecca's thoughts were whirling. The Laney stories had always been to imagine herself in a life she wanted. One she was too timid to live for real. One with fewer rules. One where there was excitement. One where she could be in control and make things happen.

Still holding the book, Rebecca sat on the edge of her bed. She had been making rather a lot of things happen recently. Some of them hadn't been too good, and even the ones that *were* good had frightened her on a deep level. Was this what it was like to be in control? Always afraid and worrying about some kind of payback? She wondered. Could she be more like the Laney in her stories but not like the . . .

Okay, say it, she said to herself.

Not like the you *who's been throwing people under the bus.* Her thought. Laney's voice.

If she did this carefully, with potential outcomes in mind—

Her line of thought was interrupted by the sound of the French doors opening on the main floor, followed by Scoundrel racing across the patio. Who could be up this early?

Rebecca peeked out her door. Lissa's door was open, and her barely rumpled bed was empty. Still in her jams, Rebecca went quietly up the stairs. Lissa was in the kitchen making coffee. She jumped when she heard Rebecca, spilling beans on the counter.

"Jeez, you scared me!" And then, "What are you doing up so early?"

"I got a text from Sam," said Rebecca.

"At this hour!"

"Well, you know. Sunrise trail ride for a bunch of city dweebs."

"She really does love horses and that ranch thing, doesn't she?"

"She does." Rebecca paused, reflecting. "She's gonna be home this weekend. I haven't seen her since school let out. I've really missed her!"

"Mmm." Lissa scooped up the spilled beans and put them in the grinder. The grinder whirred. Lissa added water to the pot, poured the fresh grounds into a cone and tucked it neatly in its place. She turned the machine on.

"I have some news too," said Lissa. The delicious aroma of the fresh brew was already filling the kitchen. She took a mug from a cabinet. "You want some?" she asked, nodding her head at the coffeepot.

"No. Thanks." Rebecca shook her head. Then she reconsidered. Why not? Try something new. "Maybe. If there's cream," she added.

Lissa smiled. "There's always cream," she said. "Mom makes sure of that."

"So what's your news?"

Lissa set another mug next to hers. She poured cream into both of them. Coffee was still dripping into the pot. Lissa leaned back against the counter, waiting.

"Mrs. Mason is back," she said. "And she's ready for you to come to work."

"OMG!" Rebecca pulled out a stool and sat down hard. "That's so . . . out of nowhere."

"You still want the job, don't you?"

"Yes!" This could really turn around a so-far-unimpressive summer. Then she sobered. "What about my interview?"

"She said she'd just try you out for a few days. Since you're my sister, she thinks you'll be just like me."

"I'm not anything like you! You have everything so together."

"Not always." Lissa smiled at her sister. She poured coffee into the waiting mugs and handed one to Rebecca. "Sometimes you have to fake it till you make it. The trick is knowing when that is."

Rebecca nodded. She had done that twice with Fat Mr. Hammond. She thought she could do it with Mrs. Mason as well. Probably. Yeah, probably she could.

"So when do I start?"

"Tuesday." Lissa's glance was a question.

"I can do that," said Rebecca. "It will cut into my pool time—"

"Right." Lissa rolled her eyes. "And then Wednesday and Thursday. I'm at The Center those days. In case that matters."

Rebecca nodded. "It's good." She grinned. "In case I screw up."

"Because I can drive you."

"Oh. Yeah."

Rebecca said to no one in particular, "And I'll have Friday and the weekend to spend with Sam!"

Lissa sipped her coffee. "We're really lucky to have these jobs," she said. Her voice was serious. "You know that, don't you?"

"I guess I will come Tuesday," said Rebecca. She sipped at her own coffee. It was hot, and sweet with cream. But still a little . . . something. She added more cream. Tasted it. "Not bad," she said.

"So long as you have coffee to go with all that cream," said Lissa. But she chuckled.

The girls sat at the island with their coffee. There didn't seem to be much else to talk about. But the silence was comfortable. Scoundrel wanted back in. Lissa let him in and filled his food bowl. Tinker wanted out. Rebecca opened the door for her.

"What time are we going to Nanna's?" asked Rebecca.

"The usual, I think," said Lissa. "Around four."

"Mmm." Rebecca nodded. "What are you doing today? Before Nanna's?"

"I'm going to The Center. There's a delivery of new crystals in." Lissa glanced at Rebecca, debating whether to say more. "And I want to get to know them."

"Get to know them? Like, 'Hello, I'm Clear Quartz, nice to meet you?'"

Lissa laughed. "More so than you might think," she said. "Stones are different. Different hardness, different makeup. And different energy."

Rebecca swiveled her stool to face Lissa full-on. "Different energy?"

"Yes. There's a signature energy about each category of stone. Azeztulite, for instance, which is in the quartz family, has a quartz vibration, but also its own signature. It's a very high frequency. Some people can feel it."

"Can you?" Rebecca looked hard at her sister.

"Turns out I can," said Lissa quietly. "And I love it."

Like Sam and Reiki, thought Rebecca, but she didn't say it. She felt like the odd one out again. Like she was missing something—only, she didn't know what, not to mention how to get it. She pushed her coffee mug away. It was still half full.

"More?" Lissa asked.

Rebecca shook her head. "There's something I want to do," she said. "Can we talk before Tuesday? About what I should do at the doll shop?"

"Sure." Lissa smiled. "But mostly, just be prepared to play with dolls."

Rebecca made a face at Lissa. She pushed back from the island and headed for the stairs. "Thanks for the coffee," she said over her shoulder. She was halfway down the stairs before Lissa could answer.

In her room, Rebecca washed her face and dressed in shorts and an old T-shirt. She straightened her rumpled covers. You couldn't really say she made the bed. She picked up the Sarah Addison Allen book again and stared at the cover. But her mind was somewhere else. She put the book back down, pulled out her desk chair, and sat in front of her laptop. She took a deep breath and closed her eyes. She unconsciously twisted a tawny lock around one finger. Another deep breath, and her fingers went to the keyboard, where they drummed a weightless staccato, too light to depress the keys. She reached for that place where the Events had come from. There was a little tickle in the pit of her stomach.

But nothing came. She couldn't quite make her fingers go.

You don't make them go. You let *them go,* whispered Laney in her head.

Rebecca didn't know how.

CHAPTER 49

That Energy Thing

June 23

IT WAS JUST family at Nanna's, plus April, but she was as good as family. Sam was still in Colorado Springs. Ty was in Steamboat. And Zoe was studying for an upcoming exam. Jimmy Norton was in trouble and grounded. Rebecca didn't mind that it was just family. Pappa grilled chicken, and Nanna and April had made fruit salad and baked yeast bread, which was yummy, especially when covered in April's honey butter, which Rebecca smeared on liberally. There were frosty glasses of lemonade and iced tea. They ate on the north deck, which was shielded from the late-June sun by a stand of lodgepole pines. The air was pungent with warm pine resin, the smell of dry summer grasses, and grilling chicken. Inkjet hung out looking expectant, anticipating that someone would reward his excellence with tasty treats.

The conversation was relaxed and low-key. Nanna talked about her book signings. She didn't particularly like to travel, but the signing tours were mandatory according to her agent. She always enjoyed meeting her readers, she said, so that was the upside. She had had signings in the big bookstores, but also in smaller, one-of-a-kind stores that managed to hang on despite the lower prices and larger inventory of the big chains. The little stores were unique and friendly, often with a tiny coffee shop where regulars came to meet and have a cuppa even when they weren't shopping for books.

April asked Rebecca how Sam was doing with her Reiki practice. The Reiki II class had been postponed because of the book tour.

"I have no idea," said Rebecca. She shrugged dismissively. Nanna and April exchanged a quick glance. "I haven't seen her since school let out," she went on. She reached for a nonchalant tone, but she wasn't sure she got it.

"Maybe you should take Reiki I," said April. "Then you girls can do Level II together. Practice on each other."

Rebecca bristled. Was it a flaming conspiracy? "What makes you think I even want to take Reiki!" she demanded.

Nanna spoke softly. "Perhaps you don't, sweetie. And that's fine. You and Sam have done everything together, or with Zoe, since you were little. That's all we're thinking."

"What, do you talk about me when I'm not here?"

"Of course!" Nanna smiled. "Don't you feel the love coming your way?"

There was no way to respond to that from a position of indignation or hostility. Rebecca bit into a chicken thigh, but it didn't have much taste. She put it down. She took a sip of her lemonade. She refused to meet anyone's eyes.

Maggie told them about the Disneyland trip. She tried to draw Rebecca into the conversation, but Rebecca stayed stubbornly mum.

Andy was quiet and down in the mouth about Jimmy's absence. He refused to tell what Jimmy had done to get into trouble. When pressed, he set his mouth firmly and shook his head, his face closed and impassive.

"It must be in the gene pool," said Pappa. There was general laughter at that, but Andy and Rebecca didn't join in.

Lissa talked about the new face of The Center, formerly the rock shop. Mrs. Mason had put a lot of money into the space, taking over leases on the adjoining sides. The increased space accommodated the various classes, such as yoga, Reiki, Tai Chi and Qigong, meditation, plus more room and better displays for the crystals. There were now also books on just about every alternative healing topic you could think of, and a comfortable seating area with a fireplace. Mrs. Mason was thinking of adding a small tearoom.

"We get shipments of crystals every week," said Lissa. "It's a challenge to keep up. Many of them are new finds."

"I'm amazed how many new crystals are presenting themselves," said April. "Even though we knew they would in the new energies."

Nanna, Lissa, and Maggie nodded thoughtfully.

"So did you 'get to know' the new stones today?" asked Rebecca.

Lissa didn't rise to the bait. "Mmm, some," was all she said.

"How do you get to know a rock?" asked Jack.

"You take it out to dinner and a movie." Andy smirked.

The explosion of laughter around the table broke the tension. It would subside, they would resume their meal, and then someone would giggle, and the whole table would be engulfed in laughter again. Andy's sulk was broken, and he looked very pleased with himself.

When she could finally talk, Lissa explained to Andy, "You can know *about* the rock," she said. "It's hardness and color." She fingered the stone at her neck. "Take amethyst, for instance. It's in the quartz family, so it has a trigonal crystal system—that means the way it was formed—and a hardness of seven. That's pretty hard. Diamond is the hardest at 10."

April and Nanna looked at Lissa in surprise. "Listen to you," murmured April.

Lissa laughed. "I've already told you more than I know," she said. "What I really like is how they feel. It's beyond cool." She smiled at Nanna and April. "I love the different energies."

There it was again. "I hear a lot about energies lately," said Rebecca. She frowned. "It's all about the energy. Everything is energy. I don't get it."

"Didn't you take science last year?" asked her father.

"Yeah, Dad. I did. We tortured frogs and mixed up nasty potions in little vials."

"Take a quantum science class," said Lissa. "Then you'll get it."

"I'd like to get it without taking quantum science," said Rebecca.

Nanna pushed her chair back and began gathering up serving bowls and empty plates. It wasn't lost on Rebecca that April did too, at exactly the same time. Rebecca was convinced, pretty much had always been, the two women read each other's minds. Or maybe they read each other's energy. Or maybe it was the same thing. There was a little tickle in the pit of her stomach. In her irritation, she brushed it off.

"I suspect you know more about it than you think you do," said Nanna. "You just haven't connected the dots. Why don't you and I have a conversation about it sometime. Just the two of us." She smiled at Rebecca, and her tone was casual.

Rebecca looked at her grandmother. The energy thing was a potentially loaded topic. But maybe she needed to hear about it. And maybe she could tell Nanna what had been going on. She wasn't sure about that part. But maybe. She nodded.

"I have cookies," Nanna said. "Nothing else for dessert. And they're from the freezer. April and I haven't had time to do anything since we got back."

"Cookies from your freezer are plenty special, Mom," said Maggie.

"Let's have them inside," said Nanna. "It's pretty toasty out here still."

So they did. Pappa and Jack headed for Pappa's den, each with a handful of cookies. Andy disappeared downstairs to play with the trains. April said her good nights, citing much to do after the extended absence. Lissa curled up in the great room with her iPhone, presumably texting James. Nanna and Maggie arranged themselves comfortably on opposite ends of a sofa, shoes off, feet overlapping in the middle, and settled in for a catch-up chat.

Rebecca noted all these pairings off and disappearances, feeling the odd one out once again. This had never happened before at Nanna's. At loose ends, she made her way up to the loft and then to the aerie. Inkjet tagged along, winding himself between her ankles. In the little room beneath the eaves, Rebecca stretched out on the bed, and Inkjet curled against her side. She intended to text Sam; maybe she'd be off work by now. But it had been a very long day. Her eyes were scratchy. She would just close them for a moment.

Almost immediately, she was asleep.

CHAPTER 50

Alfie

June 28

REBECCA HAD TEXTED Sam several times in the ensuing days, but there had been only one response, and it had been vague. Friday had arrived, and Rebecca still didn't know what time Sam was due, or even if she was still coming. She had to believe Sam was coming, though. She just did. She dressed in jean shorts and a sheer shirt, knotted at the waist, over a colored bandeau. She fastened the mustang pendant around her neck. She thought about the strappy sandals, but, in the end, she left her feet bare.

She wandered restlessly around her room and finally settled in the window seat, one leg curled beneath her. Her thoughts turned to the past few days. Things had been crazy to the extreme, what with starting at the doll shop. Lissa had taken her in to meet Mrs. Mason. Rebecca had worn the leather wrist piece with the celestite stone, and Mrs. Mason had recognized it as coming from her store, which seemed to please her greatly. The old lady was nice, and she gave every impression of having her wits about her. For this, Rebecca was relieved.

The dolls were incredible. Rebecca followed Lissa and Mrs. Mason around a large room filled with locked glass display cases. They were from all over the world and spanned more than a three-hundred-year period. Some were in pristine condition; some not so much, with a missing eye or a broken cheek. The older dolls were mostly porcelain, Mrs. Mason told her. There was another large room with many more-current dolls, and these tended to have enviable wardrobes. Rebecca was amazed, and this, too, clearly pleased Mrs. Mason. The dolls were to be handled wearing special cotton gloves. There would be no exceptions. Mrs. Mason looked hard at Rebecca, and she nodded her understanding. Lissa said they had been intending to create an index of the collection, and that working with Miss Amelia on the index (Mrs. Mason had said she would be called Miss Amelia, or Miss A., "if you don't mind, dearie") would be a good way to get up to speed.

"Are you good on a computer, dearie?" Miss A. wanted to know.

"Pretty much," said Rebecca. "Better if it's a Mac."

"And you can type?"

"I can type," said Rebecca.

Can you ever, said Laney in her head.

"Ah, excellent. Excellent," said Miss A. She smiled her satisfaction.

They would have tea together for lunch this first day, all three of them; but Miss A. usually lunched by herself, and then she napped; so in the future, Rebecca would be responsible for her own sustenance and refreshment. That's what Miss A. called lunch. Rebecca would also do a few errands and favors for Miss Amelia, the nature of which remained unnamed. "Don't worry about it," whispered Lissa, and Rebecca relaxed a little. Lissa had left them after lunch. Miss A. had skipped her nap, and she and Rebecca had worked quietly but companionably through the afternoon. Rebecca thought the old lady was really sweet. Not crazy at all. It definitely had the makings of a dream job.

The doorbell pulled Rebecca from her reverie. She flew up the stairs and to the front door. There was Sam! Rebecca threw open the door, and the girls danced around the room hugging and laughing. Finally, Sam extricated herself.

"And this is Alfie," she said.

Rebecca realized another person was there, still standing on the front porch. He was dressed like a cowboy. Boots, jeans, faded denim shirt. Western hat that cast his face in shadow. But he didn't "feel" like a cowboy. Rebecca didn't know where this came from, or even how a cowboy should feel, if you wanted to get technical. But this young man felt like he wasn't all there. Or maybe he was somewhere else. A cowboy wouldn't feel that way, would he?

"Alfie?"

"My cousin," said Sam. The girls stood side by side. "He's my ride while I'm here," she continued. She looked pointedly at Alfie. "Alfie owes me a couple favors."

Alfie smiled a kind of distant smile. Apparently, none of it was a big deal to him.

"Alf, this is Rebecca Jean," said Sam rather formally.

Alfie took off his hat and held it by its crown in one hand. He dipped his head, the smallest of nods, at Rebecca. "Ma'am." His hair was black and straight and conformed to his head in the shape of the Stetson. His eyes were dark too. He was well built and nice-looking. High cheekbones, wide mouth with full lips. But Alfie felt . . . Rebecca couldn't quite put a finger on it. And the "ma'am"! What was that? It made her feel pleased and grown-up but also irritated all at the same time.

"Alfie." Rebecca nodded back. She slipped her arm around Sam's waist. Alfie made no indication that he noticed. Rebecca considered him for a moment, and then she turned her attention back to Sam, pointedly ignoring Alfie. "What shall we do? Are you staying here tonight? Does Zoe know you're here? AJ has to work all weekend, but we can catch her at the pool. And you know Ty's in Steamboat."

Sam looked from Rebecca to Alfie. "Alf," she said, "would you bring in my kit? Just the blue bag, not the big one." She turned back to Rebecca. "I don't care what we do as long as we can *talk*. My mom's not too happy, but I'm staying here tonight. I know Ty isn't around and AJ's working. Zoe doesn't know I'm home unless you told her. I need to talk to *you*!"

"And *look* at you!" Rebecca stepped back and stared at Sam. The same tousled blonde curls in the familiar state of wild disarray, except longer. The same green eyes sparkling with life. The same jeans and boots. A faded but serviceable Beatles T-shirt. The mustang pendant at her neck. But Sam! "OMG! You look amazing!"

Sam smiled with pleasure. "Yeah," she said. "I've lost two jean sizes. The bomb, huh?"

Rebecca was still staring. It was essentially the same Sam impressively filling out the T-shirt. Just less of her. She had really slimmed down. She was also tan and toned. She was a sight!

RAINIE YORK

"You look amazing," Rebecca said again.

Sam hugged Rebecca again. "I'm also blistered, sunburned, and sore in places I didn't even know I had," she said. "But that's what happens when you work from before sunup till after dark. Not much time to eat. And sometimes it's not all that great." Sam made a face. "Turns out I'm not much into eating crap that's full of ashes and has been burned in a dirty pan over a campfire." She ran both hands through the blonde curls. "The city dudes seem to find it charming. Or romantic. Something." Her expression said, *There's no explaining city dweebs.*

Alfie reappeared with a blue duffle. He placed it on the floor just inside the door.

"Thanks, Alf," she said. She crossed to Alfie and stood close to him, a hand on his arm. "You can go. I'll see you tomorrow." Sam glanced at Rebecca. "Unless we decide to go somewhere. So keep your phone on you," she said. "And turned on and charged." Alfie nodded. "And be back here at lunchtime if you don't hear from me," she said. "That means noon. Sun's directly overhead. Got it?"

Alfie nodded again, a little smile playing around the corners of his mouth. Rebecca felt a level of intimacy in that little smile.

"Got what?" asked Sam. Her eyes twinkled at Alfie. She didn't sound condescending, more like it was a joke between them.

"Phone with me. On. Charged." The little smile. "Everything's charged." He spoke softly, his eyes meeting hers. He seemed more . . . present. Something very personal passed between them. Rebecca sensed it, even though she couldn't name it. "Back here when the sun's straight up tomorrow."

"Great!" Sam twined her arms around Alfie's neck and hugged him. Alfie held Sam by her waist, his hands making her seem small. He rested his chin briefly on the top of her head. She stood on tiptoe to speak quietly in his ear, and then she stepped back.

Alfie smiled down at her. It was like a caress. He raised his hand, as though he might touch Sam's cheek, but he stuck it in his pocket instead. He turned, crossed the porch, and ambled down the sidewalk to a waiting pickup. It was big, black, and dusty, and emblazoned with the ranch logo. He touched his hat before he stepped up into the truck.

Sam waved back, her expression pensive. The truck started up with a roar and rumbled down the street. Only after it turned the corner and disappeared from sight did Sam bring her attention back to Rebecca.

"Becks," she sighed. "Wow. Becks. Look how tan you are. Did you streak your hair?"

Rebecca shook her head. "No. Pool time. So what's up with Alfie?" Rebecca pulled Sam into the kitchen. She poured two lemonades, pushed one in front of Sam, and they sat at the big island. Rebecca fingered the mustang pendant at her throat. Sam did too.

"I haven't been wearing mine much this summer," said Sam. "It'd just get dirty. Or lost."

"Mmm." Rebecca was noncommittal. She looked expectantly at Sam. Sam tapped the end of a finger against her mouth. The nail was bare and short. All of them were. She took a sip of lemonade. Rebecca waited.

"So the cousin I told you about . . . who wouldn't ride horses. Got hypnotized?"

Rebecca nodded.

"That wasn't quite right," said Sam. "It would have been hard to explain. It's *still* hard to explain!" She scrubbed her hands through her hair again. "He was enchanted with horses. You couldn't keep him out of the stables. But he didn't want to ride. You couldn't get him on a horse. He said there had to be an agreement"—Sam hesitated—"between the rider and the horse." She shook her head. "Weird, I know."

Sam searched for words. The green eyes were focused on something far away. "I'm not so sure it was even the hypnosis. I think maybe Alfie . . . worked it out himself . . . between him and the horses. Like I said, weird."

"Like Tyler and her testing," prompted Rebecca.

"Yes!" Sam came fully back. "I think there are all kinds of ways we convince ourselves to . . . do stuff."

"Weird," agreed Rebecca.

Sam looked Rebecca full-on. "There's a shitload of weird going around, don't you think?"

Rebecca didn't know if it was a loaded comment. Maybe it was just her own paranoia. "Seems like it on the working dude ranch," was all she said.

Sam nodded. "Yeah." She was quiet for a moment. "Alfie's always been a little different. Hard to pinpoint just how." Sam pondered this for a moment. "Not afraid of horses, though!"

"He likes to be outside," Sam went on. "Spends days out in the woods sometimes. Or just takes off. He goes over to Durango. I don't know why." Sam looked thoughtful. Rebecca was even more convinced Sam was keeping something back. "He knows about all kinds of stuff. Sam shrugged. "But it's with the horses that he's so . . ." Sam shook her head. "Amazing," she went on. "He communicates with them somehow. And it's on their level, not ours. All animals, really, but especially with horses. It's like he can *feel* them or something."

"Is that the . . . um . . . the clairs thing? You know, what you told me about Reiki?"

"It's more than that," said Sam. "I'm pretty good with the horses. I can sort of sense things. And I'm getting better all the time. And that *is* the clairs. At least I think it is." She looked at Rebecca again. "I've told him everything I know about Reiki," she said. "And it's like he already knew it. Just had to remember. He's a natural. I don't even know if it's really Reiki if you haven't had the classes and the attunements." Sam sipped at her lemonade. "I could sure do with one of April's cookies," she said hopefully. "If you happened to have any lying around . . ."

Rebecca rummaged through the pantry and found a tin of chocolate cookies. She placed it in front of Sam.

Sam's face lit up. "Wow, thanks," she said around a mouthful. "Mmm, these are delish. Missed breakfast this morning."

Rebecca slid back onto her chair. "Just say it, Sam."

Sam looked at her, as if still debating. At length, she said, "Okay." She took a deep breath. "It's like he's not from here."

"What do you mean?" Chills ran up Rebecca's spine; she had had the exact thought!

"I have absolutely no idea, but that's how it feels. Sometimes he comes across as not very smart. But he is. Especially about certain things. He just doesn't care about . . . well, you know, the crap. If you can get him to focus, which isn't easy, he's amazing. He's really gentle. He gets ribbed sometimes by hands. New hands," Sam corrected herself. "He just walks away from it like he doesn't even hear it. Maybe he doesn't. A lot of the time, he's sort of . . . spacey and . . . just not really here. But when he's outside and with the horses . . . jeez! You'd have to see it to believe it. I see it all the time, and it's still hard to believe. Uncle Clint has fired hands; sent a stupid, rich customer packing for abusing a horse; changed vets; switched stalls—all on Alfie's say-so. Usually no questions asked."

Rebecca didn't know what to say, so she said nothing. She waited for Sam to go on.

"So I keep an eye on him when I can. No one messes with him if one of us is around. Me or Uncle Clint." A little pause. "And Alfie shows me stuff about the horses."

"And the favors?"

"Sometimes he sort of wanders off somewhere instead of doing his chores," said Sam. Her eyes were far off, her thoughts with them. "I find him if I can. Do the chores if I can't."

"Is that why your days are so long?"

"Sometimes. It's worth it."

"And what else?" Rebecca was pretty sure there was more.

"I thought I heard voices!" Maggie breezed into the room. Was it relief that flashed across Sam's face? "Sarah Ann! You look fantastic!" She pulled Sam into her arms for a big hug. Then she stepped back and looked at her again. "Maybe I should become a ranch hand," she said, smiling. "If it would make me look this trim and gorgeous."

"Thanks, Mom C." Sam smiled, squirming a little from the praise.

"What are your plans for tonight?" asked Maggie. "You're staying over, aren't you?"

Sam nodded.

"I thought we could maybe order a pizza and Sam and I could camp out on the trampoline," said Rebecca.

"Sounds like a plan." Maggie hugged Sam again, brushed a hand gently over Rebecca's hair, and stepped back. "I have to get back in there," she said. "Conference call. Let me know if you need me to do anything. Great to see you, Sarah Ann!" she called over her shoulder.

CHAPTER 51

I'll Tell You Mine If You Tell Me Yours

June 28

THE AFTERNOON HAD passed in a whirl of activity and catching up. The conversation never made it back to Alfie and his amazing talents. Now the girls lay propped on pillows on the trampoline, each with her head leaning on one hand. Bookends. The heat of the Front Range day was seeping slowly away, but it was still comfortably warm. They had eaten their pizza late with the sun sinking behind the peaks. The talk had wound down as the mountains faded to black silhouettes backlit by a blazing sky.

"Pretty sky," said Sam. "Solstice sunset."

Rebecca looked at her, saying nothing. Sam shrugged. "Alfie knows stuff like that."

"Mmm." Rebecca didn't know what to say to that.

Sam rolled onto her stomach and rested her chin on her arms. Rebecca waited.

"He's really special," Sam said at length. She looked at Rebecca. "I really like him."

"But he's—"

"He's not really my cousin!" Sam didn't let Rebecca finish. "He's adopted. I mean, really. Did you look at him? How could we have come from the same gene pool?"

"I did look at him," confessed Rebecca. "Hard not to. He looks like AJ."

"He does!" Sam considered this for a moment. "He says he's Zuni."

"I never heard of Zuni," said Rebecca. Sam glowered at her. "I don't mean anything by that," Rebecca said. "I'm just saying."

"They descended from the Anasazi, apparently." Sam's look had not particularly softened. "You've heard of *them*, haven't you?"

"Sure. The cliff dwellers. Advanced civilization. Totally cool. Disappeared into thin air. Or something."

There was a prolonged pause. Rebecca could feel the tension streaming off of Sam. It was palpable. She didn't need any clairs to feel it." Finally, she said, "Okay, Sam. I'll tell you mine, if you tell me yours."

And so she was committed. And if she was going to tell any of it, she was going to tell it all. Let Sam think what she would.

Sam giggled, and the friction dissolved. "Okay," she said with a sigh. She rolled onto her back again and looked up at the sky, her hands linked behind her head. "Do you ever wonder who's out there?" she asked.

"Not really," said Rebecca. "Aliens. Lost satellites. Our ancestors. Giant people-eating bugs. Are you going to tell me about your Zuni?"

"I don't know where to start," said Sam. "I've never felt this way before. Sometimes it's great, but sometimes it scares me."

"How so?"

"I guess because . . . I care so much. And it's all new to me," said Sam.

This was new territory for Rebecca too. She had no idea what to say. And she had never felt that way about a boy. Boys seemed *way* too high risk to get so close to one!

"I want to be with him all the time. If I can be with him, I don't care what we're doing. Dealing with city dweebs, feeding the horses, shoveling shit. Whatever. Riding is the best, though. When we get to ride together . . ." Sam's voice trailed off.

"So how old is he?"

Sam hesitated. "Twenty," she admitted. She hurried on, "Just turned, and I'll be sixteen in October. So we're really only four years apart."

Rebecca let the math on that slide.

"Mom would have a fit if she knew. Dad, though . . . he'd go nuclear, for sure. Uncle Clint has warned me off him. Which is funny, since Alfie's his son. Adopted or not." Sam chewed at a short fingernail. "Uncle Clint says I'm a stabilizing influence on him. So he's probably willing to look the other way, up to a point."

"How far would he have to look?" Rebecca was hesitant to follow this line of thought.

"Not *that* far!" Sam laughed. "Although I have to admit I've thought about it." She chewed on the fingernail again. "He sort of caught us up in the hayloft once. Thank God we weren't doing anything. But we could have been."

"Jeez, Sam, how did that go?"

Sam told her.

***

Sam had the morning off, but she was awake early. She was already used to waking up before dawn. She had a sweet little room under the eaves in the main house. It didn't have its own bathroom, but there was one across the hall and no one else on the floor to share it with. Alfie had grown up in a big, light-filled room at the end of the hall, but now he had an apartment of sorts over the tack room in the main barn. It was rude, but serviceable. Alfie said it suited him. He said walls made it hard for him to breathe.

Sam stretched luxuriously, enjoying the indulgence of lying in bed and the feel of the sheets soft against her skin. The sky was beginning to lighten. She thought maybe she'd take an early-morning ride. She slipped out of bed and dressed quickly. She splashed water on her face and brushed her teeth. She contemplated her hair in the spotted mirror with a frown. It was getting long, although not quite long enough to pull into a ponytail. She made an attempt to tame the wild blonde curls and gave it up as a lost cause. She padded quietly down the stairs in her bare feet, grabbing an apple from the fridge on the way through the kitchen. She quickly cut it into quarters and cored it. On the back porch, she pulled on well-worn western boots. She ate two quarters of the apple as she crossed the yards to the main barn.

The dawn air was crisp and clean. A few clouds drifted above the eastern horizon, tinted pink by the coming sunrise. She filled her lungs with the mountain air, feeling a delicious sense of being alive and at one with the world. Horses nickered when she let herself into the barn. She went into Skydancer's stall, talking softly to the mare.

"How's my beautiful girl?" she asked. She pressed her forehead against the horse's neck. "Shall we go for a morning run?"

Skydancer's head came around, and she nudged Sam. "Can't fool you for a minute, can I?" laughed Sam. She offered a piece of apple, and Skydancer ate it.

Sam slipped a hackamore over Sky's head. She'd ride bareback, with only her body and gentle handling of the reins to direct Skydancer. Alfie had taught her this. Sam didn't really even need the reins, only slight pressure on Skydancer's neck or sides, or a soft tug on her mane. She carefully closed the stall door, and then the big barn door after they were outside. Without stirrups, she needed a boost to get on. She used a fence rail. She walked Skydancer out of the main yard and headed in the direction of the mountains, which loomed high and imposing behind the ranch. Once free of the yard, Sam leaned forward and whispered to the little sorrel. "Okay, my beauty. Here we go."

"Sam!"

Sam's heart leapt. She wheeled Skydancer in the direction of the voice. Alfie was coming out of the yard mounted on his big gelding, Majestic. He trotted up to her.

"I heard you in the barn," he said. "Thought you might want some company."

"Only if it's you," said Sam.

Alfie's dark eyes lit with pleasure. His smile tugged at Sam's heart. They walked the horses side by side in companionable silence. At a shared glance, they nudged them to a trot and then to an easy canter.

Once out of sight of the ranch buildings, Alfie pulled up. Neither of them spoke. Alfie lifted Sam easily onto Majestic, and she settled in front of him, his arms around her, her body nestled into his. She looped the reins over Skydancer's neck and released her. When Majestic moved forward again, settling into a long-legged canter, Skydancer followed.

They reached a little stream and rode along its bank, now at a walk, winding around rock outcroppings and through sparse stands of lodgepole pine. At a little pool fed by a trickling waterfall, Alfie halted Majestic. He dismounted and reached up for her. She slid down into his arms.

Her back was pressed against Majestic. Alfie leaned into her, one arm casually draped over his horse, the other wrapped around her waist. She laid her cheek on his chest; she could hear his heart beating. When she looked up at Alfie, he was smiling at her.

"Hungry?" he asked.

"Starving!"

Alfie pulled two deformed-looking breakfast burritos from the pocket of his denim jacket. They walked to the creek, fingers laced, and rinsed their hands in the icy water, wiping them on their jeans. They settled comfortably beneath an ancient pine, butts settled into thick layers of fallen pine needles, their backs to the trunk, shoulders and thighs touching, and ate their burritos. The horses drank and then grazed on sprigs of grass growing along the creek. Alfie reached into the other pocket of his jacket and pulled out two pieces of chocolate.

"You think of everything," said Sam.

"I don't," said Alfie. "I mostly only think of you."

Sam's heart turned over. She looked at him in surprise. He gazed quietly back at her. His expression was questioning, and she dropped her eyes. Her feelings were such a muddle. She wanted the strength and warmth of his arms around her. She wanted to feel his lips brushing her eyes, her cheeks, her neck, warm and soft on her mouth.

But something held her back. She didn't move. And because she didn't, Alfie didn't. They sat together like this for what seemed a long time. When the horses raised their heads and snorted, Alfie got to his feet. He stood listening. Sam thought he listened with his whole body. That didn't make sense, but she didn't question it.

"Fox," said Alfie.

Sam hadn't seen it. But she accepted Alfie's word as truth.

"Let's head back," he said. He vaulted onto Majestic's back and pulled Sam up to sit in front of him once more. They walked the horses back the way they had come.

When they reached the line of trees outlying the yard, they slid off Majestic. He offered her his hands, fingers laced together. She set her boot in them, and he lifted her easily onto Skydancer. "You go in first," he said. "Meet me in the hayloft." His dark eyes blazed into hers.

Sam nodded wordlessly. She wheeled Skydancer around and trotted her toward the barn, slowing to a walk once she reached the yard. There was activity there now, but Sam didn't see Uncle Clint. She led the mare to her stall, filled her water trough, and gave her grain. She ran a brush lightly over Skydancer while the horse ate, listening all the while for the sound of Majestic's hooves.

Still no sign of Alfie, Sam climbed to the huge hay loft above the stalls. The loft was almost empty now, last summer's hay nearly gone and the new cutting not yet in. She loved the clean, sweet smell of the hay. Dust motes danced in the air. She had thought they were faeries when she was little; and when she became too old to believe, she pretended. With that memory came a stab of longing for a life that was simple and magical. She could see out through the cracks in the side of the barn, but no one would be able to see in. The sun was well up now, and shafts of strong light slanted between each timber. She stayed well back from the big opening where hay was loaded mechanically into the loft, making her way to a shadowed corner. A large knothole afforded her a decent look at the yard.

And finally, there was Alfie. He trotted Majestic into the yard and disappeared from her sight. She heard him stabling the gelding, speaking quietly to the big horse. She heard Alfie's boots on the ladder. His head appeared, and he easily leveraged himself onto the floor of the loft.

What did she want? Sam didn't know. She was filled with conflicting emotions. She loved the way it made her feel when Alfie held her or cradled her face in his hands. She loved the feel of his mouth on hers. But there was an intensity that burned in her belly that scared her. She would have happily spent every hour of every day working alongside him, but she didn't want to be committed, even to him, and so she held on to that last piece of herself. What was that about? How was it even possible to feel such opposing emotions at one time?

Sam watched Alfie move lightly across the loft toward her. He walked with the grace of a dancer or a big cat—light of foot and silent. He lowered his frame down next to her and pulled her into his arms. She went willingly. And yet she held back. Would this be the time she let her resistance slip away and her wanting take her over?

"Alfie!"

Uncle Clint!

Sam and Alfie froze. "Shh." Alfie's breath was warm against her ear. "He doesn't know we're up here," he said so softly Sam could barely hear him.

"I know you're up there, Alfonse."

They heard boots on the ladder.

"I'll go," whispered Alfie. "He only knows I'm here." He got quietly to his feet and started across the loft toward the ladder.

His father's head appeared. "You too, Sam. I know you're up here."

Sam swore vehemently under her breath. Alfie looked back at her in surprise. Alfie's body language was apologetic. He smoothed his face of emotion and moved toward the ladder.

Would she lose her job over this? Would Uncle Clint tell her father? Her father would go ballistic, for sure! Her face burned with embarrassment, even though Uncle Clint couldn't see her. She felt exposed. Caught.

Uncle Clint was still at the top of the ladder. Alfie placed himself to block his father's access. "You have to go down, Dad," said Alfie. "So I can get down." A good tactic. Alfie resisted looking back toward the shadowy corner.

Uncle Clint backed down the ladder, and Alfie followed him. Sam held her breath, waiting for Uncle Clint to call her out. She heard the two men move away, their voices low, their words indistinguishable. Only then did Sam make her way quietly to the ladder. She lay on her stomach and peered over the edge. No one was in the stalls. She quickly let herself down.

Footsteps coming back! She darted into Skydancer's stall. The horse nickered to see her again. Sam picked up a brush and began to groom the mare. And then Uncle Clint was there in the stall door.

"Come on, Sam," he said. "Let's go grab a bite of breakfast." He draped his arm around Sam's shoulders and steered her out of the stall and out of the barn.

Sam couldn't read her uncle. He didn't seem angry or upset. Just a nice guy with lots of time taking his niece to breakfast. But Sam knew better. Uncle Clint *was* nice, but he was also intensely focused when it came to his ranch or anything relating to it. And there were never enough hours in his day. He said so often. She didn't think she'd be able to eat much breakfast.

***

"Wow!" Rebecca breathed. "What did he say?"

"Oh, pretty much what you'd expect, I guess." Sam was matter-of-fact. "I'm too young for that sort of thing. I'm especially too young for Alfie. I should be with boys my own age. My dad would—" Sam didn't finish that thought.

"Yeah. I can feel that." Rebecca didn't have her head around all this, but she knew intuitively Sam's dad would be a ticking bomb if he found out.

Sam fiddled with the zipper of her sleeping bag. "I know Uncle Clint talked to Alfie," she said. "Alfie told me he did. Just not exactly what his dad said. It's interesting what Uncle Clint said to me, though. He said I was good for Alfie, kept him 'on the ground.' That stabilizing influence thing, I guess. But that Alfie wasn't good for me. He's too much somewhere else all the time. Uncle Clint said he loves him like crazy because he's his son. But that doesn't mean he doesn't see him for what he is. And that he's not always dependable."

"Do you think he's right?" asked Rebecca.

"Pretty much," said Sam. "It's just that sometimes I don't care. And that's kind of scary too. Sometimes I'm curious how it would be to . . . you know."

"So would you have . . . if your uncle hadn't shown up?"

"I don't know," said Sam. "I really don't."

"Wow." Rebecca chewed her lower lip. "Um . . . if you do, just be sure you . . . that you don't . . . that you're . . . you know. Careful."

"Yeah, I know." Sam was dismissive. "I don't really want to do it. I mean, I do, but I don't. Hard to explain. Alfie never pushes me. I mean, it might be nice and all. Kissing him sure is." Sam's eyes drifted up to the stars, and she seemed lost in thought.

She came back abruptly. "But what do I know? I don't know the first thing about . . . you know. Sex. I mean, I know how you *do* it. But that's the least of it. It's all the complicated *feelings*. You know? They didn't cover any of that in health and hygiene class."

Rebecca wanted to say she didn't know about any of this. And she wasn't sure she was ready to hear about it from Sam. It was too much information. It was an intrusion on their circle of friends, and that circle was like a rock to her. What would happen if other things, other people, came into the circle? How would it change things? Her best friend was opening her heart to her, but what Rebecca felt was loss. And she couldn't say any of these things.

Sam didn't seem to notice Rebecca's reticence. Or if she did, she let it pass. She said, "It's always been all about the horses for me, no time for anything else. Sometimes I wish it was still like that. I'm afraid it would change things, and maybe not for the better."

Rebecca started. Was Sam reading her mind?

Sam went on, "I'm afraid I'd lose myself somehow. That might be the worst part. I'm afraid I would love it. Or I'd hate it, and if I hated it, I'd be committed. To doing it . . . you know . . . more times. How could I say no if I'd already said yes? I'm afraid he wouldn't want me the same way . . . after. It's complicated."

"I guess," was all Rebecca said.

"You've never felt this way." Sam looked Rebecca straight on. It wasn't a question. It was too dark now for Rebecca to see Sam's eyes clearly, but she could feel the intensity of Sam's emotions.

Rebecca shook her head. "I did think Jackson was going to kiss me once, though." It was lame by comparison. She laughed, a tight, uncomfortable sound. "I was afraid he would and afraid he wouldn't. And he didn't. So we just continue to . . ."

"Spar," said Sam. "Wrangle."

"Yeah. I'd say that's pretty accurate."

"So tell me about the kissing thing. How did that happen?"

"Wow. Yeah." Now it was Rebecca's turn to hesitate. "Where to even start."

"Just tell me about the kissing bit," said Sam. Her face was indistinct in the darkness, but Rebecca was sure her friend was leering.

CHAPTER 52

Rebecca's Turn

June 28

"I HAVE TO tell you something else first," said Rebecca. "It puts the kissing bit, as you call it, in perspective. And now, even if I did . . . well, really like Jackson and he liked me and I thought I could trust him for five seconds around other girls, which would be a real stretch . . . I don't think I could be with him."

"Why not?"

And so there it was. Rebecca tugged at her bedding, twined a finger in her hair.

"Remember Jackson's accident? And when I fell in my room?"

"Sure. What's that got to do with anything?"

"Plenty!" She took a deep breath. "First, you have to swear, and I mean *swear*, not to say a word of this to anyone."

"Sure. I swear."

"Not anyone, Sam. Not Zoe. Not Alfie. No. One."

"Okay," Sam said. "I swear. I do!" She sounded a little alarmed.

And so Rebecca told her, starting with the fight in Home Room, writing the first Event, and the roller-coaster sequence of incidents that had followed. She told of Brittany's date story, and her own messed-up interview with Mrs. Mason. "Headless," lost and found, and ditto the iPhone. The conversation with Jackson about grades and testing and No Pass No Play. Dreamweaver, Colorado High for Ty, the stolen skit idea, High Heels. How some things seemed to offset others. How she kept hearing that everything is just energy. She needed to know something, but what? Was she influencing energy, and if so, how? Was she just basically bad to the bone? Was she losing her mind? Was she living down bad karma? Or *creating* bad karma? And WTF was karma, anyway? She told about being afraid to write a Laney story lest it backfire in some unforeseen way. Which led to the episode after their algebra exams when things had gone so terribly wrong. And how strange it felt to know things about Jackson that no one else knew, to see him in a serious light, not clowning around. She told about standing up to Mr. Hammond, how fantastic that had felt, and how Jackson had seemed to be pleased that she did. That didn't have anything to do with this new . . . ability . . . but then, maybe it did. She told of watching as Angela plunged into the koi pond and then climbed out and still walked the runway. How she feared she had misjudged Angela, so then she had written Modeling. About the sense of power and elation she felt when she was writing these little stories. But also the guilt and fear. Had she misjudged both Jackson and Angela? She just didn't know. Laney was so often in her head and talking to her. How she sometimes wondered if she was certifiable.

"So you see, don't you? How I could never let myself be with Jackson? Even if I wanted to? I made things happen to him." Rebecca had finally come to an ending. She sat perfectly still in her sleeping bag, waiting for Sam to say something.

Silence stretched out. Sam's eyes were round. "Holy catfish!" She barely breathed the words. "Jumpin' Jesus on steroids, Becks. Wow!"

"Yeah."

Both girls were silent. A sliver of moon had risen and hung like a question mark in the sky.

Finally, Sam spoke. "I need to think about all this," she said. "It's not just the stories. There's other stuff going on too."

Rebecca didn't know exactly what Sam meant, but she agreed with her, regardless.

There was another silence, and then Sam said, "You're not a bad person. I know that for sure. You're one of the best people I know. I don't know about the energy thing. Except for Reiki. That's energy. Zoe could tell you stuff." Sam paused. "Maybe you could talk to your grandmother. Or April." Another pause. "And I think you should take Reiki."

"How could Reiki help any of this?" Rebecca demanded.

"Honestly, I don't know," said Sam. "But I'd be willing to bet a lot that it would. Somehow, it would. Can't explain it."

Silence again, broken only by the sound of a dog barking in the distance and soft rustlings as the girls settled deeper into their sleeping bags.

"So you didn't really tell me the bit about Jackson kissing you."

Rebecca laughed. "Are you kidding me? After all that, you're only interested in Jackson kissing me?"

"No, I'm interested in all of it," said Sam calmly. "But I'm especially interested in Jackson kissing you."

"*Almost* kissing me."

"Oh, right."

Rebecca told that part, as well. Jackson steering her into the alcove and pressing her against the trophy case, his hand warm against her shoulder. How he leaned in so close, his eyes intense, peppermint on his breath. How she had felt completely mesmerized, unable to move or pull her eyes away. If he had meant to kiss her, she would have let him. How she could still feel the pressure of his hand on her shoulder even after she walked away.

"So I get how you can kind of want something but not want it at the same time because you're afraid it will . . . change things, or mess them up somehow. And how you can get caught in . . ." Rebecca shook her head in the dark. "How you can feel kind of trapped, almost."

"Yeah. For sure. It's like . . ." Sam didn't finish.

Rebecca didn't need her to. Even though she and Jackson were nothing like Sam and Alfie, she understood on some level how the intensity of a moment could take on a life of its own. She was a little envious of Sam and Alfie, but at the same time deeply thankful she didn't have that sort of relationship with anyone. It would be *way* too . . . extreme.

"So who all have you been kissed by?" Sam wanted to know.

"No one that counts," Rebecca said. She changed the subject. "And you kept giving me these funny looks," she said after a moment. "At the end of school. Like you knew something."

"How could I have?"

"Special powers." Rebecca laughed. The sound was a little hollow.

"You'd been acting sort of weird sometimes. I knew *that*. I'm pretty sure Zoe noticed too. You and she are, I don't know, kind of psychic about each other. I thought it might just be me misreading things. Being new to Reiki and the whole clairs thing . . ." Sam's voice trailed off.

They both fell silent.

"I love the High Heels one!" Sam said after a bit. "I'd give a lot to have seen that!" A pause, the sound of a pillow being plumped, a zipper going up or down. "And she stole your skit idea. What a bitch!"

"And there's actually one more," said Rebecca.

And she told about Louisville Slugger.

"OMG!" Sam breathed the words. "Has that happened yet?"

"I don't know," said Rebecca. "I don't even know how I'll ever find out."

"I'll bet you will, though," said Sam. "Just because of the way all the others went. And your dad seeing that TV show. That's totally out there!"

"It's pretty much *all* totally out there."

"Wouldn't I love to see that too! The Fat Man, I mean. He's a sleazoid. How'd you come up with the name?"

"You mean Louisville Slugger?" Sam was interested in the weirdest details! "It's from a Dire Straits song Nanna likes. He says, 'Sometimes you're the Louisville Slugger / Sometimes you're the ball.' Louisville Slugger is a baseball bat."

"Oh." Quiet stretched out between them. "That took guts, for sure. Risky."

"Maybe," said Rebecca. "But who would believe it? How could I ever get caught?" It was the line of reasoning she had told herself as she sat at her computer to write the Event.

Sam chuckled. "I can just hear it. Student hexes teacher. Even if someone believed it, they'd never admit it."

Quiet stretched out again. It was friendly, accepting. But maybe a little sad too.

"Everyone is changing," said Rebecca softly.

"Aren't we supposed to?" said Sam.

"Maybe." Rebecca didn't like the idea. She hesitated and then said, "I think Ty likes Travis Scott. He's been up a couple times to raft."

"He's pretty easy to look at," said Sam. "And smart. What's not to like?"

"That's exactly what Zoe said!" Rebecca exclaimed. "Did you guys rehearse?"

"How could we?"

"And now you have a boyfriend too. What happens to us?"

"Us?"

"Yeah. All of us. The five of us."

"Nothing. What do you mean?"

"I just mean . . ." Rebecca exhaled in exasperation. What did she mean anyway?

"Can't we still be us and also have boyfriends?" Sam asked.

Rebecca dodged the question. "Did you want a boyfriend?" she demanded. "Before the amazing Zuni horseman bewitched you?"

"Not really," said Sam calmly. "But there he is." She looked at Rebecca in the starlight. "Don't you want a boyfriend?"

Rebecca considered. "I'm not sure I do," she said. "Boys seem to . . . I don't know, keep things off balance. And be sort of high risk. I'm not sure they're worth all the trouble."

"What about Jackson?" asked Sam.

"Jackson!" Rebecca exhaled forcefully. "He's the worst!"

"But you have fun with him when he's not tormenting you."

"He's always tormenting me!"

"You let him," Sam said. "Why is that? Why do you let him do that?"

"Now you sound like AJ," grumbled Rebecca.

"The voice of calm and reason?" Sam grinned. "Why, thank you, Becks."

"What are you saying, Sam?"

"I'm just saying . . ." Sam searched for words. "You know it's going to happen. There are going to be other things in our lives. Like boys. College. Like Ty's rafting with her dad. And whatever she may be doing with Travis. Or some gorgeous hunk from . . . California. Wisconsin. Whatever. My Reiki. Which you should have too." She looked pointedly at Rebecca. "If we're to stay connected, really connected, then each of us has to be able to go our own way a little. We have to be able to . . . stretch. Otherwise, we'll stifle each other. And that would be"—Sam gave herself a little shake—"sort of like being buried alive."

"Yuck!" Rebecca made a face in the dark. This was pretty heavy stuff coming from Sam. But Sam had always had flashes of insight. "You could be right, I guess," she said.

"I mean, you've changed too." Sam said.

"Me! What do you mean?"

"Come on, Becks! You've got this whole other life going on where you're Snape or Professor McGonagall or something."

"It's not like that at all," protested Rebecca. "This thing just sort of happened to me!"

"Yeah, sure, like Alfie just sort of happened to me and I had no part in it." Sam took a deep breath and expelled it. "But that's not what I meant. It's that you have something else that's pretty major going on besides just the five of us. But you're still you. More, actually.

"How am I more?"

"You just are. It's like . . . it's like you're you and Laney both, and . . . one and one makes . . . more than two." Sam sighed. "It's too late for this complicated stuff," she said around a huge yawn. "I'm going to text Alfie, and then I'm going to sleep, knowing I don't have to get up before the sun." She yawned again. "Which won't be all that long."

Sam didn't sound like she was open to negotiating. And anyway, Rebecca agreed. It was too late for any more complicated stuff. "Okay," she said. "Good idea. 'Night, Sam."

"I've really missed you." Sam's voice was muffled by her sleeping bag.

"Me too," said Rebecca. Her heart swelled, and a lump constricted her throat. "Me too."

Rebecca slid deeper into her sleeping bag and zipped it up. A slight breeze ruffled the leaves in the maple tree and lifted the hair around her face so that it tickled her cheeks. She heard the *yip-yip-yip* of a hunting coyote in the distance and the answer of another one. The sound was wild and primal. It made shivers run along her spine. It also made her think of Alfie. She snuggled even deeper into the folds of the sleeping bag, instinctively rolling onto her side and pulling her knees protectively to her chest. It was comforting to have Sam right there and to be cocooned by the layers of quilts and blankets. Even so, the night felt somehow . . . untamed. Perhaps even untamable. She was pretty sure she wouldn't sleep soon.

But she did.

CHAPTER 53

In Between

June 29

REBECCA AND SAM sat at the island, their hands wrapped around mugs of aromatic coffee much diluted with cream. Maggie breezed into the kitchen to refill her own mug.

"Did you have a nice catch-up?" she asked.

"Yeah," they said in unison.

"Short night?" Maggie sounded amused.

"Of course, Mom," said Rebecca. "Don't you remember having sleepovers?"

"Oh, I do," said Maggie. "But the element of drama fades with time."

Sam's phone tinkled a little tune. "That's Alfie," she said, extracting the phone from her back pocket. She slid off her stool and stepped out onto the deck. "Hey, Alf," Rebecca heard her say before the door closed.

Lissa appeared at the top of the stairs and came into the kitchen. She poured herself coffee, stirred in cream, and sat at the end of the island. She nodded but didn't speak.

"What're you doing today?" Rebecca asked her mom.

"Oh, there's plenty to do." Her mother was vague. "Errands. Your dad and I thought we might take Andy up to Georgetown to ride the train."

"He'd like that," said Rebecca.

"What are your plans?" her mother asked.

"We're going out to the mall. Zoe said she'd meet us there. Maybe the pool later. Try to hook up with AJ." Rebecca answered her mother's unspoken question. "Alfie's taking us around. Sam's cousin," she explained. It felt weird when she said it.

Sam stepped back into the kitchen, the phone still in her hand.

"Alfie has to go back to the ranch," said Sam. Her voice was carefully neutral, but Rebecca caught the disappointment in her eyes. "Horse with an injured leg."

"So there goes our ride?"

"Yeah. Guess I'll have Alfie drop me at home before he heads down."

"I'm going out to the mall," said Lissa. "James and I might hook up, but I don't have any plans in particular. I can be your ride."

"You'd do that?" Rebecca looked at her sister with both amazement and affection.

"Why not? I'm going anyway."

"You're all of you set, then?" Maggie looked at each of them, Lissa last.

Lissa nodded. "Sure," she said.

"Then I'll round up Andy and your father and we'll get going. Have fun, girls." And she breezed out just as she had come in.

"Can you be ready to leave in thirty minutes?" asked Lissa.

There was a flurry of activity as coffee mugs were rinsed and placed in the dishwasher. "Do you want a bagel?" Rebecca asked Sam.

"Can we get something at the mall?"

"Sure." All three girls ran down the stairs.

Not quite thirty minutes and they were on the way. Sam wanted to know about Rebecca's doll-shop job and the new center, especially the Reiki. She told of the craziness of city slickers at the dude ranch and extolled Alfie's miraculous abilities with the horses.

"I swear, he can walk up to a pasture full of horses, just look at the one he wants, and it comes right to him."

"An energy connection," said Lissa. "Have you thought about learning animal Reiki?"

"Not much time to think so far this summer," said Sam. She elbowed Rebecca, and the girls giggled. "Maybe, though."

"Sam thinks I should to take Reiki too," said Rebecca.

"And what do you think?" asked Lissa.

"Don't know yet," said Rebecca. "This energy stuff, though . . . I'd like to know more about it." Remembering Lissa's remark at Nanna's, she added, "Without taking a quantum science class."

Lissa dropped them in front of The Chocolate Works. They would meet at Best Books later. The girls treated themselves to chocolate for breakfast. They slipped into a booth at the back of the shop, each with a huge brownie.

"So what are we going to tell Zoe?" asked Sam.

"What do you mean?"

"All that stuff we talked about last night. What are we going to tell her?"

"You've sworn me to secrecy about the Reiki," said Rebecca. She was pretty sure that wasn't what Sam meant.

"I'll tell about the Reiki," Sam said. "No problem. If any of us understands about energy stuff, it would be Zoe."

"What about Alfie?"

"Some of it." Sam chewed a bite of brownie, licking the icing off her fingers. "What about your stories?"

"I don't know," said Rebecca. "It just opens up such a . . ."

"You know you can't keep it locked up forever." Sam was matter-of-fact.

"I'm not," said Rebecca. "I told *you*."

"You guys are like twins practically. She'll know you're hiding something."

"Maybe." Rebecca's fingers tapped lightly on the table. "It's sort of . . . scary . . . to put it out there. That's all."

That wasn't all, really. But Rebecca didn't know how to say what she felt; that telling made it all seem more real.

Sam was quiet for several moments. Rebecca knew the look, although she didn't see it often. Sam was deciding whether she was going to say something. That in itself was a little worrying, because Sam usually just blurted everything out.

Rebecca sighed. "Okay, Sam," she said. "Let me have it."

Sam laughed. "Am I that obvious?" she asked.

"Yeah, pretty much."

"Okay, then. Here goes . . ."

Rebecca waited.

"I think some of this stuff is about changing, and maybe growing up. Finding out about ourselves maybe." Sam looked pensive. "There's tons of stuff to learn still. At least I hope so! God knows, sometimes I feel like I don't know anything about anything."

"Any more I'm not so sure growing up is a guarantee you know anything," said Rebecca. "Not anything important anyway."

Sam looked startled. "Jeez!" she said. She looked at her brownie like she'd never seen it before, and then back up at Rebecca. "Maybe grownups just know the wrong things."

"Maybe." Rebecca considered this. "Because they've stopped changing?"

Sam stared at her. "Maybe."

Rebecca stared back at Sam.

"This looks way too serious for a conversation over chocolate." There was Zoe.

"OMG, Zoe!"

"Zolly . . ." Rebecca raised her hand in the familiar gesture, and Zoe signed back.

Zoe leaned into the booth to give Sam a hug. "Mon Dieu! Look at you!" she exclaimed. Then she slid in beside Rebecca.

Rebecca pushed the rest of her brownie in front of Zoe. "I can't finish this. Don't know what I was thinking."

"The missing chocolate gene." Zoe smiled. "Mmm. I can." She looked around.

"Zoe needs a fork," said Rebecca.

Sam jumped up to get one.

Zoe tore the wrapper off the fork and took a little bite of brownie. "So what's all this seriousness about?"

"Secrets," said Sam. "I took Reiki a while back. I have a boyfriend at the ranch. We think the people running the world might not know shit from shinola." Sam grinned wickedly at Rebecca. "And Becks has magical powers."

Zoe looked from Sam to Rebecca, her fork halfway to her mouth. "Wow!"

And so it was told again. Sam told about her Reiki class and how amazing it was. How she had studied ahead and used it on Mystery Magic to heal the bruised fetlock. "Even Alfie couldn't figure it out. But she's fine now. Nothing else worked. It *must* have been the Reiki!"

"Alfie?" Zoe looked quizzically at Sam.

Sam told about Alfie, if not all of it. She told of his amazing way with horses. How she had shown him Reiki and how he seemed to already know it somehow.

"I kind of like him," said Sam. Rebecca snorted. Sam ignored her.

"He's Zuni," said Rebecca. She smirked at Sam. Two could play this game.

"Oh, Zuni!" exclaimed Zoe. "The descendants of the lost civilization of the Anasazi!" She looked at Rebecca. "This is really good," she said. "Thanks, Becks." Zoe took another bite of brownie. "What special powers?" she asked casually.

Rebecca shifted uncomfortably. There was no way she could get out of telling. It was just a matter of how much she told. She took a deep breath.

"Okay," she said. "Last May, in Home Room . . . you had a dentist appointment." She looked at Zoe. "And Sam was taking a makeup English test for a time she ditched." She looked levelly at Sam, who smirked impishly back. "So it was just me and Fat Mr. Hammond in his haven for jocks. You remember the fight I told you about. When he stole some of my story notes."

Rebecca told most of it. She would tell Zoe the rest, but not here in The Chocolate Works. It felt too exposed. She told about getting the best of Mr. Hammond in algebra class, because that felt really good. "I was scared, but I faked it. And it made me feel . . . not powerful, but at least not power*less*."

Zoe nodded.

Rebecca was pretty much finished. "I still can't believe I'm making these things happen," she said to Zoe. "But the details are so exact. And every time . . . every story I've written, this has happened. And then the stuff that's happened to me. Like it's all tied together."

"Wow, Becks," Zoe said. "I knew something was bothering you. Since before the end of school." She had finished the last of Rebecca's brownie. She moved the plate away and dabbed the corners of her mouth with a napkin.

"So is it quantum physics?" demanded Sam.

"Well, I've never heard of anything quite like this," said Zoe. "Not in physics, anyway. But there is certainly solid evidence that we create with our minds."

"So it's not some kind of—I'm not sociopathic—it's just physics?" Rebecca's voice was hopeful.

Zoe twined her fingers through Rebecca's. "You're not a sociopath," she said. "Maybe a dark wizard." Zoe and Sam laughed. Rebecca didn't.

"I think it's sort of like Reiki," said Sam. "Only we're taught Reiki can never do harm."

Zoe looked thoughtful. "I think you should talk to your grandmother," she said. "Or April. Maybe she'd know something. The Druid thing, you know?"

"So you're saying it's not science?" Rebecca demanded.

Zoe looked calmly back at her best friend. "I think science and metaphysics are overlapping here. And there's a lot more going on."

"What do you mean?" Rebecca pulled her hand free.

"What do *you* think it all means?"

"Jumping Jesus on steroids!" It was Sam's expression, but Rebecca liked it for extreme situations. She grabbed a fistful of hair. "This is turning me into Ty," she muttered. She stuffed her hands under her thighs.

"Why did you start writing your little . . . stories?" asked Zoe.

"I told you. It was after Jackson—"

"I know, I know. But what did you want to happen as a result?"

"I wanted to get even," said Rebecca. "Not the coolest motive, maybe." She clasped her hands on the table and frowned down at them. "I was so mad and felt so . . . helpless. I *hate* that feeling!"

Zoe nodded. "But underneath it all, what did you really want?"

Rebecca leaned back into the corner of the booth. She wrapped her arms around her middle. She didn't like where this was going, but these were her two closest friends.

"I wanted to feel like I'm not just a pawn in everyone else's . . . I wanted to have some sort of . . . control over my own life." It was barely more than a whisper. "That's always been why I write stories."

Sam nodded her agreement. "I get that," said Zoe. "Sometimes when Grand-mère is here and everyone is nattering and carrying on, I feel like I'm going to . . . I don't know, like, drown in it all. To lose myself. I'd do almost anything to change that feeling."

"Really?" Rebecca relaxed a little. "I've always thought . . ." She put a hand on Zoe's arm. "How could I think I know you so well and not see that?" She rubbed the heel of her other hand against her chest.

"Probably because I never did before," said Zoe.

"But—"

Sam interrupted. "I don't think we should be too hard on ourselves," she said.

Rebecca and Zoe just looked at her.

Sam shrugged. "We're sort of in between," she said.

"In between?"

"Yeah. Our old selves. Kids, you know." Sam leaned back in the booth. "And our new selves. Whatever they're going to be."

Rebecca looked at her in surprise. Was this one of carefree Sam's exceptional insights, or had she been taking Sam for granted too?

"Alfie says . . ."

Rebecca and Zoe waited.

Sam ran her hands through her hair. "Alfie says he's curious who I'm going to be, that he can't wait to know that . . . me." Sam shifted on the bench. "That kind of scares me too." She met Rebecca's gaze.

"Why?" asked Zoe.

"Because our deepest fears are what mold us." Rebecca clapped a hand over her mouth. Her eyes were wide.

Sam and Zoe stared openmouthed at her.

"That wasn't me!" It was barely a whisper. "That was Laney." Rebecca blurted it out before she could stop herself. "She just pops into my head. And sometimes out of my mouth. I don't know where her stuff comes from!"

Sam still stared. Zoe laughed. "I just love Laney," she said.

"She *is* you," Sam said quietly. "That day walking to school. I said it, but I had no idea."

"I don't have the first clue where to go from here," said Rebecca.

"Well, for starters," said Zoe, "we need to be aware of our thoughts and really careful about our intentions. That *is* quantum science." She considered a moment, and then added, "And especially the things that scare us."

"I need to walk," said Rebecca. She shoved Zoe. Zoe clambered out of the booth just in case Rebecca intended to push her to the floor. Rebecca slid out and headed for the door and the street. Zoe and Sam looked at each other and followed.

Rebecca charged out of The Chocolate Works and headed up the street with no idea where she was going. She soon found herself on the curb across from the little park, the heat from the blazing sun soaking into her body. It felt good after the frigid air in the shop. Sam and Zoe caught up with her.

"I'll think about all this later," she said. "Right now I need shoes."

"Okay, Scarlett," laughed Zoe. "Let's shop till we drop."

"Shouldn't take long in this heat," said Sam. "But I need a bathing suit if we're all going to the pool later."

The girls wandered the streets arm in arm, dodging into any store with a promising window display. Sam tried on swimsuits, settling on a daring one-piece. Very water goddess, they agreed. There was still some of the old roundness to Sam's figure; she would never be a flat-bellied stick. Rebecca thought the curves were pleasing, even sensual, and then she wondered where that came from.

She found two pairs of sandals she liked. She couldn't decide which to buy, so she got them both. Why not, she had a job now! Zoe was so far just looking.

Their conversation stayed light and easy. The Front Range sun was beating down on them fiercely now. Rebecca was hot and tired. No breakfast except half of a brownie, and the sugar rush from that had long since worn off.

Sam pulled the other two under the shade of an awning. "Jeez, it's hot!" She wiped her forehead with the back of her hand.

Rebecca shaded her eyes with one hand. Where *were* her sunglasses! The glare came from both overhead and reflected up from the sidewalk. Were the streets melting yet?

"Let's go in here. It'll be cool." Zoe tugged on Rebecca's arm.

"Where are we?"

"We're at Sizzle," said Zoe. "Sizzling outside Sizzle. What are the odds?"

Laughing, they ducked into the dim coolness of the store.

CHAPTER 54

An Apology Dictated by the Stars

June 29

T HE GIRLS STOOD just inside the door, letting the cold air
wash over them. The air-conditioning was obviously cranking;
the air felt overdry and frigid. That is to say, good.

"Rebecca." The voice was cool and familiar.

Rebecca glanced around. There was Angela, looking totally together
in a sweet little near-to-nothing top that showed off a colorful bandeau
underneath, and smart short-shorts.

"Angela," Rebecca said.

"Hey, Angie!" Sam greeted the Ice Maiden with a big smile.

"Wow, you look . . . so different." Angela appraised Sam's new
figure. "Are you doing Pilates or something?"

"Not hardly," said Sam. "Ranch hand. At my uncle's spread."

"You mean you ride horses? You look like that because you ride
horses?" Angela frowned. "Maybe I should have agreed to equestrian
classes like my mother wanted."

"Well, it's more from mucking out stalls and carting fifty-pound
bags of feed. But I do ride horses," said Sam.

Angela studied Sam wordlessly. Apparently convinced Sam was
telling the truth, her interest faded. She turned to Rebecca. She looked
like she wanted to say something. And that it might choke her.

"Rebecca . . ." Angela cleared her throat. "Rebecca . . ." She chewed
her bottom lip.

Rebecca didn't know this tongue-tied and hesitant Angela. She was
curious, but just to be safe, she schooled her face into an expression of
careful neutrality. At least she hoped she did.

Sam was looking on with interest. Zoe had moved away and was flipping through hangers on one of the displays.

Angela gestured to an empty corner of the store by the fitting rooms. Rebecca and Sam glanced at each other. They followed Angie.

Outside the fitting rooms, Angie turned back to face them. She looked from Rebecca to Sam. "Um . . . this is sort of personal," she said.

And *that* was the Angela Rebecca knew!

"Sure, Angie." Sam was offhand, but Rebecca knew she was annoyed. Sam wandered toward Zoe, idly looking through a rack of T-shirts on the way. Rebecca waited.

Angela shifted from one foot to the other. She smoothed her hand over the perfectly cut white-blonde hair. She squared her shoulders and took a deep breath. "I stole your skit idea for my last competition." She looked Rebecca square on.

Rebecca's mouth dropped open, and she stared. The neutral face dissolved and could not be retrieved. There was no point in even trying.

"It was a really good idea." Angela fidgeted. "I just couldn't admit it because . . . you all don't . . . because I don't think you . . . like me."

If Rebecca's mouth hadn't been open already, it would have fallen open then. "I don't . . . not like you," she managed to stammer. "None of us does! It's just . . . it's like you don't . . . you're so . . . in drama you're different . . ."

You're babbling, cautioned Laney.

"With all the other cheerleaders." Rebecca was incapable of a complete sentence.

Angela rolled her eyes. "Oh, them. Just a bunch of airheads. Put them all together and you won't get one interesting person."

This just got more and more surreal. Rebecca's brain was close to overload.

"Anyway, it was a really good idea." Angela looked like she might be nauseous.

"So did you win again?" Rebecca thought it might be mean to ask but didn't care.

Angela shook her head. "I was doing really great. I was pretty sure I could." She was arrogant and self-effacing at the same time. How did that work exactly? Rebecca wondered.

"But I didn't," Angela continued. "I um . . ." She brushed at an imperfection only she could see on her little shorts. "I fell off my high heels in the swimsuit competition. And into the koi pond."

"You did?" Rebecca was barely breathing. "And then what?"

The slender shoulders lifted in a nonchalant shrug. "I climbed out. And I walked the runway. Soaking wet and barefoot." Angela was getting over her discomfort and into her story. "The audience seemed to like it. And then they really loved it. The judges, not so much." Her perfectly made-up mouth turned down.

"But there was a representative from a modeling agency there. And *she* loved it." Angela smiled triumphantly. "She said she liked my ability to wing it, that sometimes the best shots are the spontaneous ones."

Rebecca nodded, but what did she know?

"And they signed me on as a model." Angie was her cool and collected self again. "I've already done a shoot. This week."

"Wow!" Rebecca struggled for something, anything, to come into her brain to say.

"Anyway, I felt like I needed to tell you this," said Angie.

"You did?"

"Yes," said Angie. "Diamonique said it was bad karma not to."

"Diamonique?"

Angela nodded. "She's my astrological guide."

"You have an astrological guide?" Rebecca thought she sounded brain-dead.

"Of course!" Angie's look suggested she couldn't fathom anyone not having their own astrological guide.

Rebecca just shook her head.

"Great name, isn't it? Diamonique." Angela spoke the name with reverence, her eyes momentarily focused on some place far off. "She said I fell into the pond because I stole the idea. But that rectified the energies. She said I created an opening when I climbed out and did the runway even though I couldn't possibly win. By overcoming my adversity, I was clear for an opportunity. My dad laughed his head off. Not at Diamonique—he doesn't even know about her. About my pond plunge. That's what he calls it. My mother still isn't speaking to him, but she's let me quit the whole pageant scene. She really pushed me to do it. She was Miss Phoenix, so she thought . . ." Angie waved one manicured hand. "It wasn't me. I didn't want to do it." Her smile was wide and beautiful. "And now I'm modeling."

"That's really—"

Angie wasn't quite finished. "It's all pretty lame, really. I don't need the money, but it's fun to have my own. The other girls are pretty much totally stupid. And mean. Even the really young ones." A look of puzzlement crossed Angie's face. "It's kind of sad, really." She snapped back to herself. "You just have to know how to handle them." It was clear she thought she did, and Rebecca had no doubts.

"But I stood up to my mom, and she respects me now. And I stood up to my dad. I don't think he respects much of anybody, but at least he leaves me alone now. I will use my own money to do whatever I want, and I don't have to take crap from anybody."

"You mean you didn't already?" Rebecca was curious. She didn't intend it to sound mean or rude.

Angie beamed. "It's even better now. Because it's my money. Diamonique says it's about personal empowerment." Angie looked her in the eyes this time. "And really, it's all because of you," she said.

"Wow! Jeez, Angie . . . um . . . that's really . . ." Rebecca still couldn't get the neurons in her brain to fire. She shook her head to clear it.

"I'm really glad I ran into you," said Angie. "Can't wait to tell Diamonique. She said I should tell you. I said I would, and boom, here you are! This really clears out all the negative energy. Well, gotta go."

Angela turned with another wave of a perfectly manicured hand and sashayed out of the store without so much as a backward glance.

Rebecca watched her go. Was her mouth still open? Yes, it was. She snapped it shut. Her legs felt sort of rubbery. She needed to sit down. There was a leather-covered stool next to a display wall. Part of it maybe—the stuff in the display was all leather. Rebecca didn't care. She sank gratefully onto the stool.

CHAPTER 55

Keeping Secrets

June 29

"I'M STARVING," SAID Rebecca. They had stepped back outside into the heat. "And I have something to tell you. Let's find someplace cool."

"Let's go to the bookstore," said Zoe. "We can get something there. I could eat too." She lifted thick, dark hair off her neck and fanned herself with one hand. "And I'm parched!"

Over cold beverages and sandwiches, Rebecca told them about Angela's apology. Zoe and Sam stared wordlessly.

"Yeah," said Rebecca. "Me too. I couldn't form a complete thought, least of all a complete sentence. I must have sounded like a total dweeb." She shrugged. "Not that Angie would notice. She's pretty focused on herself."

"Diamonique." Zoe experimented with the name. "Wow!"

"Yeah, her own personal astrological guide."

"I don't suppose we'll hear the end of the modeling gigs," said Sam. She sighed. "She'll be totally insufferable."

Rebecca didn't answer right away. "Probably," she said finally. "I've seen a different side of Angie though, with all . . . this stuff. I'd never have guessed she could pull off that runway walk. Not after her pond plunge."

They laughed. "It was pretty gutsy," said Zoe.

"And to actually apologize to you!" Sam shook her head.

"And in drama," said Rebecca, "sometimes she's still snooty and stuck-up, but she's sort of different when she's away from the other cheerleaders."

"She's always been the boss of snooty." Sam was matter-of-fact.

Rebecca wasn't so sure anymore. "I don't know," she said. "Angela and Jackson both. All that 'I don't give a flying fart,' attitude . . . What if that's just a cover for something else?" She hesitated. "I think I misjudged both of them," she said softly.

"How do you mean?" asked Zoe.

Rebecca frowned thoughtfully. She thought both Angie and Jackson used their—okay, outrageous behavior— as a cover. Jackson because he worried about getting a scholarship for college and away from—she had no clue away from what. Angela because she was basically insecure, regardless of being thin, rich, and beautiful. Maybe Angela, and Jackson too, felt like they were just pawns in a grown-up's world with no control over their own lives. If that was true, she wasn't all that different from either of them. She had sort of thought about this before but had stuffed it in the box and slammed the lid.

She needed to think about it before she tried to explain it, even to Zoe and Sam.

"I think maybe . . ." Rebecca looked at her friends. "I think it's not as simple as it looks."

Sam looked thoughtful. Zoe nodded. "None of us is," she said.

They sipped their drinks and nibbled at their sandwiches.

Rebecca's phone chirped, and she fished it out of her purse. "Lissa," she said. "She's here. At Best Books."

"Already here," she texted back. "Coffee shop."

Rebecca looked at her friends "How much of all this are we going to tell?" she asked.

"You mean to your sister?"

"No." Rebecca shook her head. "I mean AJ." She chewed on her lip. "I don't want to tell it all again," said Rebecca. "Maybe not till I know what's really going on."

"No problem," said Zoe.

"Sure," said Sam. "I get that."

And so it was decided.

Later, at the pool, after a cooling dip to combat the Front Range heat, the girls pulled loungers together under big umbrellas. A welcome breeze had come up, which fluttered the fringes of the umbrellas. They were all together for the first time since school had let out—all but Ty anyway—and it was like old times. Almost. Sam couldn't seem to *not* mention Alfie for more than a short span of time. AJ took the news of the "boyfriend" calmly.

Rebecca decided Angie's apology was too good to keep from AJ. That explained, she told them, Angela's weird reaction the day in drama when Mr. Tilson had offered to critique her skit. There was no mention, as agreed, of the High Heels story, or anything else relating to the other stories.

"I never figured Angie for that sort of thing," said AJ. "Astrology, I mean."

Rebecca nodded. "Maybe we don't really know anyone," she said softly.

No one replied. There didn't seem to be an answer to this.

No one wanted the day to end, but eventually, it did. Tom came for AJ in the battered pickup. He offered to give Sam a lift, and she agreed. Zoe and Rebecca watched as AJ slid across the bench seat with athletic grace, pulling her long legs in after her. Sam hitched herself into the truck like the ranch hand she was. The door hinge creaked before it shut with a solid bang. Rebecca and Zoe heard the truck backfire long after it had disappeared from sight. They waited for Lissa under the arching limbs of a big tree, grateful for the shade.

In front of Zoe's house, the girls hugged good-bye. Rebecca watched Zoe go up the walk, small but determined. Zoe turned at the porch and waved, making the familiar gesture. Rebecca signed back, her throat constricting. *Please don't ever let us lose this*, she thought fervently. *If we can keep this one thing, maybe I can handle everything else changing. But not this.*

CHAPTER 56

Josh Pulls Rank

July 6

JACKSON TOOK A long pull on his soda. Melting ice had diluted the sugary drink, and he made a face. He dropped onto a lounger, settled sunglasses over his eyes, and stretched out, hands linked behind his head. Water dripped from his blond hair. Blue eyes were dark with emotion, but he would have been reluctant to acknowledge it and hard-pressed to define it. Irritation? Frustration? Or maybe just boredom. Jackson lived pretty much in the moment, and that didn't include analyzing his emotions. He knew what he needed to do for a college scholarship, and beyond that, he took things pretty much as they came.

He glanced at the guard tower where Josh sat, eyes hidden behind wraparound sunglasses, a Saints baseball cap jammed on his head. Josh acknowledged by raising his chin in a nearly imperceptible nod and a slight upward twitch of one side of his mouth. Typical Josh. He didn't seem mad. Jackson's mood eased slightly.

There was no point in being steamed at Josh; he was just doing his job. Jackson knew that. Still, it rankled that Josh had called him down. The summer sure wasn't stacking up as he had expected. It wasn't just today that Jackson felt out of sorts. He had always loved summer and the freedom it brought, even with the break in sports activities. This summer, though, he had hoped to make a little money. He was envious of Josh's lifeguard job. It wasn't that Josh didn't deserve it. Josh totally did! Jackson knew his friend had the position due to exceptional ability. Jackson had his own skill set. He was good—really good—across a broad range of sports, and he loved them all. Baseball the most, maybe, even though it was football that would most likely secure college for him.

Excellence in sports didn't translate into summer jobs, though—at least not so far. He had hoped to umpire for Little League baseball, but he had no wheels; and it seemed you had to know someone to get one of those positions. He had diddled around with the idea of trying to sell some of his drawings. He was pretty good at that too. Especially big birds and dragons. His dad made fun of him, but Jackson thought there might be a market for his stuff. Tattoos, various types of boards maybe. He had done a custom dragon for a snowboard, and the guy had paid him a hundred dollars. That was pretty rad. But he didn't have a car. No way could he ask his father to help him. He had no exposure. He unconsciously fingered the small dragon tattoo on the left side of his belly. Short of parading around LoDo without a shirt in hopes someone would see his tattoo and hire him— He laughed at himself. No, people would likely assume it wasn't the dragon tattoo for sale.

He had ended up spending a lot of time just hanging around. It felt like a waste, and Jackson liked action. A combination of boredom and loyalty had moved him to tag along on a couple of Josh's mountain bike races, though he admitted to himself he didn't find it all that interesting. You didn't get to see the whole race, just the start or just the finish, mainly, and usually from some place with limited viewing potential. It was more fun to watch on TV, if you could find it, where the cameras followed the riders on their mind-numbing plunge down the side of a mountain and the races were pieced together with editing. Also, the really stupefying crashes were played over and over for the viewing enjoyment of the fans, what few there were.

With Josh on the tower today, Jackson had texted a couple of buddies in hopes of getting some sport going in the pool. Travis was in Steamboat, but Anson and Blake were both in. Things had gotten a little intense at one point. There had been some clowning around. And Jackson had violated pool rules by throwing Blake into the pool.

And this was where it had gotten sticky.

Josh had played it pretty cool. He hadn't called Jackson out in front of Express and An the Man. It could have gone down much worse. Jackson was grateful for that.

***

Josh grinned down at his friends for a moment before pulling his shirt over his head and tossing it onto the grass. He dove into the pool, his wiry body barely causing a ripple. Two loose teams formed up. In a wild exchange of volleys, the ball flew clear of the pool, and Blake and Jackson both scrambled for it. Blake snagged the ball and trotted back, with Jackson hazing him. At the pool's edge, Jackson snaked a long arm around Blake and brought his hand up beneath the ball, popping it high out of Blake's hands.

"Say good-bye, Express!" Jackson followed up by putting his shoulder into Blake's back and propelling him into the water. It was a clean, neat move. As the ball came down, Jackson snatched it from the air. Blake landed in the pool, throwing up an impressive spray of water.

The boys all laughed, but Jackson noticed Josh glance at the guard tower. The nerd was looking in their direction. He fingered the whistle around his neck, but he didn't blow it.

"Telluride, heads up!" Jackson lobbed the ball in Josh's direction, both Anson and Blake lunging out of the water in an attempt to intercept it. The game continued for several more minutes, and then Josh pulled himself out of the pool, seating himself on the edge with his feet dangling in the water. Jackson followed suit.

Josh jerked his head in the direction of the tower. "Gotta go," he said.

"Yeah, that's cool," said Jackson.

Both boys got to their feet. Josh hesitated and then pulled Jackson in the direction of the concession stand. "Look," he said, "that stunt went down, but don't pull something like that on my shift, okay?" His voice was light, but his eyes were serious.

Jackson stopped in surprise. Josh shouldered him along. At the concession stand, Josh asked for a soda. "One for my buddy too," he said. The girl behind the counter couldn't take her eyes off Jackson. She wordlessly filled and capped two cups and set them on the counter. Jackson made no move to take his. Josh grasped one in each hand and herded Jackson out of earshot of the snack stand.

He turned to face Jackson. "I need this job," he said earnestly. "Otherwise, I can't afford to race. Equipment, entrance fees. It adds up."

"You weren't on duty," said Jackson. He was puzzled, but beneath that, irritation flared.

"They watch me every minute," said Josh. "And that guy on the tower would love to get me fired. He's always taking pot shots at me with the manager. That I'm . . . not eighteen."

Jackson laughed. Josh scowled.

"It's not like there's a long list of pools that even hire life guards anymore, and most of 'em wouldn't touch me until I'm eighteen."

Jackson returned his friend's gaze but didn't speak.

"Look, Jacks . . ."

"Okay, okay, I get it," said Jackson. He clamped a hand on Josh's shoulder.

He did get it. He didn't want to make trouble for Josh. And he certainly understood about the tiresome rules adults were so fond of. "It's cool, man," he said.

"You're sure?"

"Yeah, Telluride, I'm sure." Jackson grinned. He was mostly sure.

"Thanks, Jacks." Josh thrust a soda into Jackson's hand, feigned a punch at his midsection, and headed for the guard tower.

"C'mon, Jacks!" Anson called from the pool.

Jackson set his untouched drink down and dove back into the pool. A three-man game ensued, but no wild horsing around. With Josh missing from the game, and with the sting of his reprimand fresh, the fun edge was dulled for Jackson. He tried to pretend enthusiasm for a while and then hauled himself to the edge of the pool.

"Take five," he said. He trotted over to the lounger where he had left his things and dropped onto it. He picked up his sunglasses and placed them carefully over his eyes. And here he still sat, feeling somehow off. He hated that feeling.

His dark reverie was interrupted when he heard the pool gate bang shut. He glanced idly in that direction and saw Rebecca Coleson dart into the lockers. A few minutes later, she reemerged. She scanned the pool, her gaze lingering briefly on Josh. She was wearing shorts and a tank, the top of her swimsuit visible where it was tied around her neck. A big tote was slung over one shoulder. Jackson thought she looked good. His mood ticked up.

Rebecca was fun. He liked that she was all fight and spirit when he teased her. He liked watching her eyes flash blue fire and ice, and that she never fawned like most girls. No sport in that. As he watched her from behind the cover of his sunglasses, she hesitated and then turned back to the gate as though to leave. Without thinking, Jackson called out to her.

"Rebecca!"

She hesitated before turning to scan the pool.

"Hey, Becka!"

And she looked right at him.

CHAPTER 57

Fake It Till You Make It

July 6

FOURTH OF JULY weekend, and everyone was busy. Except Rebecca. Her parents had gone for lunch together, sort of like a date. How weird was that? Zoe was tutoring a junior high dweeb in math. Sam was at the ranch. Ty was still in Steamboat. And AJ was in Santa Monica. Again.

Rebecca didn't have as much free time anymore, what with the doll shop job. Leisure had become suddenly attractive as soon as it was in short supply. Now, however, with a long weekend to enjoy, she couldn't seem to get into it. She tried to write but couldn't get into the zone—that sweet spot where the stories pretty much wrote themselves. Maybe it was the zone that was the problem. Maybe if she wrote from her "normal" self, everything would be fine. Her "normal" self, however, had not been able to write anything even remotely interesting.

The silent house seemed to close in on her. She needed to get outside! She hurried upstairs. There was a pair of flip-flops by the French doors, and she pushed her feet into them. She guessed the patio would be blistering hot. And it was.

This sucked. If only AJ was at the pool! She mopped her forehead with her hand. Okay then, she would go by herself. Yes! She could actually swim; maybe it would wash the cobwebs out of her brain. She would relax into the lazy heat and pretend she was at a remote island resort where no one knew her, even though she was famous, and the ocean was only a few feet away. She nodded to herself.

She slipped on her bathing suit and pulled her shorts and shirt back on. She stuffed a water bottle, a couple books, her towel, and suntan lotion into her big tote. The pool was only a few blocks, but the walk left her broiling hot and sweaty, and eager for the refreshing coolness of the water. She flashed her ID card under the scanner and let herself into the pool compound. The gate closed heavily behind her.

She ducked immediately into the locker room where she stripped off her shorts and tank top and stepped into a shower, letting water sluice over her hot skin. She gasped, goose bumps prickling all over her under the cold stream, but after a few seconds, it felt really good. Cooled and refreshed, she patted herself quickly with her towel and pulled her shorts and tank back on.

She paused at the door, shading her eyes to let them adjust to the glare, and looked around. She had expected the pool to be crowded on a day this hot, but there didn't seem to be many people. She glanced automatically at the lifeguard towers. To her surprise, she saw Josh Kenyon. He was perched in the definitive lifeguard pose. A whistle hung around his neck on a leather strap. A Saints baseball cap cast the upper half of his face in shadow.

If Josh was here, would Jackson be here? She didn't see him, but there were two guys in the pool tossing a ball around. Anson was one of them; she recognized the other but had forgotten his name again. B-something. Blair? Brent? Rebecca was torn. She longed for the coolness of the water, but she wasn't sure she could deal with this by herself.

Laney gave her a mental nudge. *Just have some fun with it.*

What do you mean? Rebecca demanded.

You know what I mean. Laney felt exasperated. *Think how it could play out. You, Front Range's hottest jocks. Word would get around. You'd be—*

I'd be what!

Laney was silent for a moment. *Okay. Not your scene. Then just have a few laughs. Break the boredom. That's all. Take a little chance. Pretend you're writing a story. That's it! You're the outrageous main character. Do something . . . outrageous!*

Rebecca hesitated. Laney made it sound easy, and Laney would do it in a heartbeat. Rebecca was tempted. But her wish to do something a little wild was overridden by the habit of taking the safer path. Disheartened, she turned to go. Laney sighed in resignation.

"Rebecca!"

She froze. She knew that voice. She scanned the pool. Anson and B-something were still horsing around. A few younger kids played at the shallow end.

"Hey, Becka!"

And there he was, reclining on a chaise. He raised a hand in mock salute, grinning.

Rebecca felt caught. She took in Jackson's careless grin and casual ease. There was no way she could leave now without looking like a complete lame-ass.

Okay, then. Go for it. Rebecca could feel the challenge coming from Laney. And was that a little smugness? *Pretend it's a drama exercise.*

She took a minute to gather herself. "Okay," she muttered half aloud. "Pull a moxie character out of Mr. Tilson's Stetson. See where she takes you."

Perfect, Laney encouraged her. *Fake it till you make it.*

Rebecca took a deep breath. She willed herself calm. She pictured the surprise on Mr. Hammond's face when she had refused to be quashed by his bullying, and she felt again the glow of satisfaction. She pictured Laney—herself—in casual banter with Jackson. Relaxed, detached, only mildly interested. No big deal. She took another deep breath. And then she walked leisurely but deliberately toward Jackson, stopping at the foot of his lounger. She stood there, letting her gaze wander over his long frame—the wide shoulders, the lean, muscled stomach. The dragon tattoo. Her eyes widened behind her sunglasses. They riveted on the dragon tattoo!

Oooh, whispered Laney. *Don't you just want to touch it—*

Rebecca shoved Laney ruthlessly to the back of her mind. She struggled to stay in character—whatever character she was in. Her heart was racing. She looked away from Jackson's tattoo.

"S'up?" was all she could manage. Thank the gods she was wearing sunglasses!

"Just waitin' for you, darlin'," drawled Jackson. He was grinning.

This she had heard before. She reached for that calmness again. She almost had it. She remembered Mr. Tilson lecturing them on "being" the part, especially when you were nervous. *Use your nervousness to give your acting an edgy quality.* She dug deep. She let her tote slide off her shoulder onto the end of Jackson's chaise. She pushed her sunglasses to the top of her head. She cocked one hip and planted a fist on it. She looked down at him.

"So," she said, "I'm here."

Jackson did a double take. The grin dissolved, leaving him with his mouth half open. Rebecca noted this with glee. A little smile played around the corners of her mouth.

"Uhhh . . ." Jackson crossed one ankle over the other. Bare toes tapped against empty air.

It couldn't be this easy. Could it? She tilted her head at him. "Can't even? I didn't quite catch that."

A tortured version of the FIGJAM grin played across Jackson's face. Comical, really. He crossed his ankles the other way.

Rebecca waited. She rolled her eyes. "Take a vow of silence, did you?"

"No, uh . . ."

"I'm not feelin' it," she said.

Rebecca had never seen Jackson tongue-tied. This was interesting. She relaxed a little, feeling triumphant. She smiled brilliantly at him. "So, Jackson . . ." Rebecca looked at Josh on the tower, and then at Anson and B-something in the pool. "Are you in penalty?"

"Penalty? No, uh . . ."

"Oh, that again."

She watched him watching her. He shifted in his chaise. He linked his fingers behind his head and then dropped his hands to the arms of his chair. Fierce concentration overlaid with confusion radiated off him. She could actually feel his energy. And now she was the one startled.

He sat up and reached a long leg toward the closest lounger, dragging it over with his foot. "Park it here, Becka," he said. It was the best he could do.

She perched on the end of the lounger. Now what? She was still smiling at him, but it had started to feel a little wooden. Lordy, this was a lot of work!

"Whatcha been up to all summer?" Jackson hadn't recovered his usual cocky, tormenting self, but at least he was capable of speech.

Rebecca crossed one knee over the other. She shrugged her shoulders. "Not much," she said. "Working." She let one foot swing. "Teaching my cat to levitate."

Oh, good one! whispered Laney.

Jackson chuckled. "Does that keep you pretty busy?" he asked.

"It wouldn't," admitted Rebecca. "Except I've been observing the energy patterns when she's, you know, floating . . ."

"Sort of like Einstein meets Dumbledore?"

"Well . . . it's really about the light photons. So less Dumbledore than Einstein." The side of her mouth twitched.

Jackson nodded. "Pretty much what we'd expect from a brainiac," he said.

Rebecca inhaled a quick little breath. She opened her mouth to make a denial, the cool, moxie character badly shaken. Her brows reached for each other over narrowed eyes that shot icy sparks. That would be the old Rebecca, though. The new, moxie Rebecca would never give him that satisfaction, would not rise to the bait.

The new Rebecca, however, was not practiced at this and was now at a loss. Her character and Laney were both mute. She clamped her mouth shut and stalled to buy time. She shifted her tote to her own lounger. She pulled her towel from its depths and spread it out. Reaching into the tote again, she extracted sunscreen and a paperback. She pulled out her water bottle, condensation glistening on its surface, and took a long swallow. She slid her feet out of her sandals. Settling into the chaise, she adjusted the sunglasses where they perched on the top of her head. Only then did she turn to look at Jackson again.

Jackson looked amused. Laney remained silent. The moxie character apparently had stage fright. Oh well, it had been good while it lasted. She sighed.

"I've been working," she said. "For real." She tried for nonchalant, but she wasn't sure she got it.

"Yeah?"

"Yeah."

"In your lab? Where you . . . observe photon patterns?"

"Other than that," said Rebecca.

"What sort of work?"

No way was Rebecca going to admit she worked in a doll shop! "I work for the owner of The High Health Center," she said. She could think of no smart retort, so she went with a version of the truth.

"So what do you do?" Jackson persisted.

"Oh, you know. It varies. Depends on . . . um . . . you know, stuff.

"Aren't you writing clever stories with rad endings?"

Rebecca's stomach fluttered. She looked hard at him. "What do you mean!"

"I don't mean anything. I'm just asking." Jackson relaxed into his lounger. The dragon rippled with his movements.

Rebecca didn't answer.

"Well?"

"Well what?"

Jackson's grin was solid now. "Aren't you making up stories? You do write stories, don't you?" He was definitely baiting her.

"Well, yeah. I did. Some. It's no big deal."

"It seemed like a big deal when I snatched your notes that day."

Rebecca gasped. The feel of remembered fury uncurled from her belly. She clenched her fists and glared at him.

"You were a real shit!" Her voice was low but venomous. "And Fat Mr. Hammond took your side. As always. Teacher's pet," she finished. It was the old Rebecca.

"Brainiac," he said.

"I'm not—!"

Jackson was grinning broadly now. He was playing with her, pushing her buttons. He was amazingly good at it.

Are you going to let him?

Laney's thought caught Rebecca up short. She took a deep breath and held it, her head cocked to one side. With all her will, she reached for a neutral expression. When she thought she had it, she exhaled slowly.

Jackson laughed out loud. "I love when you do that, Becka," he said. "You're a real Jekyll and Hyde."

Rebecca held her impassive face. Barely. She arched her eyebrows. She said nothing.

"You sure made ol' Hammond twitch when you pulled that face on him," said Jackson.

Rebecca lost her deadpan expression in an expulsion of breath. She laughed. "My heart was pounding so loud I was sure you could hear it across the room," she confessed. "It did sort of make him twitch, didn't it?"

"Yeah, he thought you'd have a meltdown, like usual."

Rebecca's eyes narrowed again, but she let it go. "I think he's kind of a bully," she said.

"I never thought about it," said Jackson. "Sounds about right, though."

"So what happened with him and your algebra grade? Did you end up okay?" she asked.

"Yeah." Jackson looked suddenly serious. "Yeah, I came out okay."

Rebecca nodded but didn't say anything. She didn't think she'd ever get used to that expression on Jackson's face. It darted through her mind that maybe she liked his irreverence, liked that he seemed to take nothing seriously. She wished she could just laugh things off like he did. Like Laney did. On the other hand, she knew he had struggled with tests and that his grades were important to him. She remembered the look on his face when he'd rounded on her demanding, "You ever hear of No Pass No Play?"

She suddenly felt uncomfortable knowing about this other side of Jackson. It felt too . . . exposed. She didn't want to think about it right now, sitting here in the bright sun with him two feet away. Maybe she didn't want to think about it at all. She shifted in her chair, straightening the edge of her towel. She took a sip of water.

"Jeez, it's hot," she said.

"Go in the pool," said Jackson. He said it casually, but the grin was loaded.

"*You* go in the pool," she said. She looked away, trying to ignore him.

"You're the one who's hot."

The skin on the back of her neck prickled, and her stomach turned over. Suddenly the weight of her hair was suffocating. She unconsciously lifted it from her neck, gathering it like she would for a ponytail.

"Sure, Becka's hot." The voice belonged to Josh. "You just figurin' that out, Jacks?"

Rebecca looked up, startled. She let go of her hair, and it fell to her shoulders again. Josh had come up behind them unnoticed. His eyes were hidden by his wraparound sunglasses, but his mouth was stretched in a wide grin.

Jackson laughed. Josh smirked. Rebecca bristled.

"That's not what he meant!" She squirmed in her seat and glowered at both of them.

"Sure, it's what I meant." Jackson's eyes raked her body.

"Our Becka's the only one who doesn't know she's a babe." Josh ogled her too.

OMG! Rebecca was suddenly very aware of her body. The shorts and tank top over her swimsuit provided almost no coverage. She felt nearly naked. She longed for the coolness and privacy of the locker room, but it felt light-years away. Her hand fluttered to her chest. She jerked it away, jamming her sunglasses back over her eyes.

"*Our Becka?*" With another jolt, Rebecca flashed on a memory. Josh had said that once before. What was that about? Did they talk about her? Did they *watch* her?

"Yeah?" Jackson was still grinning. "That true, Becka?"

A slow heat that wasn't from the Colorado sun crept up her cheeks. She had no idea what to say. Seconds ticked by. Both boys, complete with idiot grins, watched her.

"Can't even?" Jackson threw it back at her now.

Rebecca reached for the zone, for Laney, for anything. She clutched the paperback in her hands. The book . . . writing!

"Careful, or you'll end up in one of my novels." That was Laney. Jackson was all in. "As the totally lit hero who saves the day?"

"And gets the babe," said Josh.

"As the dark nemesis who is beset with lethal circumstances."

"Dark nemesis . . ." Jackson played with the idea.

"Beset with lethal circumstances . . ." Josh considered this. "Jacks doesn't need to be in your novel to have lethal circumstances." He laughed. "He gets plenty of his own."

Rebecca looked sharply at Josh. Was that a reference to Jackson's accident? Or was she just paranoid? Relief flooded over her when Anson called from the pool.

"Jacks! Telluride!" Anson was hanging by one hand from the end of the diving board, the ball held aloft. B-something was treading water, looking impatiently in their direction.

"Cool your jets, man." Still grinning, Jackson got to his feet.

Rebecca's head rotated up as she watched him unfold from the lounger. He stepped over to her. He bent toward her. And then everything slid into slow motion. She froze, her face turned up to him. She couldn't pull her gaze away. She tried to raise a hand . . . to hold him off? To make a fist? To what? It didn't matter; her brain refused to send any message. Jackson's face was within inches of hers. She could smell chlorine and suntan lotion on his skin. His breath smelled of peppermint. He reached for her. Rebecca couldn't seem to draw air into her lungs; the sounds around them faded as if distant. His hand curled around the back of her neck.

"Stick around, Becka," he said softly. He twined his fingers into her hair.

The shock of it brought Rebecca back to herself. A huge gasp of air filled her lungs and fired her brain. Her fist flew up in a ferocious response, catching Jackson squarely in the solar plexus. He exhaled with a grunt, nearly going to his knees.

Josh exploded with laughter. When he could get his breath, he choked out, "Not one of your regular groupies, Jacks!"

Jackson struggled to stand upright. He wrapped one arm around his middle. "You're goin' down, man," he said to Josh. His voice was hoarse.

He stepped away from Rebecca and shoved Josh toward the pool. He rubbed his stomach, his blue eyes fastened on her.

"You're breakin' my heart, darlin," he said softly. And he grinned the FIGJAM grin.

Rebecca laughed out loud. "Sure, I am, Jackson," she said. She smirked back at him, her smile wide and satisfied.

Surprise and then challenge flashed across Jackson's face, but Josh took him by the arm and hauled him off. Jackson looked once over his shoulder at her as Josh steered him away. They dove into the pool, one surfacing and then the other, tossing water from their hair.

Rebecca didn't even try to sort out her emotions. She watched the boys from the safety of her dark glasses. She was still hot, but no way was she going in the pool with them. What had just happened? Why had she frozen like a deer in headlights? Until he wove his hand in her hair; then she had come back with a blow of her own. Literally.

She stretched her legs. Took a long pull from her water bottle. She could leave, just slink away. But that would not only be totally lame, but a sign of . . . what, losing the round?

But I didn't, she thought. She reached for Laney in her mind. *Did I?*

I'd give it a draw, said Laney. *You faked it pretty well.*

Rebecca nodded to herself in satisfaction. A draw wasn't bad for a first-timer. Mon Dieu, it was a lot of work, though! Were boys really worth it? She splashed water into her hands from her water bottle and patted it onto her face and neck, wishing for a breeze. It was so hot! She upended the bottle over her shoulders and let the water run down her arms and chest. That was better. She forced her thoughts away from Jackson.

She thought about all the shared secrets from a week ago. Her own Events. She wondered what AJ was doing in Santa Monica, besides going to the beach. Sam and Alfie riding out together on Majestic, Alfie's arms around Sam. What would that be like? Having a guy you really liked hold you in his arms, his body pressed against yours. These thoughts did nothing to cool the heat from the Colorado sun. She reflexively drew up her knees.

The heat made her lethargic. Finally, a breeze! Hot wind brushed her bare skin and caused the fringes on the umbrella to whisper. She relaxed again, stretching out in the lounger. The sounds faded, and she drifted away. Into a doze and then into sleep.

CHAPTER 58

Louisville Slugger with a Twist

July 6

WHEN REBECCA FLOATED slowly up from sleep, the sun had traveled beyond the edge of her umbrella and was hot on her legs and midsection. She felt disoriented. Her mouth was dry. Sweat was beaded on her upper lip. She groped for her water bottle and found it on the grass beside her lounger. Empty. It was quiet except for a pair of voices close by. She opened her eyes enough to peek beneath her sunglasses. Jackson and Josh were sitting on the rim of the pool, legs and feet dangling in the water, both leaning casually back on their hands, elbows braced. A matched pair. Their backs to her, only a few feet away.

"You should've been there," she heard Josh say. "We creamed 'em."

"Why were you there?" asked Jackson

"Gave Express a ride," he said. "Thought I'd hang for the game."

"Not your scene," said Jackson. He punched Josh in the arm. Josh shoved him. They resettled into their relaxed poses.

"The Cougars pretty much suck anyway. No big deal to kick the crap out of 'em," said Jackson. "I never figured out why Coach set up that game."

"Me neither. But the play wasn't the best part."

"What do you mean?"

Josh looked square at Jackson, a satisfied smile splitting his lean face. "Hammond had a meltdown. It wasn't pretty."

Behind her dark glasses, Rebecca's eyes opened wide. Her heart lurched and then settled into a rapid beat. She sat upright slowly, hugging her knees to her chest.

"What was *he* doing there?"

"Who knows or cares?" Josh raised his shoulders and dropped them back down. "We were in the last inning. Blake had pitched a great game."

Blake! A corner of Rebecca's mind grabbed ahold of the name. It was a distraction from what she knew was coming. B-something was Blake Nolan. There was nowhere to go with this recall, though, and her mind locked back on the conversation at the edge of the pool.

Josh was saying, "Earned his deed to Express, for sure. Not that the Cougars made him work all that hard at it. We were up. Anson was knockin' foul balls all over the place. He wasn't even trying, y'know? We were so far ahead. The Cougars' pitcher was pretty much toast. You know that wannabe, Richards?"

Jackson made a rude noise.

Josh continued, "So the wannabe digs deep and finds a fastball. Lobs it right down the middle. Catches the Man off guard. He makes an amazing swing and really connects. You should've seen it! But he's late, and he gets under it. The ball heads over the first-base bleachers and just keeps climbing. Comes down behind the concession stands."

"So what's the big deal?" Jackson was only half interested.

Sitting behind the boys unnoticed, Rebecca knew what was the big deal. She knew exactly what was coming next. Fat Mr. Hammond was going down. The anticipation was heady.

> The stands grew quiet and necks craned as the ball climbed up and up and back over the first-base bleachers, and then began its way down, leisurely, lazy, as if in slow motion. This ball was going clear to the parking lot! And then it was no longer in slow motion. The ball sailed past the stands and hurled downward at dizzying speed. There was a dull crunch followed by a shattering crash.
>
> A man standing next to Mr. Hammond turned to him. "There goes some unlucky bugger's windshield," he said.

"The big deal, man, is that it lands on Hammond's precious Beemer." Josh smacked one fist into the palm of his other hand.

Now Jackson was interested. "No way!"

Josh chortled. "Yeah way," he said. "Made a nice crater in his hood and smashed into his windshield. Shattered it."

"Rad!" Josh had Jackson's full attention now. Silent and unnoticed, he had Rebecca's too. She smiled a tight, satisfied smile. Her eyes held cold triumph. The Fat Man had gotten his due. She was the architect of justice.

"I never saw Hammond move so fast," Josh went on. "Didn't know he could. He sort of runs and waddles out to his car. Stands there staring at it. It was sweet."

"Poor bugger." There was no sympathy in Jackson's voice. "He only just got it fixed from running me over."

Laughter, and the boys punched each other again, nearly falling into the pool.

"Must think he's snake bit."

"Someone has it in for him." Jackson punched Josh again, still sniggering.

"*I* had it in for him." Rebecca spoke quietly to herself.

A satisfying sense of righteousness filled her. There was a little tingling sensation in the pit of her stomach. She had meant to bring down the Fat Man, and she had done it. He was a bully. He was mean. It was justice. Stealing up behind her elation, however, came the niggling feeling of unease. This was followed by the certainty that there was something she needed to know, and the fear she wouldn't figure it out, or at least not in time. Whatever that meant.

"There's one more bit," said Josh.

Rebecca unconsciously cocked her head. She knew of no other bit after this.

"Better than trashing his Beemer?"

"Nothing to do with it," said Josh.

"Spill it, Telluride!"

"Hammond's been fired."

"You're shittin' me!" said Jackson. "'Cause he ran me over?"

"Bunch of stuff, I guess. Board said he's not stable, not a suitable influence on the students. Poor personal appearance. Inappropriate behavior."

"How do you know this?" demanded Jackson.

Rebecca didn't wait to hear. She had heard enough. She got quietly to her feet hoping Jackson and Josh wouldn't notice her. The tube of sunscreen fell off her chaise. Rebecca left it. Her sandals in her hand, her towel thrown over one shoulder, she clutched her tote to her chest and ran in bare feet for the gate.

CHAPTER 59

Freak Show

July 7

R EBECCA HAD FALLEN into an exhausted sleep that night, but it was not a restful one. She had smeared lotion liberally on her sunburn, which was mostly on one side. It was solid down her left leg to her ankle, where it jumped to the inside of her right foot and the top of her left one, leaving clear lines where her ankles had been crossed. She also had a funny triangle burn on her left side where her shirt had been bunched up, and a white line from the bow of her sunglasses on one temple. Her right hand had rested on her left forearm while she slept, creating an unburned splotch complete with finger marks. The right hand was, of course, scorched. Examining the damage in her mirror, she had muttered to herself, "You could be in a freak show." She would blister and peel, and her tan would be splotchy and uneven. Not that she ever had much of a tan.

The freak-show sunburn was minor, however, compared to Louisville Slugger. Or, rather, the twist at the end. Every time she had rolled onto her left side, the sunburn had jarred her from sleep. And every time she woke up, her mind had gone immediately to the Event. Was the sunburn her payback for writing the story? It seemed minor compared to Mr. Hammond's car being trashed. Or was it? Weren't people more important than things? That was a basic value she had been taught since she was little. What about his being fired, though? She couldn't make out if that was her fault or not. No question he was mean and a bully. He deserved to be fired, for sure. Adults, though, often embraced peculiar and conflicting standards on what was acceptable or deserving. What would they do if they found out about the stories? Her mind didn't identify "they." It was simply an amorphous grouping of adult power figures. She shouldn't have told Zoe and Sam. But how could she not? Maybe she should have been more adamant about them telling no one. No one! Her mind argued back, the old argument. No one would ever believe it! How could they?

Sunday dawn found her curled on her right side staring at her little patch of sky as it lightened. Tinker had become annoyed with her tossing and turning and was asleep on the window seat, snuggled against a stuffed bear. Rebecca was tired, her sunburn hurt, her thoughts were a jumble, and she felt emotionally wrecked. The barbecue this afternoon at Nanna's felt like a mountain to be climbed. If she actually made it through the day, she was sure she'd never be able to eat a bite. At least there was no Sunday breakfast to endure.

***

Rebecca did get through the day, and at last it was time to leave for Nanna's. She dressed in loose-fitting shorts and a Tee—things that wouldn't irritate the sunburn. She tucked her iPhone in a satchel and slung it over her shoulder. On the way out, she paused with one hand on her doorknob and then went back and slipped her laptop into the satchel.

Jimmy Norton was going with them, and they were picking up Zoe. Lissa was coming from The Center. It was closed on Sunday, but Lissa had gone in to inventory another shipment of crystals. So it was necessary to take both her father's truck and her mother's car.

Rebecca claimed passage in the truck. This would eliminate any opportunity for her mother to grill her about why she was acting so peculiar. She knew this was unfair. Her mother never grilled her; she was always gentle and patient. *Even worse*, whispered a voice in her head. She didn't think it was Laney. Who were all these people in her head these days!

"Dad, we can all squish in the back seat," said Andy.

"Not enough seat belts. Not legal," said her dad.

"No, Dad, Jimmy and I can stack," said Andy.

"Stack?"

"Yeah! I'll sit on Jimmy, and we can both use one seatbelt."

Rebecca laughed in spite of herself. "What if Jimmy wants to be on the top?" she asked.

"There will be no stacking." Her father was firm. But the corners of his mouth twitched.

The girls were quiet on the ride to Nanna's. She and Zoe didn't need small talk. She explained her strange sunburn with a grimace and, "I fell asleep at the pool," leaving out any other details. Zoe gave her a long, level look. Rebecca nodded toward her father, and Zoe let it go. Once at Nanna's house, the girls helped set up for the barbecue. There wasn't much to do. April was there, anticipating everything Nanna wanted or needed. Rebecca was sure they were reading each other's minds. Pappa had been slow-cooking ribs all day, and the air was redolent with the smoky aroma. It made Rebecca's mouth water. There were lots of traditional sides to go with the ribs, and it turned out she could eat after all.

When even her father and Pappa had reached their limits, April and Nanna rose in unison and began clearing the table.

"It's cooler today," said Nanna. "Why don't we clean up a little and then have dessert on the deck. Boys, do you want yours now? Then you can go downstairs." Nanna looked at Andy and Jimmy. "We have peach pie and blackberry cobbler with whipped cream." She was already setting plates out.

"Is there ice cream?" asked Jimmy. "I love ice cream."

"There is," said Nanna.

And so Andy and Jimmy ate huge helpings of pie and ice cream, everyone else watching in amazement, and disappeared to the basement and the lure of model trains and various other, seven-year-old-friendly attractions.

Later, they were all settled comfortably beneath lazily turning ceiling fans on the deck. Nanna was in her glider, pushing it gently back and forth with one foot. The glides squeaked with each push.

"I really need to get that fixed," said Nanna.

Maggie was curled in a deep wicker chair, her head leaning against the cushion. Pappa and Jack leaned on the deck rail in quiet conversation.

Lissa was in a chair opposite her mother, reading a text on her phone. "Interesting," she said to no one in particular. Then she looked at Rebecca. "Your favorite teacher got fired."

Rebecca looked up in surprise. Her stomach tightened. The ribs and sides she had eaten shifted ominously.

Zoe's dark eyes went wide. "You mean Mr. Hammond?"

Lissa nodded. "Yep."

"I heard that," said Maggie.

Rebecca stared at her mother. Maggie said, "I spoke with a member of the school board yesterday on an entirely different matter. It came up."

Pappa's phone chirped. He glanced at the display. "I have to take this," he said to Nanna. She nodded. Frowning, Pappa walked back into the house as he answered the phone. Rebecca heard him say, "What's up, Jim?" And then, "How bad is it?" before the door closed.

"So what happened?" Lissa inquired. "To Mr. Hammond, I mean."

"Was it about running Jackson over?" asked Zoe.

Rebecca couldn't seem to frame a thought, least of all words.

"That didn't help," said Maggie. "It was a combination of things, apparently. There were some complaints. I gathered it had been coming for some time."

Rebecca reached desperately for her impassive face. She was pretty sure she didn't get it. Or come anywhere close, actually. She tried for a deep breath; it came out more like a hiccup.

"Does this mean something to you?" asked her mother.

Anger flared suddenly in Rebecca's belly. It freed her mind from its arrested state. "Yeah," she said. Her voice was grim. "It means one less bully at Front Range. He's mean, he lets the jocks get away with anything, and he hates girls."

"That's quite an indictment," said Maggie. She looked at Zoe. "Do you agree with that?"

Zoe answered carefully. "I do," she said. "I never personally got targeted by him, but I know people who did." She glanced at Rebecca. "He's pretty gross."

Rebecca silently thanked Zoe. Her breath eased a tiny bit. She came a little closer to finding her unreadable face. "Even Jackson thinks he's mean and a bully," she said.

Her mother looked at her quizzically. "The dreaded Jackson the Jerk?"

"Yeah, that one," said Rebecca. "He's not always a jerk. Just most of the time. Sometimes we sort of talk."

Her mother looked like she might have something more to say, but Pappa came back at that moment. He looked distracted and tense.

"Elly, I have to leave earlier than planned." He looked apologetically at Nanna. "Meltdown in Houston. I was able to get a flight . . . but I need to leave in twenty minutes if I'm to make it."

Nanna sighed. "I understand," she said. Her look was resigned.

"Dad, I can drop you," said Maggie. "Save you a little time. I need to get Jimmy home soon anyway." She uncurled her long legs and stood up.

Pappa relaxed. "That would be terrific, Mags." He hugged Maggie gratefully. "I need to pack." And he disappeared back into the house.

"The girls and I will come too," said Jack. "I have some things to do for tomorrow."

"We want to stay!" Rebecca didn't think. It came out of nowhere. Turning to Nanna, she implored, "Can Zoe and I stay tonight?" She looked at Zoe, her eyes pleading. "Can you stay, Zolly?"

"My class tomorrow . . ." Zoe looked helplessly at Rebecca.

"I'll get you there," said Nanna smoothly. "I'd love it if both of you could stay. Make up for the party breaking up so unexpectedly. I've barely seen you since your birthday."

Zoe looked at Rebecca and nodded. "I'll call Mom. It's probably okay."

Nanna and Maggie exchanged a guarded look before their faces smoothed into carefully inscrutable expressions. Still leaning on the deck rail, Jack Coleson observed this in wonder. He had seen it many times. Becka was the best, but his wife's whole family seemed to possess this talent; even Andy could pull off a passable version. Was it something in the gene pool?

He watched as the cozy family scene on the deck dispersed, his heart filled with such love and angst for his younger daughter he thought it might bleed. Something was going on with Becka. His best instinct suggested it had to do with the "family tradition" his wife sometimes mentioned. He didn't know much about it and never asked. It felt safer that way. Rebecca had been struggling with something for several weeks, and he felt helpless to do anything about it. Was it just being fifteen? Things were so much easier with Lissa. She was more . . . solid and together, with a clear purpose and direction. She was like a steady current moving calmly toward her goals. Becka, however, his moody princess, seemed so much more vulnerable. She was one moment a quiet, reflective pond, then a deep undercurrent, the next caught up in a whirlpool, then foaming rapids with mist flying.

Jack sighed deeply and followed the others into the house.

***

After everyone left, Zoe and Rebecca excused themselves and disappeared up to the aerie. The little room had been closed up and was stuffy. They opened the door onto the tiny deck. It was only marginally cooler, but the breeze felt good. They moved around the room, bumping into each other, inspecting the books and treasures on the shelves. Zoe picked up an old doll. She gently smoothed the doll's hair and straightened its skirt.

"I still have mine," she said. "My Twin. We couldn't make out how they could be twins if one was blonde and one had dark hair."

Rebecca's eyes softened at the memory. "We thought all twins were identical," she said. "We wanted so badly to *be* twins."

"May and June," said Zoe. She chuckled. "Where did we come up with those names?"

"The mind of a five-year-old is a mystery," said Rebecca. She moved to stand in the doorway, looking out into the leafy canopy of the cottonwoods. Almost to herself, she said, "Pretty much, so is the mind of a fifteen-year-old." She turned to look at Zoe.

"So what are you going to say to them?" asked Zoe.

Rebecca was silent for a long moment. "I don't know," she said at last. She had never mentioned to Zoe what she was about to say. "I need to know what this 'family gift' thing is." And she told of the conversation she had overheard between her mother and grandmother. "Nanna realized hers when she was twelve. Realized what? And why is she writing a book about a girl who discovers how to use energy to do stuff?"

Zoe's eyes widened. "I'd forgotten about that!" Her voice was a whisper.

"Yeah, well, I haven't," said Rebecca grimly. "Everyone doing Reiki. Nanna and April communicating without ever saying a word. Laney yammering at me from my head all the time. I'm beginning to think my whole family is nothing but a freak show." She held out her arms. "Look at this sunburn! I'm a complete freak. I fit right in."

Zoe stared at her friend in dismay. She could think of no response. None at all.

CHAPTER 60

Breaking Storm

July 7

A SUMMER SQUALL was moving up from the south, forbidding clouds obscuring Pikes Peak and the ranges falling away below it and extending over the plains to the east. The air was cooler at Nanna's, but it had taken on some humidity. The breeze offered by the lazily turning ceiling fans was welcome.

They were settled comfortably on the deck. Nanna had propped pillows against the arm of the glider, and she rested comfortably against them with her legs stretched across the seat. Inkjet was on her lap. April was in Pappa's big rocker, her feet propped on the edge of the cold firepit. Zoe and Rebecca had pulled two wicker chairs to either side of a low table and sat with legs curled beneath them. Frosted glasses of iced tea and lemonade and a plate of pumpkin-pecan cookies had been brought out, but only April was enjoying any of it.

Rebecca was screwing up her courage. No easy task! She looked helplessly at Zoe, silently pleading for help.

"Nanna," said Zoe, "we need your help on something." Zoe glanced at April. "Both of you," she amended.

Nanna gently stroked Inkjet. Inkjet stretched full length on her legs and sighed. April sipped her iced tea. They looked calmly at Zoe and then Rebecca.

Rebecca reached for a lemonade. She held the glass to her lips but set it on the table without drinking. She uncurled her legs and curled them again in the opposite direction. Thunder could be heard dimly in the distance now.

She searched for words. Where to start? "This energy stuff," she said finally. "I need to know about it." She picked at a thread on the seat cushion, not meeting anyone's eyes.

"Why is that?" asked Nanna carefully.

Rebecca raised her eyes to meet Nanna's. "Because," she said, "I've been using it. At least I think I have. And I don't know what I'm doing and . . . it's turning into a real freak show. I need to know." She fisted one hand and rubbed it against her chest. It did nothing to ease the tight band that was making it hard to breathe.

"Why don't you start at the beginning, Becka," said Nanna softly.

Rebecca nodded. She took a deep breath. She began hesitantly, but soon it was coming in a torrent. The anger and the feelings of helpless frustration that had triggered the first story. The conflicting emotions. Revenge exacted, but not as sweet as she had anticipated. How even the good stories scared her. The twists to Louisville Slugger and Dreamweaver. How Laney was so often in her head and she sometimes actually talked with her. The zone, and how she seemed to just know things when she was in it—how freaky was that? The exhilaration of standing up to Mr. Hammond, the same for giving Jackson as good as he gave. Not that flirting with Jackson was a priority for her, but it was good to feel like . . . just not . . . invisible. It tumbled out in no particular order. Angela's apology. Jackson's No Pass No Play. Had she misjudged them both? Were they all—herself and her friends, Jackson, Angela—really pretty much the same? All caught in a web of adult agendas and power plays? How she felt pushed to take Reiki.

"Sam said she doesn't even know how to talk about it unless I take it too. She says she's different, and she is, but maybe that's the Alfie thing. It has taken part of my other best friend away from me, and I hate it for that! Everything is changing. Every*one* is changing. My friends, I mean. And that scares me too. What if I lose them? I keep hearing, 'It's all energy,' but I don't understand."

The sun disappeared behind an ominous thunderhead, but no one appeared to notice. The thunder was much closer now. "You can read it all," said Rebecca. "I brought my laptop. Except that's not the half of it!" She swiped a napkin under her eyes. "It's how all this makes me *feel*! I love that I can do it, but it scares the crap out of me." A glance at Nanna. "And what did you find out when you were twelve? You and Mom keep watching me and exchanging weird looks like you're waiting for my freakiness to pop out. And I think it has!"

With a last wail of anguish, she said, "And I can't even write Laney stories anymore!" Tears streamed down her cheeks. She scrubbed at them helplessly. "And that's the one place where I felt like I had some control in my life. Where I could make things happen just like I wanted."

The black clouds were directly above them now. A searing bolt of lightning leapt from cloud to ground close by, and thunder exploded overhead. The house and deck shuddered. Rebecca gasped and instinctively ducked. Nanna swore. April traced a strange sign with one hand, mouthing inaudible words. Zoe's lips formed "Mon Dieu!" Inkjet catapulted himself from Nanna's lap and fled for the house, his tail twice its normal size. The first drops of rain splattered on the roof of the deck.

And then the storm cut loose.

CHAPTER 61

No Victims, Only Volunteers

July 7

THEY SCRAMBLED FOR the safety of the house as rain gusted in horizontally from the open sides of the deck. Rebecca ran for the door. Right behind her, Zoe grabbed the plate of cookies.

"Leave it! Leave everything! Just—" Nanna shouted over the roar of wind and rain, but her voice was lost in another explosion of thunder. She held the French doors long enough for them to dash through and then closed and locked them securely.

Nanna checked the house to be sure everything was battened down, and on the whereabouts of Inkjet. She found him under a chair in the loft but was unable to coax him out. She rejoined the others in the kitchen.

"Where would we like to be?" she asked.

"Right here, don't you think?" said April. "I think this calls for something a little more stout than tea and cookies." She looked at Nanna for confirmation.

"Absolutely," Nanna agreed.

April set about preparing ice cream sundaes. Dark fudge and vanilla bean ice cream, just the vanilla bean for Rebecca, please, in deference to her "missing chocolate gene." Fresh strawberries and whipped cream. Chocolate syrup and nuts topped April's and Nanna's, no syrup for Zoe and Rebecca. Then she pulled out mugs, filled them with ice, and poured in raspberry lemonade. She added a finger from the tall frosted bottle to two of the mugs, and at a tiny nod from Nanna, a splash to the other two.

"Medicinal," she said when Zoe's eyes went wide.

"Magic bullets." Rebecca's did too. "Wait till I tell Mom!"

They dug into their sundaes, exclaiming when lightning erupted close by and thunder crashed and rolled overhead. When the bowls were empty, April gathered them and set them in the sink. She came back to the island.

"Okay, then," said Nanna. She rested her arms on the countertop and leaned forward on them. She looked at her granddaughter.

"Do you want to read the stories?" asked Rebecca.

"Maybe later," said Nanna.

Rebecca nodded. She watched as her grandmother took a couple deep breaths. Nanna seemed to settle more solidly into her chair. She looked at the big window, but her eyes were unfocused. It reminded Rebecca of what she herself did when she was getting into the zone.

When Nanna came back to the moment, she said, "Let's start with energy."

Rebecca waited.

"When we say everything is energy, that's literally correct," Nanna said. She glanced at Zoe, who nodded vigorously. "Everything—everything—is energy. Particles and matter. The universe is comprised of energy, and energy is what creates all things. It is directed by consciousness, which is also energy."

"Mind," said Zoe.

Nanna nodded. "Max Planck is quoted as saying, 'Consciousness is the forerunner of all things.'" She anticipated Rebecca's question, adding, "Planck was a German physicist, considered by some to be the father of modern quantum physics."

"Oh," said Rebecca.

"Planck is not alone among quantum scientists. Just one of the first," said April. "The concept is a hundred years old."

Nanna nodded again. "Ancient beliefs say the same thing. The first of the Hermetic Laws states 'All is mind.' Another reference to the universe being directed by consciousness."

"Doesn't it have to move to be energy?" asked Rebecca.

"It *is* moving," said Nanna. "It's vibrating. 'All is vibration' is the second of the Hermetic Laws. 'Nothing rests; everything moves;

everything vibrates.' Vibration is movement of energy through particles of matter. It's measurable. Sound occurs wherever there is a vibration. That's how we have music. Humans can only hear sounds between certain hertz levels, but there are ways to discern energy even though we can't hear it or see it.

Nanna took a sip of her magic bullet. She smiled at April. "Mm. Good."

"Science calls this universal energy a 'field,' or the 'unified field.' From a spiritual perspective, it is called God, Source, The One, Great Spirit. There are many names. All things in the field, or the universe, relate to all other things. And, in fact, are connected."

"Okay," said Rebecca. She wasn't sure she got this exactly.

"So energy is everywhere, and it's everything. That is ancient knowledge, and it is also quantum science."

Rebecca pulled a face. Nanna mirrored it back at her. "You knew we'd get to that."

Nanna waited a moment and then asked, "Has Sam talked to you about the clairs?"

"Yeah. A little."

"Can you describe them? Not individually, but in general?"

"Maybe . . ." Rebecca looked thoughtful. "I remember clairvoyance, because sometimes I do it. It's seeing stuff, but in your head. Right?"

Nanna and April nodded.

"And sometimes I just sort of know things. Or it comes to me from nowhere, especially if I'm writing. I don't know what that is." She frowned. After a moment, she said, "The clairs are a way to . . . read energy? That we can't see?"

"Exactly!" said Nanna.

"Very good," murmured April.

"We call it intuition," said Nanna. "Everyone has the ability, but often, it's unrecognized, blocked, or denied. Some people have a very strong ability, others less so, but everyone can learn it." Nanna looked directly at Rebecca. "The women in our family," she said, "seem to be . . . particularly gifted."

"You mean we're freaks!" Rebecca sat back in her chair and folded her arms across her chest. Her face was militant.

"How you look at it is a matter of choice," said Nanna quietly.

Rebecca glared at Nanna.

Nanna waited.

Rebecca drummed her fingers on the counter. "Okay, everyone can do it, but we—*this* family—we're really . . . freaky good at it." She turned toward Zoe. "Can you do this stuff?" she demanded.

"Um . . ." Zoe fidgeted in her chair. "Some," she said carefully.

"Like how?"

"Well, right now, I can feel anger and . . . denial . . . coming off you," she said. "And fear," Zoe added almost apologetically. "I can feel your stuff better than I can most people because we're so close, I think. I read Grand-mère pretty well." Zoe grinned. "That's an interesting ride at times, I can tell you!"

"I can only imagine," murmured Nanna.

"You've never told me about this," said Rebecca accusingly.

"It's just something we all do . . . Mom and Grand-mère and me," said Zoe. "I guess I thought anyone can do it."

"Anyone *can* do it," said Nanna again.

"Sometimes," said Zoe, "I just get a sense of 'It feels good,' or 'It feels bad,' without any specifics. When it feels bad, or if there's no reason to try and figure it out, I try to block it. Or move away from it."

Nanna nodded. "Smart," she said. "Okay, then, emotions are also energy. Emotions are like music. Every emotion vibrates at a particular level, or hertz, which can be measured. Sometimes emotions make beautiful music, and sometimes not so much." Nanna made a face. "The point," she went on, "is that we are all broadcasting emotions, as energy, pretty much all the time. Because we are, it can be read. We can pick up on the emotions or thoughts of another person without even knowing we are doing it. So we're back to the clairs."

Nanna waited for Rebecca to process this.

"And when we do read other people's energy, or emotions," Nanna said, "we respond to it. Sometimes knowingly, sometimes not.

Rebecca stared hard at Nanna. When she spoke, it was slowly and carefully. "So you're saying . . . I have this freaky family ability to read other people's energy . . ."

"That you are intuitive, yes."

"And what? That I somehow read . . . for starters, Jackson?"

Nanna nodded.

"And when I wrote my story, I was just . . ." She didn't know how to finish the thought.

"Mirroring back what you had picked up," said Nanna. "You wrote it because you were mad, but *what* you wrote was guided by what you had felt from him."

"I picked up on what he . . . thinks about? Without even knowing it?"

"Exactly," said Nanna. "And what he feels strongly about."

"How come I didn't pick up on . . . whatever he was feeling when he stole my notes?"

"Because emotions, as vibrations, have different levels of intensity. Fear, anger, love, compassion—these are all very powerful. They will be felt more easily. Jackson's fear of injury is very likely an ongoing thing, always there beneath the surface. At the time of your fight, however, he was just having fun—"

"Tormenting me," interjected Rebecca with a scowl.

"And you were probably not reading anything, even on a subconscious level. You were just reacting," Nanna finished.

"So what are you saying?" Rebecca spoke with deliberate care.

Nanna looked at Rebecca, her expression gentle. "What I'm saying, Becka, and this is fundamental, is no one can make something happen to us unless we first believe it's possible and we open ourselves to it; not unless we are vibrating at a frequency that supports it."

"No victims, only volunteers," said April softly. "Spellwork follows those rules."

"Why would someone allow someone else . . . to make a bad thing happen to them? That's unbelievable!"

"Basic psychology would disagree with that," said Nanna. "It's not a conscious decision. We might feel on some level that we deserve it, whatever it is. We might not be conscious of the belief at all. The human psyche is a very complex thing." Nanna paused. "Science says the same thing, in a different way. The ultrashort version is that our beliefs or thoughts create chemicals in the body, which create emotions, and we respond to those emotions with more, similar thoughts. It runs in a loop. And every thought or emotion carries its own unique frequency."

Rebecca considered this, her fingers tapping on the counter. "So are you saying it wasn't my fault? Jackson's accident? And the other stuff? Is that what you're saying?"

"Pretty much," said Nanna.

"What about all the things that happened to me?" Rebecca was puzzled.

"That's another story," said Nanna.

Rebecca sighed deeply and shook her head. Her fingers were still drumming.

"What is one thing you continually hear at home?" said Nanna.

"'What goes around, comes around.'" Rebecca didn't have to think about that one. "And Mom says to be careful what we put out there."

"Because it comes back," said April quietly.

"So . . . I believed I'd have the same sort of thing happen to me, even though I didn't know I believed it, and even though I didn't think about it, it did?" Rebecca frowned. "That's too simple, isn't it?"

"It is simple," said Nanna. "But the basic truths usually are. And you've worried quite a lot about—what did you call it?"

"Balancing karma," said Rebecca softly.

"Well, karma is another thing," said Nanna. "Karma is energy we bring in from previous lifetimes. But no matter what you call it, you were worried about having come back to you what you were putting out there. Would you say that's correct?"

Rebecca nodded.

"You worried about it—worry is an emotion. And you believe what goes around comes around. Think about it, Becka." Nanna looked earnestly at her granddaughter. "Thoughts and emotions are energy."

Rebecca said the words as though to herself, maybe getting to know them. "Thoughts and emotions are energy."

"A *belief* is a thought that we have had many times and that we accept as a truth."

"So . . . if I believe it's true, it is? Even if it's crazy?"

"Yes. For you, it's true."

"And the energy I put out there? With my stories. What about that?"

"I'm not saying you didn't give events a little boost," said Nanna. Rebecca flinched inwardly at the word *events*.

Nanna looked at April.

"It gets pretty complex," said April. "Because everything is connected to everything else. But let's say Jackson was afraid he would get hurt and so couldn't—what? What would happen if he got hurt?"

"He couldn't play sports," said Rebecca. "And get a scholarship so he can go to college."

"So there was Jackson's fear. And you wanted to have more control in your life, to make things happen. Not to mention get even. Then there was your belief that 'what goes around comes around,' as your father so succinctly puts it."

Zoe got it. "So they fed off each other? Becka's energy and Jackson's?"

"Precisely!" said April.

"OMG!" Rebecca's voice was a whisper.

Zoe ran with the idea. "Brittany was egotistical, arrogant, and a real bitch," she said. "To all appearances. But if she was really insecure down deep . . . she'd be thinking the same thing the rest of us were. Why would a college hunk bother with her? She'd be afraid he would stand her up or dump her. And he did!"

Nanna and April nodded.

"And the skit Angela stole." Zoe's small face was the picture of concentration. "She already knew what she did was crappy. That's why she held on to that binder . . ." Zoe turned to Rebecca. "And wouldn't practice the skit in class. Plus, she had her own personal astrologer telling her what she'd done was bad ju-ju, or whatever."

"Diamonique." The girls said it together. They grinned.

Zoe went on. "So she believes, whether she knows it or not, the scales are going to somehow balance. And for all her snooty arrogance, she might have been worried about that competition for some reason. Then you put out there a sweet little number about her falling into the koi pond." Zoe's expression was one of fascination. "Becks was mad, justifiably so. And like Jackson, their energies were . . . linked." Zoe nodded to herself. "Very symmetrical," she said.

"So what about her climbing out of the pond and doing the runway?" asked Rebecca. "I didn't see that."

"No, one of the places you might have misread Angela was her determination to *not* end in defeat. That's what I'd say, anyway," said April. "And it's possible she surprised herself greatly with that act. Sometimes, under duress, people really rise to the occasion."

"And the puppy?"

"Again, you wanted to have some control. Something to ward off your sense of helplessness. Ty—it was Tyler's puppy?"

Rebecca and Zoe both nodded.

"Tyler was panicked and fearful. Very strong emotions. But she had to believe—absolutely *had* to believe—the puppy would be found and be okay. There was no other way for her to deal with the situation. Again, very powerful emotions."

"And I picked up on them." Rebecca spoke softly. She was thinking hard. "I wanted it too, for Ty. And then Tinks showed up at the door, and I told her one day she was going to get trapped in someone's garage . . ." Rebecca looked at her grandmother in amazement. "So it all just connects?"

Nanna nodded. "You thought you made some things happen," she said. "But it was all haphazard. You didn't really have control."

"No," said Rebecca. "Not really. And when I thought I was doing all those things, being in control didn't feel so good. And besides, I really only wanted control of my own life. Not a bunch of other people's lives."

Rebecca fell silent. She chewed on her lip, twirled a lock of hair around one finger. "So what about Mr. Hammond?" she asked quietly. "His car I get. He was totally fixated on it. Even the jocks talk about it. But his being fired?"

Nanna waved a hand dismissively. "I talked with your mother about that," she said. "It was just a matter of time, especially after the incident with Jackson. He had been put on notice by the school board. Apparently, he responded to that with a good deal of . . . belligerence. And it's likely he already feared getting fired, perhaps because of strongly held beliefs about his own self-worth, or lack of it. Who knows? Especially after running Jackson over."

"No loss," murmured Zoe.

"For sure!" added Rebecca. And then her eyes lit up. "And accusing Jackson of cheating! He was mad because he was on notice and running Jackson over was part of the reason. In a twisted way, he could blame Jackson for his trouble with the board." She shook her head. "Plus Jackson told me he made Mr. Hammond mad. The Fat Man is *totally* about getting even! And who would have expected Jackson to ace his algebra exam? I wrote the Event, and even I was amazed when it happened!" Her amazement blazed across her face again as she spoke. "Jackson knew the stuff, just like Tyler, and on some level, he *knew* he knew it!" Rebecca was putting it together. "But he wouldn't expect other people to understand. Not with him being a jock and so cheeky about everything. So he'd expect other people to wonder how he did it."

Rebecca shook her head again. "It's circles in circles going around in circles," she said.

Nanna nodded in approval. "It is," she said. "And here's the thing. Now that you know some of these energetic truths, it would behoove you to pay attention to certain things."

"Like what?" Rebecca was suddenly wary.

"For one thing, like attracts like."

"What does that mean?"

"In the terms of energy and vibration, of which we've been speaking," said April, "it means that however *you* are vibrating determines the level of the vibration you will attract into your life. It's similar to how magnets react. We are, after all, electromagnetic beings."

"How I'm vibrating?"

"Sure. Remember we said thoughts and emotions all carry a unique frequency or vibration?" said April.

Rebecca pursed her lips, her brow furrowed. She was beginning to get it. "I'm not sure I like being reduced to just a collection of vibrations," she grumbled.

"Oh, sweetie," said Nanna, "we are so much more than that! We are an incredible symphony. We are music from the angelic realms! But remember what we said about our emotions sometimes making music that is dark or chaotic? When you wrote a story from the frequency of anger and wanting revenge . . ."

"Merde," muttered Rebecca. "So I didn't make Jackson's accident happen, or the other stuff, but I caused my own bad luck?"

"No victims, only volunteers," murmured April again.

"You said that before," said Rebecca.

Zoe had it figured out. "Jackson's case seems pretty simple," said Zoe. "It might *seem* like he was a victim. If not your victim, Becks"—she looked at Rebecca—"then Mr. Hammond's. From the standpoint of the universal laws, though, he attracted it because he operates from a place of fear of getting hurt." Zoe looked to Nanna for confirmation.

"You, my dearest," said Nanna, "are a sharp cookie."

Zoe leaned back in her chair, smiling broadly.

"And here's the kicker," Nanna said. "We get to *choose* what we think and what we believe. And that means we can greatly influence our emotions. Which means we can control the vibrations from which we operate, and thereby have control over the things that come into our own lives."

Rebecca looked at her grandmother with incomprehension.

Even Zoe was puzzled. "How can we choose what we believe? If a bunch of thoughts turned into a belief, how can we believe something different?"

"It's a conscious choice. By paying attention to your thoughts and your emotions. Your emotions are a yardstick to the kind of thoughts you're thinking."

"How so?" asked Rebecca.

"Remember the loop," said Nanna. "First the experience—the thought or belief—then the chemicals, then the emotion."

"Okay ." Rebecca tapped a finger against her lips in a very Sam-like gesture. "So if I follow it backward . . . an emotion that doesn't feel good started with a thought that is . . ." She looked at Nanna for help.

"Exactly," said Nanna softly. "A thought that is negative or limiting."

"And then just think something else?" Rebecca shook her head.

"Something that feels good." Nanna nodded. "I don't want this to get too complicated," she continued, "but the brain doesn't know the difference between what is real and what is imagined. It just notices an experience and reacts. Consider a thought to be an experience, as far as it relates to the brain. If you keep creating experiences that feel good—positive thoughts—the brain just keeps reacting by creating . . . call them happy chemicals."

"I like that," said Zoe. "Happy chemicals."

Rebecca looked uncertain.

"What happened when you decided you wouldn't let Mr. Hammond get the best of you?" said April.

Rebecca looked at April. Comprehension dawned slowly on her face. "OMG!" she whispered. "It created a whole different result."

Nanna and April waited for Rebecca to finish.

"I made that choice. *I* made it! I was just so sick of his bullying. AJ says the best defense is to not let them see that you're mad." Rebecca was following her own line of thought. "And Laney says to 'fake it till you make it.' I did that with Jackson, and it totally shut him down." She shook her head again.

"It sounds like it could be a lot of work," said Zoe.

"Yeah," Rebecca agreed. "I did great at first. . . giving it back to Jackson, but I couldn't keep it up."

"You're right," said Nanna. "Both of you. But look at it this way: how much work is it to constantly deal with the unwanted things that come into your lives because you are unaware?"

"Mmm. I guess so." Rebecca thought about it. Zoe nodded.

"So," said Nanna. She rubbed her hands together and then clasped her fingers. She smiled. "To sort of summarize all this—it's about awareness and conscious choice. You pay attention to your thoughts. You investigate what you really believe, and why. Question where beliefs come from. Many are from other people. So our lives are being affected by what someone *else* believes! And that's crazy!" Nanna took a deep breath. This was all very close to her heart. "By becoming aware," she repeated more calmly.

"The skills to do this are really pretty simple, once you know them. They become a habit. And then it becomes easy." Nanna looked from Rebecca to Zoe. "And *then*, my dearest ones, you really do have control over your lives! And it's not just philosophy. It's science."

Zoe nodded thoughtfully. "I've read that," she said. "Who said it?"

"Okay, Einstein," teased Rebecca.

"That's it!" Zoe declared. "Albert Einstein said . . ." Her mouth pulled into a little pout of concentration. "I can't quite remember."

April did. "Einstein said:

'Everything is energy, and that's all there is to it. Match the frequency of the reality you want, and you cannot help but get it. It can be no other way. This is *not* philosophy. This is *physics*.'"

Nanna chuckled. "Einstein was pretty confident in his beliefs."

"So whatever frequency we're creating, whether we want it or not—that's what we pull into our lives. That's what you're saying." Zoe looked from Nanna to April.

"It is." April and Nanna said it in unison.

"Wow!" Zoe's eyes widened. She said softly, "This could be very—"

"Empowering," said Nanna.

"Wow!" Zoe's face glowed.

Rebecca's face was clouded. "I need to think about all this."

"You do, my sweet. No question." Nanna walked around the island and wrapped her arms around Rebecca. She leaned her silver head against the tawny one.

CHAPTER 62

Light Show

July 7

"LET'S TAKE A break," said April.

They stood as one and moved toward the French doors. Was it a common thought they all shared? Inkjet appeared on the stairs, where he sat surveying the scene below him with distrust. The storm had moved past them, its fury now being spent somewhere else. The deck was wet and littered with leaves and twigs. Nanna unlocked the doors and opened them. A blanket of humid air hit them.

"Yuck!" Rebecca stepped back from the door.

"OMG, that's awful," exclaimed Zoe. "I can almost hear my hair frizzing!"

"It is, at least, cooler." Nanna stepped out and walked to the edge of the deck, looking around. The trees dripped, and water could be heard trickling in the downspouts. Clouds roiled over the Denver skyline, dark and threatening. Lightning flashed almost constantly, and thunder rolled, but distant now and moving away from them.

Zoe and Rebecca joined Inkjet on the stairs. April and Nanna talked quietly. April's gray braids were wound around her head as usual, the hairpin bobbles dancing and catching the light each time her head moved. Her head was lowered toward Nanna. Nanna's face was turned up to hear what her friend and companion was saying. Rebecca watched them from the stairs. Powerful emotions washed over her, along with a sense of déjà vu. Wonder, safety, power. These two women, her grandmother and April, had always been a presence in her life. Rebecca realized one of her earliest memories was of the two of them in quiet conversation, just as they were in the present moment.

A hazy halo of light seemed to surround both women. With a flash of insight, Rebecca realized she had seen this before too. She saw herself as a toddler, bouncing in her crib, laughing at the sparkly lights dancing around April and Nanna.

This wasn't a new gift. It was one she had forgotten.

"Can you see that?" she whispered to Zoe. She wrapped her arms around her middle and hunched low over her knees.

"What?"

"The colors around them." Rebecca indicated Nanna and April with a nod of her head.

"Kind of sparkly?" Zoe whispered back.

"Yeah."

"Mon Dieu!" Zoe stared.

"*Nan*na . . ." Rebecca's voice was wary and, at the same time, resigned.

Nanna looked up at them. The light halo swirled and settled back into place.

"We can see . . . um . . . your . . ." Rebecca didn't quite know how to say it.

"Lights," said Zoe. "We can see a halo around you."

Nanna's face lit up. "You can see our auras!" she exclaimed.

"Whatever you say," said Rebecca. "Pretty freaky," she added.

"It's just the energy field around us," said Nanna. She laughed up at the girls. She stepped away from April, and the light separated into two distinct halos extending out several feet from their bodies. "Have you seen this before?" she asked.

Rebecca just nodded. "Another thing I need to learn about."

Nanna laughed again. "It will be fun," she said. "I promise. But not tonight." She moved briskly about the kitchen. "April and I are going to straighten up a bit. You two need anything?"

"A more normal family?" suggested Rebecca.

"Mmm. You're stuck with this one, I'm afraid," said Nanna. "You'll just have to make the best of it." She opened the dishwasher, turned on the tap, and began rinsing dishes. She handed them wordlessly to April, who stacked them neatly in the appliance.

"There's one more thing we want to do." Nanna wiped her hands on a towel. "Then we'll call it a night. I'd prefer to wait until tomorrow, but no matter. We'll work with it and get Zoe to her class on time. And it will help you sleep. And let's go to my office," she added. "It's cozier, and I like the energy there."

Rebecca and Zoe trailed after Nanna to her office. April followed.

Nanna's office was lined with bookshelves on three sides, and the fourth was a wall of glass opening onto an intimate walled garden. Subtle uplights lit a small fountain, a piece of garden art, and two small ornamental shrubs. Low mats of groundcover paved the garden with a softly textured carpet. A big maple outside the wall spread its branches over the garden like a protective cloak. Light from the garden softly illuminated the room; Nanna didn't turn on the overheads. Two straight-backed chairs sat to the side. Nanna pulled the chairs to the middle of the room and indicated that Rebecca and Zoe should sit. They did.

Zoe's phone hummed. She pulled it from her pocket and inspected the display.

"It's a text about school tomorrow," Zoe said.

"You must read it," said Nanna.

Zoe read the text, her face taking on a look of astonishment.

"I don't have class tomorrow," she said. "It's been canceled. It doesn't say why."

"How incredibly fortuitous," murmured April.

Rebecca stared at April, her eyes narrowed. "Did you do that?" she demanded.

"You think very highly of my abilities," said April. Her head bobbed, and the hair bangles danced, throwing little sparkles of light.

"Let's get this done so you two can go to bed." Nanna diverted the conversation. "Think of seeing auras as just another way to read energy," she said. "The aura is an extension of the body's energy field. It's measurable scientifically. Negative energy can get trapped in the aura. Including other people's energy sometimes."

"Eew!" Rebecca wrinkled her nose. "That sounds nasty."

"It can be, actually." Nanna said. "We want to give you two a little house cleaning."

"You're saying we have—" Zoe didn't finish.

"Klingons?" said Rebecca. The girls looked at each other and burst into wild laughter at the reference to the old Star Trek movies and the more current and inelegant allusion to . . . unwanted hangers-on, you could say. It was comic release. Once they started, they didn't seem able to stop.

Nanna and April exchanged glances. It was time to wrap this up for the night.

When she could speak, Zoe looked ruefully at Nanna. "Sorry," she said. She wiped her eyes. "Couldn't help it."

Rebecca hiccupped, still incapable of speech. Nanna and April waited. When she had it back together, at least somewhat, Rebecca said, "Do you have a magic potion to keep all this from giving us a . . . mental meltdown? Another magic bullet maybe?"

"Another magic bullet would harm more than help," said Nanna firmly. "The best thing to help you assimilate all this would be Reiki, but I could not possibly do it without your consent."

Rebecca sighed. "If you're asking for my consent—"

"I'm not, Becka," said Nanna. "I would not pressure you."

"I was going to say go ahead," said Rebecca. "Sam will talk me into it sooner or later, and the sooner she and I can talk about it, I guess the better."

"Not unless you are absolutely sure."

"I am. Seems like maybe I need it. Don't know what makes me say that."

"It's your higher self," said Nanna. She raised her hands to ward off Rebecca's protest. "Just think of it as a cool, supersmart Laney who's looking out for you."

"Yeah? Cool. I can do that." Rebecca nodded.

"Me too?" asked Zoe. "I want it too."

Nanna looked at April, who seemed to be communing with . . . the ceiling? Rebecca realized April was off in that same place she had seen Nanna go before all the discussions had begun a few hours ago. What seemed like days ago, actually. Talking with their higher selves? Could that be right?

"It's the same as the zone, isn't it?" Rebecca asked with wonder in her voice.

"What is?" Nanna looked perplexed.

"When I write . . . used to write . . . I'd take some deep breaths and let my mind sort of slip away. Into the zone. That's what I call it. That's where all the . . . Events came from. That's how I wrote stuff I didn't even know. That's what you did before you started telling us about energy. And that's what April was just doing. Isn't it?" Rebecca looked from her grandmother to April and back. "You're listening to your higher self, aren't you? That's how you know stuff you don't know how you know." Rebecca shook her head—little quick shakes as if to clear it.

Nanna looked at Rebecca Jean in surprise and with new respect. This child—no, not a child any longer—was going to become a force to be reckoned with. In fact, she already was. She had stumbled onto her gift, used it, refined it, experienced the consequences, learned from them, experimented, and kept it all together, if barely at times. She had tiptoed through an energy minefield and emerged bruised and sunburned, but intact. A little frightened, a lot wiser, and asking the right questions. She would need some guidance, but she was already figuring things out for herself. What would she do with her gift? That was the million-dollar question.

Nanna's heart expanded with love and pride. She acknowledged a tickle of trepidation but gave it no power. "You are absolutely correct," she said. "The zone. A good term."

"You can use it for pretty much anything, can't you?" Rebecca nodded to herself. It wasn't really a question.

"You can," said Nanna.

They were all looking at Rebecca. She leaned back in her chair. Her smile was enigmatic. Clearly, she was rather pleased with herself. The silence drew out. Outside, a light rain had begun to fall. Prisms of light floated around each uplight. Inkjet wandered into the office and sat by the glass wall. He looked out at the garden. Contemplating universal law, perhaps? Or maybe he just sensed a mouse out there.

April broke the silence. "Shall we proceed?" she asked.

Nanna nodded. "Just the Reiki and a clearing?"

April pursed her lips and steepled her fingers, tapping the index fingers together. "I was thinking Attunements and a clearing," she said. "And we want Level II, for the mental/emotional symbol."

Nanna considered this. "Quite right." She nodded.

She turned to the girls. "April is one of my Reiki Master Teachers, and I defer to her exceptional intuition and judgment. Okay, then, we're going to give you Reiki Attunements, and the classes will follow along later, if you so choose, at which time you'll learn how to use the symbols. For now, it will support you with the clearing of your auras . . . of all sorts of things, including Klingons, and will help keep you from going into overload with all of this."

"What do we have to do?" asked Rebecca.

"Just sit quietly," said Nanna.

CHAPTER 63

Couldn't It Just Be Magic?

July 25

REBECCA RETRIEVED HER lunch from Miss A.'s refrigerator and took it outside. Her feet carried her involuntarily to her favorite place on the estate. She had found a hidden garden one day when she had seen a half-grown kitten dart into the bushes. Following the kitten, she had made her way along a barely discernible path through a tangle of overgrown shrubs. This had led her to the garden, where she had found Miss A., the kitten curled in her lap. Rebecca had pulled up with a little gasp of surprise. Miss A. had regarded her calmly.

"We heard you coming," Miss A. had said. "You've found my favorite place. Come and meet Boo."

Boo was a tortie-on-white, a splotch of orange surrounding one eye on an otherwise-mottled black face. Her tummy, chin, and three paws were white. Her sides and back were stippled black and orange. Her eyes were large and green. She had gingerly sniffed the hand Rebecca proffered and then completely ignored her.

The secret garden was a good place to think. And there was a lot to think about. Rebecca settled comfortably into a chair. Birds were busy at a feeder and often swooped in to drink or bathe in a fountain. It was all very tranquil. There was no sign of Boo. She leaned her head against the back of the chair and let her mind wander.

Rebecca was beginning to come to terms with the concept of "all is energy." In practical application, however, it was another thing entirely. She had attacked the idea with the logical part of her brain—the part that liked math with its neatness and predictability. The problem was that everyday life was anything *but* neat and predictable, especially when thoughts and emotions were factored in. She didn't know who she was anymore. She wasn't the shy, frustrated someone she had been before the Events. She wasn't the confident, making-it-happen someone she had been when she wrote them. And, thankfully, she wasn't the guilt-ridden, worried person she had often been after the fact. Laney was still there in her head, but she felt kind of distant.

Rebecca nibbled on her sandwich and tossed a piece of bread to a bird by the little pond. The bird snatched up the morsel and flew away with it.

Except for Mr. Hammond, of the "bad" stories she was relieved not to have been the cause. She still liked thinking of herself as the "architect of justice" as far as the Fat Man was concerned. In fact, she wanted it. She felt she had lost something in assigning Mr. Hammond responsibility for his own misfortunes. She hadn't experienced any fallout from writing that Event, and Nanna said she wouldn't. Because of her own awareness, and also because of the Reiki and the energy clearing. She should be relieved by that. But somehow, it felt like a loss, a battle scar she had earned.

Since Jackson had created his own situations—at least according to Nanna and April's theories, and she trusted them, she did—there was no reason to avoid a relationship with him. That was twisted thinking, however, because she didn't *want* a relationship with Jackson. It was okay to kid around and flirt, maybe even talk honestly once in a while. But seriously! Where could that lead? She was curious, though. How might it go with Jackson, given what she knew now? She realized Jackson had lost some of his bigger-than-life luster. It was a letdown.

Think of yourself as being more, rather than Jackson being less, Laney whispered in Rebecca's head.

It comes out to the same thing, Rebecca answered. For that, Laney had no response.

Some days she felt it would have been better if Nanna had told her the family gift was magic. That she was really a wizard, and a very talented one. Like in *Harry Potter,* or the witches in the movie *Practical Magic.* Magic was pretty cool. And magic would be a whole lot less work than figuring out all this energy stuff! From somewhere came the thought, though, that Harry Potter and his friends, and the sisters in *Practical Magic* had gotten into all sorts of trouble with their spells, and it had been a lot of work to straighten it all out.

It was a muddle. Sometimes she wished she could just be the old Rebecca. But she didn't know how to unknow what she now knew. In fact, she was pretty sure she couldn't.

And there was one more thing. April had said Sam's Reiki II class would be before school started up, which was less than a month away. Zoe and Rebecca needed to have Reiki I first if they were to take Level II with Sam. So she and Zoe were to have their first class with April this weekend. Rebecca had agreed. She couldn't turn back now. And she really did want to have that connection with Sam. With all three of them having Reiki—that would be totally the bomb, wouldn't it? She told herself it would, but she didn't understand how it would work.

She had done no writing, and she hadn't been in the zone since the storm. The zone felt as distant as did Laney. She had to believe that would work itself out, that she would get them back. They were a part of her now, and she missed them both.

CHAPTER 64

The Magic of Reiki

July 27

THE REIKI I weekend had proven to be sort of fun. It wasn't at all like a regular class. Nanna or April would present something, and they all would talk about it. Some of it, like the history of Reiki and the Japanese guy who had perfected this particular system, was what it was. A lot of it, though, was subject to interpretation and was very personal. In those areas, Nanna said there was no wrong way to go. It really had to do with respecting the energies, honoring that they were sacred, and learning about yourself.

They talked about the chakra system. Nanna said science called them energy centers. And there was more information on the clairs. Rebecca was coming to sort of like the clairs. She already knew she had clairvoyant abilities. She had seen auras. And when she wrote stories, she pictured them in her mind, almost like a movie. Nanna said that was a form of clairvoyance. When they meditated in class and focused on life force energy, Rebecca could "see" the energy, which was cool. A sixth clair had been identified, called claircognizance. That was when you "just knew" something but didn't know how you knew. Rebecca really liked this one, because it explained how being in the zone worked for her. Nanna said that scientifically, claircognizance came from being tapped into the universal field.

"I wonder if that's how Alfie does it," Rebecca said to Zoe. "Is that how you and your mom and grandmother do it?"

"I don't know," said Zoe. "They've never talked about it."

"Hmm. I just assumed. A hunch, I guess." Rebecca was thoughtful.

"That can be another form of claircognizance," said Nanna. "Sometimes people will say they have a strong hunch, or they just feel something in their gut."

"What is it when you know what someone is going to say before they say it?" asked Zoe.

"It could be claircognizance," said Nanna. "But it would depend on how you 'know' it. It's interesting to know about the individual clairs, but the important thing is to recognize your signals. Your 'tells.' The niggles, tingles, shivers—whatever it is you feel or see or sense that accompanies esoteric information. Learn to respect it and how it works for *you*."

"Becks gets a tingle in the pit of her stomach." Zoe looked at Rebecca, who nodded. "Especially when she has a story idea."

"You guys all know about my tingles," said Rebecca. She grinned.

"I get little prickles. All over my body. Like shivers," said Zoe. "I never associated it with . . . psychic powers." She grinned back at Rebecca and elbowed her in the side. "The clairs are so lit!"

They were given the first Reiki symbol, told its meaning, and then they had to practice until they could draw it correctly.

"Think of it as your Reiki Power On switch," said Nanna. "The symbol invokes Reiki to flow through you. It's also a power booster."

"How does it work?" asked Zoe.

"Ah . . ." Nanna glanced at April. They wore twin expressions of wonderment. "No one knows exactly," Nanna said. "Part of it is usage and intention. Any place where rituals have been performed over and over again, an energy builds that is aligned with the frequency of the intentions. A Wiccan ritual, a church ceremony, a Druid circle, the national anthem before a sports event. The stronger the intentions and the more alignment there is of the emotions, the stronger the energy that will build. Reiki symbols have been used for thousands of years for the purpose of healing. They are tremendously powerful."

April nodded her agreement. "Beyond that," she said, "Reiki crosses from the understanding of science and into the metaphysical realm. It is ancient, sacred, and mystical. There is, however, more and more scientific evidence of its effectiveness." April and Nanna put their palms together over their hearts and executed little bows to each other.

"But wouldn't it be like my . . . um . . . stories?" Rebecca's brow was furrowed in puzzlement. "You said they worked because of the person . . . not because I intended for it to happen, but because they already worried it would. Or were afraid. Whatever."

"You are absolutely correct!" Nanna practically glowed with pleasure.

"Then how?" Zoe was puzzled too.

"All healing comes from within the one being healed. No healing will work if the receiver doesn't accept it or doesn't want it. Bottom line. One of the most important things to know about Reiki is that the practitioner is only the channel for healing energy. Like a straw. We can intend healing, and we offer the energy. The results are up to the client."

"So you can't force it on someone . . ."

"Absolutely not. And it would be unethical to try."

"What about with animals?" Rebecca asked. "Like when Sam did it on Magic?" She clamped a hand over her mouth. Sam had read ahead—she wasn't supposed to do Reiki yet on anyone but herself.

Nanna nodded to herself. "Yes, we thought she would. We attuned her to the Level II symbols, as we did with you two," she said.

"So . . . it's okay she did it?"

"Intention is so significant," said Nanna. "And you *cannot* harm with Reiki."

Rebecca wasn't sure that exactly answered her question. There seemed to be some gray areas with the rules. Typical.

"Let's take a break," said Nanna. "Anyone hungry?"

"I am," said Zoe. "Starving."

Apparently, everyone was.

At the end of the day, Nanna drove the girls home, each with an armload of books, manuals, and notes. It was a quiet ride. Zoe scraped her mass of waves away from her face. Rebecca watched her thoughtfully.

"You'd look really great in a pixie cut," she said. "You already look like a faerie."

Zoe's eyes widened, and she stared hard at Rebecca.

"What?" said Rebecca.

"That's so *weird*," said Zoe. She dropped her hair and fished for her iPhone. "I'm going to on Monday. It's just with all the Reiki stuff, I forgot to tell you—"

"No way!"

Zoe pulled up a picture. "Like this," she said. "If my hair will do that."

"That's so . . ." Rebecca looked from the picture to Zoe and back. "You'll look amazing! She glanced at Zoe, her expression curious.

"Just say it," said Zoe.

Rebecca chuckled. "Okay, so now that I know you're totally psychic, and even which clairs you have, you won't surprise me anymore when you do stuff like that." Then she sobered. "So tell me—do you know what I'm thinking, or just that I'm thinking about *something*?"

"Just tell me," said Zoe.

"Okay." Rebecca didn't know how to put it. She drummed lightly on her thigh with one hand. "Remember that day at lunch, when I told you my dad said we're an odd little group?"

Zoe nodded.

"We agreed that we're all unique. Like what Luna said. We're together because we choose to be, not because we're exactly the same."

Another nod from Zoe.

"We're not cookie-cutter friends. Like the cheerleaders." Rebecca was remembering what Angela had said at Sizzle. "Who might not even *be* friends, really. But that day, AJ said we should celebrate our individual strengths . . . I'm not saying this very well," said Rebecca.

"You're saying it just fine," said Zoe. "I totally get it. We agreed we shouldn't apologize for being different from each other, for being who we are." Rebecca nodded. "And you're thinking that now we're even more different than before," said Zoe. "You and Sam and me."

Rebecca nodded again. "What about Ty and AJ?" she asked. "Will we still be solid with them? Or are we going to be . . . *too* different?"

"I guess we'll find out," said Zoe."

"Maybe we all have some of this energy stuff. The clairs. Whatever."

"Maybe." Zoe was thoughtful.

Rebecca added, "And maybe that's part of why we're together." Her face lit up. "What a cool story," she said. "A band of energy wizards doing whatever good wizards do!" She hadn't figured that part out yet.

"Listen to you," murmured Zoe. "Just a couple weeks ago, you were wishing things wouldn't change. Now look at you!"

"Yeah. Look at me," sighed Rebecca. Her voice was sad. "Lost and freaky and confused."

"Are you going to go all moody on me now Becks?" said Zoe.

"Jeez, Zolly!"

"If I may interject something here," said Nanna from the front seat, "this would be a time to take a deep breath and surround yourself in Reiki. A time to start learning how to use Reiki—and energy in general—in your everyday lives. To smooth out some of the rough edges. So as to not go all moody, as you say," she added.

Rebecca met Nanna's eyes in the mirror. Then she looked at Zoe. "Okay . . ."

Rebecca closed her eyes and took a deep breath. She took another deep breath and pictured herself sinking into a cloud. They had done this meditation earlier in the day. The cloud was soft and floaty, but it supported her. She pictured that cloud filled with Reiki. She could "see" both the energy and the Reiki symbol in the cloud. She let her mind relax and drift. Without realizing it, her body settled more comfortably into her seat. She found herself floating in the zone. It felt so comfortable and so "home" it took Rebecca a moment to realize she was not alone.

Welcome back, whispered Laney in her head.

Rebecca's eyes flew open. "OMG!" she said with a gasp.

"Quoi?" Zoe's eyes opened wide. "What?"

"Laney's back," said Rebecca in wonder.

"I didn't know she was gone," said Zoe.

"Ever since the night of the storm," said Rebecca. "All this energy stuff—I've been trying to figure it all out, and Laney has hardly been there. Like she's . . . I don't know . . . blocked from me or something."

"Wow, Becks," said Zoe. "That's . . ."

"Yeah, totally," said Rebecca.

In the front seat, Nanna smiled to herself.

CHAPTER 65

Figuring It Out

July 30

THE DAY AFTER the Reiki class, Rebecca woke feeling drained and wrung out. Nanna had warned about that possibility, but even so, it caught Rebecca by surprise. Zoe texted and said she had a headache, and she never got headaches! Their instructions had been to honor however they felt and just go with it. It hadn't made sense at the time, but Rebecca totally got it now. She was too wrecked to even practice her Reiki.

Don't worry, Laney whispered. *You have plenty from yesterday.*

By Monday morning, Rebecca felt almost like herself. The house was quiet; everyone already gone to wherever they were going, except her mother, who would be at work upstairs. She stretched luxuriously and threw back her blanket. She padded barefoot to the closet. Partially dressed, she inspected her sunburn in the mirror. She was still peeling, but she hadn't blistered. She shrugged it off. She turned away from the mirror but, on impulse, turned back. She inspected her scantily clad form critically. Good hair. That was a real plus. Big blue eyes. Another good feature. Not beautiful, but certainly not coyote ugly. A few too many freckles, and now, of course, the freaky sunburn that had left her a little blotchy, but that was temporary. Not skinny, not fat; unremarkable, but no serious flaws. She assessed her figure, twisting to see her backside. Reasonably good butt and legs. She cupped her breasts. Generous curves rounded above the top of her bra. She dropped her hands, but most of the fullness remained. When had this happened? She stared hard at the girl in the mirror.

"So who are you anyway?" she asked softly.

Whoever you make me into, whispered Laney. *Who do you want to be?*

Rebecca pursed her lips, her brow furrowed in concentration. So, of course, did the girl in the mirror. "I want to be . . . I want to be . . ."

Rebecca stepped away from the mirror. "I'll get back to you on that," she said. Interestingly, she felt okay with the response. It wasn't like the many things she had stuffed in the box because she couldn't deal with them. She *could* deal with this. And she was. She just didn't have the answer yet.

Rebecca pulled on shorts and a Tee and ran up the stairs. Her mother was in the kitchen refilling her coffee mug.

"Want a cup?" her mother asked.

Rebecca shook her head. "Too hot." She poured herself a glass of orange juice, added some ice, and perched on a stool at the island. Her mother slid a bowl of fresh strawberries toward her, and she nibbled on one. Her mother leaned against the counter sipping her coffee and watching her calmly.

"So what all did Nanna tell you . . . about my . . . um . . ."

"Adventures and misadventures?" Her mother smiled.

"Yeah. And my amazing supernatural powers."

Maggie Coleson laughed. "Welcome to the tribe, Becka," she said.

Rebecca frowned. She still wasn't sure how she felt about her freaky family.

"Let's go sit on the front porch," said Maggie. "It's still shady on that side of the house."

"You don't have calls or anything?"

"Nothing that can't wait."

Coffee in hand, Maggie walked to the front door. Rebecca followed, her eyebrows raised. The front door! Had she achieved a rite of passage? But no, even the adults didn't use this door.

"Maybe it's time to . . . relax about certain things a little." Her mother looked pensive for a second, but then she smiled.

"Mom?"

Her mother turned to face Rebecca and waited for her to continue.

"Do you want to read the stories?"

"I would very much like that," said her mother. "If you're comfortable with it."

Rebecca nodded. She hurried downstairs to get her laptop and came back to the front porch. She pulled up the files and wordlessly handed the computer to her mother. Maggie adjusted the angle until the screen was free of glare. She read through all the stories without commenting. When she was finished, she closed the laptop, folding her hands over it on her lap.

"Wow," she said. There was a long pause. "Thank you for trusting me, sweetie."

Rebecca sipped her orange juice. "Did you do anything like that?" she asked.

"No. Not like that. Nanna and I talked about . . . uncommon things. And I could see auras from the time I was little."

"How come you didn't talk to me about it?" Rebecca tried to keep a note of accusation from her voice. She was remembering her realization at Nanna's the night of the storm—that she had seen auras when she was just a toddler.

"When you were really little, I was sure you could see . . . something. You were too little to talk. When you could talk—by then you completely shut down when I brought it up," said Maggie. "So I decided to wait until you were ready. No choice, really."

There didn't seem to be a response to that, so Rebecca made none.

"Do you plan to keep on with your writing?"

Rebecca considered this. She hadn't tried since the night of the storm, but she wasn't afraid of it anymore "Yeah, I think so. It's always been . . . I don't know how to explain it, exactly. I think it has kept me from going bonkers a few times."

"I get that," said her mother. "It's also a good method for creating who we want to be."

Rebecca looked sharply at her mother. She couldn't know what Laney had said only a few minutes ago. Could she?

Maggie watched her daughter but didn't say anything.

"That's not a bad idea," Rebecca said slowly. "I could play around with different . . . situations and . . . characters. Practice, sort of. See what feels right. Get a little crazy, even."

Her mom nodded. "Being very careful with your intentions, of course."

"Yeah, for sure." This was new ground still, but Rebecca understood its importance. She contemplated this idea. "And then just write the new me into existence?"

"Something like that," said Maggie.

"So which side are you on?" Rebecca changed direction without so much as a hand signal. "The quantum science side or the metaphysical one? The more magical one?"

"Why do I have to take sides? Can't I be on both at once?"

"I don't know," said Rebecca. "Can you?"

"Of course. Most of the time, they overlap, just saying the same thing in different language. Quantum science has yet to catch up with some of the less conventional thinking, but ancient and indigenous cultures are on the same page."

"So we're the ones out of step?"

"It looks that way."

Rebecca chewed on her lower lip. "I wish it could just be magic," she said at length.

"Why?" asked Maggie. "What is the draw of magic?"

"More fun," muttered Rebecca. "*Harry Potter* and *Practical Magic* and all."

"Well, two things," said her mom. "All societies have described as magic the things they don't understand. Science will always be behind the curve, because it is bent on proving things. And that takes time. Not to mention sometimes it's wrong."

"And the second thing?"

"Fun is where you find it," said her mother.

Rebecca grunted. Nanna had said something like that. *How you look at it is a choice.*

"You don't have to choose between science and metaphysics," said Maggie. April and I are pretty crossover. She loves both the science and

Druidic sides, and she's very knowledgeable in both. Your grandmother loves the scientific validation, but she's pretty solidly on the metaphysical side."

"She is?"

Maggie nodded. "She is. She's pretty far outside the box in some ways. Things she has probably never talked about in front of you. I used to think . . ." She shook her head.

"What?" This was intriguing. Rebecca had always thought her mother and grandmother were pretty much alike. No. That wasn't right. It was a belief she had never really thought about at all but just accepted. She had a sudden insight; it gave her shivers all over her body. OMG! This is what Nanna had meant about beliefs we held without even knowing it!

"Huh," Maggie was deep in thought. "You know," she said slowly. "I think I'm more comfortable on the science side. But circumstances have nudged me toward a sort of balance. And the balance is tremendously persuasive."

Rebecca looked at her mother with new eyes. Until recently, she had never considered that grown-ups didn't have it all figured out. Oh, she had seen all sorts of evidence that they lived with contradictions! It had long been a source of her own frustration. But here was her mom, acknowledging new insights about herself.

"We're never done, are we?" she said.

"Done how so?"

"Figuring it out," said Rebecca. "You know, kids think being grown-up means you have all the answers. But you don't, do you?"

Maggie laughed. It wasn't a particularly humorous sound. "Oh, good God, no!" she said. "We are all most definitely works in progress!"

Rebecca studied her mother. "That's kind of scary," she said. "But I think I can live with it. And it means I don't have to have it all figured out right now, either."

Maggie looked at her daughter in admiration. She was going to have to get to know this new Rebecca Jean. Her little Becka was transforming before her eyes into a remarkable and intuitive young woman. It filled her with pride and tugged at her heart at the same time. She sighed, brushing her eyes.

They sat companionably until the July heat found them. Maggie stood up, wiping her brow. "It's getting hot," she said. "What are you going to do?"

Rebecca considered for a moment. "You know," she said, "I think I'll write."

They went into the house. Through the front door.

CHAPTER 66

Back in the Zone

July 29

REBECCA STRAIGHTENED HER room a little, organizing the things on her desk, tossing her jams into the closet, straightening the pillows on her window seat. She yanked her blanket up. You couldn't say she made the bed, exactly. She paused, looking at the still-rumpled covers. Then she pulled the sheets tight and smooth and neatened the blanket. She rescued the comforter from the floor at the foot of her bed and tugged it into place. She plumped her pillows and leaned the shams against them. She retrieved a small pillow from the window seat and placed it in front of the shams. Better. She nodded in satisfaction. She put some books on the shelves, her fingers lightly tracing the spines of several novels.

She took her laptop into the sitting room—the room no one ever used—and sat on the little couch, the computer resting on her thighs. The room was cheerful. It had a better view of the backyard than her own room.

She took a couple deep breaths, exhaling slowly and settling into the cushions. She closed her eyes and pictured a cloud, the Reiki symbol embedded in it. She let her mind go to the cloud and then drift as it would. She slipped into the zone. It was different somehow, although she didn't try to analyze it. She felt peaceful and . . . comfortable in her own skin. She sensed Laney was present, but Laney felt a little different too. Bigger? Closer? More? Rebecca let her mind drift past the questions and settle more deeply into the quiet place where she floated. She felt anticipation, but without the edgy quality she had always felt when writing an Event. Was she okay with that? She had liked that edgy place.

She waited for the little tingle in the pit of her stomach. It did not disappoint. When she felt it, she took another deep breath and opened her eyes.

"What is my intention?" she whispered.

Deep in thought, she twined a finger through her hair and twirled a honey-blonde lock around and around. "My intention is a story that harms none. That is just for fun. To make . . . Andy smile." That was pretty simple. Was it specific enough? She thought it was. All she wanted was a fun little story to see what she could do from the zone.

She placed her fingers on the keypad, where they tapped a feather-light staccato—too light to depress the keys. She took another deep breath and thought, *Here goes.*

She began to type, at first slowly, and then fast and sure. Her fingers seemed to move of their own will, flashing across the keys. Her eyes were on the screen, but they were focused . . . somewhere else. Words appeared before her, growing into sentences and paragraphs, and then pages, and along with them, the scenes played out in her mind's eye. When she finished, she set the laptop aside and stretched. She stood and walked around the little sitting room before going back to the computer to read what she had written.

It was the story of a little boy and his dragon. The boy was blond and blue eyed. His name was Adam. Adam had a big mutt of a dog named Rogue. The dragon was blue and named Peeves. With Adam and Rogue safely belted into a unique basket strapped to Peeves's chest, the trio traveled the galaxies in search of trouble, which they always remedied. They were known as Star Mates. Star Mates traveled in other dimensions, in which they could span many light-years in mere seconds. They met other dragons and Star Mate teams, strange creatures, horrifying monsters, and peculiar human-like beings, all the while navigating through meteor storms and dodging black holes, exploding suns, and lost satellites.

The Star Mate trio communicated telepathically, an all-around handy talent since Adam didn't speak dragon. Or dog, for that matter. Rogue continually got himself into trouble, from which Peeves or Andy would then extricate him. He ambled through the galaxies in seeming oblivion, but in a pinch, he displayed rare flashes of genius and a knack for dumbfounding (interesting choice of words) the bad guys.

At the end of their adventures, Peeves, Andy, and Rogue would slip back to the Earth dimension through a portal high in the Rockies and into a dragon stronghold, which was energetically concealed and protected with powerful dragon forces. Secure in the stronghold, they would rest and recuperate, readying themselves for their next intergalactic mission.

When she came to the end, Rebecca shook her head in wonder. Where *did* this stuff come from! She titled the piece simply, "Peeves." Andy would like the story, she was certain.

She hollered up the stairs, "Mom, can I use your printer?"

"Go ahead," came the reply.

She printed out the story. Then she hunted the Internet for pictures of outer space and mythical dragons, printed out several, and inserted them in the story pages where they seemed to fit the best. She created a cover page with a picture of a blue dragon, the title, and "For Andy." As an afterthought, she added "by R. J. Coleson." She bound them into a report folder. She returned her laptop to her desk, leaving the folder next to the Mac.

Pleased with her little project, Rebecca ran up the stairs.

"Mom," she called. "What's for dinner?"

CHAPTER 67

Dragon Tales

August 4

THE REST OF the week went smoothly. Miss Amelia spent mornings with Rebecca, leaving her at lunch and not returning in the afternoon. Rebecca worked on indexing the doll collection. It was meticulous work, especially with the older dolls, but she found it somehow soothing. Weird. But she was from a totally weird family, was she not?

It was Sunday morning before Rebecca presented the story to Andy. It wasn't a full-fledged Sunday breakfast. Lissa wasn't there. Breakfast was a simple egg scramble with toast and bacon. The gods willing, there would be no week's highs and lows.

Andy opened the folder carefully. He looked at the cover and the pictures with interest. Then he pushed it back toward Rebecca.

"Read it," he demanded. And then, "Please? You read faster than me, and that way, I can have my toast."

Rebecca laughed. She read the story. Andy listened intently until she finished. Then he bombarded her with questions about Peeves, the dragonhold, the Star Mates, how they traveled through dimensions. She did her best to come up with answers. Everyone contributed ideas for future episodes. It made Rebecca's head spin; they seemed to assume she could just crank out more stories on demand. The truth was, she thought the story might be a one-off; there might not be more stories about Peeves. She just never knew what was going to come out of the zone.

"Rogue is Scoundrel, isn't he?" Andy asked. "And is Adam me? That's a cool name." Andy looked imploringly at his mother. "Could I change my name?" he asked.

Maggie looked back at Andy, one side of her mouth tweaked down. She shook her head.

"Jimmy could be a Star Mate, couldn't he? Do they have to always be in threes? We couldn't leave Scoundrel, I mean Rogue, behind." Andy considered this. "I think we could all fit in Peeves's basket thingy."

"You might have to stack," teased Rebecca.

"But we could!" Andy glanced at his dad. "I mean, it's dragon rules. Right?"

"Absolutely!" It occurred to Rebecca that maybe Andy, too, felt rebellious about three-dimensional and house rules.

Andy helped himself to another piece of toast. He smeared on jelly and munched on it thoughtfully. "Dad could be a Star Mate!" His face lit up. But then he reconsidered. "Hmm, I don't know," he said. "Dad might be too old."

Jack looked offended.

"No, not old exactly!" Andy squirmed. He shrugged apologetically. "It's just that . . ." He frowned in concentration. "Oh, I know! You're needed here!" He grinned. "It's pretty risky out there, you know."

It was totally transparent, but Jack let it go.

Andy still had questions. "Who's Peeves?" he wanted to know.

"He's not anyone," Rebecca said. "I just made him up."

"That's so cool!" Andy beamed at her. "Read it again?" he pleaded.

"Later, maybe," said Rebecca. She was beginning to wonder if she'd opened a Pandora's box. Just what she needed—another box!

Andy was finally finished with his breakfast, and he left the kitchen with the story clutched tightly to his chest. Maggie said quietly to Rebecca, "The story is really very good."

It was Rebecca's turn to beam. "You think so, Mom?"

"I do," her mother said. "Have you considered showing it to Nanna?"

"Not really. Why?"

"Because I think it could be published."

Rebecca's mouth dropped open. "Seriously?" she spluttered. "Really, you're serious?"

"I am." Her mother nodded. "Why don't we take it this afternoon?"

And so they did.

Pappa was traveling. Jack disappeared down to the train room with Andy after snacks. Lissa made her excuses; she was meeting James later. That left Rebecca, her mother, and Nanna sitting beneath slowly turning fans on the deck. Rebecca had a lemonade. Nanna and Maggie sipped iced tea. Nanna read the little story, nodding and smiling, but not commenting, all the while gently pushing her glider with one foot. There was no squeak!

Nanna seemed to read Maggie's mind. "I had some things done around here," she said.

"I kind of miss it," said Maggie. She was laughing.

Nanna closed the folder. She regarded Rebecca gravely.

"What do you think, Mom?" asked Maggie.

"It isn't good enough to publish, is it?" said Rebecca. "I mean, I only wrote it for fun."

"Quite the contrary," said Nanna. "I think it's rather exceptional for children's literature."

"You do?" Rebecca stared. Her heart hammered.

"I do." Nanna nodded. "Is this something you want to consider?"

"I don't know. I hadn't even thought about it." Rebecca drummed her fingers on the arm of her chair. "What would I have to do?"

"For starters, you'd need some illustrations." Nanna thumbed through the story. "Illustrations are critical for this age bracket. I would suggest one source and style."

"I only meant it for—"

"I know, Becka," Nanna patted Rebecca's knee. "I'm not criticizing." She pursed her lips. "I have an idea about who can help us out. Unless you know someone."

Rebecca shook her head. This was taking on a life of its own.

"Would you like me to speak with Lucille about this? My agent," Nanna added.

"Um . . . sure. I guess."

"Tell you what. You think about what you'd like to do." Nanna glanced at Maggie, who dipped her chin once in agreement. "This is amazing, Becka. A very respectable work. I'm exceedingly proud of you."

CHAPTER 68

Truth Is Stranger Than Fiction

August 6

TWO DAYS OF musing, and Rebecca still didn't know what she wanted to do with Andy's story. Should she publish it? Would Andy mind? She'd have to ask him. She could dedicate it to him. He'd think that was cool. Would she be expected to write more stories? What if she couldn't? What if the pressure completely froze her up? She wasn't sure she wanted to take on anything of such magnitude. It might not be fun anymore.

Oh, good God, Rebecca Jean! Laney was so exasperated Rebecca thought she might pop right out of her head. *This is exactly what you've always wanted!*

It was. Rebecca had no argument. *I more thought . . . later on*, she sent back at Laney. The whole thing was pretty overwhelming.

Laney made a rude noise.

Now, sitting in Miss Amelia's secret garden, Rebecca tried not to think about it. She nibbled on her sandwich without really tasting it. A rustling in the bushes pulled her from her musing. Across the little garden, beyond the fountain, she saw Boo emerging from the shrubbery. Rebecca froze. Boo looked in her direction and also froze. After a minute or two, Boo moved cautiously towards Rebecca.

Rebecca waited. She carefully relaxed into her chair. She wanted her energy to be calm and nonthreatening. She didn't wonder where this came from; it was an instinct. That was enough to know. Slowly, she worked a piece of meat from her sandwich, tearing off a little bite. Boo was between her and the fountain now.

"Hello, little one," Rebecca said softly. "Aren't you a pretty girl!"

Boo hunched down, belly to the ground. The tip of her tail twitched. The green eyes regarded Rebecca cautiously.

"Are you hungry?" coaxed Rebecca. "I have a nice treat for you."

Boo held her wary pose, observing, but she raised her nose to sniff. Rebecca leaned forward ever so slowly, her arm outstretched, the piece of turkey between her fingers.

Without thinking about it, Rebecca pictured the Reiki symbol and a soft ball of light surrounding herself and the kitten. *Calm*, she thought. *Safe.*

Boo stretched her neck in Rebecca's direction.

"Just try it." Rebecca continued to softly coax. "If you don't like it, you can leave it."

Boo took the proffered bit of meat and slunk back. She dropped it, looked at Rebecca, sniffed the treat carefully. And then she ate it.

"Good girl!" Rebecca cooed. "Do you want some more?"

She offered another piece. Boo approached her carefully. This time she took it daintily and ate it without moving back. When she had swallowed it, she considered Rebecca with big green eyes. And then she jumped onto the chair beside her.

"Oh, my goodness!" Rebecca breathed in awe. "What a brave girl you are." She fed Boo the rest of the turkey from the sandwich. Boo licked her paws and cleaned her face, and then she curled up on the chair beside Rebecca. Very gently, Rebecca ran her hand down Boo's back. Boo sighed, purring softly. Rebecca continued to pet her, fingers light on the mottled fur. She kept the Reiki image around them. It made her palms tingle. Laney was in Rebecca's head, but she was silent. Just there. They remained that way for a piece of time—the kitten, the girl, and the cool, supersmart, sort of a guide in the girl's head, surrounded by the ball of Reiki energy.

***

Rebecca didn't want to leave, but she eventually had to go back to the house. When she shifted in the chair to gather her lunch things, Boo jumped down and moved off. She disappeared into the bushes, but in no particular rush. Rebecca was eager to tell Miss A. she had befriended the kitten. When she reached the doll studio, however, Miss A. had a guest. Two actually.

"Come and meet my grandson," said Miss A. "Rebecca, this is Anthony."

Anthony nodded. "Tony," he said. "And this is Rupert."

"Hello," said Rebecca to Tony. She looked at the dog. "Aren't you . . . big!"

"He is. But he's a great guy." Tony ruffled Rupert's fur, and the dog sat on Tony's foot leaning against his leg. His head came well above Tony's waist.

Tony looked at Rebecca. "You can pet him." He nodded encouragingly.

Rebecca extended a tentative hand toward Rupert.

Rupert butted his nose into Rebecca's outstretched hand and licked it. He stayed where he was on Tony's foot, but his tail thumped the floor. Apparently, they would be friends.

"I have a special job for you," said Miss A. "Anthony is leaving Rupert here for a few days while he and his family are on vacation. You will walk him for me."

"I don't know," said Rebecca. "I mean, I'd be happy to!" She looked first at Rupert, then at Miss A. "But he's as big as me almost! What if—"

"Rupert is a good dog and well trained," said Tony. "Aren't you, big fella?" Tony ruffled Rupert's fur again.

Rebecca knew only two dogs well. Scoundrel and Headless—beg pardon, Anne Boleyn. Neither of them gave a whit for training or obeying. She had seen work dogs at the ranch, but they seemed to pretty much do what was required without any instructions at all.

"What is he?" she asked.

"Rupert is Labrador and golden retriever," said Tony. "With a little mystery thrown in. He's obedience trained to me, to my wife, and my two daughters. I'd guess they're about your age. He is handled by strangers periodically and responds well. I'll get you two acquainted this afternoon. You'll be fine. You'll see." Tony was confident.

Rebecca was not.

It turned out, for all his size, that Rupert was pretty much a peach. He instantly obeyed commands, seeming to anticipate what Tony wanted of him. Rebecca practiced with "come," "sit," and "stay," and Rupert was a champ. Maybe this would work.

Tony dropped to his knees and took Rupert's head in his hands. "You be a good boy for Miss A. and Rebecca," he said. Rupert licked Tony's face and looked at him in adoration.

"Give him lots of praise," said Tony. "Rupert is a love. Aren't you, boy?"

Tony gently hugged his grandmother, ruffled Rupert's fur one more time, nodded at Rebecca, and took his leave. Rupert lay down facing the door, his head on his paws. He sighed deeply. He looked sad and resigned. Rebecca knelt beside him and gently rubbed his head.

Miss A. stayed in the studio the rest of the afternoon. An hour before Rebecca was due to leave, Miss A. suggested she take the dog out. "There's a private park three blocks down," she said. "Hardly ever anyone there. Wrought iron fence all around. Huge old estate. House burned down decades ago and was never rebuilt. You can take him off his leash there."

"Okay." Rebecca wasn't sure about letting Rupert roam free. What if she couldn't get him back? But she kept her trepidation to herself.

Rupert was eager to be off, prancing and smiling, but he fell right in on the leash. "Left from my front gate," said Miss A. "Then three blocks."

Rebecca tucked her iPhone into the pocket of her jeans, hoping she wouldn't need it to call for help saying Rupert had run off and was probably in Golden by now. They set out. Rupert was curious and wanted to smell everything, but he stayed at her heel. Another dog appeared across the street, barking and lunging on its lead, impervious to the commands of its owner. Rupert strolled calmly along like the champ Tony had said he was.

"Good, boy!" Rebecca patted Rupert's head gratefully. He butted her hand and licked it, as before. "Good, Rupert." She rubbed his neck with both hands. He licked her face but didn't jump up, like Scoundrel always did. She wiped her face with the hem of her shirt, and they continued up the street, Rebecca much encouraged.

She found the park with no problem. She punched in the code Miss A. had given her, and she and Rupert went through the gate. She closed it securely behind them. A bark-mulched area in the center of the huge lawn offered some play structures. Several stray balls were scattered around. Benches were placed around the area, and there was a spigot where you could give your dog water. The back of the property was thick with mature trees and large shrubs. A path meandered from the play area to disappear into the trees, and she and Rupert followed it. Rupert was clearly excited, but she kept him on the leash, and he stayed at heel.

At the edge of the trees, Rebecca chose a bench and sat down. She took Rupert's head in her hands and addressed him earnestly. "If I let you go, do you promise to come back when I call you?" Rupert smiled, panting, tongue lolling, but didn't commit. "Okay. Here goes." Rebecca unclipped the leash.

Rupert continued to sit there, gazing up at her.

"You can go," she said. "Just come when I need you to."

Rupert trotted off.

She watched him go. Nose to the ground, he trotted back to the play area. A squirrel caught his eye, and Rupert tore across the lawn. The squirrel was long gone before Rupert was anywhere near, but he didn't seem to care. He nosed about in the shrubs. Rebecca watched him for a while. He disappeared into the bushes, and fear spiked in her chest. What if there was a hole in the fence in there? Where she couldn't see it?

"Rupert!" she called to him.

Rupert's head popped out of the bushes, and he looked intently in her direction. "Come, boy!" Rebecca commanded.

Amazingly, Rupert did! He loped across the broad expanse of grass and bounded up to her. Rebecca ruffled his fur and kissed him on the top of his head. She praised him profusely. She let him go again, and he gamboled off. Rebecca relaxed. Maybe this would be okay.

She was more comfortable when she could see the dog, and she kept an eye on him. He would periodically lope back to her, get his rubs and praise, and bound off again. Rebecca wished she had brought a book to read, or one of her notebooks. Something. She checked messages on her phone. No pings. She sighed. Rupert was somewhere in the trees. She had lost sight of him, and she couldn't hear him.

"Rupert!"

The dog came bounding out of the trees. He saw her, stopped, barked, and turned and ran back the way he had come.

"Rupert!"

Rebecca followed him, feeling a little anxious. Once through the maze of overgrown shrubs, the path led into a park-like area, a firepit at its center. It was very quiet and densely shaded. Rebecca hurried along the path. Another bark. "Rupert!"

Benches encircled the firepit. And there was Rupert. But he was not alone. A young man was sitting on one of the benches. Rupert's front feet were on his shoulders. Was Rupert attacking him? Her breath caught. What should she do? Her hand went to her iPhone, but who would she call, and what would she say? "My dog is attacking someone! Oh, never mind, he'll be dead by the time you get here."

"Rupert! Down!" she commanded. Rupert dropped to his haunches, sitting without being told. He looked at Rebecca and back at the other person.

"Rebecca . . .?"

Rebecca stared, her brain resisting what her eyes told her. How could anyone know her here? She commanded Rupert to come, and he did, sitting at her side and leaning against her. She draped her arm around his shoulders. He *so* showed up Scoundrel!

The young man stood up. "Becka?"

"Jackson! What the—" Rebecca's mouth dropped open. She was still staring.

Jackson walked toward her, his expression relaxed but curious. He stopped in front of her. Rupert nuzzled Jackson's hand. Jackson rubbed the dog's head. "Becka," he said again. And then, "You know Rupert."

"*You* know Rupert?" Rebecca couldn't fathom it. "What are you doing here?"

The grin again. It was just a big grin, not the FIGJAM or "I'm a jock you gotta love me" smirk. "I come here all the time. What are *you* doing here?"

"You come here?" Rebecca was having trouble completing a thought.

Jackson was perfectly at ease. "I live around here," he said.

"You *do*?" Rebecca finally managed to close her mouth, but she was still staring. "How do you know Rupert?" It was all she could think to say.

"I know Tony," said Jackson. "And his grandmother. Bit eccentric. Likes dolls. You know Miss Amelia?"

The familiar use of Miss A.'s name jarred Rebecca sufficiently to clear her brain a little. "I work for her," she said.

"No way!" It was Jackson's turn to gape. "Since when?" He brushed blond hair from his eyes. "Wait, you said you worked for the guy who owns that health center." He looked at her accusingly.

"I said owner, not guy." Rebecca was able to breathe a little more easily now. You couldn't say she was relaxed, but her shock had been diminished. It was just Jackson, however convoluted a universe that tended to suggest. "She owns The Center."

"She does?"

Rupert had sat quietly long enough. He butted Rebecca's hand as if asking for permission to leave. "You are a really good boy," Rebecca said to him, kneading her hands through his ruff. "You can go. Good boy." Rupert nuzzled Jackson's hand again, was rewarded with an ear scratch, then bounded off. They watched him go.

Rebecca still wasn't thinking with lightning speed, but her mind was beginning to work at least a little. "That day you missed the bus and we walked . . . after school." She frowned at him. "Kind of a long walk to here," she said.

Jackson shrugged again. "We moved," he said. "A while back. Changed school districts."

"How long ago did you move?" Rebecca smelled a secret, if not a rat.

"A while." Jackson was noncommittal. "Front Range has the best football program in Denver metro," he said. He walked back to the bench where Rebecca had first seen him.

"What's a while?" Rebecca followed him.

"Um . . . maybe three years."

"You moved here three years ago and you still go to school in the eastern burbs?"

Jackson didn't reply. He pushed his things to one side and sat, leaning back comfortably, his arms draped along the backrest.

"How does that work exactly?" she asked

"My mom works at the Tech Center. We use that address."

"And it's all so you can play football at Front Range?"

"Well"—Jackson grinned, and this time it was the old smirk—"they also have the best curriculum."

"And you care?"

Jackson's look measured her. His eyebrows climbed to disappear under blond hair.

"Oh, right. I forgot you're an athlete with a brain." But she said it lightly. Apparently, Jackson *was* an athlete with a brain. She moved to stand at the end of the bench. Jackson shifted his position. His leg brushed against a battered notebook, knocking it onto the ground. He bent to pick it up, nonchalant, no big deal.

Rebecca was quick as a cat. Reacting on pure instinct, she snatched up the notebook and stepped away from Jackson. He was on his feet immediately. She sprang away, putting the bench between them. He reached for it. She turned her back to him, thumbing quickly through the pages. It was filled with drawings. Some in color, but mostly in black-and-white. And all of big birds. Or dragons.

A quick glimpse was all she got. Jackson stepped onto the bench and vaulted over its back. Rebecca yelped and ducked instinctively. His long arms snaked around her, his lean body tight against hers as he pinned her from behind. She fought him, giggling, but she didn't fight very hard. He was going to nick it anyway; she was caught and, under the present conditions, really no match against him. She quit struggling. For just a moment they stood that way, Jackson's arms around her, their bodies pressed together, his breath on her hair. Rebecca's heart thudded. She let go of the notebook. Jackson stepped away, looking flustered. He brushed the hair from his forehead. He smoothed the pages of the notebook, folded it in half, and stuffed it into a back pocket in his jeans. He walked back around the bench and resumed his seat, arms draped on the backrest as before. Now, though, the fingers of one hand tapped restlessly against the wood.

Rebecca followed, watching him closely. She was getting one of her tingles. An idea was forming. The tangle of emotions triggered by being caught in Jackson's arms was relegated to the box by the import of this idea. That overflowing box. She could look at it later—if she wanted to look at all. Right now, she was thinking about the drawings. Did she want to go there? She looked at him, calculating.

"What?" Jackson propped one ankle on the other knee. The toe of his trainer tapped against nothing but air.

Rebecca twined a finger into her hair and coiled a lock around it. She pursed her lips. She sat gingerly on the end of the bench, facing him, and just beyond the reach of his arm.

Jackson watched all this. He had been watching Rebecca for a long time. She had a lot of faces, and he had seen a lot of transformations. This felt different; he would never have been able to describe how. But he was pretty sure he hadn't seen this Rebecca before.

"What?" he said again.

"Did you do all those drawings, Jackson?" Her voice was calm. Solemn almost.

"Yeah. So what?"

"So nothing," she said. "Can I see them?"

"Why?"

"Jeez, Jackson! I'd like to look at them! Is that a criminal offense?"

Jackson grasped his ankle with both hands. The foot tapped a little faster. He frowned. He brushed hair from his eyes in the so-familiar gesture.

"I'd just like to look," said Rebecca gently. "Please."

Jackson didn't know what to make of this calm, reasonable Rebecca. He didn't. The foot tapped a bit longer. Reluctantly, he pulled the notebook from his pocket. He extended it gingerly in her direction but didn't let go.

Rebecca gave the notebook a tug, and Jackson let it slip from his hand. She unfolded it and smoothed it out. It was pretty abused. She opened the cover and thumbed slowly through the dog-eared pages. Lots of birds. There were eagles, hawks, what she thought might be a condor. Birds that could only be mythical or right out of Jackson's imagination. Several versions of a phoenix. All amazing. But the dragons!

She looked up at him and asked again, softly, "And you drew all these?"

Jackson looked defensive. "Yeah. I did."

Rebecca turned more pages. She came to a blue dragon, its expression lifelike. The body language spoke to her of gentleness masked by enormous power. And . . . playfulness? That felt right. She let her fingers trace the arch of the neck, the scaled back, the long tail.

"These are amazing."

"You like dragons, I take it." Jackson's defensiveness had softened, but only a little.

"I never really thought much about them," said Rebecca. She turned pages until she reached the back of the notebook. It was nearly full. She exclaimed softly over several of the drawings, but she returned to the blue dragon.

"Have you ever thought about . . . selling any of these? Or publishing them?"

"What do you mean?" Jackson was wary again.

"I mean," Rebecca spoke slowly, enunciating carefully, "have you ever thought about selling your drawings?"

Jackson looked at her sharply. This was an idea dear to his heart, but he didn't have the first clue how to make it happen. And he had never shared it with anyone. "Like how?" he demanded. "A tattoo shop or something?"

"Maybe, or boards of some sort." She was thinking of Jimmy Norton's hoverboard, of which Andy was extremely jealous. Or—" Rebecca's eyes opened wide. "You designed your tattoo, didn't you?"

"How do you know I have a tattoo?"

Rebecca laughed out loud. "I saw it a couple times at the pool," she said. "It was pretty much in my face." She remembered Jackson lounging in his swim trunks, the dragon rippling every time he moved. How he had leaned over her, his face close to hers, the smell of suntan lotion and chlorine on his skin, peppermint on his breath. Okay, she hadn't been looking at the tattoo in that moment. No, her eyes had been locked on his. Laney had seen the dragon too. It was Laney who had wanted to trace her fingers over it.

The memory brought warmth to her cheeks and scattered her thoughts. She lifted her hair off her neck and fanned herself with one palm. *Get a grip!* she said fiercely to herself.

Rupert trotted up to them and dropped to the ground, panting. He lowered his muzzle to his paws and sighed deeply. He looked quite pleased with himself. Rebecca and Jackson both looked at him. Rebecca leaned forward and patted Rupert on the head.

"Hot," she murmured. "Gotta love the dog days of summer."

Jackson watched her, curious but baffled. This girl was a complete mystery. A collection of contradictions and ever-changing personalities! He could hardly keep up with the shifts of thought train, focus, mood, disposition—any of it.

Rebecca was thinking hard. If she said what she was contemplating, would she be committed in some way? To going ahead with Andy's story?

You've already made up your mind, breathed Laney. *If little Boo can take a risk . . .*

"Boo." Rebecca said the name to herself, under her breath. She nodded.

Just go for it, whispered Laney. *He already knows you write.*

Jackson waited. This was fascinating. If he was into films instead of drawings, he'd want to capture "five minutes in the head of Becka Coleson." It would be a weird film, for sure. A roller-coaster ride into shifting perspectives of psychedelia.

Rebecca turned to face him again. She held the notebook gently in her hands. "Okay, I'm going to tell you something and hope you—" What did she hope? Who could he tell that it could possibly make a difference to her? Rebecca Coleson writes stories. Yeah? So flaming what! She shook her head and changed her tack.

"I wrote a story for my little brother," she said. "You were right that day at the pool. I do write stories." She gathered her thoughts. "Andy loved it. No big deal—he's seven. But I showed it to my grandmother. And she thinks it's good. Really good." She looked at Jackson full-on.

"And?"

"My grandmother is an author," said Rebecca. "She has written more than twenty books."

"Oh." Jackson waited.

"She says it's good enough to publish."

"Way to go," said Jackson. He looked at her with mild interest.

Rebecca exhaled forcefully. Was he dense? Or playing hard-to-get? She spoke with measured purpose. "Children's literature," she said, "is all about the illustrations. Often way more than the actual text." She held Jackson's gaze. "It's a story about a dragon."

"Cool."

Rebecca couldn't believe it. She leaned toward him. He just looked at her.

"I need an illustrator." She spoke slowly and carefully.

Jackson's eyes widened. "No shit!"

"No shit," said Rebecca. "Until today, I wasn't even sure I wanted to do it. To have it published, I mean. I wrote it for Andy, not for . . . But I've always wanted to be an author." Rebecca's focus went inward, to something personal and guarded. Jackson couldn't follow her there. "Like Nanna," she said softly.

Jackson tried to take in Rebecca's words. What would this mean? "And you think my drawings . . . you might want to . . . they could be . . ."

"I love the blue dragon," said Rebecca. She looked wistful. "But I don't know exactly how it all works. If you're interested, maybe you could read the story and draw what comes to you." She looked at him curiously. "Is that how you draw? Just . . . what comes to you? From a place you . . . don't even understand?" This felt a little vulnerable, but it was out.

Jackson shifted on the bench. He uncrossed his ankle. Stretched out his legs. Studied the toes of his trainers. He had never really thought about how he did the drawings. "Something like that, I guess." He glanced at her. "I sort of dial down the chatter. Like a pitcher throwing a no-hitter." He shrugged.

Rebecca raised her hands, palms up, in a gesture that said she had no idea what he was talking about.

Jackson's brow furrowed. How to explain this . . . "If I'm on the mound," he said, "the pitching mound, it's about focus." He looked at her to see if she was following. She nodded, and he went on. "I clear my mind of everything that isn't . . . everything except the pitch. What's going on in the stands, the game, the guys around me. I dial down the chatter," he said again. "Till it's just me in a place—"

Rebecca nodded again. "It's like going into the zone," she said, almost to herself.

"The zone?"

"Yeah. That's what I call it."

"The zone." Jackson nodded. "Yeah, I can feel that."

"So . . . you'd maybe do that?" She looked at him a little warily. "Read Andy's story and draw some dragons especially for it?"

Jackson drew his legs in. One heel tapped the ground. "I don't know," he said. "I'm not sure I want to be known for drawings in a little kids' book."

"Why on earth not!"

Jackson stood up. Paced to the firepit. Came back. He knelt down by Rupert and scratched his ears. He sat back on his heels, looking at Rebecca, but he didn't quite meet her eyes. "It's not exactly the—"

Rebecca guessed instinctively where Jackson was going. So did Laney. Laney was in her head, feeling something like disgusted outrage.

"*Image* you want?" Rebecca finished Jackson's sentence.

He looked at her in surprise.

"Not tough-guy enough?" she mocked him. "Not secure enough to let your talent speak for itself?" Rebecca couldn't see it. Boys were so stupid!

Go easy, cautioned Laney. *If you want that little blue dragon . . .*

"I need a football scholarship more than I need to get my drawings published," said Jackson. His jaw was set. The look in his eyes said clearly, *Wanna make something of that?*

Rebecca took a deep breath. "Sorry," she muttered. She chewed one side of her lower lip, thinking hard. "Okay then . . ." Her face lit up. "Why not both?" she said. Her smile was brilliant. "Use a pseudonym." The smile was replaced by a meaningful look. "So long as people who want to hire you, to *pay* you for your drawings"—she let that hang there for Jackson to consider—"can find you."

"A pseudonym . . ."

"Sure. A pen name. A made-up name."

"I know what a pseudonym is." Jackson threw her a dirty look. He came back to the bench and perched on the edge of it. "Who does that?"

"Lots of people. J. K. Rowling has. Stephen King. Benjamin Franklin. Just for starters."

"You gotta be kidding!"

"I'm not!"

Maybe this wasn't going to work. Maybe she should just forget it. She wasn't going to waste her energy trying to persuade him. What time was it, anyway? She pulled out her cell phone to check.

"Merde," she murmured. Then to Jackson, "I know this has sort of come out of nowhere. It has for me too." She looked at him, her expression calm. At least she hoped it was. She didn't feel particularly calm. "Just think about it. No harm in that."

"Yeah. I can do that." He was still skeptical.

"I have to get back." She stood up. So did Jackson. Rupert sat up. The big dog leaned into her, nudging her off balance. She took an involuntary step, catching ahold of Jackson's arm to steady herself. She looked up at him.

"Your drawings are good, Jackson," she said softly. "*Really* good."

"So you're an expert on . . ." He fished for a word to describe his drawings. He didn't find one, because he didn't have the slightest idea how to define them.

"No, I'm not." Rebecca was honest. "But I read a lot," she said. "A *lot*." She stepped away and clipped the leash on Rupert. She became all business.

"What should we do? I can talk to Nanna to see how this might work. If we collaborate." She liked that word. She looked at Jackson. "So do you want to read the book? It's not a big commitment. Take you all of ten minutes. I think you should. I mean, if you're interested in . . . Are you here a lot?"

Jackson struggled to keep up with her erratic train of thought. "Some." It seemed a safe response.

"We could meet here Thursday, maybe. About the same time. You can think if you'd want to do something like this."

It wasn't really a question. Jackson nodded. "I guess," he said.

"You guess?"

"Okay. Sure. I'll think about it, and I'll meet you here Thursday."

"We should have each other's cell numbers."

Jackson just looked at her.

"So I can call you or text you late at night and say silly things like how wonderful you are and can I sign the bottoms of your shoes or something." One side of her mouth was drawn down; the other side twitched up.

He looked at her, his eyes a little glazed.

Rebecca let him hang out there for a minute, and then she was all business again. "So we can confirm, or let the other know if one of us . . . can't make it, or doesn't want to do it, I guess. But I'll be here with Rupert."

"Okay." He told her his number, and Rebecca repeated it as she typed it into her iPhone. "I just texted you to confirm," she said.

"So I'll maybe see you Thursday," he said.

She looked up from her phone, but her gaze went beyond him into the trees. There was a faraway look in the blue eyes. Those eyes clouded, cleared, shifted to regard him. She nodded her head as if to herself. She looked at him like she'd never seen him before. Jackson got that. It was pretty much how he felt about this whole surreal afternoon.

"Jackson." She inclined her head almost formally. "See you Thursday." And she turned and headed down the path at a brisk pace.

"Rupert, heel," she commanded. Rupert did.

Jackson thought it would be a brave, or very foolish, dog who didn't. And an equally brave or foolish person who underestimated Rebecca Coleson. He watched them go. Trotting alongside Rebecca, Rupert looked back at him once. Rebecca did not.

CHAPTER 69

Endings

August 10

S UMMER WAS OVER, or would be in a few more days. Rebecca wasn't ready for the demanding schedule of school to begin, but at least she would see her friends every day. Summer had been a crazy roller-coaster ride with extremes in all directions and no calm center. She thought a second summer to get over the first summer would be ideal; then she'd be up to the whole new crazy of the next school year. Maybe.

That could not be, however. All the calendar allowed was a weekend getaway with everyone together in Steamboat Springs.

It didn't seem possible summer was almost over. The dream of lazy days and a slow rhythm of leisure with her friends had not materialized. Not even close. The girls' attentions had been scattered. Rebecca wondered if their core connection had been diminished in some way. Her own focus had been fragmented between the Events and their repercussions, the family gift, quantum science, and Reiki. Just for starters. And then there was the doll shop, Andy's book, and figuring out who the new Rebecca was. AJ had her job, had been to California, and had come back full of beach stories and movie star sightings. Sam had always been all about the horses, but now there was Alfie. Zoe's attention was on her college admission to Boulder, thus the summer class. Rebecca didn't think Zoe needed to worry about getting into Boulder, or any university; her grades were nearly perfect, and she was awesomely smart. Maybe there was something else that prompted Zoe to concentrate so hard. Was there something Rebecca had missed? She and Zoe had been inseparable for most of their lives. Could she be operating off assumptions about Zoe with no solid basis in reality? It was an unsettling thought.

Do I really know her? wondered Rebecca.

Can we really know anybody? That was Laney.

Rebecca stuffed that thought in the box, but then she pulled it cautiously back out. She barely knew herself anymore. Were the friendships merely a safe launching pad for each of them to catapult off in different directions? Rebecca had thought the friendships made her *more*. Maybe that wasn't quite right. Maybe they just gave her the security to . . . what? Explore being more on her own? Was that just semantics?

She didn't feel the Events had made her more. But they had been a platform for her to experiment with something completely new and unfamiliar, and they had led her to scientific and metaphysical revelations, which had most definitely made her more. Rebecca thought her summer had fallen pretty much into two periods, and they had been marked by a significant divide—the night of the storm at Nanna's. She thought of it as *before the storm*, and *after*. Before the storm was the "OMG I'm losing it—I must be totally wacko" period. On the overall, she felt this could accurately be defined by her fears, both named and unnamed, and an overriding sense of ricocheting through life completely out of control. It had not been pretty.

And then . . . *after*.

That's where she was now. She didn't know what else to call it, and anyway, it was still in the process of forming up. After the night of the storm. After she had spilled it all to Nanna. After learning of the "family tradition." Freaky. After all the quantum science explanations. After realizing Laney was a sort of guide, albeit a smartmouthed one, and that the zone was an element of claircognizance and was a connection to the unified field. After learning she wasn't twisted and demented, but neither was she a cool wizard. After Reiki. After. *After* put control of her life squarely in her own hands, and that was nearly as frightening as the wacko, out-of-control feelings.

Reiki fell chronologically on the *after* side of summer, but it seemed to be in a category all its own. It didn't feel the same as the "freaky family tradition." She kind of liked the Reiki stuff; certainly the clairs, even though they weren't technically part of Reiki. Reiki didn't fit neatly into a logical, defined-by-the-precision-of-math box. The ancient, sacred, mystical aspect of Reiki seemed to thumb its nose at science. But who knew? Science might discover tomorrow how Reiki worked. On the whole, though, it didn't feel wacko like the Events and her family tradition, and she thought it would probably be a long-term thing. She was comfortable letting Reiki stand on its own.

She was beginning to understand the science aspects, and to come to terms with the mystical side, of some of the energy weirdness. Nanna said this would evolve into a fundamental understanding of how everything in the world worked that would be very comforting. So far it wasn't. It was requiring that she completely redefine her belief in who she was. This was kind of exciting at times. Like Andy's story. And the (potential) collaboration with Jackson—talk about bizarre. But it was a lot of work! And there was no taking a break from it. She was constantly being forced to decide how to react to things—from the old perspective or the new. There were times she wanted to just drift until she could get some kind of grip. Occasionally, she took a passive attitude and let habit take over. The old Rebecca, however, felt as foreign as the new Rebecca was a mystery, and trying to coast between the two left her feeling like she had a foot in two different worlds. Worlds that were drifting farther and farther apart.

She thought about all the things she had stuffed into the box. That bulging, imaginary container where she had crammed all the troublesome or scary things she didn't want to face. The box was no longer threatening to explode. Which didn't mean it was empty, or even close to being empty! Many of the issues had been satisfied *after*, even if she didn't care for some of the answers. She kept the box, though. She would pull something out to look at it and decide how it related to an energy principle, or just her life in general. And it was a good temporary holding place for things she wanted to consider when she wasn't under pressure. So she could think them through at her leisure. Like her thoughts of a few moments ago about not seeing Zoe completely. Like how she really felt about Andy's story being published. Like how it felt that Ty and AJ were slipping away.

That was actually a brand-new thought, and Rebecca stuffed it into the box with her heart thumping. Where had that come from? She forcefully diverted her thoughts to something else.

She thought about the scuffle with Jackson at Miss A.'s park, how it had felt to be encircled by his arms, even though he was just trying to get his notebook back. What was that about? Was she actually attracted to Jackson? Or did she just want something like what Sam and Alfie had? It all flew in the face of what she had always said about boys—that they were too much work and risky in the extreme. She had pulled that out of the box several times to study it. And really, that's all she was doing. Studying it because it was interesting.

She didn't let Laney weigh in on this topic. Rebecca didn't want to hear what Laney would say. She might say the fact that Rebecca was confused about all this didn't mean she wasn't sending out energy. She might say it would be a good idea to clarify what that energy might be, and how it could be interpreted by Jackson. Laney might say it was time to take Jackson off his "star" pedestal and look at him as he really was, rather than in a vacuum. Laney could raise a lot of questions Rebecca wasn't quite ready to look at. She reasoned that sometimes it was good to figure things out on her own, without the cool, supersmart, sort of a guide. And it was definitely good to keep that box around.

Sometimes she felt like she was outside herself, watching a stranger. What would that girl do? What would be the consequences? Nanna said she was learning to set intentions for her outcomes, to be the designer of her own life, and that it was very powerful. Maybe so. But she missed being impulsive and just diving into a situation and living it to the max.

And when did you ever do that? Laney demanded. *Except when you ran off at the mouth and got yourself into trouble. Is that what you call living to the max?*

Sometimes the cool, supersmart, sort of a guide, was a real pain in the ass.

"Just try to relax and enjoy the process," Nanna had said.

That was proving difficult. It meant going from a life where she had felt she had no control and was constrained by too many rules to one where she was the architect of her own destiny. It was a big leap. Sometimes she practiced in her mind, but most of the time, things came up with no warning, which left her with no time to rehearse.

Like the jaw-dropping news from Ty and AJ the last day of the Steamboat reunion.

***

The weekend had been fun, but a little strange. Restrained, maybe. Rebecca felt it but couldn't define it. There were a lot of outward changes. Zoe's pixie haircut; Sam's trim, ranch-hand figure and short, bare nails. Ty was wearing her hair down her back instead of in a ponytail. Rebecca thought she herself *looked* pretty much the same, but she was definitely a different person otherwise. Her sense was that the same held true for AJ, although Rebecca had no idea of specifics. She was getting a lot of tingles, and they weren't all good.

The last morning in Steamboat, the girls had taken their breakfast out to the deck and circled comfortable chairs around a low table. Sam propped bare feet on the table in a familiar posture. All that was missing was a pair of western boots. AJ stretched her long legs and crossed her ankles. No high-heeled sandals. Rebecca and Sam sipped coffee; Zoe nibbled on a strawberry. The river babbled happily. No one spoke. Rebecca looked around the circle. What had happened to them? Why this reserve? What was being held back? And why?

Okay, then, whispered Laney. *You start. Shock the shit out of them.*

Rebecca nodded to herself. Okay, then. "I've been seeing Jackson Middleton," she said. That should be a good teaser.

It was. It stopped them in their tracks. Rebecca smiled inwardly.

"You have *not!*" gasped Ty.

"I knew it! I always knew there was something—"

"But he always makes you so mad!"

AJ and Ty talked over each other. Sam was giving her that assessing look. Zoe's expression was bland, but the corners of her mouth twitched up.

When she could get a word in, Rebecca told them about walking Rupert and the chance meeting at Miss A.'s park. That she had seen him there a couple times. He and Rupert were already buds. How weird was that? It felt strange and out of context, but also okay. "He has a dragon tattoo. On his side. Sort of low down." She leered at them.

"And you know this how?" Sam leered back at Rebecca.

Rebecca laughed. "I saw it at the pool," she said.

"Yeah, me too," said AJ. "It's good."

"He designed it," said Rebecca.

"No way!" AJ was impressed.

Rebecca let it all sink in a minute. Then she said, "And I've written a story for Andy. It's about a boy, a cool dragon, and a big dumb dog. They go chasing around the galaxy knocking out villains. Nanna says it's good enough to publish."

"That's so the bomb!

"Way to go, Becks!"

"Definitely the gene pool."

"So how'd you do that?" asked AJ. "Keep your cool when Jackson messes with you."

"Well, you said to never let them know if they get to you," said Rebecca. "And Laney says to 'fake it till you make it.' So I've faked flirting with him a couple times. It's pretty cool."

"What happens when you do that?"

"It totally shuts him down," said Rebecca. "It's beyond awesome! He is *not* used to girls who don't just fall down in a heap at his feet. Or who have a brain." She glanced at Zoe, who nodded her agreement. Rebecca leaned back in her chair, a satisfied smile on her face.

"I did it a couple times with Fat Mr. Hammond too," she said. "The 'fake it till you make it' thing. It totally made him twitch." And she told them about the day in algebra.

"Oh, and he got fired," Rebecca added.

"No way!"

"How do you know that?"

"Someone texted my sister," said Rebecca. "We were all at Nanna's. Lissa told us. Turned out Mom already knew about it."

"Why?" asked AJ. "Because he ran over Jackson?"

"Partly that. There was some other stuff too."

"Lucky freshmen."

"For sure."

Ty rewound to Jackson. Her expression was dismissive. "So you've seen Jackson a few times," she said. "That's not the same as you're seeing him. Like a boyfriend or something." She looked at Rebecca, her heels tapping on the deck.

Rebecca looked back in surprise, and then her face closed down. In her head, Laney's voice whispered, *She's kind of a bitch. How come I never noticed that before?* It was quiet around the circle.

After a couple minutes Sam said, "I sort of have a boyfriend."

"When have you had time to find a boyfriend!" AJ actually sounded a little rattled!

"At the ranch," said Sam.

"The amazing Zuni horseman," said Rebecca. She winked at Sam.

"*Absolutely* amazing with horses! It's like he can communicate with them. I can't describe it." Sam shook her head.

"Never mind the horses," said AJ. "Tell all!"

"I've known him since we were kids," said Sam. "I just never paid much attention. Then he was away at school for a while. This summer, we worked together. Mucking out stalls. Feeding the horses. Driving hay out for stock. And we did some trail rides. With the dudes, you know. Sometimes we rode together, just the two of us. And things got a little different."

"So how come he was always around? It's not exactly like your uncle has neighbors anywhere close." Ty was pushing buttons, for sure.

Sam tapped a finger against her lips. "Um . . . well, my uncle raised him."

"Raised him? You mean, like, he's your cousin?" Ty pressed. "You can't have a boyfriend who's your cousin!"

"He's not really my cousin. He's adopted!" Sam ran her hands through her blonde curls.

"You should see him." Rebecca stepped in smoothly. "Dark eyes. Dark hair. Chiseled cheekbones. Clearly not the same gene pool!"

Sam sent her a silent look of gratitude.

"Easy to look at, I can tell you," Rebecca added. "And very mysterious."

Ty looked sullen. Sam tried to move them on. "Really, guys, there wasn't time for much of anything. I worked my butt off this summer!"

"We took Reiki," said Zoe. "Sam and Becks and me. We're Level II certified."

AJ pushed her glasses up her nose. Tyler's expression was blank. She reached for the ponytail that wasn't there, tucked her hair behind her ears. The amazing Zuni horseman was temporarily forgotten.

"I've never heard of that," said Ty eventually.

"I have," said AJ. "Some of the massage therapists Aunt Tillie works with use it. She said she might take it."

"Way to go, Aunt Tillie," said Sam. "I think I'd like to meet her."

"So what is it?" Ty frowned.

"It's an Eastern energy healing system," said Rebecca. "That's how Mom describes it. You know alternative stuff is her job. She says to think of Reiki as acupuncture without the needles. But there's more to it than that."

"In Eastern medicine, it's all about energy flow," said Zoe. "If energy gets blocked, it can cause dis-ease, or dysfunction."

"And Reiki can unblock the energy and balance out your chakras," said Sam.

"And then the body can heal itself," said Zoe.

"Chakras?" Was there an edge in Ty's voice?

"Yeah," said Rebecca. "Surely your dad and"—she almost said "Looney Luna" but caught herself in time—"Luna have mentioned chakras."

"Yeah," admitted Ty. "I just never expected to hear it from you." She stared hard at Rebecca and Zoe.

"In quantum physics, they're referred to as energy centers." Zoe's voice was mild, but Rebecca saw the tightness at the corner of her mouth. Why was Ty being so argumentative?

"You can do it on animals," said Rebecca, trying for an angle that wouldn't provoke. She wished they hadn't brought it up. "I do it on

Tinker, although I can't tell if she likes it. Nanna says Inkjet is a Reiki junkie." She was kind of babbling. She looked helplessly at Zoe. "And Sam healed Magic's foot with it."

"Fetlock," said Sam. "But yeah. Even Alfie hadn't been able to figure it out. If it hadn't been for the Reiki—"

"And you all just decided to do this?" Ty wasn't smiling. "Together?"

Rebecca and Zoe exchanged glances. Sam looked at Tyler.

"It started with Magic," said Sam. Rebecca could see the glitter of annoyance in Sam's eyes. "No one could figure it out. And everyone— *everyone*, including animals—pulls their weight on a working dude ranch."

Rebecca understood the reference, although she wasn't sure Ty would. *I like dogs that earn their living*, Sam had said when Rebecca asked her why she didn't like Anne Boleyn.

"Even so—"

Sam shut Tyler down. "The ranch foreman wanted to have her put down." Her voice was flat. She looked levelly at Tyler. "I'd have tried just about anything. So would've you, if it was Headless."

Ty gasped. One hand flew to her mouth. The tension in the air was palpable. Sam's green eyes challenged, and her usually smiling mouth was pulled into a straight line. Zoe and Rebecca glanced at each other. AJ looked uncomfortable.

"So what's going on here?" asked Zoe. She looked at Ty and then at AJ. She combed the short hair around her face with her fingers. "Something's bothering you, Ty. What are you two not telling?" she said quietly.

Ty and AJ both looked startled. And maybe a little guilty.

"What do you mean?" Ty's heels tapped.

AJ shifted in her chair and looked down at her hands.

"I said it in plain English," said Zoe. "You two are holding stuff back. And whatever it is, it's crapping onto everything else." She looked at AJ. "You've hardly said three words since we got here. Spill."

AJ's face clouded. She slouched lower in her chair, fingered a hair extension. Then she sat up straight. She took a deep breath and blew it out with force. "You're right," she said. "I don't know how to tell you."

"Just say it, Alexa," said Zoe.

Rebecca nodded. There was a hard knot in the pit of her stomach.

AJ didn't say anything for what felt like a long time. Then she said, "Tom's been offered a football scholarship." Ty looked at the deck. Rebecca, Sam, and Zoe looked at AJ.

"So?"

"From UCLA. It would help a lot with costs. He's always wanted to play for UCLA."

"And?" said Zoe.

"We went out to Santa Monica a couple times." AJ uncrossed her ankles and crossed them the other way.

"Your Aunt Tillie," Rebecca said. This wasn't making any sense.

AJ nodded. "Since my uncle died last winter . . . Aunt Tillie has this big house, and she's all alone in it. She's been after Mom to come out. Live the California lifestyle, you know?"

"What's wrong with the Colorado lifestyle?" demanded Rebecca.

"And?" Zoe said again.

"She got mom interested in essential oils. They use them at the spa where Aunt Tillie does massage." AJ glanced at Ty. "Mom and Aunt Tillie have always been close. It would be good for her. For Mom, I mean." AJ bit her lips. She looked at them apologetically. "So with Tom's scholarship . . . we're moving to LA."

"You mean the one in California?" Sam was stunned. "That LA?"

"Wow." Zoe's eyes opened wide, and she blinked twice.

The knot in Rebecca's stomach twisted. "OMG." It was all she could get out.

"UCLA is only a few miles from Santa Monica," AJ said. "It would be really convenient. For Tom."

"And high school . . .?"

"They have a few in LA," said AJ dryly.

"What about . . . us?" Rebecca still couldn't get her head around this.

"I know," said AJ. It was a whisper. "But what about me?"

"What do you mean?" asked Zoe gently.

AJ looked at them helplessly. It was unsettling to see this expression on her face. "I want to go," she said quietly. "I've been . . . sort of lost here. I feel stifled."

"But you're our—" Rebecca couldn't finish.

"Yeah, strong, all-seeing, all-knowing rock." AJ laughed. It was a brittle sound. "You know what I always say," she said sarcastically. "Never let them see how you really feel. Well, I'm tired of hiding everything. I want a change. I love the beach, I hate winters here, and I want a change."

"Wow . . ."

No one moved or spoke for what seemed like a long time. Sam broke the silence. "I'd do it," she said. "I mean, if it was something to do with horses. I totally get it." One finger tapped her lips.

AJ looked at Sam gratefully. "I don't have any idea how this is going to play out," she said. "But it feels right."

There didn't seem to be anything to say to this. All eyes were on AJ. She sat up straighter and calmly folded her hands in her lap. However difficult it was to believe, it seemed AJ's mind was made up.

Ann Boleyn nosed the screen door open and let herself outside. They watched her trot across the deck, her tags jingling, and scrabble against Ty's chair. Ty picked her up, settling the little dog in her lap.

Zoe turned a calm gaze on Tyler. "And you?" she said.

Ty looked at Zoe almost defiantly. "Me what?" Her eyes didn't quite meet Zoe's.

"What are you not telling?"

Ty huffed and grabbed a handful of hair. "What are you, the resident psychic?"

Zoe just looked at her. Now Sam and Rebecca did too. AJ looked down at her hands. She picked at the polish on one nail.

"AJ already knows," said Sam. "You have to tell us too."

Ty glared at AJ. "You told!"

"I did not," said AJ emphatically. "I did *not*."

Ty turned her defiant gaze on Sam, and then at no one in particular. Her heels tapped restlessly. She cradled Ann Boleyn against her chest.

"I'm going to school up here this fall." She blurted it out. Her stony look defied any of them to argue with her. "For the year."

No one spoke. Zoe opened her mouth. She closed it again.

Rebecca thought she should feel surprised, but her foremost emotion was resignation. What else was going to come out today? "Okay, Ty," she said. "Spill it all." She ran a hand through her honey-blonde hair and then dropped it to her thigh where the fingers rested quietly.

Ty took a deep breath. "Well, Dad suggested it. And we've been doing photography together. He thinks some of my pictures . . . one of the local galleries . . . there's zillions of them up here." She smiled, but she looked nervous. "Stupid tourists," she said. "They'll buy almost anything. Especially from a real Coloradan. I'm going to be part of a nature photo exhibit."

"That's really cool, Ty," said Zoe.

"And you have to go to school here to take pictures and show them?" Rebecca didn't see the connection.

"Luna says she wants me to stay too," said Ty. "We've really hit it off this summer. She says Dad's more grounded when I'm here. Whatever that means. Mom's not too happy, but she's busy with the baby and what's-his-name." Ty wasn't crazy about her stepfather. "I think she's mostly mad she'll be losing a built-in babysitter."

Ty was babbling. Rebecca wondered what she was covering up. "Get to the real point, Ty." Her expression was unreadable. You could read the edge in her tone though.

Ty fiddled with her empty plate. She dabbed at some crumbs and licked her finger. "And there's this guy I've sort of been seeing." She reached for the ponytail again, pushed the hair behind her ear.

"I thought you were seeing Travis Scott," Rebecca said.

"Um . . . well, I sort of was," admitted Ty. She smiled shyly. "But Gabe . . . that's his name . . . Gabe lives here and takes lessons from Dad in the winter. He's an amazing skier." She looked around the little group. "He wants me to stay."

"And you'd drop all of us for a stupid boy?" The anger in her voice surprised even Rebecca. She took a deep breath, tried to hold the neutral face. She wasn't sure she did. "Aren't there enough boys to choose from at Front Range?"

"I like this one." Ty's face set stubbornly. "And I'm not dropping you," she said. "I'm just expanding my . . . it's like AJ going to California . . . and your book."

"It's not." Rebecca had a stubborn streak too. "We're actually *doing* something."

"Well, it's like Sam and *her* boyfriend!"

"Sam's not going anywhere."

AJ had been silent. Now she broke in. "Writing, boyfriends, whatever . . . things are going to move forward, with us or without us," she said. "It's just another chapter. I don't want to be the same when I graduate as I am now." She looked at Rebecca. Her face was soft. "I love you guys," she said. "I don't know how I feel about the whole California thing. But it feels like a real opportunity for me." Her eyes pleaded for understanding. "I love . . . us." She gestured at them all. "But doing something of my own . . . it makes me feel so *alive*!" She shook her head. "I'm sorry to be breaking us up."

"You don't have to apologize," Zoe said quietly. "Do *not* apologize."

"I get it." Sam looked at AJ. "When the Reiki healed Magic—" Sam brushed at her eyes. "I can't tell you how that felt. I'd give up almost anything in order to keep that."

"It doesn't have to be a trade-off," said Zoe. "Does it?"

Rebecca and Zoe exchanged glances. AJ and Sam locked gazes, an understanding passing between them. Ty sat a little apart, Ann Boleyn clutched in her arms. The Yampa River babbled softly. A mountain jay screeched. A jet droned high overhead.

Rebecca pushed her chair back and went to the deck rail. She leaned over the railing and stared down at the river. She didn't know what to think about any of this.

CHAPTER 70

Beginnings

Late August

FOR ALL PRACTICAL purposes, summer was over. They had seen Ty when she came down to collect her winter clothes and some personal possessions. She had been withdrawn, and there had been an underlying tension. AJ, her mother, and Tom had packed up what personal belongings would fit into a car and Tom's battered pickup and headed west. There had been some hasty text messages full of promises to send pictures and stay in touch, but they had not seen AJ again before she left. Rebecca found this hard to accept, even though a part of her felt it was easier than a prolonged series of good-byes.

Rebecca had a sense of things . . . shifting. It would all be so different without Ty and AJ. But maybe it would be simpler. They had all changed. That had been abundantly clear in Steamboat. Even if Ty and AJ were still at Front Range, things would be different. Rebecca was excited for Alexa. AJ was exploring something totally new. Creating it, in fact, both literally and figuratively. That thought pulled Rebecca up short.

Way to go, Alexa! she said to herself.

She was confused about the situation with Ty. And bottom line, hurt and kind of mad. Rebecca knew Ty's separation from her father had long been a source of distress. If living in Steamboat could smooth that out, Rebecca was happy for her. The three of them, though—Mr. Lane, Luna, and Ty? It felt off somehow. Ty had always been strung pretty tight, and a little insecure. Maybe she tried too hard. Maybe she did what she thought other people wanted her to do instead of what she wanted for herself.

Maybe she has no idea what she wants for herself, whispered Laney. *Maybe she's just trying to figure it out.*

Maybe. Rebecca thought she could cut Ty some slack, if that was the case. But it still felt like Ty had blown them off over a stupid boy. Maybe it was an unrealistic expectation, but Rebecca wanted the connection with her best friends to transcend other relationships.

Does that mean exclude them? Laney's thought was a sigh in Rebecca's head.

I don't know, thought Rebecca. But she kind of did know, and the knowing made her uncomfortable. In truth, she wanted the freedom of her writing and her—whatever else, but for things with her friends to stay the same. Was she willing to grant them the same freedom?

Rebecca put that in the box.

There would be one more day at the doll shop before her job took a hiatus until her school routine was established. Working after school instead of days would be different. Would Tony and Rupert still come by? Would she run into Jackson at the park? Park time was diminishing; already, the days were noticeably shorter. She would have homework. Jackson would have football practice. She could imagine all sorts of scenarios with Jackson at the little park, but how about at school? A lot had changed. She had changed, and she liked the new Rebecca who was emerging. How would things be between her and Jackson? She had no idea.

Rebecca sat in the little sitting room by herself. She was trying to get all the changes and revelations in some sort of order in her head. Sam had her horses and Alfie. Zoe had her college aspirations. Rebecca didn't question that those two were also creating their own dreams. Beyond Andy's book, Rebecca didn't feel she had anything as compelling. Jackson was interesting, and the situation was a curiosity. But it hardly compared with Alfie and Boulder.

So figure out what you want and just go for it! Laney felt exasperated.
I don't know what I want! Rebecca thought back.
Then let me tell you.

"Nervy," Rebecca muttered aloud. But she found a journal to make notes. She chewed on the end of her pen. How to do this? She took a deep breath and reached for the zone.

You want to write, Laney said unequivocally. *Not just the dragon story, but other, more significant stories. There are many.*

Rebecca nodded to herself and wrote it down.

You want to understand all this energy stuff. Not just how it works, but how to use it.

Definitely. Nanna and April would help her. She wrote it down. And the Reiki . . .

Laney was on top of it. *Yes. You want to see where Reiki takes you, and that means just do it and see what happens.*

Rebecca wrote, "Reiki—Just do it!" She drew a crude Nike symbol. She chuckled to herself. It looked more like a toboggan than the Nike icon.

You want to grow and expand as yourself.

Rebecca's gut reaction was *How?*

Just write it down! said Laney. *It will come to you.*

Also grow and expand in your relationship with Zoe and Sam. There is something special about the three of you. Three is a powerful number.

Rebecca didn't understand this, but neither did she disagree. She wrote it down.

And you want to see what an honest relationship with Jackson would be like. Just getting to know him. Like Reiki, see where it takes you.

Really? That's up there with writing books and three powerful Reiki wizards? Rebecca was skeptical. *I'll consider it, but I'm not writing it down,* she thought to Laney.

"And anyway, since when do you get to give me directives?" Rebecca said this out loud under her breath.

Since I'm in your head, sweet pants. Laney didn't pull any punches. *And you asked. It's up to you what you do with it.*

There didn't seem to be a response to that. And Laney didn't seem to have anything more for the list.

Well, maybe one thing. *The list is not static. New things will appear. Some things may fall off.* Before Rebecca could protest, Laney added, *Just go with it.* And she disappeared.

Rebecca chewed again on the end of her pen. She thought her cool, supersmart, sort of a guide could be pretty pushy.

The next morning, Lissa dropped Rebecca at the doll shop, her last day for probably two weeks. She had been thinking about Ty and AJ, and all the changes, and it had left her out of sorts. At lunch, she headed for the hidden garden. She settled into one of the chairs and opened her lunch bag. A rustling in the bushes caught her attention, and she watched as Boo appeared, first pouncing on a leaf, and then at a dangling vine. Boo didn't worry about things. She took them as they came, moment by moment. She stretched out in the sun and groomed one paw. Rebecca sighed. She envied Boo her calm acceptance. Maybe that should go on the list.

Rebecca was surprised to find Tony and Rupert in the doll shop when she returned. Rupert greeted her with well-behaved enthusiasm, thumping his tail energetically on the floor and butting her hand with his nose. Tony and Miss Amelia were deep in conversation.

"Do you want me to take Rupert to the park?" She tried to sound offhand.

"That'd be great." Tony smiled. "Wouldn't it, fella?" He ruffled the big dog's fur with affection. "Miss A. and I have some things to discuss."

And so Rebecca found herself slipping through the tall iron gate and into the park. She unleashed Rupert, and he trotted off, never going far before he circled back to her. Rebecca walked slowly along the trail toward the firepit. She didn't expect to find Jackson there. She only meant to sit in the shade and think. She and Jackson hadn't communicated since the day she'd brought him a copy of Andy's story. That had been just before the Steamboat trip almost two weeks ago. Jackson had said he would read it and play around with some drawings. He had tucked the story in a back pocket in his jean shorts. Grinning the old FIGJAM grin, he had tweaked her hair and said he'd get back to her, but right now, he had football practice. She had watched him jog away, feeling a strange mix of emotions. So what else was new?

It was hot. The shade felt good under the canopy of trees. Rupert trotted ahead of her, his nose to the ground, his tail wagging.

When she heard Rupert bark, her heart did a little hiccup. Still, she didn't let herself hope. Jackson was probably at football practice. Rounding the bend in the path, however, she saw him sitting on the same bench, Rupert overjoyed to see him. She approached slowly. She didn't know how to play this. She didn't feel like faking anything, and what did that leave?

Why not just be yourself, Laney whispered in her head.

Which self, Rebecca thought back.

Oh, for God's sake, Laney shot back. *You make everything so complicated! There must be a real you under there somewhere.*

For a cool, supersmart, sort of a guide, you can be a real bitch, thought Rebecca.

Laney had a smart retort. Rebecca could feel it. But she shut her down. She put a composed, neutral expression on her face—at least she hoped she did—and walked calmly up to the bench and sat.

"Jackson," she said.

"Hey, Becka! Didn't expect to see you today."

"No? Me either. I mean, I didn't expect to see you." She bent to rub Rupert's ruff to hide that she was rattled. *Get a grip!* she told herself fiercely.

"So what's up, Becka?" Jackson asked casually. "You seem sort of . . . in a funk."

She looked at him sharply. "What do you mean?" she demanded.

Jackson chuckled. "You're so touchy," he said. "I don't mean anything. I'm just asking what's up?"

Rebecca frowned at him for a moment, and then she sighed. "I am in a funk," she said. "Ty's going to school in Steamboat this year, and AJ has moved to California."

"Friends of yours?"

"Two of my *best* friends," she said through stiff lips.

"Oh. I thought Sam and Zoe—it's Zoe, right? The little, smart one? I thought they were your best friends."

"Is there a limit to the number of best friends I can have?" She knew she sounded irrational. Testy.

Jackson looked like he might debate this, but he wisely decided against it. "No," he said. "No way. Wow. That bites."

"Yeah."

"Look at it this way: You can go up and stay with her. Ski that champagne powder Steamboat is so famous for."

"I didn't know Steamboat was famous for champagne powder. I don't even know what champagne powder is."

Jackson studied her. He seemed to be debating with himself again. "It's superfine, superdry, superamazing powder that skiers come from all over the world to ski on," he said.

"Really?"

"Really."

"Huh." She shrugged. "Ty never mentioned that. Her dad's a ski instructor, though."

"So you could go up there, and he'd give you lessons, because you're his kid's best friend or something. And then you could ski some of the world's best champagne powder. Wouldn't happen with her down here, would it?"

"It could have!" She scowled at him. She played with a smart remark. Changed her mind. "Are you always this chirpy about everything?" It was as much an accusation as a question.

"Beats being in a funk," said Jackson. Then he changed the subject. He picked up a package beside him and pulled out a sketchbook. "Do you want to see some drawings for your little brother's book? I didn't know if you'd be here, but I brought them just in case."

"You did? Sure!" She turned to look at him. "So you're going to do this?"

"I might." He pushed blond hair from his forehead.

From the back of the sketchbook, he pulled the copy of Andy's story. It was pretty abused. That seemed to be a trademark of Jackson's. The sketchbook pages, however, were pristine. Jackson folded back the protective cover to reveal the first drawing.

Rebecca looked in amazement. There were simply drawn images, sometimes only a line or two, suggesting a boy and dog soaring through space on the back of a dragon. The dragon, though, was beautifully executed and detailed. It leapt off the page at her. The two types of images shouldn't have worked together, but they did.

"I don't know how to draw all that other stuff." Jackson was matter-of-fact. "So I just did it real simple. It was the dragons you wanted, anyway, wasn't it?" He looked at her inquiringly.

Rebecca continued to stare at the images. She couldn't seem to form words.

Jackson turned the page. "No big deal if you don't like them," he said. He rested one ankle on the opposite knee, the toe of his trainer tapping against nothing.

"You said illustrations are really important for a kid's book, so I did quite a few." He flipped to the next page. "I numbered them so you can tell where they go. I numbered the story pages too. Hope you don't mind my writing on it."

He flipped up the page. "This is where they meet the first bad guy." He turned quickly to another page. "And the meteor shower."

Rebecca scooted closer to Jackson and reached for the sketchbook.

He held on to it. "If you don't like them, it's no big deal," he said again.

She tugged on the pad, taking it gently from his hands. "Jackson," she said.

"What?" He crossed his arms over his chest. The toe continued to tap the air.

"I won't know if I like them until I can actually see them," she said. "Let me look." She set the pad on her lap and turned back to the first drawing. She let her fingers trace the shape of the dragon, the suggestion of the boy, hair flying, and the dog, tongue hanging out the side of his mouth. She turned to the next page.

"Oh!" She smiled.

Another page, and another.

"Awesome! Way to go, Peeves!"

There was Peeves in sweet flight. Peeves with flame spewing from his mouth to stun a thug. Peeves with a wing protectively around the boy and the dog while he battled huge, bird-like creatures. Two dragons fighting, flames swirling and stars exploding.

Jackson glanced at her each time she turned a page. He gripped his ankle with both hands. He crossed his arms again. He brushed the hair from his forehead. Through it all, the toe continued to tap.

Rebecca came to the end of the drawings. Jackson still fidgeted. She laid her hand on his ankle, pressing down hard. The tapping stopped.

"These are amazing," she said softly. "I love them!"

"You do?" He looked at her. He searched her face for any suggestion of duplicity.

"I do. Honest." She skimmed through the pages again "They're amazing! Really." She came to the drawing of two dragons fighting. "This one . . . I never thought . . ." She turned the page. Abruptly, she went back to the first drawing.

"Give me the story," she demanded. "I want to match them up."

They rested the sketchbook between them on their knees. Jackson unfolded the story and smoothed the rumpled pages. One by one, they went through the drawings. His shoulder leaned into hers as he pointed out a detail. Her fingers brushed his as she turned a page.

"The story doesn't say this exactly, but this is how I saw it," he said of one drawing.

"It's perfect!" she said. She turned to another page. It was the two dragons fighting. "I totally didn't see this," she said. "But it's perfect. Of course, this enemy is another dragon. It represents—"

A part in each of us we don't recognize, whispered Laney.

"That's pretty heavy stuff for a seven-year-old," said Jackson.

Rebecca looked at him, startled. "Did I say that out loud?"

"Well, yeah, you did."

"Wow," Rebecca whispered. "That's . . ."

Jackson studied her. "Is that how it works with your zone?" he asked quietly. "It just sort of pops out?"

"Sometimes, yeah. That was—" She caught herself before she spilled to Jackson that she talked with Laney, a disembodied voice in her head. She turned another page. "So that's how you did these? You dialed down the chatter and they sort of came to you?"

"Isn't that what you wanted?"

"That's exactly what I wanted. I just didn't know they'd be this good." Deep in thought, Rebecca drummed her fingers on the sketchbook. She looked at him. "Next, I think I need to show these to Nanna. So she can . . . do whatever she does. Can I take the sketchbook? I'll make copies. You can have the originals back if you want."

"You think this is really going to happen?"

She nodded. "Feels like it is," she said. "I mean, I think the story could get published anyway, but it doesn't hurt that Nanna is, . . . you know, known, . . . and . . . supportive."

Jackson considered. "Yeah. That's good. You take the drawings," he said. "Whatever happens, happens."

"You're sure?"

"Sure."

She thought for a moment. "You need to sign them," she said. "Every page. And put a date on them."

Jackson took the pad and turned to the first page. He looked down at it, but his eyes were distant. Rebecca thought he might be going into his own zone. Dialing down the chatter. It was like he had slipped away. After a moment, he was back, and he slashed a signature in one corner. It was the initials EJM, and with a few extra loops and whirls they flowed subtly into the shape of a dragon. Quickly going through the sketchbook, he signed every drawing. He handed the pad back to her.

"Just like that . . . you create a dragon. That's so cool!" Amazement shone on her face. "EJM. What's the *E* for?"

"Um . . ." Jackson looked sheepish. "My first name. I don't use it."

"But what is it?"

He studied her. "I don't like it," he said.

"I figured that," said Rebecca. "Just tell me it's not Andrew."

Jackson laughed. "It's not," he said. "It's an *E*, not an *A*. He relaxed against the bench and stretched his arms along the backrest. He looked very pleased. And he was watching her.

Rebecca looked back at him. She suddenly became aware—really aware—of his closeness. She tried to relax; she didn't want to come off as a dweeb. She slowly breathed in and carefully let it out. She resisted the urge to run her hand through her hair. She held the pad on her knees, her fingers drumming lightly against it. She clenched her hand to still the tell.

Jackson watched all of this. "You're a piece of work, Becka," he said casually. "About a dozen different people. Sometimes two or three at the same time. It's hard to keep up."

The comment caught her by surprise. "It's hard for me too," she admitted. "To keep up sometimes." She wasn't trying for the neutral expression; she was being honest.

"So who are you now?" he asked.

She looked at him. She didn't really know. A part of her felt like a detached observer, and from there none of this felt quite real. From there, she found amusement in all this—sitting here on a bench, alone with Jackson Middleton, legs touching, his arm not quite draped around her shoulders. One corner of her mouth twitched up, just the tiniest bit.

***

Jackson returned her gaze. She wasn't pulling that impenetrable poker face, but even so, he was clueless to read her. She was perfectly still; none of her usual tells gave her away. One corner of her mouth twitched up. What did that mean? He suddenly wanted to kiss that little twitch. She would probably grab him by the hair, throw him to the ground, and kick the shit out of him. But it might be worth it. He leaned a little closer and curled his hand hesitantly over hers, the one that had been drumming on the sketchbook and was now clenched in a fist. She looked at it, and then back up at him. Jeez, this girl was a riddle. She flaming made him crazy! She didn't move away or pull her hand back. And she didn't slug him. So he kissed her. Just a brush of his lips on that twitchy corner of her mouth, and then his lips gently on hers.

For a heartbeat, another, she didn't respond. He was waiting for all hell to break loose. And then her mouth answered his, and the world seemed to fade away. His entire body hummed with an electric charge. He heard a rushing like a wave in his ears, all around him. Her hand relaxed beneath his, and he curled his fingers into her palm. He wished he could float like this indefinitely with his lips pressed lightly against hers, her mouth answering back. When her hand tightened into a fist again, he thought she was going to let him have it. He reluctantly pulled away and withdrew his hand.

***

Rebecca experienced this on one level and observed it from another. She didn't know any more than Jackson which was the real Rebecca. Was it the one with the thumping heart? Or the amused, calmly detached one who merely watched? Jackson leaned toward her, ever so slightly. He curled his hand around her fist, the one she had clenched to still the telltale fingers. One of the Rebeccas glanced down at it, and then back up at his face. She couldn't read his expression. He leaned a little closer. She didn't move. His lips brushed the corner of her mouth. And then his lips were on hers—warm, soft, questioning. He tasted of peppermint. For a heartbeat or two, she was absolutely still. There was no time, no space. And then her mouth responded to Jackson's of its own accord. Her eyes drifted shut. Her fist relaxed, and his fingers curled into her palm. She felt an incredible sweetness. At the same time, lightning seemed to explode through her body. Every corner of it tingled. Her hand trembled, and she balled it into a fist again to still it.

Jackson pulled away. She felt a pang of disappointment in her belly. She opened her eyes. His face was only inches from hers. She could still taste peppermint.

"Are you going to punch me now?" he asked softly.

Rebecca felt a slow smile spread across her face. She couldn't help it. She was light-headed. She shook her head no, her eyes never leaving his. She didn't seem able to speak.

"Not even if I did that again?"

Jackson smiled back at her. She could feel the smile on his mouth as his lips met hers. And then their smiles faded away, lips still gentle, exploring. Jackson took her by the shoulders and pulled her closer. She relaxed against him. Time seemed to stop again. She didn't hear the sound of flying feet until Rupert hit them.

The big dog bounded up exuberantly and thrust his head between them. His back half wriggled with pleasure for the sheer delight of life. He licked both their faces.

"Rupert!" Rebecca broke away from Jackson and wiped her cheek with the back of her hand. "Eeew! Sit!"

Rupert sat, his tail wagging enthusiastically. He looked from one of them to the other, barely able to keep his haunches on the ground because life was so good.

Rebecca ruffled the fur on Rupert's neck, trying to gather herself. Panting, tongue lolling, Rupert nuzzled her hand and then Jackson's. He butted his head against the sketchbook, nearly flipping it out of Rebecca's grasp. She grabbed for it, pages fluttering, and pressed it to safety against her knees. Her arms rested on the two dragons fighting, her fingers curled around the edges of the pad.

"Ah, there you are, boy!" Tony appeared on the path, coming around the bend and approaching them.

Panic flooded over Rebecca, followed by relief. What if Rupert hadn't come bounding up when he did? What if Tony had seen them that way?

"Hey, Tony," Jackson greeted him casually, settling against the bench and moving slightly away from Rebecca. He rested one ankle on the other knee. The toe of his trainer tapped.

"Jackson." Tony nodded at him. "You two know each other."

"From school," said Jackson. "Us both knowing Rupert, though—that's totally weird."

"Should I have come back already?" Rebecca's cheeks flamed hot. She bent over the sketchbook, flipping the pages to close it, to hide her agitation. Thank the gods Rupert had showed up when he did!

"No. No problem. I'm just going. Thought I'd gather up Rupert and give you a ride back if you want." Tony jingled his car keys in one pocket, looking from Jackson to Rebecca and the sketchbook. "What do you have there?" he asked.

Jackson pulled the pad from Rebecca and put it on the bench beside him, his leg partially covering it. "Just some drawings," he said.

"Oh?" Tony was curious. "Mind if I look?"

Jackson hesitated. "I guess not."

Ignoring Jackson's reluctance, Tony helped himself to the sketchbook. He glanced at several pages. "Always interested in this sort of thing," he said. "For my board shop in LoDo."

"You have a board shop in Lower Downtown?" asked Jackson. "What sort of boards?"

"Hover, skate, snow. Pretty much everything. I don't sell actual boards. We just do artwork." He handed the sketchbook back to Jackson. "These would be great for kids. There's talent here. But my customers are mostly older."

"These are for a story I wrote for my little brother." Rebecca tried for a calm voice, but it was difficult to contain her excitement. "You should see his other drawings."

Tony looked only mildly interested.

"Show him your tattoo." She prodded Jackson's shoulder. "You should see it," she said to Tony.

Jackson hesitated. He glanced from Rebecca to Tony. He didn't want to push Tony, but he sort of wanted to stay in Rebecca's good graces. Maybe more than sort of, given what had just gone down. Reluctantly he stood. He lifted the edge of his shirt to expose the dragon tattoo.

Tony looked at it. "Did you design this?" He leaned in for a closer look.

Jackson nodded.

"And you have more . . . of this caliber?"

"Yeah." Jackson pulled his shirt back into place.

"I *would* like to see them, if that's the case," said Tony.

"Yeah?"

"Always looking for fresh talent. What's your focus?"

"Mostly dragons. Big birds. Some mythical creatures."

Tony smiled broadly and clapped Jackson on the shoulder. "I'll contact you, and we can set up a time to meet." He jingled his keys again. "I need to move," he said. He whistled for Rupert, who had wandered off. "I'll contact you," he said again. "Come on, let me drop you kids. Rupert!"

Rupert fell to heel. So did Rebecca and Jackson.

CHAPTER 71

Departure

Late August

S AM SLIPPED A hackamore over Skydancer's head with a heavy heart. School started in two days, and that meant she would only get to ride on weekends. Things were always strained at home—another reason working the ranch was so good. And lately, she had been feeling a little edgy with Alfie. Was it her, was it him, was it them? She didn't know.

She was officially off the clock today and was going for a long ride. She needed time to think. About Ty and AJ leaving. About summer ending. About Alfie.

She didn't know what to do about Alfie.

She clambered onto Skydancer from a fence rail, patted the horse's neck, and they left the yard. Sky frisked in her eagerness. Sam held her gently back until the horse had time to warm up, and then let her move into a canter. Sam settled into the rhythm, her body moving easily with the horse.

The feel of Skydancer beneath her eased her heart and quieted her mind. She let her thoughts drift until there was nothing but her and Skydancer, the rhythmic beating of hooves, the wind in her face, and the vast Colorado sky. Reaching the cover of pines, she pulled Sky back to a walk. She came to the little creek and followed its bank. At the pool, she slid to the ground. She left the reins loose so Sky could drink and graze, and she settled herself against the ancient lodgepole where she and Alfie had sat together. They hadn't been back since that day. Since the day Uncle Clint had found them in the loft. Was that day the turning point? Sam didn't know.

She thought about Ty and AJ. She totally got AJ moving to California to live with her aunt. She considered what sort of circumstances in her own life might warrant such a major step and couldn't come up with anything. But in concept, she was on AJ's page. Ty was another matter. That whole situation seemed to be laced with an underlying desperation. She thought Ty was lost—making her decisions based on what other people wanted and what she thought, or hoped, they wanted her to do. Sam figured it would all blow up in Ty's face. It was just a matter of time.

Was she doing the same thing with Alfie? She laughed at herself. How could she be? Since she had absolutely no idea what Alfie wanted. Still, was some of it the same? She was crazy about him. She really was! But she couldn't give herself completely to him. For her it would be a commitment, not a casual thing. She barely knew who she was; how could she commit to someone else? There was too much to learn and explore first. Lately, she had started to worry that maybe Alfie *did* know what he wanted. That he cared for her in a different way than she cared for him. She felt caught between letting him down and leading him on, between not committing to him and losing him altogether. She didn't want any of those things. She realized she had been hoping the end of summer would settle the situation. At least for a while.

So I'm not doing what Ty's doing, she thought. *I'm doing the opposite. I'm running away!* Was it true? Was she just a chicken?

Sky raised her head and nickered. Sam sat perfectly still, listening. The wind sighed through the trees overhead; a pinecone dropped to the ground. A bird flitted from branch to branch, chirping as it went. And then the soft *thud* of a horse's hooves on the needle-strewn forest floor. She turned her head in that direction and waited.

Majestic appeared from the cover of some undergrowth, Alfie sitting easily in the saddle. Her mind absently noted the saddle. She watched as they approached. Alfie swung a long leg over Majestic's rump and dropped to the ground. He loosed the reins, as she had done with Sky, and walked to where she sat. Sam marveled, as always, at his easy grace. She loved to watch him. He moved with the lightness and stealth of a big cat. He seemed to be a part of the earth, rather than to merely walk upon it. He settled beside her. Neither of them spoke.

At length Alfie said, "I thought I might find you here."

Sam just nodded.

Alfie pulled two misshapen chocolates from his pocket. He handed her one.

"You think of everything," she said.

"I don't. I mostly only think of you."

Her heart fluttered, and she smiled wistfully, remembering. Things had been much simpler then. She unwrapped her chocolate and bit off one corner. She barely tasted it.

"Just say it, Alf," she said quietly.

Alfie sighed. He rested his hand gently on her knee. "You're really something, you know that?" His voice was soft.

Sam waited him out.

"I'm going over to Mesa this winter," he said finally. "As soon as things settle down for Dad. With the dudes."

She looked at him in disbelief. And yet a part of her had already accepted this. All those trips to Durango. Not Durango, it seemed, but Mesa.

"Why?"

"Two reasons, mainly," he said. "I want to find my biological parents, if it can be done." Alfie raised a hand to ward off her objection. They had had this discussion before. "It's more about my heritage," Alfie went on. "Even if I can't find them, and I know it's a long shot, I still want to know all I can about being Zuni. And I need to be with Zunis to do that."

"But where—?"

"There are communities around the Four Corners. I've been in contact with a couple that would be willing to put me up in trade for work. With horses, if I'm lucky. Maybe let me study with a shaman. If not . . ." Alfie was accepting. What would be, would be.

Sam let this sink in. "But you'll be back to see your folks." She looked up at him. "Me."

Alfie didn't move.

Sam could feel the tension in him. Something awful was coming. "And the second reason?" Her voice was a whisper.

Alfie shifted against the tree. He withdrew his hand from her knee. Without it there, her leg felt cold. Sam noticed this with heightened awareness. She unconsciously wrapped her arms around her middle.

"The second reason is you," said Alfie quietly.

"Me!" She rounded on him, her hands clenched into fists. "How could you be leaving because of me!"

Alfie caught her fists in his hands and held them. She struggled against him, but Alfie was strong. "It's because I love you!"

"Wouldn't that be a reason for staying?" Hurt, outrage, bafflement filled her heart and spilled across her face.

Alfie took a deep breath. "Will you hear me out, Sarah Ann?" he pleaded.

At the use of her real name, the struggle bled out of Sam. Her gut was tight, and she was trying desperately to keep herself together. Alfie let go of her hands, and she instinctively wrapped her arms around herself again.

Alfie shifted so he could more easily see her face. "I love you, Sarah Ann," he said softly. "I want to be with you. Every day. I can't imagine my life without you in it." Sam opened her mouth and Alfie put a finger to her lips. "And the way I want you in my life is in my arms and in my bed."

Sam's throat closed in panic. She struggled to get her breath. "OMG! Alfie, I—" Her voice was a croak.

Alfie unfolded his other fingers against her mouth. They smelled like leather and hay and horse and outdoors, and an unnamable something else. They smelled like Alfie.

"You're only fifteen," he said. "And I'm twenty."

She shook her head. "Uncle Clint has warned you off me, hasn't he?" The green eyes were a mile deep and darkened by anger. "And I'm almost sixteen!"

"Would you listen to me!" Alfie's raised voice transmitted his agitation. Majestic turned his head in their direction and snorted. "You can't know what you want for the rest of your life! I'm not even sure I can. I know what I feel right now. But even if we were sure, there are some things that have to happen first."

"Like what!"

"Like knowing more about my heritage. About who I really am. I have no idea what direction that will take. I just know I have to take that path. At least for now."

Sam looked at him. "And what else?" The boot was going to drop. She could feel it.

Alfie weighed his words carefully. "And the bigger thing, really—you need to turn seventeen."

"So Uncle Clint did—"

"It's *your* father I worry about, not mine!" Alfie picked up a pinecone and hurled it. Both horses skittered. "You know he's a hothead. And he doesn't like me. He never has."

"No, Alfie—"

"Sam!" Alfie's voice was desperate. "He would ruin this for us. He has *never* accepted me! What he would do . . . that sort of thing follows you the rest of your life. You can't outrun it!" Alfie scrubbed his face with his hands. "And I could not survive in jail. I could *not*."

She gaped at him. What sort of non sequitur was he babbling? What could he possibly be thinking? Deep inside, though, she knew what he was thinking. And she knew her father was mean enough to do it.

"If we have something real, we can give it the time for these things to work themselves out. But we both need to grow up some first."

"You think *you* need to grow up?" She looked at him in surprise.

"Of course I do!" Alfie hurled another pinecone, this time away from the horses. "You're the only thing that keeps me grounded. I need to learn if I can achieve that without you. And maintain it. How else can I . . ."

"Can you what?"

But Alfie refused to say.

"So what do we do next?" Sam's question was a whisper.

"You go back to Denver." He wouldn't look at her. "You focus on school and whatever it is you want. On doing what you love." He took her hands. His eyes were tormented, but his hands were gentle. "The

Reiki. That's magic for you. And the horses. Your friends. Love those things." He placed her hands gently in her lap. "And I go to Mesa."

"Do we . . . text? Or talk? What? Will I run into you here on weekends?"

"I don't know, Sam." Alfie raised his hands helplessly. "It might be better if we don't."

"So, for now, you just toss me aside." She clambered to her feet and stood staring down at him, her fists planted on her hips. Disbelief battled with fury on her face. Bitterness tasted like bile in her throat. She knew her reaction was unfair, especially given her own confusion about the relationship. But hurt tightened her heart. "And then fourteen months from now, we just pick up where we left off?" She kicked at a rock. "Like nothing ever happened?"

"Jesus Christ on steroids, Sam!" Alfie surged to his feet. "I am *not* tossing you away! I'm trying to preserve us from certain disaster!" He wrenched a dead branch off the pine and heaved it into the forest. "I cannot maintain the facade that you are just another ranch hand to me. Hands talk. Your father could—*everything* could be ruined for us."

"But we haven't—"

"It doesn't matter! And we might. *I* can't pretend anymore." Alfie dropped his head and stared unseeing at the ground, his shoulders slumped. "It doesn't matter," he said again.

He came to stand in front of her. "In fourteen months, we decide if we want to pick it up again," he said. "And then we start from the beginning. Go easy. See how it goes. Until you're eighteen. And then no barriers. That's what I want." Dark eyes pleaded with her. "I want you and me with no barriers."

Sam looked up into his face. Her thoughts whirled. She shoved her hands into the pockets of her jeans. "Sounds like you have it all figured out," she said. Her voice was flat.

Alfie didn't respond.

"So this is it, then? For fourteen months?"

Alfie nodded helplessly.

"Do I at least get to kiss you good-bye?"

"My God, Sam!" It was a whisper. Alfie's eyes burned into hers. Sam could feel his hunger, felt hunger of her own respond to his. It caught her by surprise. It kindled a warmth deep in her belly and made her legs weak. Alfie dragged her roughly into his arms. He pressed his cheek against her hair, holding her so tightly she could barely breathe. She didn't resist him. Her body felt at home there, tight against him and encircled by his arms. He took her face in both of his hands, turned it up to his, and crushed his mouth against hers. She wound her arms around his neck and tangled her hands in his hair. She kissed him back, melting into him. She had never felt like this before, never felt so alive!

Alfie tore his mouth from hers with a moan, still holding her fiercely to him. His hands cradled her head to his chest, his lips pressed against her hair. She could feel his heart pounding, his ragged breathing. Every nerve in her body was zinging. He set her away from him, holding her at arm's length. She felt like a rag doll in his hands. The anguish in his eyes made her heart contract. He couldn't feel this way and leave her! Could he? Alfie shook his head once. He released her; he turned and stumbled to Majestic. He reached blindly for the reins, missed them, grabbed again, and swung into the saddle. He was urging Majestic forward before he found his seat. Majestic sprang away with a snort and was at a gallop in a few paces, Alfie hunched low over the big horse's neck.

He did not look back.

Stunned, Sam listened to the sound of retreating hooves until she heard only an unnatural silence in the forest. She was reeling. She could still feel Alfie's arms around her, his mouth hungry on hers. He had never kissed her like that before. This had not been the "kind of spacey, not all there" Alfie she knew. This Alfie was very present and a very real force. She touched her fingers to her lips. If he had kissed her like that before— She leaned her back into the ancient lodgepole, her hands against the rough bark for support. She let herself slide down the trunk to the gnarled roots at the base of the tree. She drew her knees up, wrapped her arms around them, rested her forehead on her arms. She sat that way, her mind numb, her heart aching. Tears came slowly at first. And then in a torrent.

Sam cried until there were no more tears, and then she simply sat with her head resting on her arms, her eyes closed. She had no idea of time. At some point, Skydancer nuzzled her leg, bringing her back to reality. She lifted her head to find Sky standing by her, head lowered.

"Okay, my beauty." Sam got stiffly to her feet. She stumbled to the creek and washed her face in the cold water, wiped it with her shirt. She led Sky to a boulder and clambered onto her back. The pines whispered overhead. The waterfall murmured. A songbird warbled; another answered. Calm, peaceful, soothing sounds. Sam felt none of those things.

She gave Sky her head, and the mare trotted steadily toward home. When was Alfie going? Would he be cleared out of the barns already? She didn't think she could bear seeing him. She wondered if he had solved her dilemma for her. If so, why did she hurt so much? And if so, shouldn't she feel relief? She didn't. He was right. They could not go on as they had been. She had been a fool! They had been headed for a train wreck that involved not just herself and Alfie, but both of their families. That was why he was leaving, not the Zuni thing. She slowed Sky to a walk. She needed time to think and to gather herself.

Sam was still numb when she reached the outer ranch buildings, but she was resolute and outwardly calm. She could not speak of this to her parents. She would be circumspect with Uncle Clint if he questioned her. She would do as Alfie suggested. She would *not* think about what might happen in fourteen months. She would not! When she allowed herself to think about Alfie, it would be of easy times. Riding side by side, holding hands; bareback on Majestic, Alfie's arms around her. Mucking out stalls and laughing at some little thing they shared. Racing Sky and Majestic across the high plains, the wind tossing their laughter behind them, pulling up breathless and delighted, the horses blowing. She wasn't sure she could love high school, but she thought she could love aspects of it. Reiki would ground and sustain her. Maybe it would ease her heart. She would do the meditations every day. She would study and practice. She would become very, very good at it, and she would love it. She already loved it! Sky, Zoe and Becks, Reiki—she would do her best to love life. But would that be enough?

Ty and AJ leaving paled in comparison to this. This made Steamboat seem like another lifetime and insignificant. AJ was creating her own dream. Sam could celebrate that. Whatever Ty was doing, she would have to figure it out for herself. It was just Becks and Zoe and her now. They could see each other through anything. Had done so before. True, there had never been anything like this, but they had been kids.

Sam realized something else. She might not be a grown-up, but she was no longer a kid.

CHAPTER 72

Plans

Summer's End

L ISSA PULLED HER father's big pickup to a stop in front of Uncle Clint and Aunt Jo's farmhouse, Zoe and Rebecca riding shotgun. They would load Sam's things in the bed, and the girls would all fit in the double cab for the ride back to Denver.

Sam came out of the house with a duffel in each hand. Uncle Clint was behind her, lugging some boxes. They stashed everything in the bed of the pickup. Aunt Jo followed with a few last items. Everyone queued around the truck, except Sam and Uncle Clint. They stood a little apart from the rest, close together in quiet conversation. Rebecca watched as Sam's uncle pulled her into his arms for a long hug.

Rebecca wondered what was going on. Sam looked different. Rebecca realized the wild curls had been scraped into a tight ponytail. The ponytail was short and curly; too-short wisps escaped around Sam's face. Her green eyes were shadowed. Rebecca felt . . . heaviness.

"Anything in the barn, Sam?" asked Aunt Jo.

"I think I have some books up in the loft," she said

Aunt Jo nodded. "Melissa, why don't you come in for a few minutes while the girls get the last of Sam's things." She hooked her arm through Lissa's and guided her toward the house. Lissa walked away, glancing over her shoulder at Rebecca. Sam headed resolutely for the barns.

Rebecca was getting a tingle. This didn't feel like "Bye, I'll see you next weekend." She glanced at Zoe. Zoe shook her head, her dark eyes concerned. They followed Sam.

In the dimness of the stables, Rebecca and Zoe saw Sam sidestepping off the ladder into the loft. Rebecca had played up there with Sam when they were little. She remembered a big, dusty sweet-hay-smelling space with cobwebs in all the corners and sun slanting through the cracks between timbers. A barn cat with a litter of kittens. A magical place. She hadn't been up there in years. As she maneuvered herself off the ladder, she saw that the loft was full nearly to the rafters with huge bales of hay. A narrow gap barely allowed for movement around the sides. Sam was sitting on a broken bale at the edge of the big loading door. Zoe and Rebecca edged their way to her, seating themselves on another bale across from her.

"You didn't come for books." Zoe was matter-of-fact.

Sam shook her head.

"It's Alfie, isn't it?" Rebecca asked softly.

A deep sigh from Sam. She nodded.

"Do you want to talk about it?"

"There's not much to say. He's gone."

Zoe gasped. Rebecca felt anger curl in the pit of her stomach. She shoved it down and reached for Reiki energy, picturing a soft ball of light around the three of them.

Zoe shivered in surprise. Sam gave herself a little shake and looked at Rebecca. "That's nice, Becks. Thanks."

Rebecca felt her tingles increase. She knew Sam and Zoe were adding to the Reiki energies. Sam sighed again. And she told them.

"I already knew it was coming," said Sam. "I just wouldn't admit it to myself. I thought maybe my coming back to Denver for school would sort of solve things."

"But it wouldn't for Alfie," said Rebecca.

"No." Sam shook her head.

"Do you love him, Sam?" Zoe asked quietly.

"I don't know!" Sam reached up to run her fingers through her hair. No curls. She smoothed the sides of her head and tugged the ponytail tighter. "I barely know who *I* am. How can I be in love with someone else? I'm crazy about him, but is that the same as love?"

"How do you feel about his leaving?"

"At first I was mad. I couldn't believe—it felt like he was dumping me. To do his Zuni thing. I sort of wanted to drown him in the creek!" Sam brushed a knuckle under her eyes. "But he was different. So intense! And he felt really . . . all there. Not spacey at all." Sam stood up and paced. The area was too small for pacing. She sat back down on her bale.

"And anyway, it doesn't matter how I feel. He's gone. And I'd bet Skydancer on his not being back for at least fourteen months." Sam's expression was grim. "And however hard this is, it's not as bad as if we went on . . . the way we were and my dad . . . " Sam didn't finish. She dropped her head into her hands.

Rebecca wasn't sure if she should ask the next question. But she did. "Do you really think your dad would go down that whole . . ." But she couldn't finish either.

"Yeah." Sam's eyes were flat, her voice venomous. "I do. And everything—*everything*!—whatever Alfie and I had, have, would be ruined. Forever. And d'you want to know the best part?" she said. "Alfie and I never . . . I'm still a virgin!"

Sam reached for her hair again, tugged at the little ponytail instead. "I remember some stuff now, since Alfie said what he did. That my dad doesn't like him. I never paid any attention before. Why would I? And once I started thinking about it—it's not just Alfie. I can't decide if my father is just a stinking redneck or a Neo-Nazi!"

"Mon Dieu, Sam!"

"You don't really think—"

Sam did think. Her fierce expression made it clear. She stood up and paced to the big loading door again. She stood looking out toward the mountains. She paced the two steps back.

"I just want to graduate and get the hell out of Dodge," she said grimly. "Let him be who he is, but so that it's not my problem."

"Could you live down here? With your aunt and uncle? If things got too bad—"

"Probably, but that would make it even harder for Uncle Clint. Between him and my father, I mean." Sam tapped a finger against her lips. She looked from Rebecca to Zoe, her attention lingering on Zoe. "I'm even thinking about trying to graduate early."

"Get out!"

"OMG!"

Sam laughed. It was a brittle sound. "I'm not stupid," she said. "I just never gave much of a shit before."

Zoe stared in disbelief at Sam, and then her look turned thoughtful. She fingered the pixie hair around her face. "If you're serious about that," she said, "I have an idea."

Rebecca and Sam waited.

Zoe focused on something far off. She nodded her head, just a slight inclination of her chin, as though she was listening to someone. "Okay . . ." Three quick little nods. "Okay." She smiled at them, a wide, radiant smile.

"I've been practicing the meditations," she said. "And after what Nanna and April said about the unified field and energies and all that intention stuff . . ." Zoe glanced at Rebecca and then went on. "I think I can use Reiki and the unified field . . . well, to be smarter."

Rebecca snorted. "Okay, Einstein," she said. "If you think you need it."

Zoe ignored her. "I think Reiki comes from the unified field. I mean, where else? If the field is . . . creator, supreme power. Do you know what I mean?"

Rebecca and Sam looked at Zoe curiously. "And?" Rebecca prompted.

"And," said Zoe, "if I can do it, so can you." She looked at Sam. "So we meditate, and practice getting into"—now she glanced at Rebecca— "your zone, Becks. We do it with Reiki, and we set the intention to learn."

Rebecca suddenly saw it with crystal clarity. "More, faster, better!" She was a little breathless. "We use the first symbol to boost—"

"YES!" Zoe's eyes blazed.

Sam was going a little more slowly. "So you're saying we can use Reiki to . . . get better grades?"

"Not just grades," said Zoe. She waved a hand dismissively. "To learn more. Learn it faster. Retain it better. I read a study about Transcendental Meditation—there are hundreds of them, actually—and it said doing TM all the time does that." She looked at them. "Reiki, TM, quantum science. What's the difference? It's all about connecting to that . . . field of creation, that sweet spot. Isn't it? Reiki *is* that sweet spot!"

Rebecca didn't know from dog doo-doo about TM, but she got the picture. So did Sam.

"Okay, then," Sam was thinking hard. "I need to know more about the stuff your grandmother told you," she said to Rebecca.

"Oh, she'll be delighted to teach us," laughed Rebecca. "I'd bet the farm on that!"

"I have a CD," said Zoe. "This guy tells how science works in the body." Rebecca frowned. So did Sam. "No, it's easy to understand. Promise! It tells how thoughts release chemicals that create emotions. It's like what Nanna said . . . a whole chain reaction of stuff. We can choose certain thoughts and levels of emotion. The high-frequency ones, you know? To create whatever we want." She fingered the wispy hair at her temple. "You guys could get it too. The CD, I mean."

Sam nodded. "We get our plans in order," she said. "We finish high school." She looked at Zoe. "End of junior year?"

"Doable." Zoe nodded. "Summer session latest."

"I want to get certified on some equine bodywork practices. Reiki will really make that zing. I'll use all the stuff Alfie taught me . . ." Sam's voice faltered.

"You might be able to get credits for some of that," said Zoe.

Sam nodded. "Maybe."

"We get our Reiki Master certification," Zoe continued. "All of us. As soon as April says it's okay. And we do it every day. No exceptions."

"Wait a minute." Rebecca had a sinking feeling. "So Zoe gets Boulder, no doubt on full scholarship," she said. "And Sam gets . . . what, a Reiki massage clinic for horses?"

"I get freedom," said Sam softly. "I get to be me. Whoever that turns out to be."

"And I get senior year all by myself?"

"You get whatever you want," said Zoe. "You write. You get Andy's story published. You coauthor with your grandmother and go on book tours with her. You get to be prom queen on Jackson's arm. That would tweak some cheerleaders, for sure." Zoe grinned a wicked grin. "Whatever you want. You wanted to be in control. You said you did."

"Sam!" Aunt Jo called from the yard.

"Coming, Aunt Jo!" Sam waved at her aunt from the loading door. It was time to break this up. She edged her way back to the ladder, Rebecca and Zoe following.

At the bottom of the ladder they dusted themselves off. Sam's step was lighter. There were still shadows in her eyes, but now there was also clear purpose.

"I put everything into this," said Sam. "And let the Alfie thing work itself out. When he comes back—and right now it feels like that's what I want—I'm in my own place of power, aren't I?" It wasn't a question for her friends, exactly. "And if we get together, it's what he said—no barriers. But either way, I know who I am, and I'll be creating what I want."

They walked into the hot August sunshine, shading their eyes with their hands when they stepped out of the dimness of the stables. Sam looked toward the pine-covered mountains. "Goddess willing and the creek don't rise," she whispered. "Godspeed, Alfie."

"I think I'll want at least two majors," said Zoe, almost to herself. "Cell biology, of course. And maybe astrophysics. The micro and the macro." She giggled.

"Of course you will, Einstein," laughed Rebecca.

"So what was that bit about prom queen with Jackson?" Sam had come at least partially back to them.

Rebecca threw a look at Zoe. Zoe grinned that wicked grin again. "Becks has been . . . tormenting Jackson. You should tell it, Becks."

And so Rebecca did. "Remember in Steamboat I told how I faked flirting with Jackson and how it completely shut him down?" She nodded to herself. "That was sweet, I can tell you. That's when I saw the dragon tattoo. Up close, anyway. Laney wanted to trace her fingers over it. I was pretending to be in some moxie character to, you know, give it back to him, and that just about knocked me out of the role!"

She told how Jackson had gotten it back together and then she had lost it. Josh had come over, and she had felt outnumbered.

"He said I'm hot," said Rebecca. She shook her head in amazement. "Josh did."

"Everyone but you thinks that," said Sam.

Rebecca wasn't ready to accept that. It was too alien to her. She went on with her story, skipping to the end where she had thought Jackson was going to kiss her, right there in front of Josh and the lifeguards and everybody! How she had punched him, that Josh had found it hilarious and Laney had agreed it was a standoff and not bad for a first-timer.

"And he has a whole notebook full of amazing drawings. Dragons and other stuff. But the dragons!" Rebecca shook her head. "Amazing! And I need illustrations for Andy's book. I had to convince him, but he said he'd think about it. And then to give it a try. And this is so cool! You know how I go into the zone to write?"

Sam and Zoe nodded.

"Well, he does this thing—he calls it 'dialing down the chatter.' Like when he's on the mound pitching." Rebecca grabbed each of them by the arm. "And you have to swear you won't breathe a word of this!"

They just stared at her.

"Seriously!" she said. "Not a word! It's not mine to tell. It's Jackson's. Do you swear?"

Zoe swore. So did Sam.

"And that's how he did the drawings for Andy's story. I can't wait till you see the finished book. This is so amazing! I can hardly believe it's Jackson!"

She told how they had talked like two regular people some of the time. That he had said she was like a dozen different people and it was hard for him to keep up.

"And I get it. I feel that way myself sometimes. Kind of schizoid, you know? And here's the thing—I think maybe he gets me."

"Well, that would be something," said Zoe. "Since most of the time *you* barely do." Zoe looked sheepish. "Sorry, Becks."

"No, it's okay," said Rebecca. "I can feel that."

She told them about going through Andy's story and matching up his drawings. How they had been really close on the bench. And then he had kissed her under the canopy of huge old trees in the dog park.

How she had let him. She had *not* punched him. And she had let him kiss her again, and she had kissed him back, and it had been sweet and thrilling and pepperminty.

"And then Rupert showed up and just about knocked us off the bench. Thank the gods, because Tony was right behind him!"

It made a good story.

CHAPTER 73

I Can Do This

Later that Day

THAT EVENING, REBECCA sat in the glider on the front porch and watched the light behind the Rockies fade from purple to lavender to pale turquoise, the serrated silhouette of the mountains etched in sharp relief against the late-summer sky. The air was warm and soft. She breathed in the fragrance of flowers in bloom and damp earth. Her mother must have watered earlier. The swirl of thoughts triggered by the conversation with Zoe and Sam was forming up into something clear. Something solid. At least some of it was.

Rebecca didn't know that she wanted to finish high school in two more years. She was pretty sure she could, if she set her mind to it. But then what? She had always assumed she would go to college. It seemed to be what her family did. She would look at that belief to see if it was what *she* wanted, rather than what was expected of her. She couldn't quite get a picture of school without Zoe and Sam. And she *really* couldn't get a picture of herself as prom queen on Jackson's arm! That idea made her laugh. She *could* see the possibility of some sort of . . . evolution in her interactions with Jackson. She didn't want to call it a relationship. That was too fraught with implications. She really didn't want a boyfriend, but sitting in the dusky light alone, she could admit to herself that she definitely wanted to kiss him some more.

What if she was already an established author by the time she graduated from high school, the world hers for the plucking? What if she didn't do the usual and predictable? What if she made up her life to fit what she envisioned rather than what others expected? What path might she follow? If she could go anywhere and do anything, what would she choose? She had no idea. And that seemed to be all right. She would figure it out.

Let's not go too fast, whispered Laney.

You're right, Rebecca thought back. She felt Laney's surprise. It made her smile. *Let's savor every kiss along the way.* That shut Laney up, for sure.

She thought about Zoe and Sam. Her heart hurt for Sam. But Sam had showed a strength at her core that Rebecca found amazing. There was a new element to their relationship. Without Ty and AJ, they had circled the wagons, the three of them. She sensed that they all felt it. And Reiki . . . who knew where that might take them? Rebecca was curious how it would play out, but she was comfortable not having the picture yet.

She had an idea for a story. It would be about three friends who were wizards. Strong in the power. Yes, magic. Magic would be fun. And first of all, this story was meant to be fun. She didn't feel she understood the science angle of energy sufficiently to write from that perspective. Not yet. Writing about it from a magical aspect . . . well, if it was magic, it could be anything she wanted. Anything! She would learn as she went. And anyway, it seemed it was mostly a question of semantics. The story—"No, let's say book," she said aloud to herself—would be as good as her imagination. She would draw on real experiences. *But let's be real here,* she thought. *I'm only fifteen!* She would need a lot of help from imagination and from Laney, and from that field of creation. She was counting on all of it.

"You figure out what you want and write yourself into it."

Who had said that? Her mom? Nanna? Laney? She couldn't remember. But it felt like a truth. And she didn't have to decide immediately. In fact, that was the whole point. Writing different stories could help her decide. She was sure of it.

Rebecca sat on the porch until full dark. A bright light over the western horizon gleamed softly at her. Venus maybe? She really had no idea. She could look it up, but it was time for bed. As she snuggled into her covers, she pulled Tinker close, and the big cat curled into the curve of Rebecca's body, purring softly. Rebecca's hands gently cradled Tinker, and her palms tingled with Reiki energy.

"So you *do* like Reiki!" she whispered.

Tinker uncurled and stretched out. The tingling in Rebecca's palms turned into real heat. She set her intention to include a ball of Reiki energy. "A Reiki Ball," she said softly to herself. She surrounded herself in the Reiki Ball, and she sent one to Sam and also Zoe. As an afterthought, she sent it to Alfie as well, even though she didn't know where he was. And then to Ty and Alexa. It seemed the right thing to do.

When Tinker had had enough, she moved away, settling herself at Rebecca's feet. Rebecca's thoughts turned to her story ideas. Laney whispered to her, and she put Reiki on "the book." Could she do that? She'd have to ask Nanna. But it felt right.

As Rebecca drifted off to sleep, Laney was an alive presence in her head. Not pushy or bitchy or rude. Just there. Rebecca could feel her. "I don't know who I want to become," she said half aloud and to herself. "But I can't wait to figure it out."

THE END

July 2019
Milton, Georgia